Kate High is a graduate of the Faber Academy, as well as a contemporary artist, working in metals. She has exhibited internationally, with her work having been shown at the V&A, the Design Council, and also selling through outlets such as Liberty's and Chelsea Crafts Fair. Kate is a former voluntary branch administrator for the RSPCA and she co-founded a charity that aims to support older animals, Lincs-Ark.

Also by Kate High

The Cat and the Corpse in the Old Barn

The Man Who Vanished and the Dog Who Waited

THE
MISSING
WIFE AND THE
STONE FEN
SIAMESE

Kate High

CONSTABLE

CONSTABLE

First published in hardback in Great Britain in 2022 by Constable
This edition published in 2023 by Constable

1 3 5 7 9 10 8 6 4 2

Copyright © Kate High, 2022

The moral right of the author has been asserted.

*All characters and events in this publication, other than those clearly in the public
domain, are fictitious and any resemblance to real persons, living or dead,
is purely coincidental.*

A CIP catalogue record for this book is
available from the British Library.

ISBN: 978-0-34913-520-5

Typeset in Adobe Caslon Pro by SX Composing DTP, Rayleigh, Essex
Printed and bound in Great Britain by Clays Ltd, Elcograf S.p.A.

Papers used by Constable are from well-managed forests
and other responsible sources.

Constable
An imprint of
Little, Brown Book Group
Carmelite House
50 Victoria Embankment
London EC4Y 0DZ

An Hachette UK Company
www.hachette.co.uk
www.littlebrown.co.uk

For all the animal lovers who have given a home
to a rescue dog or cat

Chapter 1

The creature leapt from the blackness of the sodden dyke, travelling at speed into the light. Momentarily startled, Clarice Beech hit the brake and at the same time dipped the headlights. The hare, landing on the single-lane track a few feet in front of her car, did not pause. Instead, with its front legs out, it pushed upwards, stretching its long hind limbs to jump again and reach the dyke on the opposite side of the track before disappearing back into the darkness. The elegance and coordinated grace of the creature stayed lodged in her mind for the remainder of the journey.

Classes for the new term of Tuesday-evening ceramics had begun in the third week of September. It was a twenty-minute drive on unlit country lanes from the town of Castlewick, in the Lincolnshire Wolds, to Clarice's home. Now that British Summer Time had ended, dusk came early, and she always left and returned home in darkness.

Often at the end of September it felt that one foot was still planted in summer, with sunny days that drifted into mellow evenings. This year, it had been cold and autumnal from the beginning of that month, so now, one week into

November and six into the term, the chill of winter had taken a firm hold.

The class had been running for eleven years, mainly attracting people who worked during the day. The workshop's size imposed a limit of eight students; six of the current group had attended from the very beginning. As they'd attained a greater knowledge of techniques, their work had developed, and with friendships deepening over time, the small group had evolved to become tight-knit.

Clarice marvelled at how well such an eclectic bunch had bonded; their backgrounds and life experiences could not have been more different. There was an accountant, a tattooist, a mechanic, a shop worker, a solicitor, a teacher, a nurse and a retired secretary. Their ages ranged from thirty-five to seventy-four.

The students shared their successes and failures. If, after firing, a piece came from the kiln with a crack, the disappointment was collective. Each was aware of the effort that had gone into its production. And there were often deadlines, the ceramics designated as gifts for birthdays, Christmas and weddings. If a piece failed in the firing, it would mean starting again.

There was always banter and laughter during classes as the group discussed family and work problems and caught up on what had occurred over the time since their last meeting.

Tonight, the class was down by one student, Colin Compton-Smythe, a middle-aged accountant, one of the six who had signed up from the first class. He'd told Clarice he was unsure if ceramics would really suit him, but he'd give it a try for a term.

Colin was short, slim and, as befitted his profession, conservative in attire. On joining the class, he'd initially given the impression of being extremely shy. But over time, as his relationships with fellow students developed and his assurance in producing top-quality ceramics increased, his confidence grew, and he flourished. As he'd shed his reserve, Clarice had noticed changes in his appearance. In the first year, he'd abandoned his tie, and in the second, he had acquired a pair of jeans. The most significant transformation came after three years, when he'd replaced his regular conventional glasses with elegant kingfisher-blue frames. It was an act of rebellion – as if he'd suddenly decided he would no longer be invisible.

Everyone in the group had met Colin's daughter, Emily. Over the years, she'd attended end-of-term social gatherings and parties. Clarice had watched her transformation from an eight-year-old schoolgirl to a nineteen-year-old university student. She'd inherited her father's shyness, but managed to put up a good front; only the heightening of her facial colour – blushing – gave her away.

Earlier in the day, Clarice had received a call from Emily confirming that her father, had gone into Lincoln Hospital, as arranged, and would later undergo surgery for a bowel problem.

After asking the girl to pass on her good wishes for a speedy recovery, Clarice had taken a Get Well card to class; all the students wrote in it, with messages designed to cheer.

After signing and passing the card on, Gill, the retired secretary, had bitten her bottom lip, her face pinched with worry. 'He will be OK, won't he?' she asked, addressing the class as a whole.

'Course he will,' Micky, the town's tattooist, reassured her. 'Told me he didn't like the idea but wanted to get it over with; he'll be right as rain in a couple of weeks.'

Knowing that Emily was staying at her father's house on the outskirts of Lincoln, Clarice intended to leave the card on his doorstep the following day, along with some flowers. She could pass them on to her dad on her next hospital visit.

As she drove carefully in the darkness along the narrow lanes, her thoughts moved to Rick, hoping he might have beaten her home. As a detective inspector with the Lincoln police, her husband's working hours were not always predictable. Clarice generally ate her evening meal early and alone, leaving Rick's for him to warm up later.

He had begun work on a new case related to an incident in a Lincoln nightclub over the previous weekend. An argument between two groups had flared, leading to a knife being produced and a fatality. Due to a trivial falling-out, a man of twenty-three had lost his life. With his usual stoicism, Rick was now occupied with the minutiae of what had happened in the minutes leading up to the death. The area in a hallway near the toilets where the altercation had occurred was not covered by the club's CCTV. And there were conflicting accounts of who had been carrying the knife and had inflicted the fatal wound to penetrate the heart.

Driving out of the last of the winding lanes, Clarice came to a main, unlit carriageway. Hidden by the darkness of late evening, agricultural fields and undulating hills flanked either side of the road. The beam from her car headlights pierced the blackness, and ten minutes later, she reached an unmarked exit leading down an incline onto a rough track.

Following the curve of the bend, she saw the welcoming lights of home.

Built in the 1850s and added to by various incumbents over the years, her cottage was surrounded by three acres of garden and a number of outbuildings, which included her ceramics workshop and a barn converted for rescue animals. Some years ago, Clarice had founded a charity called Castlewick Animal Welfare, known locally as CAW; the barn housed animals she fostered until they found permanent homes.

She parked her blue Range Rover next to Rick's white BMW estate. That he was already at home lightened her spirits. Walking to the cottage, she pulled tight her heavy grey winter coat to keep out the whip of the wind and the cold night air, and caught the welcome smell of drifting woodsmoke: Rick had put a match to the fire she'd laid that morning.

Before she reached the door, the sounds of joyful yelping came from the dogs. The noise of the car engine, signalling her arrival, had sent them into welcome mode. The door opened, allowing Blue, a sturdy Labrador cross, black with a white chest, and Jazz, a smaller, rough-coated brown dog with a long body and short legs, to run out to greet her. Blue, as usual, carried a present clamped in her mouth, a battered tennis ball. Jazz, close behind, without a gift, wiggled her body while swinging her long tail.

Behind the welcome-home committee, filling the door frame, blocking out the light, stood Rick. At six foot four, tall, solid and broad, he had a height advantage of three inches over his wife.

'Good class?' he asked when the dogs had calmed, allowing Clarice to get inside.

'Not bad,' she said, before telling him about Colin's absence, and the reason for it.

'Was it something that was expected?'

'He knew he had to go in,' Clarice said. 'Yesterday he had lots of tests, and today he's having the surgery, but he seemed unfazed by it.'

Rick poured two glasses of South African Shiraz, and he and Clarice drifted into the sitting room, followed by the dogs, to the welcoming warmth of the open fire. In her childhood, this space had been two smaller rooms. After inheriting the property from her mother, she had changed it to make it into one long room, with windows now covered by heavy red drapes at the far end. On the walls were large, colourful framed posters of jazz and blues musicians, with the room lit by several table lamps and the glow from the fire.

Clarice took up her usual spot, reclining on the sofa in front of the hearth, while Rick sat at an angle in a nearby armchair. Toots, a long grey cat, stretched along the back of the sofa, lifting her head to acknowledge their arrival. The dogs spread themselves on the floor in front of the open fire, and as the group relaxed, other cats wandered in to join them.

'Sandra left a note,' Rick said. 'She and Bob left about seven. They've fed and watered all the cats in the barn.'

'Great.' Clarice smiled, wondering how she'd manage without the support of their friends Bob and Sandra, who acted as volunteers for her rescue charity. 'Tell me about your day. Anyone admitted to the stabbing?'

'No.' Rick stretched his long legs out as he talked. 'We have footage from the CCTV in the club, and outside, just not the area where the stabbing took place. We can identify each individual involved and have fourteen witness statements, including everyone in the hallway where the victim died. We've narrowed it down to two possible suspects.'

'What about fingerprints on the knife?'

'We don't have it. Whoever used it took it away.' Rick was pensive. 'Also, everyone involved had the victim's blood on their clothing. We'll need to work out from the blood spatters who was nearest to the victim at the moment he was stabbed.'

'What was the argument about?'

'Bearing in mind they were all half-cut, it comes down to one bloke accidentally knocking someone's arm, causing him to spill his drink.' Rick raised his eyes. 'It progressed from swearing and name-calling to the two men and their friends moving away from the bar area to the corridor outside the toilets.'

'Unbelievable,' Clarice said. 'Twenty-three and his whole life ahead of him.'

'And a pregnant girlfriend.'

'No. That's awful.'

'It is pretty depressing.'

The ringing of the phone cut into the conversation.

'A bit late.' Rick looked at his watch. 'It's probably for me – more problems.'

'I'll get it.' Clarice lifted Big Bill, a large, friendly ginger cat, from her lap.

'Hi, Clarice, it's Emily – Colin's daughter from class. I'm sorry to phone so late.'

'Emily,' Clarice said with surprise, glancing at Rick, who, realising the call was not for him, sat back in his chair, relieved. 'How did Colin's operation go – well, I hope?'

There was a long silence before Emily responded. Clarice could tell that she was struggling to keep calm.

'It seemed OK,' she said. 'But Dad was in theatre a lot longer than they said he'd be. When he came out, I was allowed to sit with him for a while.'

Clarice waited to hear what was coming, aware from the tone of Emily's voice that it would not be good news.

'He didn't come round while I was there, and the staff told me to go home and get some sleep – to go back tomorrow.'

'So you went home?' Clarice asked gently.

'Eventually. I didn't want to leave him alone.' Emily stopped abruptly. Again Clarice waited. 'I'd only been home ten minutes when they phoned to tell me that Dad had died. I wish I hadn't left him …' Her voice was a wail.

Clarice remembered Emily's age, and her mind flicked momentarily to the twenty-three-year-old man murdered in the nightclub. Colin's daughter was younger, only nineteen, studying social history at Nottingham University. Being young was no protection against bad things happening.

'It isn't your fault, Emily,' Clarice said. 'The staff at the hospital would have believed that the operation had gone well. They wouldn't have suggested you go home if they thought he wasn't going to pull through.'

'They said he'd had a heart attack – the operation was obviously too stressful.'

'I am so sorry,' Clarice said. She waited for Emily's sobs to subside before she continued. 'Are you alone? Is there someone with you?'

'I've sent Jake, my boyfriend, a text. He's in Nottingham, but I think he'll phone and come over when he picks the message up.'

'Are you going to be OK until he arrives?'

'Yes …' Emily's voice trailed away. 'I have to phone my mum. She lives in France – she and Dad are divorced – and then my grandfather, Dad's father. Jake should have got back to me by then – I'll be fine.'

Later, after having done her last check of the rescue cats in the barn, Clarice walked the dogs around the garden with Rick, thinking about poor Colin's unexpected death.

'Are you worried about her?' Rick asked.

'Yes,' Clarice said. 'The poor girl is in shock. I hope her boyfriend gets there quickly. She needs someone she loves and trusts to offer a shoulder to cry on. No one should be alone at a time like this.'

Chapter 2

The following morning, low grey clouds lay like a dirty rumpled duvet over the fields and hills, heavy with the threat of rain. Rick and Clarice walked the dogs around the outer boundary of the garden. Blue, with a new treasure, a short, stout stick clamped in her jaw, oozed joy, while Jazz ran in circles around them; the morning walk was always her favourite of the day.

After doing three laps of the boundary, Clarice kissed Rick goodbye and watched as his car disappeared to make its way onto Long Road. Going back into the house, she fed the animals and breakfasted on toast with honey and a cup of tea before returning outside to cross the garden to the cat barn.

The barn, divided into three sections, allowed Clarice to separate or isolate animals when necessary. During the spring and summer, the numbers of cats and kittens were high, but there had been a good home-visits rate, with animals finding new homes. Also, Clarice had recruited four new foster carers in and around Castlewick. The downside to entrusting a cat to an ardent cat lover was that they invariably fell in love with the first one they looked after, and when a prospective adopter was found, could not bear to be parted from it. The upside was that although Clarice lost a foster carer, the cat found its perfect, loving home. The upsurge in rehoming and the extra foster homes meant that there were currently only ten feline residents in the barn.

Walking across the garden, Clarice heard the cry from the most recent of these, an apricot-coloured Persian. Entering the barn, she found that Sassy, having pushed his bedding around the floor, was sitting in the centre of the room emitting a loud, croaky indignant howl. The old cat was completely deaf and unaware that he was not alone; he appeared to be shouting at the wall.

Three days earlier, Clarice had received the type of call she dreaded: Sassy-Boo, a seventeen-year-old cat, had been left behind when social services took her elderly owner into a nursing home. A neighbour had been tasked with feeding her and finding an animal rescue charity to take her, but due to the animal's age, this had proved impossible. Clearly distressed, the neighbour had telephoned Clarice from a Lincoln veterinary practice, having taken Sassy-Boo there to be put to sleep. One of the vet's nurses had given her Clarice's number; she was using the vet's telephone to ask if the charity might help.

Clarice had taken Sassy-Boo to be examined by her friend Jonathan Royal, the Castlewick vet.

'You are a niffy old girl.' Jonathan spoke gently to the cat.

'Her teeth,' Clarice said. 'I noticed as soon as I picked her up.'

'What do you know about her?'

'Not a lot. The neighbour told me the owner was ninety-one. She'd had Sassy for fifteen years. She's actually a sweetie,'

11

Clarice looked at the animal as she spoke, 'but she has the grumpiest expression I've ever seen on a cat.'

'Unfortunate name.' Jonathan lifted his eyebrows.

'Yes,' Clarice grimaced, 'and apparently the owner used to tie a small pink ribbon in a bow on top of her head.'

They stood silently side by side looking at the sour face; the belligerent eyes stared back as if to challenge them.

'Leave her with me.' Jonathan smiled. 'I'll check her over and sort out any problems with her teeth. You know I'll need to put her under?'

Clarice nodded. 'I'll come back later.' She was aware that anaesthetic with an elderly animal carried risks, but there was no other option. If the cat was in discomfort with rotten teeth, her quality of life would be affected.

When she'd returned to the surgery, a sleepy Sassy-Boo had been brought into the consulting room in her travel basket. Jonathan, short and sturdy, with a mass of curly white hair, stood in his regular pose, arms folded, head angled to one side.

'She's still a bit dopey,' he said.

'How many—' Clarice began.

'Ask,' Jonathan interrupted with a raised index finger, 'not how many teeth I have removed, but rather how many I've left in.'

'How many have you left in?' Clarice complied.

'Four.'

'They *were* bad.'

'Awful,' Jonathan agreed. 'I could practically pull them out with my fingers. They must have been causing her a lot of irritation. And I think I've discovered the reason for the grumpy face.'

'Go on,' Clarice said.

'If you were a big butch boy, how would you like to have to wear a pink ribbon and have everyone calling you a pretty girl?'

'*She* is a he?'

'*He* is a neutered tomcat.'

Carrying Sassy around the barn now, listening to his full-on purr, Clarice remembered the conversation.

'You may have the grumpiest face, but you also have the loudest purr.' She scratched behind his ears. 'From now on, I'll call you Sassy, and we can forget the Boo and the ribbons.'

Sassy drooled with delight.

'You do kick up when you're left alone, even though you have your own hiding box.' Clarice put the cat down thoughtfully. 'I imagine your owner was with you for most of the day.'

Sassy stopped purring and stared disgruntled as Clarice headed to the door.

'Don't worry, sweetheart, I'll be back,' she said quietly, 'and just remember to work your magic on the big man I bring in later.'

Back at the house, she left a note for Bob and Sandra telling them she would be visiting Emily and would be back later. Snug in her chunky waterproof dog-walking jacket, she pulled on a matching tan-coloured woollen hat, tucking her shoulder-length auburn hair inside. Outside, the grass was wet, the rain that had threatened earlier coming down in a fine drizzle.

It was almost 8.30 a.m. when she reached the outskirts of Lincoln. She had looked at the flowers in her garden and judged the wind-battered autumn perennials not good enough to give as a gift. She drove directly to a florist near Colin's home, and from a large selection chose a bouquet of bright yellow chrysanthemums and white carnations. After putting them on the front seat to join the card expressing her sympathy, she made her way through the maze of streets in the Nettleham area to reach Colin's bungalow.

Over the years, Colin had gone from being just another of her adult students to becoming a good friend. He'd spoken so often of his daughter, an only child. He and Emily had been in touch daily with phone calls or texts, and she frequently visited him for Sunday lunch. Clarice had thought of their closeness as a joy for Colin, but with his sudden death, his being such a big part of her life would only deepen the sense of loss for Emily.

Turning into the quiet cul-de-sac, she drove slowly between the two rows of bungalows facing one another across a narrow road. Built within the new millennium, they were outwardly smart and well maintained. The gardens to the front of each property already looked barren in the onset of early winter. Trees had shed their leaves, with those remaining a variety of colours on a theme of brown and gold. The ground below the trees was for the most part clear, suggesting a tidy neighbourhood.

As she drove towards the end of the cul-de-sac, Clarice remembered her last visit, in May; she'd brought ceramic plates fired in the college kiln for Colin and stayed for a cup of tea. She recollected an orderly house, Colin's output of dishes, plates and vases adorning his hallway and sitting room. He'd had a love of roses and had decorated many of his plates with abstract red shapes resembling flowers; quite an achievement given that red glazes were notoriously difficult to fire successfully.

She parked outside number 72 and picked up the flowers and card. The curtains were closed, and she imagined that Emily and Jake, after a late night of conversation, were having a lie-in. Tucking the card under the flowers to one side of the porch, she slipped quietly back down the path.

'Clarice!' Emily's voice reached her as she left the garden.

Chapter 3

Clarice turned to retrace her steps. 'I didn't want to bother you,' she said.

Emily was pretty, petite and slim. Clarice thought of a delicate, spindly whippet. She understandably did not look her best today. She'd half emerged from behind the door, wearing creased pink pyjamas, her long brown hair scraped back into a ponytail, her skin pallid and eyes puffy.

'Is Jake still here?'

'He didn't make it.' Emily was blunt, not expanding with an explanation. 'Come in, Clarice.' She held the door open. 'And thanks for these.' She cradled the flowers in the crook of her arm as she led the way into the sitting room.

The room had not changed since her last visit. Clarice looked at the plates and vases displayed on the sideboard and windowsill; Emily followed her gaze.

'He so loved your classes.' Putting the flowers and card down on a table, Emily attempted a weak smile. 'And I gained a whole new family in his classmates. He included me in all the social events.'

'He told me at the first class that he'd try ceramics for one term – and then he was hooked,' Clarice said.

'Yes, I don't think he'd ever considered himself artistic or creative, but he was.' Emily's voice held a note of surprise.

'He just had to find a way to let it out, and ceramics did it for him.'

Emily nodded, the smile wobbling before she dissolved into tears.

'I'm so sorry.' Clarice put an arm around her shoulders and waited as the younger woman, her hands now filled with tissues pressed against her face, sobbed loudly. When the tears were finally reduced to sniffling, she guided Emily to the sofa and sat down beside her.

'I guess you didn't get any sleep last night?' she said.

Emily shook her head. 'I was wandering around the house. I couldn't settle.' She blew her nose, then sniffed as if trying to regain her composure. 'It's just so unfair. Dad was only fifty-five. Grandpa – Dad's father – is still going strong in his mid eighties.'

'It isn't fair,' Clarice said gently, 'but then, that's life.'

'Grandpa said that last night. He said Dad was too young.' Emily pondered. 'I think he was crying, but I don't know. He isn't the type to cry.'

'If he's in his eighties, he'll have lost a lot of people, friends and family, over the years, but Colin was his son – a special bond. Did your dad have siblings?'

'No.' Emily was calm now, twisting the tissues between her fingers. 'He was an only child, like me.'

'Me too.' Clarice smiled. 'It has good points and bad.'

Emily nodded agreement. 'Let me make you a cup of tea or coffee.'

'A cuppa would be great.' Clarice followed her into the kitchen, encountering a sleek black cat in the hallway. 'Hello, you.' She knelt as she spoke, watching as the cat pushed its head against her proffered hand.

'That's Josephine,' Emma said. 'Napoleon's on Dad's bed.'

'I've met them before – siblings. I couldn't tell them apart.'

'They're best buddies,' Emily said. 'I was four when Dad brought them home as kittens, so they're over fifteen now.'

Ten minutes later, the two of them sat with steaming mugs of tea at a round white Formica table in the kitchen. Like other parts of the property, the kitchen with its pine units and white wall tiles looked pristine. Three misshapen papier-mâché pigs of varying sizes squatted in a line on top of the fridge.

'I made those for Dad,' Emily pointed at the pigs, 'when I was at school.'

'So Colin wasn't the only artist in the family,' Clarice teased.

'They're a bit rubbish – but I was only seven.'

'Your dad didn't think they were rubbish.'

'No,' Emily said, her voice serious, her eyes glassy with unshed tears.

'What's happening about the funeral?' Clarice changed the subject.

'Grandpa will organise it.' Emily brushed her hand across her face as she spoke, attempting to banish the tears. 'The Compton-Smythes have a family plot at Sealsby church. I know Grandpa would want him there, and he'll arrange a church service … though that's a bit awkward.'

'Colin wasn't religious?'

'No.' Emily grimaced. 'I know you can have non-religious funerals, but that won't happen with Grandpa. I don't feel strong enough to fight him about it.'

'Is the family home near the village?' Clarice asked.

'It's quite close, about five miles away. Stone Fen Manor is on the edge of the Fens, one of the last houses before the Wash. It was built in 1890, on reclaimed land. A couple of hundred years before that, it would have been part of the Wash. Dad described it as "the end of the bloody world". He didn't mention it to you?'

'No.' Clarice pondered. 'I can't remember him mentioning the house or anything about his family – apart from you. He loved to talk about you.'

'He must have bored the pants off everyone.' Emily's face suddenly lit up. 'I could never have any secrets. Dad told the whole world about every aspect of my life – but then I was a real daddy's girl.'

'He was so proud of you.'

'I know.' Emily nodded. 'You're welcome to attend the funeral, and any of his friends from the class. I know some of them would have to get time off work, so they might not be able to come.'

'I'll drive down,' Clarice smiled, 'and after I've put the word out to Colin's classmates, I expect there'll be others.'

'I would have been surprised if Dad *had* mentioned his father or talked about his childhood,' Emily said. 'It wasn't happy. He always said he'd *survived* his childhood.'

'I'm sorry,' Clarice said, surprised. 'I didn't know. Was his father violent?'

'No, no – never.' Emily hesitated, thoughtful for a moment. 'Dad's parents, my grandparents – Ralph and Avril – had what Dad described as a loveless marriage.'

Clarice nodded, waiting to hear more.

'When Dad was five, he caught his mum crying. She told him, "Daddy doesn't love me, he loves someone else." A few days later, she took Dad to a school friend's house for an afternoon in the garden. She was due to collect him at teatime, but it was evening when Ralph came. He told Colin his mum had gone away – she'd left.'

'How awful,' Clarice said. 'It must have been a terrible shock – and something that would've stayed with him all his life.'

'Yes, and worse still, Dad said he'd seen Avril the previous day in the garden talking to Ralph's business partner, Major Freddie Baxter. Everyone always referred to him as the Major. Avril was in tears, and the Major was holding her hand.'

'She might have been confiding in him,' Clarice said. 'If she'd found out about her husband's affair, perhaps she needed an adult shoulder? Confiding her troubles to a five-year-old wouldn't have worked!'

'Mm.' Emily gave Clarice a knowing look. 'The Major went missing the same day as Avril.'

'Ah, I see. So he wasn't married?'

Emily sipped her tea thoughtfully. 'No, he was separated. His wife had left him a few weeks earlier.'

'That does alter the picture – a bit coincidental them going at the same time,' Clarice said, her interest stirred.

'Grandpa said they had left together, but Dad never believed him. He said that his mum would have taken him with her.' Emily gave a half-smile. 'According to Dad, Avril was loving, gentle and shy, and she would never have just gone without even saying goodbye.'

'He didn't find out more?' Clarice probed. 'From Ralph, after the dust settled?'

'No. Avril was a taboo subject. Dad said if he ever talked about her leaving, or even mentioned her name, Grandpa went mad. Grandpa said that he'd lost two people on the same day. He'd thought of the Major as a close friend – the brother he'd never had.'

'And did Colin like the Major?'

'Very much. He'd thought the world of him until the day he disappeared with his mother.'

'Poor Ralph, and poor Colin. That's so sad.' Clarice thought for a few minutes. 'What about Ralph's relationship – who was he having an affair with?'

'Well … his girlfriend moved in about four months after Avril left. Her name's Tessa Dinkler. She and Grandpa had a daughter called Dawn, twelve years younger than Dad. She still lives with them at the manor.'

'So Colin had a half-sister?'

'Dad would never have described her like that; he told people he was an only child. They didn't grow up as siblings. Dad was sent away to boarding school when he was twelve. Dawn was born a couple of months after he'd gone. After leaving school, he went off to university.'

Clarice could not suppress the thought that Colin's dislike of his half-sibling might have been due to jealousy. He'd gone away, and Dawn had taken his place in the family home.

'It must have set tongues wagging with the locals,' she said meditatively. 'Ralph's wife left, and shortly afterwards, the girlfriend moved in?'

'Yesss.' Emily drew the word out. 'My great-grandfather and great-great-grandfather were both known to have kept mistresses. It was something Grandpa thought amusing but perfectly normal – my dad said that the Compton-Smythes saw themselves as red-blooded males. *He* thought they were hypocrites.'

'Really?' Clarice was starting to see a different side to Colin.

'Front row in church on Sunday with the family, and visits to the mistress during the week.'

'I can see your dad's point.' Clarice tactfully brought the conversation back to the matter in hand. 'So you're waiting to hear from your grandfather about the funeral arrangements?'

Emily nodded.

'What about your mum? You said she lives in France?'

'She moved there six years ago, after the divorce.' Emily sounded matter-of-fact. 'She was pregnant when she left. She had twin sons by her French husband. When she left, I stayed here with Dad.'

'Will she come over for the funeral?'

'Good God … no chance,' Emily huffed. 'She did give her condolences, but she said Colin is her past – she has her boys to think about.'

But, Clarice thought, looking at Emily's indignant face, she also has a daughter who is now suddenly alone.

'Did you stay at Stone Fen Manor with your dad while you were a child?'

'We went for the weekend twice every year. I'm not sure if I'd call it ritual or duty. I was often curious, wondering what Avril – my grandmother – might have been like.' Emily paused in contemplation. 'I'm not too fond of Tessa, or Dawn. I think Tessa sees me as competition.'

Clarice looked at her, puzzled.

'For Grandpa's affections. I took attention away from them. And then there's Great-Aunt Ernestine – Ralph's spinster sister – who is completely barking, and that was before she was diagnosed with dementia.'

'When was she diagnosed?'

'Within the last year,' Emily said after a moment of thought. 'She has a heart condition too, but then she's nearly eighty.'

Clarice nodded, thinking that Emily was probably contemplating again how young her father had been when he died.

'I should go.' She hesitated before asking, 'When is Jake coming?'

'He won't be.' Emily looked awkward. 'I finished with him two days before I came home. I told you he was coming because I thought you were concerned about my being alone. I lied.'

'I am sorry, Emily – breaking up with your boyfriend and then your dad dying two days later,' Clarice said with sympathy.

'Yeah, my timing was rubbish.' Emily cast her eyes downward.

'Are you going to be OK here on your own?'

There was a long silence. Clarice thought the girl was weighing something up.

'Can I ask you a huge favour?' she said at last.

'Go on.'

'Grandpa said he'd organise the death certificate for the funeral director. I have to wait until I hear from him about a date. And I'm not up to doing anything about the bungalow or the things in it.'

'Probably too soon to think about all that. You only lost your dad yesterday; give yourself some time,' Clarice said gently.

Emily nodded. 'It's my first year at uni. I'd like to go back.' She pressed her fingers to her lips briefly, as if trying to hold back more tears. 'That way I can be with my friends for a bit before the funeral.'

'That sounds like a good idea,' Clarice encouraged her.

'I need to speak to my tutors, let them know what's happened, why my assignments will be late.' Emily paused. 'I don't suppose you would take the cats home with you for a couple of nights, three at the most. They've never been to a cattery ...'

'Yes, if it helps, of course I will,' Clarice said immediately.

'Thank you so much, Clarice.' Emily's face had suddenly brightened, showing her natural beauty. 'I don't want them rehomed; they're my last link to Dad. I just need a few days.'

'A good idea to be with friends, and you can't do much here anyway.'

'There is one other thing.' Emily twisted her face into a grimace. 'I hope I'm not asking too much.'

'What is it?' Clarice was intrigued.

'You'll probably think it's a bit silly ...'

'Try me.'

'It's about Avril, my grandmother.' Josephine wandered in yowling as Emily spoke, and she bent to scoop her onto her lap. 'Dad never believed the story about his mum running away with the Major. He hoped he might find her one day, and about ten years ago he even paid a private detective agency to try and trace her.'

'No success?'

'Unfortunately not. Last night I came across the box where Dad kept his mementoes of his mother. It also has the agency's report.'

Clarice nodded.

'Would it be possible while I'm in Nottingham for you to go through it? Dad told me you had the sharpest mind of anyone he knew – and he said you are a bit of a sleuth.'

'Well ... I'm *very* nosy and inquisitive,' Clarice began.

'Just give me an opinion. I don't expect anything else – it's half a century since they went missing – but if you could take a look?'

'Yes.' Clarice spoke the word decisively. She found herself already fascinated by what Emily had told her.

'Great.' Emily stood up, passing Josephine to Clarice. 'I'll get the cat baskets first.'

Twenty minutes later, the cats were in their baskets on the kitchen floor, and Clarice had a carrier bag full of their food. Emily came into the room carrying a small brown wooden box.

'Here we are.' She opened the box to bring out two photographs. 'This was Dad as a child with Avril.'

Clarice looked at the photograph of Colin at perhaps four or five years of age. He stood with his arms around the skirts of a pretty woman, who was smiling, with one hand raised to shade her face from the glare of the sun. She had fair wavy hair and wore a white lacy blouse and a locket.

'The locket Avril is wearing is in the box ... and this is my dad with Grandpa.' Emily passed the second black-and-white photograph to Clarice. Behind the family group, dwarfing them, stood an enormous, worn but still majestic stone Siamese cat in a sitting position, its paws lined up out in front.

Clarice looked closely at the picture. 'Who are the others?'

Emily leaned in to point. 'This is Grandpa and Avril, with Dad in front; this is Major Freddie, and Great-Aunt Ernestine. Probably it's Johnson behind the camera. He works for the family, does most of the cooking.'

'What's his other name?' Clarice asked.

'I don't know. I've only ever known him as Johnson,' Emily said. 'Ralph's eyesight is poor, so Johnson drives him about. He does a lot in the house, and instructs the cleaning lady who comes in weekdays, and the gardener.'

'And the two black Labradors?'

'Grandpa always has two black Labs. It's a family tradition, that and having Siamese cats.'

'It sounds like a busy household. The stone Siamese is stunning.'

'She's called Bellatrix, which is Latin for a female warrior,' Emily said. 'The first breeding pair of Siameses came to the UK in 1884; they were called Pho and Mia. Dad said my great-great-grandmother Emily, my namesake, was bonkers about Siamese cats, and in 1890 she acquired a pair of kittens, descendants of the first breeding pair. Because she loved them so much, Great-Great-Grandpa George said when he commissioned the stonemason that the stone cat's features had to be recognisable as being Siamese.'

'Which is why the family continues to have that breed of cats … what an interesting history.'

'Bellatrix stares out to the Fens, and beyond to the Wash.' Emily warmed to telling the story. 'According to family legend, she guards the house and protects its inhabitants.'

Clarice smiled, thinking that poor Colin didn't seem to have been overly protected in the course of his lifetime.

After they'd talked for a further ten minutes, Clarice made a move to leave. Emily helped her carry the cat baskets to the porch, though Clarice told her to stay indoors, as she was still in her pyjamas. The sky had darkened, with rain falling; it was clear from the puddles that it had set in some time ago.

'Thanks for coming.' Emily hugged her. 'I appreciate it – and you will have a look through the things in Dad's box?'

'I will,' Clarice promised, 'and when you get back from Nottingham, you must come over to the cottage for lunch. We can talk more about it then.'

Clarice drove home, aware of Colin's cats in the back of the car. She had not raised the subject with Emily, but the younger woman's insistence that she intended to keep the animals was problematic. It was doubtful she could have them in her room in the hall of residence. It was something she would discuss with her the next time they met.

She glanced at the brown wooden box on the seat next to her. She found it hard to stop her mind from roaming over the details Emily had given her about the Compton-Smythe family. She realised she was itching to get home and explore the box's contents and the investigator's report.

Chapter 4

Later, over a lunch of vegetable soup and home-made bread, Clarice told Bob and Sandra about her visit to Emily.

'Poor girl.' Sandra was sympathetic to Emily's plight. 'Dad dying so young and unexpectedly, and her mum with a new family, not having time for her!'

Clarice imagined that Sandra might be thinking about her own daughters, Susan and Michelle, and how awful it would have been if they'd ever been in that position. But Sandra's girls were now in their forties, with half-grown children of their own.

'And then splitting up with the boyfriend.' Sandra sighed.

Clarice nodded as she looked at her friend. In her seventies, Sandra was small and feisty, always beautifully turned out; her make-up and every dyed-black hair perfectly in place, and as usual wearing bright pink lipstick.

'Don't forget it was Emily who did the dumping!' Bob interrupted. He was an inch taller and a year younger than his wife, rotund and with little hair.

'I can still feel sorry for her. She's not much more than a kid,' Sandra shot back.

'We've got Colin's cats for a few days,' Clarice interrupted. 'Although Emily did open up with me, she'll be happier with her uni mates.'

'You have a way of getting people to open up.' Sandra looked at Bob, who nodded. 'And by the way, we're both in love with Sassy. What an old fusspot.'

'I love the way his front paws turn outwards, like the legs of an antique chair.' Bob demonstrated, making his hands into fists to mimic Sassy's. 'He stamps and rumbles when I go in, like he's ready to argue, but when he's picked up, he goes into melting purr mode.'

'A lion in disguise. He has a big personality,' Clarice said.

'I doubt you'll find anyone to take him,' Sandra said. 'He'll be one of the stickers – too old to rehome, and you and Rick said you couldn't take on any more yourselves.'

'If we can't find him a home, we'll have a rethink. Rick might change his mind.'

'Good luck with that!' Sandra rolled her eyes.

'So.' Bob put his elbows on the table to lean in. 'When are you going to look through that box?' He glanced at his wife and winked.

The three collectively turned their gazes to the wooden box that had been displayed on the dresser since Clarice's return.

'I'll have a look later today.'

'It's not like you to wait,' Bob teased. 'You're usually on to something immediately. Have you still not sorted out those business accounts?'

'Nope.' Clarice shook her head ruefully.

'If there's a mystery, it's sure to pull you in. But it all happened too long ago, darlin'.' Sandra sounded dubious. 'They'll all be dead. You won't get to the bottom of it after fifty years.'

'Mm.' Bob nodded. 'Sandra's right, and if the detective agency couldn't find out what happened to Avril, you'll probably be wasting your time.'

'I promised Emily I'd look at the stuff in the box.' Clarice shrugged. 'I'll go through what's in there – it's my own time I'm wasting.'

After they had cleared the table and washed the bowls and plates, Clarice followed her friends outside, chatting until they left, then set out to walk the boundary of the garden with the dogs. The day had brightened up and the rain had stopped, with the sun splitting through the clouds. The dogs moved ahead of her, across the grasses of the wildflower meadow, happy, like Clarice, to be outside.

Back in the cottage, she headed upstairs to the study to catch up on phone messages. Blue and Jazz squashed together on the small sofa at one end of the room, Jazz, the smaller of the two, resting her head in the centre of Blue's back.

The room was spick and span, having undergone a tidy and deep clean a few days earlier. After finishing the phone calls, Clarice sat in front of her computer, working through columns of figures. She needed to get all the paperwork for her ceramics business in order before sending the accounts to Douglas Bains, whom she'd used for many years. Her mind returned to Colin Compton-Smythe. Douglas was in his mid sixties, and she had often thought that when he retired, she would ask Colin to take over as her accountant. It was not to be.

Her eyes kept creeping to the dark green folder with *Brown, Davidson and Simpson* in black letters on the cover. Inside, the first page was headed *Client, Colin Compton-Smythe*, and below, *Purpose of Investigation – Missing Persons*.

With an effort, she pulled her eyes and thoughts back to her accounts. She generally sent the paperwork for the previous year's income from her ceramics business in June. This year time had somehow spooled out, and she knew she must complete this tedious task today. Douglas expected to receive the accounts before the end of the week. The sooner she got it done, the sooner she could read the investigator's report.

Blue started to snore, a deep, contented rumble. The wind was getting up; Clarice could hear it whispering. Outside the window, the clouds moved, and leaves danced. Ignoring all the distractions, she switched her total concentration to the accounts.

Over two hours later, as A4 sheets of paper collected in the tray of the printer, she sighed with relief. She put the paperwork, bank statements and receipts into a large manila envelope and addressed it to Douglas. She would take it into Castlewick the following day and drop it in at his office.

Downstairs, while the kettle boiled for a cup of mint tea, she opened the door to allow the dogs to wander in and out for a few minutes. Taking her tea into the sitting room, she flopped down onto the sofa to open the dark green folder – then, with a change of heart, put it back into the box and brought out the battered black notebook that was underneath it.

Opening it, she smiled as she recognised Colin's neat hand-writing, remembering the deep blue fountain pen ink he'd been fond of using. There were several pages of notes under the heading *Investigative Agency*. They started with a list, possibly written before the initial meeting with the investigator, to remind himself of questions to ask and what his requirements were.

Tracing the whereabouts of Avril

Tracing the whereabouts of Major Freddie Baxter

Did they leave Stone Fen Manor together?

If finding them proves to be impossible, follow the trail as
far as possible

Janice Baxter – wife of Freddie – left before her husband. Her
trail might lead to the Major. Find more information

Contact Avril's friends

There should be no contact with my family members at
Stone Fen Manor

The notes then continued with an account of his first meeting with Dennis Simpson, who had assured him that the agency had a high success rate and that he would be given a detailed account of all the time spent on the investigation.

Clarice flicked slowly through. The next list appeared to be memories of Avril. Further on, there were addresses. As she turned the pages, there was the sound of a car engine outside. Both dogs ran to the door in a frenzy of barking. She switched on the outside light; it was dark, with day creeping into evening.

'Rick,' she said as he climbed out of his car while being welcomed home by the dogs. 'You're early.'

'Don't sound so surprised. It's gone six, though I suppose that's early by my standards.' He grinned as he followed her inside, looking forward to a comfortable evening.

Later, after dinner, having moved into the sitting room, they sat in companionable silence for a few minutes. The only sounds were the fire crackling, spreading its warmth. Blue and Jazz lay sleeping, back to back on the hearthrug. Reposing around the room, on chairs, the windowsill and along the back of the sofa, were five of the seven family cats.

Rick had told Clarice about his day, with little more to add on the murder case.

'You haven't told me – how did you get on with Emily?' he asked.

Clarice repeated everything Emily had told her.

'Have you gone through the report, and what's in the box?'

'I ran out of time. I had to finish the hated accounts. I've only read through what I suspect Colin was going to instruct the investigator to look into. I'll get stuck in properly tomorrow morning.'

'It sounds like your sort of mystery.' Rick smiled.

'Bob and Sandra thought that after fifty years it would be unsolvable.'

'I agree with them, but that's not going to stop you trying.'

'That sounds like a thumbs-up – not the usual disapproval?'

'I'm never disapproving – quite the opposite. I'd like to think I've always supported you.' Rick sounded defensive.

'You always help.' Clarice gave her sweetest smile.

'I know – eventually.' Rick appeared to reassess his position. 'I'm generally cautious because the puzzles you delve into have brought you into contact with some unpleasant characters.' He paused momentarily. 'But I don't think something that happened half a century ago will be dangerous; no mad murderers lurking in the shadows. Avril and her major have probably been dead for years.'

'Quite possibly,' Clarice agreed. 'It might be that when I've gone through the box and the report, I'll feel that it's a no go – a complete dead end.'

'That's for tomorrow.' Rick stood up, and the dogs, reading the signs, preceded him to the door.

'While you take the girls around the garden, I'll do my last check-in at the cat barn,' Clarice said.

'I'll come with you,' Rick offered.

'Are you sure? It's getting late. You're up early tomorrow.' Clarice spoke gently. 'Don't you want to get to bed?'

'Let's do it together, Clarice. Anyway, I've not met Sassy yet.'

After taking a turn around the garden with Blue and Jazz, they headed into the barn, leaving Sassy until last. As Clarice walked towards the cat, it came at pace to meet her. But on reaching her, the animal let out a yowl of joy and ran straight past her to Rick.

Rick stared down; the cat gazed up, giving its best vocal offerings, half shout, half purr.

'I had to pick him up to get that reaction,' Clarice said, green-eyed.

'He's got good taste.' Rick bent to scoop the cat up. Sassy immediately tucked his head into Rick's neck, putting his paws on either side.

'I think you're his chosen one.' Clarice smiled.

'He has the most amazing old-gentleman set of handlebar whiskers. They curve to meet in the front.'

'Old cats are beautiful in ways not always obvious.'

'I hope you can find him a good home; you know we can't take another one into the house.' Rick gently rubbed his fingers down Sassy's back.

'Yes, I know.'

* * *

Back at the cottage, Rick went to bed while Clarice headed for the sitting room to open the brown box. It had turned into a strange week: Sassy, Colin's death, and the meeting with Emily.

Taking out the two photographs, she held them under the bright circle of the table lamp to examine them more closely. Ralph and the Major were both in their prime, Ralph broad-chested and rugged, the Major, half a head taller, elegant and handsome, with chiselled features. Looking at each of the faces in turn, she ruminated over where Avril and the Major might have gone on that fateful day fifty years ago. Her eyes finally came to rest on Colin, a child, but recognisable as the man she'd known. They had spent numerous hours together over the last eleven years. She had known him first as a pupil, then as a friend, and their discussions had covered many aspects of life. They'd laughed together often. She'd considered him a decent person, kind, funny and thoughtful; she felt a stab of profound sadness.

'All those internal hidden scars; you carried such misery for most of your life.' She spoke quietly to the image of the child in the photograph. 'I might not be able to get to the bottom of it – but I promise I'll try.'

Chapter 5

The following morning, after Rick had left for work and Sandra and Bob had taken over the cat duties, Clarice took in the view from her study window as she unpacked the contents of the box onto her desk. A slash of white along the horizon topped an angry black sky. The wind moved the trees in a frantic jig and the first drops of rain hit the window.

As she glanced at the items in front of her, the phone rang.

'Clarice – hi, it's Emily.' Her voice sounded more upbeat than the last time they'd spoken.

'How are you?'

'Much better, thank you. Are Napoleon and Josephine all right?'

'Perfect,' Clarice said.

'I heard from Grandpa. Dad's funeral has been arranged for Thursday of next week, at Sealsby village church.' Clarice heard the tension in Emily's voice.

'I'm glad he's got a date.'

'I'm meeting one of my lecturers in about fifteen minutes, but I'm going to be cheeky and ask if you'd mind my returning to pick the cats up on Saturday, rather than tomorrow.'

'No problem,' Clarice said. 'You did say it might be three nights. If you're coming on Saturday, have you time to join Rick and me for lunch? It'll probably only be soup, bread and cheese.'

'Brilliant. I'd love to meet your husband, and you can tell me what you think about that report, if you've managed to take a look.'

'About twelve thirty, then. We can talk over lunch.'

'I'll see you then.'

Clarice returned her attention to the items from the box: the locket, a postcard, the green folder from the investigative agency, and the notebook.

She judged the delicate gold locket to be Victorian, perhaps inherited by Avril from a family member. Inside it was a photograph of the infant she knew to be Colin, with his mother. Picking up the photographs one at a time, she examined each closely, using a magnifying glass from the desk drawer. The locket worn by Avril in the photo was the one she was now holding. Emily had confirmed it. The postcard was from Ilkley, addressed to Colin, the postmarked date illegible. Scrawled in spidery writing were the words *It is a mistake, do not come. I will not be there.*

Moving back briefly to Colin's notebook, she realised that it might be harder than she'd imagined to decipher his short sentences and scattered words. While in the beginning the notes had clarity, and she could work out their purpose, as she went further, it became more difficult. Surprising, as she had always thought Colin so exact. Still, the issues and subject matter were personal, and he might have preferred to use a shorthand only he understood. The notes were for his guidance, after all, never intended for anyone else's eyes. She set it to one side to look at later. Relaxing into the backrest of the office chair, she at last opened the green folder bearing the words *Brown, Davidson and Simpson* in bold black letters on its cover.

The first page gave information about the agency, which had been founded in 2001. It had both male and female investigators. All had backgrounds in the police force, army or security, and each had been CRB-checked and was insured.

There was a brief CV for Dennis Simpson, the agent used by Colin. He had joined the army aged eighteen years, and at twenty-seven became a police constable. Ten years later, having risen to sergeant, he'd gone on to work for BBR Security, a company used by department stores. Starting first as a senior security manager, he had worked his way up, over ten years, to top management level. He had then joined Francis Brown and Daniel Davidson as a partner in the detective agency.

The most common cases undertaken by the agency were tracing family members or friends and helping adopted children who wanted to find their birth family. They also obtained evidence regarding marital and adultery matters, and traced debtors who had absconded. They claimed to tailor their investigations to the specific needs of each client. They used the latest technology, combined with surveillance and GP vehicle tracking. Clients were assured that the investigators were reliable, knowledgeable and discreet. An in-depth report would be given with findings, together with video and photographic evidence.

Colin's report began with a detailed background account of those living at Stone Fen Manor, along with anyone who had a relevant connection to the Compton-Smythe family.

Ralph Compton-Smythe had been born at the manor. Privately educated at boarding school, he became an investment banker in the City of London. He inherited the house on his father James's death, and returned to live there. Once settled, he founded a company known as CS Investments. His mother, Elizabeth, who had severe arthritis, moved to Italy after her husband's death.

Ernestine Compton-Smythe, also born at the manor, was five years younger than her brother. She had been educated at local schools, and had never married or left home. There was little other information about her: no mention of a career or a share of the inheritance. It was – Clarice twisted her pen absent-mindedly – much like many farming families in Lincolnshire. The oldest son would inherit the house and any acreage. Sisters would get the money to pay for a decent wedding. If they were fortunate, they might also receive help with the deposit to buy a property with their new husband. It looked like Ernestine hadn't got either of those – the word *spinster* followed her name in bold letters. Still, while not owning a share in the house, it had continued to be her home.

Freddie Baxter had gone to Sandhurst and risen to become a major, serving in the Royal Fusiliers. He was described as handsome and self-assured, and able to draw female interest. It was clear that he had led a charmed life, with no shortage of money. There was no information concerning details of children or siblings. After leaving the army, he had, for a short time, been a partner in CS Investments. He had received a payment from Ralph for his share in the business before he left the manor for the last time. The Major had been married to Janice (née Reading), who was two years his junior. They had lived in Sealsby, the nearest village, but they sold their property there and Janice moved to Leeds. Freddie had then moved into Stone Fen Manor. The arrangement lasted only a few weeks; Freddie and Avril then left together.

Dennis Simpson gave the names of seven people said to be friends of the Major. Four had died, one had proved to be untraceable and two had refused to comment.

Avril Compton-Smythe (née Blake) was born in Spalding, Lincolnshire, the younger of the two daughters of Ken and Helen. The sisters both attended the local grammar school. Avril left school, aged sixteen, with five O levels. She went to work in a clerical position in the offices of a local seed merchant.

Helen, already a widow when Avril married Ralph, died eight months after her daughter's wedding, having suffered a stroke.

Seven months after he'd returned to live at Stone Fen Manor, Ralph Compton-Smythe had met Avril Blake at the local tennis club. It was a whirlwind romance, with the couple marrying less than six months after their first meeting. Colin was born a year later. Avril was thirty-one years of age when she left. Ralph would then have been thirty-five, and the Major forty.

Clarice sat for a few moments considering the information. It seemed that Ralph had been fortunate, with everything coming conveniently together. His father died, and he'd inherited Stone Fen Manor. Within a few months, he had met and married Avril. Had he been in love with her, she wondered, or had he decided that having the house and a new business, he also wanted a wife, child and two Labradors to complete the picture?

Tessa Dinkler was given only a one-line mention. The report stated that she had moved in with Ralph four months after Avril had departed, but that she and Ralph had never married; their daughter's name was Dawn.

Bernard Graham Johnson, always known as Johnson, had been born in Liverpool of a Scottish mother and an African seaman father. His mother, Hannah Johnson, had returned to Glasgow when her son was five years of age. She had died two years later, at which point Johnson had become part of the care system. He was five years younger than Ralph and employed in London in hotel management before moving to the Compton-Smythe household. Within two weeks of Ralph's return to the manor, he had hired Johnson to manage staff and run the place. Johnson was now eighty years of age.

Clarice remembered Emily saying she didn't know Johnson's Christian name. Had she read the investigator's file? Perhaps it was only after Colin's death that she had looked through his possessions and found the box. In which case, in her confused and upset state of mind, she would only have glanced at the report.

Dennis Simpson made observations about conversations with many people contacted as part of the inquiry. They variously described Avril as being quiet, intelligent and shy. She had been in love with Ralph and appeared to be content. But the picture painted was sketchy; it had no depth. The information gained could be a description of anyone. It felt as if the investigator had discovered a shadow in his search for Avril, not a rounded, complete person. She did not appear to have had many friends, and the ones she had were vague. It had not been possible to contact Pattie Freeman, named as a close friend.

Two hours later, after reading the comments of friends and relatives connected to Ralph and Avril, Clarice was interrupted by Sandra, who asked her to join them for lunch. She reluctantly put the folder and her notepad to one side.

'Is this for the accountant?' In the kitchen, Sandra held up the manila envelope that was on the dining table. 'We can drop it in to Douglas for you when we leave – we're going to Castlewick.'

'Thanks, it'll save me a journey.' Clarice beamed at Sandra as she went to the table. 'Ooh, fresh bread. You have been busy.'

'And your favourite soup.' Sandra looked pleased.

'Yes, thank you.'

The two dogs, having followed Clarice downstairs, settled on the floor nearby.

'Have you learned much from the investigator's report?' Bob asked when they were seated around the table, each with a steaming bowl of the carrot and coriander soup in front of them.

'Yes and no. Avril's friends paint an interesting picture of Ralph. There are small observations about him: he seems to have been detached, distant, antisocial. A bit of an oddball.'

'And Avril?' Sandra asked.

'Quiet, reserved and shy, not many close friends. But there are conflicting opinions about the marriage. While there were some comments that Avril married for love and appeared content, other people said the relationship was cold.'

'That's confusing.' Sandra paused, thinking. 'I suppose it depends who they talked to; people can be nasty if they have other reasons not to like someone.'

'Mm, you may have a point. I get the impression that Ralph saw himself as a cut above. That's a sure way to be disliked. Pattie Freeman might be more interesting, but they couldn't reach her. She didn't return their calls. And it would have been good to have Pamela's opinion – Avril's older sister – but she refused to talk to Dennis.'

'Did she give a reason?' Bob asked.

'No. She said it was something that had happened a long time ago, and she didn't want to talk about it. She told Dennis to bugger off!'

'She didn't sit on the fence, then!' Sandra laughed.

'Quite,' Clarice said. 'There's also mention that Colin was specific in his request that the investigator must not under any circumstances contact those who were living at the manor house.'

'From what you told us,' Bob paused mid dip, his spoon raised in the air, 'Ralph, Colin's father, didn't want any talk about Avril and Freddie.'

'Which,' Sandra joined in, 'is understandable if she dumped him for the business partner.'

'But did she?' Clarice said, perplexed. 'If Ralph was in a relationship with Tessa, and Avril found out about it, why would she suddenly take up with Freddie?'

'You don't think she was carrying on with him before she found out about Tessa?'

'I haven't read all Colin's notes yet, but according to Emily, Colin said that when Avril found out about Ralph's affair, she was completely devastated. If she had been having an affair too, why would she be so distraught that her husband was doing the same? Something doesn't add up.'

Chapter 6

After Bob and Sandra had departed, Clarice returned to the investigator's report.

The afternoon slipped away as she continued to go through the file, making notes with queries in her pad. On the computer, she fed the names of Avril's friends into the electoral roll. When the investigator had made contact with them, they'd all had Lincolnshire addresses. But that had been ten years ago, and none of them now showed up as being voters at the addresses in the report. Given their ages, if they were alive, they might be in nursing or retirement homes.

She had better luck with Pamela Snell, née Blake, Avril's older sister, who would now be eighty-three years old. It might be worthwhile trying to contact her again. Clarice put a tick next to her name and moved on.

'So, how are you getting on, tell me?' Rick asked later that evening when they were sipping their nightcap.

'I've five that I want to make contact with,' Clarice said. She turned the pages of her notepad to come to the lists of those she had eliminated as possible contacts and those she thought might be worth a try.

'Are these people you intend to phone?'

'I would like to. I need to ask for Emily's permission, and I'll try to catch her tomorrow morning before she goes to classes,' Clarice said. 'She's coming for lunch on Saturday. I might be able to arrange meetings for Monday or Tuesday.'

'And Colin's funeral is on Thursday?'

'Yes, so Emily will have whatever new information we can glean before she goes to stay with Ralph and the family.'

'Do you believe it possible to find any new information?' Rick said doubtfully. 'From what you said earlier, you can't even trace some of the people Dennis interviewed – they're all dead?'

'Not all, and I won't know unless I make a few phone calls.'

'Who's on your list?' Rick leaned back in his chair. 'You said five?'

'I'd like to speak to the investigative agent, Dennis Simpson, although I'd have to tread carefully. I don't want him thinking I'm trying to suggest he didn't do his job properly.'

Rick nodded.

'Avril's sister Pamela lives in Lincoln. She's the one who wouldn't speak to the investigator. We might find out something new from her.'

'Or she might tell you to bugger off, like she did with Dennis!'

'I'll take the risk,' Clarice said. 'Then there's Gerry Pillar. He was an acquaintance of the Major, and is still at the same address in Spalding where he was ten years ago.'

'I though Simpson couldn't trace any friends of the Major?'

'Yes.' Clarice looked at her notes. 'The friendship was through the wives, Janice and Ann, Gerry's wife. Ann died eleven years ago, a year before the investigation.'

'He's not going to help much then.'

'Probably not.' Clarice looked again at the notes. 'According to the report, Gerry said, "I only met him a couple of times. He was nice enough but wasn't my type." He went on to say, "He seemed the kind of man who would enjoy flirting with the ladies, and because he was a good listener, they told him all their little secrets. Janice, the Major's wife, appeared resigned to his flirtatious ways, and they seemed close as a couple, so it came as a surprise that he'd run away with Avril."'

'Gerry gave a lot of information; what more could he tell you?' Rick asked.

'Probably not a lot.'

He nodded his agreement. 'So that's three – two more?'

'Pattie Freeman, if she's still alive. I'm desperate to speak to her.'

'Why?'

'In Colin's notes, he has her as "Mum's closest friend". She's on the electoral roll at the time of the investigation, but never returned calls. Not there now, according to the voters' list, although I do have a telephone number for the address from ten years ago. And I did also hope I might be able to trace Janice, if she's not dead.'

'The Major's wife?'

'Ex-wife, I believe.' Clarice nodded. 'Janice moved to Roundhay in Leeds after she left him, and according to Dennis Simpson, she was still there ten years ago. There are photographs taken of her from across the street. She looks doddery even back then.'

Clarice opened the file to show Rick a tall, stooped woman, then in her mid seventies. She'd made no attempt at trying to disguise her age. Her hair was white, and she wore no make-up; her clothes had the appearance of giving comfort rather than being fashionable or flattering. In each of the four shots taken in the street, she'd been using a stout walking stick.

'The investigator's report said she had arthritis. Again, she's no longer on the electoral roll for that address, and there isn't a telephone number.'

'Maybe check for a death certificate,' Rick suggested.

'I've done that, but no luck. I don't have either her date of birth or a date of death, and I don't want to spend all my time looking for death certificates. I'd rather talk to the living.' Clarice put her empty glass on a small table.

'She might still be alive, in a nursing home.'

'Possibly. According to the report, she had a brother called Peter, who returned to the UK from Australia after a divorce. Might he have possibly moved in with his sister?'

'Not on the voting list?'

'Nope – and an extra complication is a second address in Colin's notebook, in Oakwood in Leeds, West Yorkshire, which is just down the road from …'

'Roundhay,' Rick finished.

'And don't forget the postcard is from Ilkley – in Yorkshire.'

'You only have Janice for the Yorkshire connections?'

'So far,' Clarice said, frustrated, 'but I haven't started digging yet.'

'What time are Bob and Sandra in tomorrow?'

'They won't be. They're going to have lunch with their daughter, Michelle. They'll be back on Sunday when we go to Norwich to deliver the ceramics to the gallery. Go to bed, Rick. I'll be up in a minute.'

Going upstairs to the study, she picked up the investigator's file and Colin's notebook, and went to relax on the small sofa usually claimed by the dogs. A low background sound of snoring from the bedroom indicated that Rick had taken her advice. She opened Colin's notebook again, and turned to the page relating to his first meeting with Dennis Simpson.

The words *street savvy* under Simpson's name and *understands what is required* suggested that to begin with, Colin had been content with the investigator. Later, however, he had noted, *Janice Baxter – nothing to report*. Then, *A dead end. Janice does not know of the whereabouts of her ex*. He had queried whether Janice and Freddie Baxter were divorced, since he had not seen the evidence. The response from Dennis Simpson had been that it was irrelevant to his inquiry.

Having received the final report from Simpson, Colin had noted, *Conclusions unclear, disappointing result*.

The notebook also had a page devoted to sets of figures. Two numbers, then a group of five, then seven, and so on. It was impossible to ascertain what they related to: telephone numbers, distances, or something else entirely? Elsewhere, Colin revisited the days before Avril had left. There was mention of her talking to the Major in the garden, with him holding her hand. On the day she left, he'd written, *the hottest day of the year*.

The most intriguing information was a before-and-after section. The 'before' list, Clarice assumed, related to the period when his mother was still at the manor. It included types of food, things she might have done or they'd done together, such as kite flying, skating, dancing, and items of clothing. The 'after' section, presumably when Avril had gone, was shorter, but both lists included jewellery, shoes and dancing. Clarice pondered on Colin's state of mind when he'd made the lists. So much time had passed since Avril's disappearance, but he'd still been mentally locked into that period of his childhood.

Resisting the temptation to read further, she put the paperwork aside and sat quietly, trying to muster her thoughts into some sort of order. With her mind swinging from one subject to another, she realised she was past her mental sell-by – it was time to join Rick and get some sleep.

Chapter 7

Later the following day, after she'd had her lunch and all the animals were settled, Clarice went into the study to begin her phone calls. She'd caught Emily, early in the morning, before she went to classes; she had agreed that Clarice should contact the people mentioned in the report, and said she would be happy to meet with them on Monday or Tuesday of the following week.

Clarice had felt a sense of foreboding after talking to Emily. The younger woman's response had been so optimistic and upbeat that she could not help but feel that if the enquiries did not lead to an outcome or a positive conclusion, she would feel deflated. Might she use the focus of looking into what had happened to her grandmother to evade her sorrow for her father? It would be a mistake; grief was a visitor that would not be ignored.

The investigative agent, Dennis Simpson, sounded non-plussed by her call. It took several minutes to get past a female receptionist keen to build on his importance. She needed to know every aspect of the caller's enquiry, the implication being that the company would not tolerate time-wasters. Clarice, undaunted, pushed her case. When he eventually came to the phone, Simpson's voice, with an Essex drawl, was measured. He claimed not to remember the case, but said he would call her back when he'd had an opportunity to look at the file. Clarice realised that it was reasonable for him not to immediately remember Colin Compton-Smythe and his family, with so many clients over the last ten years. But there had been something in his tone that caused her to think he had not been entirely truthful.

Next, she called the number given beside the name of Pattie Freeman. That Pattie was no longer on the voting list was not a hopeful sign. However, the call was answered by an amiable woman, who said she knew her.

'I bought this house from her. I'm Karen Jones,' she said. 'Although, when I arrived to view the house, Pattie and I didn't know each other, we got chatting and realised our daughters were good friends, and she and I got on so well we've turned into ladies who lunch – she's such a sweet person.'

'What a happy coincidence,' Clarice responded, pleased to find a thread that might lead to Pattie.

Mrs Jones chatted on, moving from one subject to another. Clarice felt it might be easier to stop the sun rising and setting than halt her in mid flow.

'I'd better go. My husband thinks I'm never off the phone,' Karen said, suddenly giving a high girlish laugh. 'I can see his car coming up the drive. I have Pattie's number here in my phone book. She lives with her daughter Olivia in Stamford.'

Having tried the number twice, Clarice left a brief message asking if Pattie would return her call, before moving on to Avril's sister, Pamela. The phone was answered on the second ring, as if the elderly lady was seated nearby waiting expectantly for a call. When Clarice explained the nature of her enquiry, there was a long silence.

'Are you from the same place as the people who contacted me years ago? Colin paid for an investigation into my sister's disappearance.'

'No.' Clarice explained again. 'Colin died last week. It's his daughter Emily, your great-niece, who asked me to look into it.'

'So you *are* another detective?' Pamela's voice was sharp.

'No.' Clarice kept her voice level, realising that the woman was confused. 'I was a friend of Colin's, and Emily asked me if I would look at the investigator's report.'

'You're half a century too late to catch up with Avril,' Pamela said. 'My sister and I didn't get on that well; we had little in common and nothing to do with each other after she married.'

'I understand,' Clarice said.

'I live in Lincoln.' Pamela spoke after a moment of hesitation. 'If you want to bring Emily to visit, that will be acceptable – I've never met her.'

'Thank you. I have your address. When can—'

'You can't come at the weekend. I'm busy,' Pamela cut in haughtily. 'Come on Monday morning at ten thirty.'

'We'll be there on Monday, thank you,' Clarice said.

The line was already dead. Pamela had hung up. Clearly, it was only her curiosity to meet Emily for the first time that had made her agree to their visit.

'One down, three to go,' Clarice said to Blue, who responded by lifting her head to yawn.

The conversation with Gerry Pillar felt initially like a dead end. 'I can't tell you any more than I told the man from the agency,' he said to Clarice. 'The Major was nice enough, but he wasn't a mate – I only met him twice. His wife, Janice, was a friend of my late wife, Ann.' There was a long pause. 'It was awkward. He was rich and posh, and we weren't in the same league – I could never be comfortable with him.' He laughed, 'It would have been the same for him. I wasn't his type any more than he was mine.'

'But your wives were close friends?' Clarice said.

'Janice grew up in Spalding. She wasn't posh, that's why she and my Ann got on well,' Gerry said. 'I wouldn't have said this in front of Ann, but Janice was a cracker; she was a real beauty, and boy, did she have style – she looked amazing.'

'Did you know of other friends of the Major or Janice who I might contact?'

'You mean the ones who aren't already pushing up daisies?' Gerry rumbled, laughing at his own joke. 'I don't know of anyone, sorry, love.'

'Ann didn't keep in touch after Janice moved to Yorkshire?'

'Not that I recall.'

'You heard nothing about her remarrying – a new man?' Clarice waited.

'No.' Gerry was firm, 'Sorry, I can't remember any bloke's name. Ann laughed about it. She said Janice would never be brave enough to take on another boyfriend after the debacle of her first marriage.'

'Why? Did Ann think the first marriage was a disaster?'

'She did.' Gerry laughed again. 'If I'd believed what Janice told my Ann, they were a perfect match. That was before she went to Leeds to look after her old mum. She trusted him on his own, and in no time, he was gone – he'd left with Avril.'

'I didn't realise she originally left to look after her mother,' Clarice said.

'Her father was from Leeds, and when he retired, he and Janice's mum moved up there. The mother had cancer, and before she married, Janice was a nurse.' Gerry paused before commenting. 'Trusting her husband while she nursed her sick mother just goes to show that there's no such thing as perfect.'

He took Clarice's number, promising to call if he thought of anything new.

After putting the phone down, Clarice flicked through the investigator's file to look at the image of Janice she had shown Rick the previous evening. She felt a flicker of sadness. The girl Gerry had described as being a beauty had turned into this stooped, white-haired woman. Struggling, like many other elderly people, with disability caused by arthritis.

At least she had a chance of gleaning something more from Pamela on Monday. The new information from Gerry, about Janice going to Leeds to care for her mother before her husband vanished, might lead nowhere. But it was another piece of what she envisaged as a vast jigsaw. Once she had all the pieces in place, she might have more understanding of what had happened to Avril.

Later, while pulling the drapes closed in the sitting room, Clarice considered whether to make a vegetarian lasagne for supper or zap something from the freezer in the microwave when Rick arrived home. As she finally settled on a lasagne, the phone rang.

'It's Dennis Simpson, returning your call.'

'Great!' Clarice enthused. 'Thank you for getting back. Did you manage to find the file?'

'Yes indeed. Was there something specific you wanted to know about the investigation?'

Clarice explained that with Colin's death, his daughter had come across the investigator's file and was keen to probe further into Avril and the Major's disappearance.

'There isn't anything I can add to what's in the report,' Dennis said, sounding ready to terminate the call.

'Would it be possible to have half an hour of your time?' Clarice asked. 'Just to ask you about any impressions you might have had of the main characters involved. I know it would mean so much to Emily.'

There followed a long silence.

'It was such a long time ago, and I've had numerous cases over the last ten years. I doubt I'll be able to tell you anything new after all this time.'

'We would appreciate it,' Clarice persisted.

'I realise that Mr Compton-Smythe's daughter must be grieving for her father. His death is so recent, and decisions taken at these times are not necessarily rational. Perhaps,' Dennis spoke as if reasoning with an awkward child, 'when the dust has had time to settle, she may read the conclusions of the investigation and realise everything has been dealt with.'

'I don't think that will happen. Emily needs to follow her instincts now.' Clarice was polite but firm. 'Will you see her, Mr Simpson, if I bring her over next week, perhaps Monday or Tuesday afternoon?'

'Well, let me think – and please call me Dennis.'

Clarice sensed he was playing for time.

'I can't do Tuesday. I'm away on a case. It will have to be Monday at three. Do you know where we are in Lincoln?'

'Yes, I have your address. Thank you so much, Dennis.' The battle had been hard won. The case was ten years old and had no further financial value to him. Dennis didn't want them wasting his time.

'See you on Monday at three,' Clarice said.

Chapter 8

The lunch had gone well. Emily had been subdued and quiet on arrival, but Rick had worked his magic, coaxing her out of her gloom. Observing him, Clarice thought about those he dealt with on the wrong side of the law. His height and bulk might intimidate, and the hair cropped tight to his skull, merging into the permanent five o'clock facial shadow and rugby-damaged nose, added to his rough, rather menacing appearance. But he was a good listener and utterly disarming when he so chose.

Clarice had returned Colin's box to Emily, adding a typed sheet with her thoughts about Colin's comments in his notebook and the investigator's report.

Later, having finished lunch, they moved into the sitting room with coffee.

'Thanks for arranging the meetings for Monday,' Emily said.

'I don't want you to get your hopes up,' Clarice warned. 'We can talk to family and friends, but it might not lead anywhere.'

'We didn't know Janice originally moved to Leeds to look after her sick mother.' Emily was upbeat. 'That's new information.'

'Perhaps, but it might not take us any nearer to solving the puzzle.' Clarice spoke gently. 'I don't want you to feel deflated if we hit a dead end.'

'She's right,' Rick added. 'Remember your dad was desperate to solve the riddle for fifty years. Even the employment of an investigator didn't get to the bottom of it, so don't build up your hopes.'

'I understand where you're both coming from.' Emily looked from one to the other.

Clarice nodded, getting up to top up the coffee cups. 'The funeral is on Thursday; you said your grandfather asked if you would go on Wednesday and be there for two nights, is that right?'

'Yes, if I get there Wednesday mid morning, I'll be able to help get the house ready for people coming back after the funeral for food and booze. It'll be around an hour and a half's drive to get home, but I can't drive back later on Thursday if I've been drinking.'

'Quite right,' Rick said.

'Think you might be tired anyway; it sounds exhausting. Are a lot of people expected? I didn't think Colin's family was that large.'

'It's not family. It includes anyone who wants to attend the funeral, mainly from the village,' Emily explained. 'There'll be the usual church service, ending with the coffin at the grave. There will be quite a crowd, and as Grandpa puts it, "They'll expect to be fed."'

'Is that traditional?' Clarice asked.

'Yes, it goes back to when the Compton-Smythe family thought they were something special, in Great-Great-

Grandfather George's day. They gave money at Christmas to provide for the poor of the parish and they had a big standing in the community. Their pew has always been on the front row of the church. Woe betide anyone who dared not to turn up for the Sunday-morning service.'

'They held a lot of power and influence then?' Clarice said.

'Yes – but that was back then. Dad said that George and his son, my great-grandfather James, both had a lot of authority locally. I don't think Grandpa Ralph realises that apart from people attending the funeral, our family now means nothing to the villagers. His idea of how the Compton-Smythes are perceived comes from his father and grandfather, back in the dark ages.'

'If you'll be gone for two nights, do you want me to take Napoleon and Josephine? You can leave them here early Wednesday morning.'

'Yesss.' Emily dragged the word out.

'Only if you want to.' Clarice sensed a 'but'.

'I hope you won't think me too rude in asking – but you said you would be going to the funeral. Will you come with me and be there for the two nights?' Emily's face had turned a rosy pink.

'Me?'

'It would be brilliant if you could be there. Dad was a friend of yours,' Emily babbled, as if getting the words out in a rush might win her case. 'And with the mystery of Avril and the Major, if you get to know the key players and spend time with them, it could help to get to the bottom of things.'

'I'm not sure your grandfather would approve.' Clarice smiled kindly to soften the blow.

'He said yes!'

'You've already asked him?'

'I thought it better to ask him before I asked you – in case he said no.'

'I see.' Clarice could feel Rick's eyes on her as she spoke.

'We would have to share a bedroom. Grandmother Avril's room is now the guest room; it has single beds.' Emily was babbling again.

'The problem I have is that apart from our family animals, two dogs, and seven cats,' Clarice glanced at Rick, 'I've also got a cattery – not overflowing with cats, but still enough to take up a lot of time. Rick will be working in Lincoln.'

'I'm sorry.' Emily seemed to have shrunk with embarrassment. 'It was a silly suggestion.'

'But I imagine you do want to go, Clarice?' Rick asked.

'Yes,' Clarice said, 'but with so many commitments …'

'Do you think Bob and Sandra might agree to move in for a couple of days?'

'You wouldn't mind?'

'Of course not. Bet you Sandra will bite your hand off. She'd love the chance to be in charge.'

'Don't forget they've already agreed to come tomorrow when we go to Norwich, and again on Monday, while I'm out with Emily,' Clarice reminded him.

'Are these the volunteers you told me about?' Emily asked. 'The ones who were friends of your mother when you were a child?'

'Yes,' Clarice said wistfully. 'Sandra and Mum were the best of friends. They used to go to all sorts of classes together – watercolour painting, flower arranging, ceramics. Bob and Sandra are a lovely couple. When they both retired, Bob said he thought there was a possibility they might die of boredom, so they offered their help with the rescue animals. Rick and I think of them as family.'

'Your mum was also a ceramicist?'

'For Mum it was a hobby. Though it was called pottery back then, rather than ceramics.'

'But,' Rick cut in, 'Mary, Clarice's mum, did steal the name for her daughter from ...'

'Clarice Cliff,' Emily finished. 'Of course, I love the pottery from that period.'

'The 1930s was a productive period for ceramicists.' Clarice spoke as she stood up. 'Well, there's no time like the present. I'll give Sandra a ring. I know she's at home now.'

She left to use the phone in the study, and when she returned fifteen minutes later, Emily looked at her hopefully.

'Sandra said she'd be delighted. She'll get Rick all to herself, although she did suggest that Bob would undoubtedly muscle in for a game of chess.'

'Bob and I do enjoy chess,' Rick said.

'That's great.' Emily stood up, grinning, 'I'm so glad you can come with me, Clarice.'

'Me too,' Clarice said. 'Don't forget about Monday; it might be easier if I come to you at your dad's house.'

After Emily had said goodbye to Rick, she went with Clarice to the barn to collect the pair of cats. Clarice said farewell to the departing guest before stepping back into the shadow of the barn. She watched as Emily glanced around before driving away. Her mouth drooped, and her expression became taut and wretched. It was as if believing she was alone, she felt she could remove a mask.

* * *

'She puts up a front, trying to hide the desolation,' Clarice said. They were standing together in the kitchen, Clarice washing the lunchtime crockery with Rick drying.

'Yes,' he agreed, 'she does.'

'It was good of you to suggest asking Bob and Sandra to move in.'

'Don't tell me the thought hadn't already crossed your mind.' His eyes twinkled.

'Well – yes. I was surprised she asked me to go to the funeral, but I didn't want you to feel abandoned.'

'I won't. Bob and I will have a couple of whiskies while I let him beat me at chess, and Sandra will play mother hen to all the animals and us.'

'Let him beat you – ha!' Clarice laughed.

'And …'

'And what?'

'Emily is a lovely girl, but she's so young for her age, nineteen going on twelve.' Rick scratched his head thoughtfully. 'Maybe she wants you there as a support.'

'That did occur to me.'

'It's odd she was hanging out with her dad's mates. Most kids over the age of eleven want to be with their own friends, not their mum or dad's.'

'I wondered about that too.' Clarice nodded. 'I was thinking about how her mother leaving to live with her new French family must have affected her. She would have been thirteen when that happened.'

'Sounds like history repeating itself. Colin was five when his mother left.'

Clarice nodded again. 'I was also thinking how everything so far points to the Major being charming and charismatic. Emily told me Colin had liked him.'

'And according to the investigator's report, he was wealthy.'

'You've had the same thought,' Clarice said.

'I don't think it's what Emily wants to hear, but it is a strong possibility. Avril might simply have fallen in love and left with the Major.'

They continued their chores in silence, lost in their thoughts.

'The mystery of the disappearance of Avril and the Major is fifty years old.' Rick spoke eventually. 'What possible harm could come from you asking a few questions after all that time?'

Clarice nodded, smiling. Her mind had already moved on to another place, imagining the people she would meet on Monday, and later in the week, the rest of Colin's family at Stone Fen Manor. She wondered how well Emily was going to cope. It was clear that she could not manage to put on a brave face indefinitely.

Chapter 9

Sunday passed quickly, with Rick and Clarice travelling to Norwich to deliver fresh stocks of ceramic plates and vases to one of the city galleries. This was followed by lunch at their favourite Italian restaurant, where Clarice was able to try out her rusty Italian on Alberto, the proprietor, before their return home.

On Monday morning, arriving at Colin's house, Emily came out to greet her.

'Coffee?' she asked as she led Clarice indoors.

It was a different Emily today, unidentifiable as the washed-out, ashen young woman of five days ago. She was dressed smartly in slim-fitting black trousers and a long grey tunic top. Her make-up was perfect and her brown hair, brushed and shiny, tumbled down over her shoulders. Only the sadness lurking behind her smile indicated her state of mind. She had, Clarice realised, put her mask firmly in place for the day ahead.

Clarice accepted the mug of coffee proffered to her in the kitchen before, stalked by the two black cats, they went into the sitting room.

'What a lot of flowers!' She looked at the vases filled with blooms of all types on tables and the windowsill. 'I noticed more in the hall and kitchen.'

'They're mainly from friends and neighbours. Dad was popular. He always seemed to be helping someone with shopping or gardening, or filling in paperwork. There are lots from his ceramics mates.'

'Your dad was a one-off.' Clarice smiled, remembering. 'So many people loved him.'

'I know,' Emily said sadly. 'I was always proud of him.'

They sat in silence drinking their coffee, and Clarice sensed how hard it was for Emily to put up a front.

'We've got half an hour before we need to leave.' She spoke while stroking Josephine's ears. 'Have you thought about anything, however trivial, that your dad might have told you about your great-aunt Pamela?'

'I was thinking about it before you arrived,' Emily said. 'On the rare occasions I can remember him mentioning her, he never referred to her as aunt – or auntie. I believe Avril met up with her once when Dad was a small child. I'm fairly sure it's something someone told him. I doubt he'd have been old enough to remember it for himself.'

'Who would have told him?'

'I'm sorry, I really can't remember.'

'Do you know why Pamela and Avril fell out?'

'No, Dad said it was a mystery.' Emily shrugged. 'I imagine there would have been a lot of things he would have found out from his mum when he was older, had she stayed.'

'And,' Clarice added, 'if Ralph were more forthcoming, Colin could have asked him, but Avril was a taboo subject.'

'Yes, Ralph flew into a rage if Dad ever mentioned his mum. I'm sorry I can't tell you more.'

'It doesn't matter. Pamela might tell us, although,' Clarice warned, 'she came over on the phone as rather grumpy, so she might not be very forthcoming,'

'At least we'll have tried.' Emily appeared to be attempting to put a positive spin on the situation.

'Quite right,' Clarice said.

'And I've bought her a box of chocolates.'

'Soften her up!' Clarice grinned. 'I like your style.'

Almost an hour later, they reached Fiskerton, east of Lincoln. Pamela's home was on a small retirement estate, comprised of rows of single-storey bungalows. Outside the doorways of many of the dwellings were sloping ramps for wheelchair use, and to the front of each house was a small, neat square of grass. Clarice noticed a slight movement of the net curtains and realised that Pamela was probably peeking out, weighing them up.

The door opened as they reached it.

'Hello.' Emily spoke hesitantly. 'Auntie Pamela, I'm Emily.'

'I'm your great-aunt – but auntie will do.' The white-haired woman looked Emily up and down with sharp, unfriendly eyes. She was short and ramrod thin, wearing a navy-blue woollen dress, her tiny feet encased in grubby pink moccasin slippers. 'You must take after your father's side; you don't look a bit like Avril.' She sounded pleased with her assessment.

She turned, waving to indicate that they should follow her. Inside, the property was compact. Straight ahead, Clarice saw through an open door to a kitchen-diner. There were two closed doors on the right, probably the bedroom and a bathroom. She followed Pamela into the room on the left, where the elderly woman pointed towards the two-seat sofa.

'Sit there,' she instructed.

'I brought you these.' Emily held out the box of chocolates, which Pamela took from her, holding them in front of her as though she'd been handed an undetonated bomb.

'You shouldn't have.' She sniffed. Her tone and demeanour made it plain she was not using the words to be polite. She placed the box on top of a sideboard crowded with old newspapers, envelopes, invoices and the TV remote control.

As Clarice and Emily sat beside each other, Pamela took the only other seat, an armchair opposite.

The focal point of the room was an electric heater, turned on low. There were no family photographs, nothing personal, and the place had a stuffy, unpleasant smell, as if devoid of fresh air for a long time. On the faded, yellow-flower-patterned wallpaper hung several small frames containing images of castles and stately homes.

Pamela leaned forward to stare for a long time at Emily before speaking.

'What did your father tell you about me?' Her face, previously mobile, was now set, her voice sly.

'Only that you saw him once when he was small.'

'*Small!*' Pamela guffawed. 'He wouldn't have remembered that. His mother must have told him. He was in his pram.'

Emily looked confused, and Clarice sensed her awkwardness.

'Avril, your grandmother, was in Spalding. She was pushing the pram. Colin was a baby. She was with Ralph's sister, Ernestine.' Pamela straightened herself as if remembering a battle fought long ago. 'I didn't speak to them; I just had a look into the pram. He was an ugly little bugger. All babies look either like chimps or Winston Churchill; Colin was a chimp.'

She fell silent, as if reflecting on the long-ago meeting.

'Is she still alive – Ernestine?' she asked eventually.

'Yes.' Emily nodded. 'She lives at Stone Fen Manor with Ralph, her brother – my grandfather.'

'Didn't escape then, poor bitch.' Pamela slurred the words before falling silent again, like a wound-up toy that had suddenly closed down.

The atmosphere hung between them like a barrier of fog.

'You didn't get on with Avril?' Clarice asked, her voice seeming suddenly loud in the confines of the small room.

Pamela turned to look at her, as if aware of her presence for the first time.

'Who are you?'

'I'm a friend of Colin's,' Clarice said. Then, glancing at Emily, she added, 'And Emily's. I spoke to you on the phone and arranged this visit.'

For a moment, watching the mobile, twisting face, Clarice was reminded of an angry, cornered weasel, and was unsure if she might suddenly hiss or screech.

'I didn't get on with Avril.' Pamela was sharp. 'I told that man years ago – we didn't get on.'

'The investigator?' Clarice asked.

'That's what he called himself. And I'd told her it would never work when she agreed to marry Ralph – take something that's not yours, and it'll come back around to bite you on the arse.'

'What was it she took?' Emily's face was alight with confusion.

'Ralph – he wasn't hers!'

Emily and Clarice looked at Pamela as she stood up, pulling her small frame taut.

'He was mine. I met him first.'

'At the tennis club?' Clarice asked.

'I was a member, and Ralph and I played doubles most weeks, then our mother said Avril wanted to join the club, foisted her onto me. I took her along – I was kind, did her a favour.'

'She met Ralph through you?'

'The first week she joined, he asked her out.' Pamela's face twisted with emotion. 'I'd known him for six months. He would have asked me out if she'd not put her oar in.'

'You felt Avril stole him from you; that was why you didn't get on?' Emily gasped.

'She did steal him,' Pamela wailed. 'It should have been me living in that big house. I'd have been the lady of the manor – and he wouldn't have looked elsewhere if he'd had the sense to marry me.'

'But if you'd seen him every week for over six months, and then he asked Avril out the first time he met her, doesn't that tell you something?' Clarice boldly stated the obvious.

'It tells me that Avril was a slippery bitch.' Pamela's voice rose with each word. 'That little white mouse act – everyone thought she was shy and sugar-sweet. It fooled Ralph into asking her out and marrying her, but he soon got bored.'

Emily looked at Clarice, her embarrassment evident.

'I think we should go.' Clarice stood up, towering like a giant over Pamela. Emily copied her, following her to the door.

'Yes, go, bugger off. I didn't ask you to come.' Pamela

elbowed her way in front of them to throw open the front door. 'Ralph had had enough of her simpering ways, and he had a hell of a temper. You ought to have seen what he did to his tennis racquet after losing a game. He probably killed her and dumped her in the Wash – and good riddance.'

Clarice and Emily walked out of the house towards the car, Pamela's rant following them like a bad smell.

'They didn't even invite me to the wedding. Our mother went, but not me, me, her only sister.' Her voice turned into an unrelenting howl.

Getting into the car, Clarice started the engine. In the rear-view mirror, she could see that Pamela had gone back into the bungalow, but a moment later she reappeared. As the car pulled away, there was the noise of a small impact from the rear.

'Did you hit something?' Emily asked, suddenly fraught.

'No,' Clarice said, again using the mirror. 'It was your chocolates – Pamela threw them at the car. I'm surprised she had the strength, but her aim is good.'

'What a waste,' Emily said, then, as an afterthought, 'and we didn't even get offered a cup of tea.'

'Thank God for small mercies,' Clarice said. 'It'd probably have been laced with arsenic.'

Later, back at Colin's bungalow, Clarice and Emily lunched on toasted cheese.

'Strange that she wanted to meet me,' Emily said, 'just to be so rude.'

'Curiosity got the better of her, I imagine,' Clarice said. 'When I phoned, I thought she'd say no, but she couldn't resist the temptation of meeting Avril and Ralph's granddaughter.'

'She came so close, I thought she might try to yank open my mouth to examine my teeth.' Emily laughed.

'Yes, that thought had occurred to me,' Clarice agreed. 'She was almost on your lap in the sitting room.'

'It's sad she's so bitter.'

Clarice nodded. 'Fifty years of hate because she thought Avril had stolen her boyfriend, while it was clear he never was interested in her romantically. And it was hardly a surprise, with her attitude, that she didn't get an invite to the wedding.'

'Do you think we've learned anything?' Emily asked uncertainly.

'An amazing amount. Two matters have become clear.'

Emily looked at her, uncomprehending.

'Go back to last week, how you described Avril to me from your dad's point of view.'

'He said,' Emily spoke slowly, 'that his mother was loving, gentle and shy.'

'Think of how Pamela described her.'

'A slippery bitch.' Emily looked at Clarice again. 'A white mouse, quiet and shy?'

'Yes.' Clarice balled her hand into a fist and placed it on the dining table. 'Forget the first part – that was Pamela's jealousy. Pick the bones out of the second part, and you have Avril.'

'Quiet and shy.' Emily paused to think. 'Or loving, gentle and shy, as Dad put it.'

'We now know Avril's character from two sources, your father and her sister.'

Emily nodded.

'Ralph might have liked Pamela as a tennis partner. I'll bet she matched him in the aggression stakes on the court.'

Clarice nursed her coffee cup. 'But he didn't want a dominant, forceful wife.'

'He wanted someone gentle and loving.'

It was Clarice's turn to nod.

'So he picked Grandma Avril.' Emily pondered this briefly. 'You said two matters?'

'It's what she said about Ralph. It sounds like he has a short fuse.' Clarice looked intently at Emily.

'Yes, as I've told you, Dad said Ralph would fly into a rage when he asked him about Avril.'

'Apart from what your dad told you,' Clarice pushed, 'did you have any personal experience of his bad temper when you stayed at Stone Fen Manor?'

'Yes.' Emily spoke without hesitation. 'I saw him angry on several occasions. My mum once told Dad that if his father continued to act up, we wouldn't go again.'

'What did Colin say?'

'It was when their marriage, Dad's and Mum's, was on its last legs; they disagreed about everything. Mum often used the expression "red-blooded male" against him – said it didn't apply to him; he was a blip in the male line of the Compton-Smythes. Dad ignored that. He said we'd visit his family a maximum of twice a year and keep the visits short, so that's what we did, but still Mum wasn't happy about it.' Emily stopped for a moment, looking down into her coffee cup before adding, 'Mum disliked Ralph and Ernestine.' There was a sense of discomfiture, as though she was revealing something distasteful. 'Ralph likes to believe that whatever he says is right; his anger can drag on, but it's usually a sudden flare-up, and then it's gone.'

Clarice looked at her silently, appearing to consider.

'You think that when Avril wanted to leave, Ralph really did kill her and dispose of her body in the Wash?' Emily asked.

'We have to consider it a possibility,' Clarice said.

Chapter 10

After discussing the contents of Dennis Simpson's investigative report again, Clarice and Emily set out for their second meeting of the day. Clarice had made a list of the points to review with the investigator.

With the address on the satnav, they reached their destination with ease. The three-storey concrete building was occupied by several companies, with Brown, Davidson and Simpson sharing the third-floor space. Inside the building, a sign in bold red lettering stated that no smoking was allowed on the premises; a second, attached to the lift door, announced that it was out of order.

As they walked silently up the concrete staircase, Clarice remembered her late teens when, after leaving school, she'd undertaken employment in similar office buildings. Her emotions sank at the memory of the grey premises that might have been interchangeable with this one, displaying no sense of design or originality. It seemed that the architects, and those who occupied these blocks, strove to eliminate any sense of warmth or attractiveness, perhaps for fear that beauty in any form might overstimulate the senses.

The stairwell's grey ambience continued to the top floor, with the windows on each level overlooking a busy street. On the third storey, they found a door bearing the legend *Brown, Davidson and Simpson – Detective Investigators*.

Clarice recognised the overly genteel voice of the receptionist she'd spoken with when making the arrangements for today's visit. She was older than she had imagined, mid thirties rather than twenties, petite, with short, spiky honey-blonde hair. The high, artificially refined voice was still in play, clearly used not only for the telephone but also to greet clients in person.

There were four doors in the reception area. The receptionist tapped gently on the nearest, leading them into a small office and announcing their arrival.

The double-glazed windows running one length of the room acted as barriers against the sounds and smells from the street below; stale cigarette smoke and coffee permeated the air. Three walls were crowded with shelves, overflowing with files and books.

Clarice had imagined that with his army and police background, the investigator might be muscular and fit. She was, on first sight of Dennis Simpson, instantly disabused of the notion. In his late fifties, he was tall and round-shouldered, a protruding stomach overhanging his trouser belt. He came around the desk to shake hands, and Clarice noticed a yellow smear at the bottom of his blue tie, possibly from his breakfast egg. The smell of cigarette smoke radiated from his clothes and skin, though not from his hair, of which there was very little. The top of his head resembled a shiny white egg, with a narrow band of short grey hair around the back.

'Dennis, call me Dennis,' he repeated, his voice jovial.

He indicated two seats before returning behind his desk.

'I'm sorry for your loss.' He addressed his remark to Emily, his tone of voice professionally sombre. 'Clarice told me on the phone that Colin had passed. He couldn't have been old?'

'Fifty-five,' Emily said.

'Very sad. I remember him – he was …' Dennis sought for suitable words, 'very pleasant. How do you feel I can help you?' As he spoke, he lifted a grey folder to place it before him on the desk.

'You still keep everything on file?' Clarice asked, looking around the room.

'No, after two years, the record of the investigation is saved to the computer.' Dennis tapped his fingers on the folder in front of him. 'I've downloaded this to run through and refresh my memory.' He looked at Emily. 'What specifically did you want to talk about?'

Thinking the statement made no sense, Clarice decided to plough on. Glancing at Emily, she saw her complexion turning pink, as if she was suddenly feeling awkward.

'We wanted to ask about the Major, who went missing at the same time as Emily's grandmother, Avril.' Clarice smiled encouragingly. 'It seems odd that having shown no previous interest in the man, she would suddenly run away with him.'

'Not necessarily.' Dennis sounded wary. 'Nobody but Avril and the Major would have known when their relationship changed. When the affair began. She obviously kept it well hidden from her husband.'

'Indeed, if they actually had an affair.'

'These things happen all the time.' Dennis drummed his

fingers on the folder. 'I understand the Major was not only handsome, but also charming and quite wealthy – family money. Ralph Compton-Smythe had been one of his closest friends; it must have been a double betrayal for him.'

'You had no contact with Ralph?'

'No.' Dennis was oily. 'The instructions from our client were that we were not to contact his father, aunt or any other member of the household at Stone Fen Manor.'

'What about Janice?' Clarice persisted. 'The Major's wife? Did you have much contact with her? She told you that she'd not seen her husband since she moved away. Did you believe her?'

'It was what she told me.' Dennis lifted his shoulders, implying he had done all he could. 'I had no reason to disbelieve her.'

'Did you know if there was a new man in her life?' Clarice caught a sideways glance from Emily. She had informed Emily of her conversation with Gerry. 'I ask only because I was told Janice was quite a beauty. It would seem strange if her husband had dumped her that she didn't move on, meet someone new. Perhaps remarry?'

'I wasn't aware of a new man.' Dennis closed and reopened the file absent-mindedly. 'Though I know that her brother, Peter, moved in with her when he returned to the UK.'

'No.' Clarice did not drop her gaze. 'I was wondering about a relationship that was more of a romantic nature.'

'It might have happened that she took up with someone. She could quite reasonably have considered it to be nobody else's business.'

'Yes, we thought that too.' Clarice looked at Emily for confirmation. 'There was a postcard from someone Colin had arranged to meet in Yorkshire, cancelling the meeting. Janice is the only Yorkshire connection.'

'I don't think she'll be around any longer, so that one will have to remain a mystery.' Dennis stared unblinkingly. 'You saw the photographs in the file. She was using a stick to get about ten years ago. She had severe problems with arthritis.'

'Yes, she would be in her eighties now, possibly in a nursing home,' Clarice said.

'But why would Colin want to meet her?' Dennis opened the folder again to flick through it casually. 'As far as I was able to ascertain, it was all clear-cut. Janice left. The Major then moved into the manor with the family, began a relationship with Avril, and left with her. He'd already dissolved the business relationship. He received a payment that amounted to a refund of his full investment in the firm. Forty years after the event, it was impossible to trace either of them. Their whereabouts were unknown.' He closed the file firmly, resting his hand on top. 'Cut and dried.'

'Don't you think it's strange that if the Major was so wealthy, friendly and popular, he couldn't be traced? They must have had friends in common?'

'Ralph Compton-Smythe must have chosen, fifty years ago, not to follow that route of enquiry. Perhaps it was too humiliating. By the time his son started to dig around, most of the people who knew the Major were dead. The ones who weren't wouldn't talk to us.'

'I don't know if I believe that Avril and the Major were in a relationship.' Clarice was blunt. 'Colin said his mother was devastated when she found out about her husband's affair.

Then – what a surprise – within twenty-four hours, she was supposedly having a fling herself, only to run away without taking her small son. It doesn't wash!'

'Colin was only a child.' Dennis had dropped the oily voice; he matched Clarice for bluntness. 'A five-year-old is not much of a witness. And it was common knowledge that the Major was one for the ladies; it was said he could charm the birds from the trees. As a small boy, Colin wouldn't have understood his mother's attraction.'

'You never discovered who Ralph was having an affair with?' Clarice changed tack.

'That wasn't what we were employed to do, but my money would have been on Tessa Dinkler. She moved in on him pretty damn quick after Avril left.'

'You said it was cut and dried, but you found out nothing.' Clarice gave her sweetest smile. 'Colin was no further forward in finding what had happened to his mother, although he was several thousand pounds worse off.'

'I'm sorry if he felt disappointed.' Dennis's face had become drawn and unreadable. 'I can assure you that we did our utmost to trace Avril and the Major, but some cases prove to be more difficult than others. Investigating a forty-year-old disappearance was never going to be easy. It clearly states in our policy that while we do our utmost, there is never a hundred per cent guarantee.'

They stayed for a further fifteen minutes talking about Avril's friends. There were no near neighbours to the manor house, and if there had been, it might have proved difficult; the neighbours could have relayed any discussion back to Ralph Compton-Smythe and others at the manor.

It was unmistakable from Dennis's curtness on their departure that he was glad to see the back of them.

Driving back to Colin's house, Emily was clearly disheartened. 'That was a dead end.'

'Still, it was worth a try.'

'The office was a bit smelly, even though it was a no-smoking building,' Emily said. 'There was a sign near the lift.'

'I spotted that,' Clarice agreed. 'I did think the stale tobacco smell was coming from Dennis. Maybe he's a heavy smoker and lights up in the car; in an enclosed space it hangs on the clothes. He doesn't inspire great confidence – all those folders, when everything is computerised these days.'

'I noticed from the notes you gave me with Dad's notebook that you contrasted how Dad saw Dennis in the beginning, when he'd been so hopeful of finding Avril, and how that had changed by the end.'

'I think your dad was disappointed.'

'You didn't take to Dennis?'

'I didn't trust him.' Clarice took the route leading to Nettleham. 'Being realistic, he probably has explored all possible avenues of interest. Although I didn't warm to him, being sloppy in his personal and business habits doesn't necessarily mean he's a con man.'

Chapter 11

The following day, Clarice savoured being alone, knowing that from tomorrow she would be in the company of others for three days.

Returning to the cottage after the dogs' morning walk, Clarice went upstairs. She sorted out toiletries and looked through her wardrobe for the clothes she would need for the trip to Stone Fen Manor. As well as a light woollen black trouser suit for the funeral, she included two chunky sweaters. Emily had warned her that Ralph had a phobia about wasting money on heating. If anyone complained about the cold, he would tell them to add another layer of clothing.

She ate her supper alone, leaving a vegetable pie for Rick to warm up in the oven on his return later. It was a week since she'd taken Emily's call telling her that Colin had died. So much had happened since then that it felt much longer.

The phone rang as she was about to leave, and Olivia, daughter of Pattie Freeman, introduced herself.

'You left a phone message for Mum,' she said. 'Sorry not to have got back sooner, but we only came back today from a visit to my husband's cousin. Mum asked me to call and invite you to come to us for coffee or lunch. She'd love to meet Avril's granddaughter.'

Clarice explained the circumstances: Colin's death, the funeral details, and their research into Avril's leaving Stone Fen Manor. 'Emily and I are driving there tomorrow morning,' she concluded. 'It's a bit short notice, but might we call in then? You're only about twenty-five minutes further on from Sealsby, which is where we're heading. We'd be with you between nine and nine thirty.'

Olivia readily agreed, and after hanging up, Clarice called Emily to rearrange the time she'd need to arrive the following day.

After the flurry of activity, she brought her mind back to the present, the Tuesday-evening ceramics class. During the week, she'd phoned each of the students, explaining what had happened. Later, driving through the dark back roads to Castlewick, she knew she was not looking forward to the evening.

Although the students made little progress in their work, however, the class proved more uplifting than Clarice had anticipated. When she arrived, the group had already pulled chairs around the main table, and the kettle was boiling to make coffee. Diane, a retired nurse, brought out fairy cakes. Gill, once a secretary, also now retired, helped her. Micky, the tattooist, short and bald, with a green, blue and black snake tattoo creeping around his neck and up to his bald head from behind his left ear, was unpacking a home-made lemon drizzle cake.

'This is Colin's recipe,' he said as he cut into the cake, while Denise, who worked in a chemist's shop in the town, moved the slices onto small plates and passed them around.

'Colin loved baking.' She smiled. 'I've got a great recipe for his walnut and prune cake.'

'The cake he made for our end-of-term bash last Christmas?' Micky asked.

'That's the one.' Denise nodded.

'He made some amazing plates, lots of red,' interjected Simon, a solicitor from Louth, 'and he was always eager to share his methods with others.'

There followed a thoughtful silence while they all munched cake.

'He was a lovely bloke.' Gabriel, a large black man with a deep, rumbling voice, was reflective. His family had originated from Nigeria, and he was a mechanic in Castlewick. 'The work he produced was stunning – what that man could do with clay.'

'Loved the way he changed over the years. Remember the kingfisher-blue frames on his specs?' Mandy, a geography teacher, said with affection.

'His mum left him when he was a small boy.' Denise spoke after another pause. 'It must have been a sad time.'

'I didn't know that, the poor little sod.' Micky drew his blue-and-red tattooed fingers across the table to sit upright.

Clarice looked around the group; it appeared that everyone was surprised by these revelations.

'Did you know that, Clarice?' Micky asked.

'No, Colin didn't tell me anything about his family. Since he died, though, I've found out a lot more from Emily.' This was intriguing. Clarice wondered what else Colin had told Denise. 'What did he say about it?'

'That was all really,' Denise said. 'It was after I'd lost my mum. I was telling Colin, and he told me that he was five when his mum walked out … he said it was the hottest day of the year.'

'Funny thing to remember,' Mandy said.

'I suppose the heat would have stuck in a child's mind, with his mum going on that day,' Denise said.

There was a murmur of agreement.

'How is Emily taking it?' Micky asked. 'She's such a shy, sweet girl.'

'Poor kid, she can blush.' Gabriel smiled.

'She's coping as best she can,' Clarice said. 'It was a shock – so unexpected.'

'And she's not that old.' Denise looked glassy-eyed. 'We've all watched her growing up. Colin brought her along to all the social dos, didn't he?'

'You must tell her, Clarice,' Gabriel said, 'that if there's anything we can do – anything …'

'She only has to ask.' Diane took over, looking around the group. 'Colin always did so much for everyone else – came to the rescue in times of trouble. My Alan cried his eyes out when I told him.'

By the end of the class, it had been decided that Micky and Denise would definitely go to the funeral to represent Colin's classmates. The others would also try to attend; they would phone one another the following day. Clarice gave them the details of the church and the time.

At home, Rick had already eaten his supper and put a match to the fire. He stretched his legs out, looking at the flames. On his lap, Toots, the long grey cat, yawned contentedly.

'Are you packed and ready for the morning?'

'Yes, as ready as I'll ever be.' Clarice filled him in on her evening, including the call from Pattie Freeman's daughter, and their earlier start the following day. 'I'm sorry to leave you on your lonesome.' She smiled warmly at her husband. 'But it is only for a couple of nights.'

'I'll have Bob and Sandra. Don't worry about me, just look after yourself, and remember the two golden rules.' Rick was suddenly serious.

'I won't forget: phone in at least once a day, so you don't worry about me, and don't under any circumstances leave my phone lying around, in case someone takes it.' Clarice considered for a moment. 'I don't think you need to worry.'

'It's not you. I completely trust your instincts to stay safe,' Rick said. 'It's the unknown – Colin's relatives – that I don't trust. You're going into uncharted territory.'

'Sounds like a space flight!'

'Don't joke. Be careful and watch your back.' Rick stroked Toots. 'You didn't tell me how the class went.'

'A lot better than I had anticipated.' Clarice told him about her evening.

'I can't see that Colin's baking skills or it being the hottest day of the year when Avril went away would have any relevance,' Rick mused. 'You might find out more from Pattie. But it's good that some of his classmates will attend the funeral – it shows his family that people cared about him.'

Clarice gazed into the fire, thinking about how they would all miss Colin.

'Any other news?' Rick asked.

'No, only that Sandra said she's doing a steak and ale pie for supper tomorrow night – she knows it's one of your favourites.'

Clarice got up from the sofa, putting Big Bill, the large ginger tom, onto the floor. Toots, knowing the routine before bedtime, jumped from Rick's lap.

'I said you didn't need to worry about me. Sandra's steak and ale pies are unbeatable. She always uses those big individual metal pie dishes, and she makes her puff pastry for the top.'

'Mm, maybe you'll enjoy me being away a bit too much,' Clarice teased.

'As if.' Rick grinned.

Chapter 12

The weather forecast had warned of heavy showers. As well as the rain, slow-moving tractors were coming from the fields. They pulled trailers laden with broccoli and cabbages and brought mud onto the roads. Clarice found herself stuck behind long lines of haulage trucks throwing up arcs of dirty water in their wake, as the journey to Stone Fen Manor made slow progress.

As promised, Bob and Sandra had arrived at seven that morning, in time to see Rick before he left for work. Sandra then helped Clarice to feed the cats in the barn and change the litter trays. They joined Bob for a cup of tea in the house to go over the lists, which included food and medication requirements for individual animals.

Emily had arrived half an hour after Bob and Sandra. Bob took Napoleon and Josephine into the barn in their baskets, while Clarice transferred Emily's case to her car.

Emily looked drawn, her skin wan and her eyes bloodshot. It was clear she had been crying. Clarice imagined her wandering around Colin's house during the night. Now that the day had arrived to drive to Stone Fen Manor, the forthcoming funeral was an unhappy reality. Her chat, as if trying to distract herself, bounced lightly from one topic to another.

'It is so good of you to drive. I love my Mini Cooper, but it's a bit of a squash,' she said as Clarice negotiated a roundabout.

'It's OK, I enjoy driving.' Clarice smiled, imagining Emily's small car to be perfect for her tiny frame. For someone of Clarice's height, the journey might have proved less than comfortable. A quiet fell between them for a few minutes. Catching sight of Emily's wretched expression from the corner of her eye, Clarice dredged around for a subject that might capture her imagination. 'I expect the birdlife around your grandfather's house will be amazing.'

'Absolutely. Dad and I would go out for long walks with binoculars. We were both twitchers. I wanted to be the first to spot the different types of waders – redshanks, avocets, ringed plovers.'

'What about winter birds?'

'Geese,' Emily said immediately, 'hen harriers and short-eared owls.'

'You know your birds,' Clarice said.

'I loved that time spent with Dad, just the two of us out walking, talking about birds – although I do admit that my favourites are swans.'

They drove for a while in companionable silence, Clarice thinking about Colin and imagining Emily doing the same.

'Tell me,' she said, 'about the manor. You said it was built in 1890, but I always associate manors as being from a much earlier period, with lords or feudal barons, and surrounded by great parks.'

'It does have twenty acres, mainly filled with trees, but I agree.' Emily nodded. 'Dad said that George, my great-great-grandfather, who had the house built, made his money in London. He was someone the upper classes would have looked down their noses at, called new money.'

'Nouveau riche,' Clarice added.

'Yes, that's it. I think the problem for George was that he had a sharp brain. He'd worked hard and acquired wealth, and he also married the only child of a rich merchant.'

'So acquired more money,' Clarice said.

'But because they were regarded as trade, they would never have been accepted by the old-money City crowd. He could never be special in London, whereas in a backwater like Lincolnshire, he could play the big man.' Emily gave a short laugh. 'The lord of the manor might have built a church locally, or a chapel attached to his manor. George didn't do either of those things, but he was regarded as the local squire. He'd bought land, tended by tenant farmers. James, his eldest son, inherited the house and most of the money. And Ralph inherited everything from James. Sadly, the farms and land are all gone now, sold over the years.'

'What's the house like?'

'A bit unusual, style-wise – but I'll say no more. See what you think,' Emily said teasingly.

'I couldn't make out much of it from the photographs you showed me. One of them's a close-up of Colin with Avril, and Bellatrix, the Siamese stone cat, is the focus of the main family snapshot. Built in 1890 by someone with no shortage of money … might it be Empire style, considered to be the second phase of neoclassicism?'

Emily smiled. 'I don't know anything about Empire style or neoclassicism.'

'Think tall, straight columns,' Clarice said, smiling.

'Nope.'

'OK.' Clarice pondered. 'So if not that, it might be Victorian Gothic. An amazing number of buildings and churches in Lincolnshire fall into that category. It's called Stone Fen Manor, which suggests it might be Bath stone, mined in Somerset, or more likely closer to home – Lincolnshire limestone?'

'No good guessing,' Emily said. 'I know nothing about history and architecture. I'm going to make you wait and see. It won't be long.' She changed the subject. 'You said you didn't speak to Pattie, just her daughter?'

'Olivia,' Clarice said. 'She sounded lovely, and is looking forward to meeting you.'

'I hope I don't disappoint – and that it's not a repeat of Pamela!'

'I'm sure it won't be. Your dad did write the words "best friend" next to Pattie's name.'

They were driving south on the A17, bypassing Sleaford and Boston. The weather finally cleared as they came closer to Stamford.

Olivia's house was one of eight on a private estate on the north side of the town, each individual in design, and all with extensive enclosed gardens and carports.

'I adore Stamford.' Emily sighed. 'Dad used to take me to the George for Sunday lunch on treat days – his or my birthday.'

'I've always liked the architecture, and the light colour of the Stamford limestone; it was mined in Lincolnshire, as I mentioned earlier. The older timber-framed townhouses go back to the sixteenth and seventeenth centuries. Film companies love the town, because it's ideal for filming period pieces.' Clarice drove slowly, looking at the house names.

'Did you know Stamford was originally called Stoney Ford – a completely useless piece of information?'

'No, I didn't. So you do know some history!' Clarice laughed. 'And I like new pieces of information; I never think of them as being useless.'

As they pulled into the drive of The Lodge, a slim woman in her mid forties came out of the house. She wore faded jeans, and her blonde hair was tied high into a ponytail that swung as she walked.

'Hello.' She took them both in with a sweeping glance. 'I'm Olivia, Pattie's daughter.'

Clarice introduced herself and Emily. 'We spoke on the phone.'

'Good to meet you.' Olivia waved her hand towards the house. 'Come in. Mum's been so looking forward to meeting you and Avril's granddaughter.'

Inside, they were immediately jumped upon by two identical West Highland terriers, each determined to outdo the other in barking.

'Lulu and Lupin have welcomed you!' Olivia laughed.

She took them into a long room with wall-to-wall burnt-yellow deep-pile carpets. A brave choice, Clarice thought, thinking of the dogs bringing in mud on their paws from the garden. But, she noted, it was spotless.

'This is Pattie, my mum,' Olivia said as they reached the smiling elderly woman, seated with a hand extended.

Pattie Freeman was, in looks, an older version of her daughter, but as she stood, it was clear that she had stooped with age. Her hair was coiffured in a way that made Clarice think of the 1960s. Her orange dress, worn with a neat boxy black cardigan, showed that she still had style.

'I'm thrilled to meet you, Emily.' Pattie cupped Emily's face in her withered but still elegant hands, staring at her as if to absorb every detail of her features. 'I can see a lot of your grandmother in you; you have her eyes.' She smiled sweetly. 'Please sit down. It's so lovely – a treat – to have guests.'

They settled in deep armchairs with lattice backs and plump cushions that matched the carpet in colour. Clarice imagined that the French windows at the end of the room, leading out to the garden, would be open in the summer, allowing the family and their dogs to spill out onto the mani-cured lawn.

'She was a lovely person.' Pattie warmed to the subject of Avril. 'I first got to know her in our last year at school; my parents had moved the family here from London, because of my father's work – he was a vicar.'

Clarice stored away this information.

'We hit it off straight away. I think we had a similar sense of humour. Avril had a very dry, deadpan delivery.'

Olivia gave her mother a knowing look. 'Sounds like you, Mother.'

'And it sounds like someone we knew too,' Clarice said to Emily.

'My dad was just like that,' Emily said shyly.

'He must have inherited it from his mum,' Pattie said kindly. 'A lot of the people we came into contact with as children were quite serious. They had high opinions of themselves. Avril taught me to be an observer of the human condition.'

'Dad said Avril was shy, gentle and kind,' Emily said.

'A perfect description. She was.' Pattie nodded. 'Her sister-in-law, Ernestine, was quite a lonely soul; she never went out much, and Avril had nothing in common with her personality-wise, but she always tried to include her in her social activities.'

'Dad said that Avril and Ralph – my grandpa – had a loveless marriage.'

'No – not at all.' Pattie's tone was confident. 'I can't say what happened at the end, but when they got together and married, it was without a doubt a love match.'

'I didn't know that.'

'They met at the tennis club. It was Pamela, Avril's sister, who introduced them. Ralph asked Avril out almost immediately. I was never into tennis, but of course I'd met Pamela when we were still at school. I'd gone to their home quite often.'

'We met Pamela,' Emily said. 'We visited her the other day.'

'Oh my word!' Pattie's face broke into a wide grin. 'That was a mistake. I bet you wished you hadn't!'

Emily told her about the meeting, and its ending, with the chocolates being thrown at the car as they'd driven away.

Pattie laughed uproariously, bringing her hands to cover her face. 'I wish I'd been a fly on the wall to see that. Did you know she's been married four times?'

Emily shook her head, throwing Clarice a surprised glance.

'The first lasted the longest, about five years.' Pattie nodded, her smile lighting up her face. 'Pamela was besotted with Ralph before he took up with your grandmother – or should I say she was in love with his money. She thought he was wealthy and might be a bit of a catch. And,' her eyes were suddenly impish, 'he was really rather good-looking back then.'

'*Mother!*' Olivia scolded playfully.

'I wasn't always old.' Pattie nodded at her daughter, who rose to replenish the teacups.

Clarice felt the inward tug of melancholy, witnessing the natural bond between the elderly mother and daughter. Her own mother having died nearly twenty years earlier, she always felt an inner ache in these situations.

'Pamela was furious with her mother,' Pattie continued. 'Helen was a widow – a lovely lady. It was she who had insisted Pamela take her sister to the tennis club, and Pamela never let her mother forget that it was her fault Avril had stolen her man. The poor woman died not long after Avril married.'

'I don't think he was ever *her man*, was he?' Clarice asked.

'No – he never had any interest whatsoever in Pamela.'

One of the Westies wandered over to Clarice to lie across her feet. Clarice looked down at the adoring eyes gazing up at her as she leaned down to stroke the little dog's head.

'What made you think it was a love match?' Emily quizzed.

'Well, firstly, Avril told me, and she wasn't someone who exaggerated or bragged; then I saw them together as a couple.'

Emily waited.

'I remember I went to Stone Fen Manor to visit Avril a few months after they'd married. They were in the garden, standing close, laughing. Ralph was resting his hand on her waist, and she had her head back, looking up at him. It was pure joy – apart from …' Pattie chewed her bottom lip, looking melancholy.

'Apart from?' Clarice prompted gently.

'Further away, near the house, I noticed the man who worked for Ralph – they called him Johnson, I think,' Pattie said vaguely. 'It was such a long time ago. He was watching Ralph and Avril. His expression was cold – not that that was anything out of the ordinary. Avril said she'd never seen him crack a smile – he was always sour. Then he saw me watching him, and he turned away and went into the house.'

'Did you tell Dennis Simpson, from the agency that was trying to trace Avril, about her relationship with Ralph – that it was a love match?'

'I've never come into contact with him.' Pattie looked puzzled.

'Yes, of course,' Clarice said, remembering that Dennis Simpson had been unable to contact Pattie. She explained that ten years earlier, Colin had paid for an investigation.

'I'm afraid I know nothing about that; he didn't contact me.'

'Might it have been when you were in Malta, Mum,' Olivia interrupted, 'with Dad before he died? That was around ten years ago.'

'Yes, it could have been. We spent a lot of time in Malta.' Pattie glanced at Clarice. 'The warm weather suited my husband.'

'Your name was on the investigator's list as "unable to make contact",' Clarice said. 'We got your old number from Colin's notebook. He had "Avril's best friend" written against it.'

'We *were* best friends,' Pattie said, her face serious. 'That notebook sounds intriguing.'

'It is.' Clarice reached into her handbag. 'Do you mind if we ask about these "before" and "after" lists? We think they refer to when Avril was still with Colin, and after she'd gone.'

'Show me.' Pattie leaned forward, then to her daughter said, 'Darling, would you fetch my glasses?'

Glasses on, she silently read down the lists. 'My goodness, there are such a lot of things. From food – Yorkshire puddings, apple pies – through activities and clothes, hair and places.' She fell silent again as she read the second list. 'I suspect that you're right: the things he did with his mother, then other things after she'd gone. Why did he make these lists? What do you think he hoped to achieve?'

'I believe he was searching through his past to find clues about what happened to Avril,' Clarice said.

'I know she cooked puddings and pies for him, his favourite things.' Pattie looked again at the lists. '"Dancing feet" – that would be his mother; she loved dancing – and "buckled shoes". She once bought a pair that were a little unusual – they had gold-coloured buckles.'

'Dancing feet are in both before and after,' Clarice said.

'Yes, so are pearls and diamonds, feathered hats, Siamese cats and black Labradors. Ernestine might have liked to dance, also the second Mrs Compton-Smythe. They might also have liked jewellery and hats, and I'm assuming Ralph continues to have black Labradors? Avril said it was a family thing, the dogs, and always one or two Siamese cats.'

'Ralph never married Tessa,' Emily interrupted. 'He was only ever married to my grandmother.'

'I didn't know that,' Pattie said. 'I didn't believe that Avril had run away with the Major. That was what Ralph told me had happened. And I understand from what you're telling me that Colin, despite paying the agency, never got to the bottom of it?'

'No. The agency proved to be a disappointment. Can you remember when you last spoke to Avril? Was it long before she left?'

'It was two days before she disappeared.' Pattie rested her hands together in her lap, her voice sombre. 'We had a long phone chat. She was upset and said she had a problem, but she wouldn't open up and tell me what it was. I asked if it was related to Ralph, and she said it was. She suggested we meet a couple of days later. She said she would find it easier talking face to face.'

'Dad said his mother told him that Daddy didn't love her any more.' Emily spoke quietly. 'He said he saw her talking with the Major, holding his hand.'

'Mm.' Pattie nodded. 'He might have just been consoling her. He was charming – a very good listener. When you talked to him, he listened attentively, as if your opinions really mattered. He was also incredibly good-looking, with dark floppy hair.'

'He sounds very attractive,' Clarice said. 'But you didn't believe they'd run off together?'

'Never! Not then and not now. It was all too sudden.'

'And you heard nothing more from Avril?'

'Not a word. I phoned several times, until Ralph got nasty with me. He said that if Avril dared to show her face again, he'd point her in the direction of the door. There was nobody really to fight her corner. I did my best. Her parents were both dead, and Avril only had a small circle of friends – she was reserved, and a lot of the people she knew were not solid buddies, more like acquaintances.'

'What did you make of the family, how Avril fitted in?' Clarice asked.

'As I've said, Ralph seemed in love with her as much as she was with him,' Pattie answered. 'Ernestine was mad as a box of frogs but harmless enough, and she adored both Avril and Colin.'

'She's very greedy,' Emily put in.

'Oh my God, I remember – was that woman greedy! But always so skinny; she never put on weight. Avril said she must have a tapeworm.' Pattie smiled at the memory. 'Ernestine had the strangest sense of humour, laughed at the oddest things.'

'She hasn't changed,' Emily said. 'She never stops talking. She was diagnosed with dementia about a year ago.'

'Poor Ernestine, she seemed confused at the best of times. Dementia, that's sad. Avril said she thought Ernestine's parents probably mollycoddled her as a child because she had a heart defect. But she's still going, and is a good age.' Pattie was quiet for a while, as if considering. 'Johnson was the one I worried about.'

'What worried you?' Clarice asked.

'His life revolved around his work, but he also had a private life. He was apparently a whizz at bridge, and Avril said he would disappear three or four evenings a week to go into the town. Ralph hinted to her that Johnson had a special lady friend, but he never brought her to the house.' Pattie looked from one face to another. 'Avril believed Johnson would do anything for Ralph. In fact, she said something once, as a joke – that if Ralph told Johnson he'd just killed someone, Johnson would reply, "I'll get the spades."'

'Was that seriously a joke?' Emily sounded shocked.

'I think what she was saying was that whatever Ralph told Johnson to do, he would never question it. She told me the last time we spoke that she found him threatening.'

'I can't imagine that could be true,' Emily said. 'I know Johnson is the grumpiest of men, but if he had threatened her, why didn't she tell Grandpa?'

Pattie lifted her hands and lowered them in a calming gesture. 'I thought about it afterwards and understood what she meant. I believe Ralph would have confided in Johnson about his affair, knowing his secret would be safe. Understanding Avril as I did, I realised that would have been humiliating for her, and she would have felt threatened. For heaven's sake, she was his wife, and they had a son.' She paused. 'I never had an opportunity to see or talk to her again. She was so in love with Ralph, and no one will ever convince me that she ran away with the Major.'

Chapter 13

After saying their goodbyes and Emily promising Pattie that she would call her after Colin's funeral to tell her how things had gone, they went on their way.

'We are heading upwards and east now; only another half an hour,' Clarice said.

'She was lovely.' Emily smiled contentedly. 'Meeting her did make me wish I'd known Avril. I'll bet she was as charming as Pattie.'

'Yes, I think you're right. It's obvious how highly Pattie thought of her. She gave us a very thorough picture of your grandma – I believe we can trust what she told us to be accurate.'

After twenty minutes, they left the main route to take numerous minor roads before approaching the village of Sealsby. Passing through, Clarice took in its quiet centre. There was a baker's, a butcher's, a vegetable shop, a post office and store; also a tall column she took to be a war memorial. Heading out of the village, Emily turned her head to look at the church.

'Is that where the funeral will be?' Clarice asked.

'Yes,' Emily said quietly. 'St Peter's. The cemetery's behind it, and the Compton-Smythe family plot is in the centre, opposite a massive oak tree.'

Clarice looked at the girl as she put her hands to her face and leaned forward. Pulling into a side street, she stopped the car.

'Are you all right?' she asked, turning the engine off.

'No, I'm bloody not!' Emily rooted in her bag for tissues as tears ran down her cheeks.

'It is OK to show you're upset. Nobody is going to expect you to put on a happy face and cover up what you're really feeling.' Clarice rested her hand gently on Emily's shoulder. The younger woman sobbed, her body shaking as she pressed the tissues to her face.

Clarice waited.

'Grandpa will,' Emily said eventually, after noisily blowing her nose. 'He hates shows of emotion, and once I start crying, it's hard to stop.' She hiccuped.

'You are allowed to grieve.' Clarice's voice was gentle.

'I'm cross with myself.' Emily spoke quietly.

'Why?'

'Because I'm wasting my time and yours with this ridiculous rubbish about Grandma Avril.' She looked at Clarice with reddened eyes. 'She fell in love and ran away — end of story. If she didn't, does it matter after all this time?'

Clarice nodded understanding.

'Dad is dead, I'm burying him tomorrow, so why I am bothering about ancient history — something that happened fifty years ago?'

'I think it might be a distraction,' Clarice said.

'I thought about that last night,' Emily agreed. 'It takes my mind away from the real world, and Dad no longer being in it.'

'If you feel it works better for you, maybe you should forget about Avril for the time being.'

'No.' Emily's voice was certain. 'I need to find out what happened – for Dad.'

'It might be better to concentrate on your dad's funeral. You can't bury all the pain you're feeling by chasing ghosts.'

Emily blew her nose again. 'I know I'm not making sense,' she said. 'I'm contradicting myself, and now I've got hiccups.'

'Don't be silly, you're making perfect sense.' Clarice smiled. 'There are some bottles of water in the back, shall I get one?'

After Clarice brought the bottled water, Emily alternated swigs with holding her breath. 'I've still got to work out what to do with Napoleon and Josephine.'

'I thought about that,' Clarice said. 'You won't be able to take them to your halls of residence. Would you like—'

'No, Clarice, I don't want them rehomed, or for you to feel you have to foster them. I can't think about it right now; there isn't enough room inside my head.'

'Put it on the back burner then – until after the funeral.'

'Yes,' Emily stared out of the window, 'that's what I thought.'

After sitting quietly for twenty minutes, they set forth again. The hiccups had stopped and Emily remained silent for the rest of the journey.

The main difference between the undulating Wolds, where Clarice had her home, and the Lincolnshire fenlands was the flatness. The sky dominated the unbroken vista, now clouded over grey and white. She imagined it during other times of the year, especially on summer evenings, when the big sky would reveal magnificent sunsets.

The further they progressed from the village, the narrower the lanes became, as if the verges were pressing them inward. The drains, water inlets along the lane edges, were fringed at the top of the banks with brown and autumnal gold grasses, while lower down, just above the water's edge, fresh, tall, vibrant lime-green growth sprouted in abundance. Beyond the dyke, Clarice could see fresh-water scrapes and reed beds. And then the sun suddenly spat through the white clouds to enliven the fields around them.

A few minutes later, the satnav instructed her to turn left, with the message 'You have reached your destination.'

The entrance of the private driveway led to a track. They entered an avenue of trees of various species, plunging them into shade.

As they followed the curve of the track, there were glimpses of stone and chimneys between the trees, and Clarice realised that the trail she was following was working in a diminishing circle around to the front of the manor house.

Slowing to a crawl, she pointed. 'Who's that?'

'The gardener, I think.' Emily peered. The man walking through the trees did not seem curious about their presence. He continued to walk, head down, his hands pushed deep in his jacket pockets, not acknowledging them.

Clarice brought her attention back to the woods. She glanced upward. The leafless limbs of the trees looked barren and forlorn, with weak sunshine filtering through to form moving patterns on the dirt track beneath.

Leaving the wooded area, driving back out into the sunshine, she saw the facade of Stone Fen Manor. It was nothing like she had anticipated. In front of it was an expanse of lawn, with the track continuing through the centre to the front of the house.

From the corner of her eye, she saw Emily turn her head to watch the expression on Clarice's face.

'Yes – I understand.' Clarice found herself unable to take her eyes from the building. 'In the eighteenth century, the neoclassical style was associated with radical liberalism. Your great-great-grandpa wouldn't have wanted that. He needed to be accepted, and the Gothic revival was all about tradition, conservatism and the monarch. And it's the yellow Lincolnshire limestone; there were five quarries back then that produced it.'

'Yes, you got it with your second guess. It is Victorian Gothic.' Emily flipped down the passenger-seat mirror and checked her face, her voice positive, as if determining to be upbeat. 'I don't know about radical liberalism versus conservative values, though. Both George and James were known to have kept mistresses, and they didn't attempt to hide it. I'm not sure how that fits in with being conventional or traditional.'

'That's rich men misbehaving, and how they wanted to be perceived by other rich men. A tradition in its way, I suppose – what they'd call being "red-blooded males", as Colin put it.'

'Yes. A bunch of hypocrites.'

Clarice smiled vaguely, all her attention fixed on the manor.

Years of neglect, plus salt from the Wash, and beyond that, the sea, had eaten into the yellow stone. It had added shades of brown and orange, giving the building a sense of torpor, as if it might be a magical place deep in slumber.

She felt a frisson of excitement. It was lovely.

The facade stretched in a line, the windows and entry sharing a pointed arch design. At the centre, the castellated tower, with four sets of windows, one above the other, gave a dramatic sense of height. High above, gargoyles peered out to leer downward with menace. On either side of the central tower, the building continued on two levels, balancing each other in length. Bellatrix, the majestic stone Siamese cat, reposed below the central tower, proud and dominant, her head held high, her front legs outstretched.

Clarice recalled Emily telling her that Bellatrix stared out towards the Fens, and beyond that, to the Wash. From this position, all she could see was the dense foliage of trees. Drawing closer to the building, she noticed that the leaded glass windows were ornate, possibly containing religious or mythical scenes.

To one side of the house, some distance away, was a block that might once have been stables. Nearer the house stood a two-storey modern building, its doors open to reveal cars.

As if reading her thoughts, Emily pointed to indicate this building. 'Johnson lives in a flat above the garage.'

'How many bedrooms does the main house have?' Clarice asked, her eyes drawn back to the manor.

'Eleven,' Emily said. 'There are three in the central tower section, and four on either side of the tower. The four on that side are unused.' She pointed to the right-hand side of the building. 'Dad told me that really grand Victorian Gothic country houses are much more significant, with twenty-five bedrooms or so – but don't mention that in front of Grandpa.' She nodded her head to a figure walking from the manor's main entrance. 'Look, here comes Johnson.'

The man coming towards them was tall and thickset. His hair was a combination of grey and white, combed back from his face; his bearing was upright, his tread sure and confident.

As they climbed out of the car, dead leaves danced in the breeze around their feet, and the *caw caw caw* of rooks nesting in trees near the garage resonated above them. The cold wind bit at Clarice's face; she was thankful that Emily had suggested she bring warm clothing.

'Good morning, Emily,' Johnson said as he reached them. He looked closely at her face, but if he noticed the telltale blotchy signs that she had been crying, he didn't show it. 'I hope you enjoyed a pleasant journey. I assume this is your guest, Mrs Beech.'

His voice carried a thin underlay, betraying his Scottish origins. Clarice remembered what she'd learned from the investigator's report. He had been born in Liverpool to mixed-race parents, his mother Scottish, his father an African seaman. Brought up in Glasgow. Christian names Bernard Graham. He was now eighty years of age.

'Yes, the drive was OK, thanks,' Emily responded. 'This is Dad's friend, and mine, Clarice.'

'A pleasure to meet you, Mrs Beech.' He moved his head in an acquiescent half-nod. He was tall, his height similar to Clarice's own. As she stepped forward, away from the car, their eyes met on a level. His, deep brown, pierced into hers. The dark skin of his face was rough and pitted, the pockmarking possibly due to childhood infection. So penetrating was his stare that she thought fleetingly of the farmers at Castlewick summer fairs when, as a child, she'd watch the 'guess the weight' competition in the main marquee. Johnson shared the look of intensity those men had had when calculating the piglet's weight.

'Good to meet you,' she responded, but he didn't offer his hand to shake. Instead, he walked past her to the back of her car.

'Let's get your bags inside.' He waited while she came to open the hatch.

As she and Emily followed him through the main entrance, Clarice watched his progress carrying the two bags; despite his age, his movement was fluid. Perhaps he'd felt it professionally incorrect to shake her hand. It seemed he'd been looking out, awaiting their arrival, and she realised that in the few moments of their meeting, she'd become aware that he was on his guard. Was it because of her friendship with Colin? Whatever the reason, Johnson didn't trust her.

Chapter 14

Clarice and Emily followed Johnson into the deep porch, walking under a stone arch, with its embellishment of carved roses, to reach the main entrance.

Behind the heavy oak door lay the great hall. Along one wall were fabric hangings, once vibrant reds and blues, now threadbare in places, dusty and muted with age. Below them was a row of chests with straight wooden backs, useful for storage or, when the lids were down, bench seating. On the opposite side of the room, a black marble fireplace with a pyramidic top reached the panelled ceiling. The light from oblong stained-glass windows fell in long lines to pick out the cracks in the old stone floor, and at the far end of the hall, the dark metal balustrades of the staircase curved in dramatic style to take the eye upward.

Clarice turned full circle to look around, absorbed in the drama created by the scaled-down Victorian mimicry of grand medieval Gothic.

'What do you think?' Emily's voice reminded her that she was not alone. A few feet away, Johnson also waited and watched. The look on Emily's face was joyful, while Johnson observed her much as a cat might scrutinise a mouse soon to become its dinner.

'It's amazing.' Clarice's voice held awe. 'It's not at all what I'd imagined.'

'I know it well, but I'm always excited by other people's reactions when they see it for the first time.' Emily started to progress towards the staircase. 'Let's dump our bags, and I'll give you the full guided tour.'

'Your grandfather is in his office.' Johnson, who had remained stationary, spoke quietly; the expression 'an iron fist in a velvet glove' stole into Clarice's mind as his words inhabited the space between him and Emily. 'He will expect you to let him know you have arrived and to introduce Colin's friend.'

'Yes – of course.' Emily looked flustered, the colour in her face heightening. 'I should have thought of that. Is it OK if you take our bags upstairs while I say hello to Grandpa?'

'Yes, you'll be together in the guest room.' Johnson walked away with their bags towards the stairs.

'It's Grandma Avril's old bedroom, but the family always refer to it as the guest room,' Emily said as she guided Clarice towards the far end of the hall.

Clarice nodded. 'You told me we would be in what used to be Avril's bedroom.'

Emily turned left when they reached the staircase to leave the great hall and enter a dark panelled corridor with a window at the end. Halfway along, she pointed to a door on the left. 'That's Grandpa's private sitting room – when he wants to escape from the world and everyone in it.' She stopped and tapped on the door opposite. 'And this is his office.'

A male voice boomed, 'Come in!', followed by an instant chorus of barking.

Inside the office, they were jumped on immediately by a young Labrador, its black coat as glossy as burnished silver, its rear end swinging back and forth with delight. An older dog, of the same colour and breed, with a greying muzzle, sat behind, watching the newcomers through milky clouded eyes.

'Sit, boy, sit! Damn you – sit down!' As he shouted at the young dog, the elderly man, dressed in thick brown corduroy trousers and a grey sweater, manoeuvred himself from behind the desk. He was of average height, solidly built, with a barrel-shaped girth, and wore dark-framed spectacles. Clarice saw no resemblance to Colin in his father. Ralph's short white hair, bristling moustache and heavy eyebrows gave him an angry, demented look. It became more exaggerated as the young dog wiggled to push himself first against Emily, then Clarice.

The room smelled of wet dog, coffee, and something Clarice could not identify. Along with the leather-topped desk and curved-back chair, the room had bookcases filling two of the walls, with additional piles of volumes in front of each; it seemed Ralph had too many books and not enough space. Next to the window overlooking the driveway was a battered brown leather armchair, both arms worn and damaged, with two shabby grey cushions squashed into the seat – a prime position from which to observe arrivals and departures.

Clarice watched for a few moments as Ralph continued to shout, trying to make the young dog obey his command. Then, as he turned, walking away muttering, she suddenly clapped her hands – her unexpected action silencing both dog and master. Bending quickly, she pushed the dog's rear onto the ground while lifting its head with her other hand under its chin. 'Sit.' She used a firm command, and the startled Labrador stared at her but stayed seated. She swiftly brought something from her pocket to reward the dog, who swallowed it within a moment and sat waiting for another treat.

'Well.' Ralph turned around as he spoke, seeming taken aback. 'So, Emily, this is your friend?' He stared at Clarice.

'Yes, Grandpa, this is Clarice Beech. She was a friend of Dad's,' Emily said, as Clarice found herself pushed by the young Lab, who had realised another treat would not be forthcoming and forgotten the command.

'Pottery lady?' Ralph said, moving forward to shake Clarice's hand.

'Yes.' Clarice smiled. 'I teach evening classes in ceramics at Castlewick College. Colin came to my Tuesday class for eleven years. He was very talented.'

'He told me he enjoyed the classes.' Ralph scratched his chin thoughtfully. 'Didn't think it would be his sort of thing. Eleven years – my goodness.'

'Yes,' Clarice said.

'Your dad.' Ralph spoke to Emily as he lifted his liver-spotted hand, the fingers swollen with arthritis, to pat her on the shoulder. 'Bad business, too young – unfortunate.'

It was clear he was uncomfortable with expressions of emotion. Emily caught Clarice's eye, as if aware of what she was thinking. Clarice imagined Ralph patting his Labradors in much the same way.

'I see you're used to dogs,' he said.

'Very much so. What are their names?'

'The young 'un pushing his face into your hand is Ben, eight months; the old girl is over fourteen – Floss.'

'Clarice runs a rescue charity,' Emily said. 'She takes in dogs, cats and other things – even rabbits.'

'Yes, we get all sorts coming in – the odd ferret, guinea pigs and hens.'

'Good gracious!' Ralph stared aghast. 'Potter and animal rescue – you are a busy lady.'

'I enjoy what I do.' Clarice smiled again.

'Well, you are welcome here. I don't know if Emily explained that we're setting up the long trestle tables in the great hall for food and drink for tomorrow?'

'Yes, she told me – I can help,' Clarice said.

'That's good, all hands on deck.' Ralph moved towards the door. 'Why don't you go and unpack? I'll see you at lunch – it's at one. Emily will show you the way.' He took hold of Ben's collar as they went out, to stop the dog trying to follow. 'After that, we'll all crack on together.'

Back out in the corridor, they retraced their steps. Before they reached the door leading back into the great hall, Emily stopped, pointing to the left.

'It's a cloakroom.' She slid out of her coat as she spoke before hanging it up inside the small room. 'It saves dragging up and down the stairs for our coats if we want to go out. And there's a loo next door to it.'

Clarice hung her own coat up before following Emily back into the hall and up the curved staircase.

'It must be the Clarice effect. I've never seen Grandpa so polite – friendly even!' Emily, speaking over her shoulder, trotted ahead.

'Maybe I'll see his other side later.'

'I don't think he'll be able to keep up the charm offensive for long.'

Clarice paused on each level, remembering her visit to Dennis Simpson's office. The views from here were of more interest than the roads and buildings in Lincoln, and the stained-glass windows were exquisite. She was aware of Emily watching as she took in the windows' themes, which included flowers, snakes and dragons.

'They often depicted religion,' she said.

'Yes, these don't, but if you look at the ones in the great hall, they have a religious content – halos, and hands clasped in prayer.'

'I'll have a close-up look later,' Clarice said.

Several of the windows had damage, probably due to weather and salt from the Wash. Outside, each would have a shallow ledge above, part decorative but also a practical feature, intended to divert rainwater to run down the sides rather than over the panes. Over time, though, they could not fully protect the windows and lead from wind and water. Clarice wondered how Ralph managed financially; the cost of upkeep for a house of this type would be huge.

Reaching the fourth floor, they stopped as Clarice studied a sculpture of a cat. It sat elegantly on a stone plinth positioned above the well that looked down to the ground floor. It was about four feet in height, its body elongated, narrow at the bottom, where the feet came together, and expanding up to the shoulders. The patina of the bronze might have started light, but with time had become dark brown.

'I love the eyes,' Clarice stroked her hand down the body,

'and the way the artist has extended the body gives it an abstract, contemporary feel – it is quite clearly a Siamese.'

'Great-Grandfather James commissioned it in the 1930s for his wife, Elizabeth, and it survived a fall.' Emily looked over the edge of the balustrade. Clarice joined her to see Johnson passing below.

'It's so heavy, I'm surprised anyone could lift it,' Clarice said.

'No, it was pushed, really hard, by a very naughty school friend of Grandpa's when they were only ten years old.'

'Yes, it is top-heavy.' Clarice moved to the side of the sculpture. 'Its height and weight would make it topple and go down at a tremendous speed. Bronze is a tough metal, though; it would survive the drop, but I bet it made a big hole in the floor!'

'Apparently it did. Luckily there was nobody below for it to land on.'

'I expect it's been fixed in place now – health and safety and all that …'

'You are joking, and don't mention health and safety – Grandpa would have a meltdown.'

Clarice followed Emily into the bedroom opposite the sculpture. Her eyes went immediately to the vaulted ceiling, with its arched wooden roof trusses. A row of floor-to-ceiling windows swept upwards, reaching a point where there was a separate arched panel, the design and ornate colouring in heightened detail. She stared out over the treetops.

'I see what you mean now about being able to look out across the fenlands towards the Wash.'

'Yes.' Emily, having dropped her handbag, came to stand next to Clarice. 'It's a lovely view from up here. Driving in through the woodland surrounding the house, you don't get a sense of the nearness of the Wash, and Bellatrix is directly below these windows.'

'This is level four. With the one below, it forms the top of the central part of the tower.' Clarice looked out. 'They don't have corridors that lead anywhere.'

'No, it's just the stairwell up and down,' Emily agreed.

Clarice stepped to lean nearer the windows.

'I can't see Bellatrix. We're too high up. I guess I would need to open a window?'

'Yes, but it's a bit cold.' Emily touched the handle catch of one of them. 'These open inwards. Dad told me that if the weather was warm, Avril would have this pair open wide to let a breeze blow through.' She smiled at the memory of his words. 'Avril had a double bed there, against that wall.'

'You said it was Avril's room. Did she not share it with her husband?'

'No, Grandpa's room is just below this one. We passed it on the way up.' Emily pulled her lips downwards. 'I think the two rooms were near enough for Grandpa to come up – or maybe she went down. Dad said they liked their own space.'

'Well, the house is certainly big enough to give them that.' Looking about her, Clarice took in the furniture, mainly antique Victorian mahogany: a large double glass-fronted wardrobe and a matching chest of drawers. The two single beds must have replaced Avril's double. In between was an occasional table with a modern steel lamp and there was a matching pair of bedside cabinets. Near the window stood an inlaid Victorian desk chair with an embroidered seat cover. The only items of furniture not in mahogany were the two beds, which had pine headboards. Why, Clarice mused, would Ralph have got rid of Avril's double bed, presumably in matching mahogany? Guests would generally come as couples or on their own, so putting in two single beds was unnecessary. Was there some significance: had Avril died in the bed? Clarice reined back her thoughts; there was no reason or evidence to suppose anything like that.

'Did you say there are two rooms on this level?' she asked. 'And on the one below?'

'The second room is smaller. It was once Avril's dressing room,' Emily replied. 'There's a single put-me-up, where I slept when I was small and came here with Mum and Dad, and again when I came with Dad after Mum left us.'

Following her over, Clarice looked in as Emily opened wide the door.

'There's a commode.' Emily pointed to the dark-coloured bedside cabinet. 'It has a chamber pot inside if you get desperate during the night. The nearest bathroom is two floors down. Sadly, there are no en suites in this house.'

'I wouldn't have expected there to be bathrooms up here,' Clarice said.

'Do you want to have a wander around before lunch? It looks like work will take up the afternoon – setting up for tomorrow.'

'Sounds like a plan.'

'Grandpa has a family photo album. There are quite a few of Dad,' Emily said, heading towards the door. 'I'll ask if he can get it for us to look at later, before bedtime.'

Chapter 15

Going down one flight of stairs to reach the next landing, Emily hesitated. 'That's Grandpa's bedroom.' She pointed as they passed the door, stopping again on the next level. 'And this is Tessa's.'

'I guess she wanted her own space too,' Clarice said. 'I'm surprised she didn't want Avril's old room. The view must be much better.'

'The reason was more prosaic.' Emily pushed open a nearby door leading to a corridor and pointed. 'There's a bathroom practically next to Tessa's room.'

'Ah.' Clarice smiled. 'A sensible consideration.'

Keeping the door open, Emily looked along the corridor. 'After the loo, there are two other rooms on each side. The first door on the right is Ernestine's bedroom, and on the left is Dawn's. They each use the room next to their bedroom as a private sitting room. In Dawn's case, she shares it with Tessa.'

Crossing the landing to push open the door on the opposite side, she said, 'There's the same number of rooms on this side, and that will be our bathroom. The family use the other one when they have guests. And I've shown you where the downstairs loo is.'

'Well, I shouldn't get caught short now.' Clarice grinned. 'I realised that everything is on two levels, apart from the central tower.'

'Yes, that's right.' Emily nodded. 'There are four levels to the tower.'

'OK,' Clarice said, 'I'm getting my bearings. So who uses the bedrooms on this side?'

'The rooms in this half are for storage. Dad called it the cemetery for dead furniture – Grandpa won't throw anything away.'

'That sounds like Colin's sense of humour.' Clarice laughed. 'He called the college the assimilation of facts factory.'

'I will miss his funny phrases.' Emily sighed.

They stood for a moment, Clarice imagining Colin walking up and down these stairs as a child with his mother.

'That's the serious information out of the way.' Emily moved to go down the final flight of stairs. 'Let me show you the rest of the house.'

As they descended to return to the great hall, Clarice caught a movement nearby and heard the distinctive cry of a Siamese cat.

'Hello, Ruffian,' Emily said, bending to stroke the animal as it emerged from the shadows.

'You are so beautiful,' Clarice said.

'He loves a fuss.' A woman in her mid forties appeared behind the cat. She had pale skin, a wide mouth enhanced by deep red lipstick, and an abundance of brown curly hair that bounced above the shoulders of her black padded jacket.

'Hi, Dawn,' Emily said. 'This is Clarice Beech. She was one of Dad's friends.'

Dawn walked toward Clarice with her hand outstretched.

'Good to meet you, Clarice. You're the pottery teacher?'

'Yes.' Clarice shook the offered hand. 'And you're Emily's aunt.'

'Yes, it's complicated.' Dawn cast a sideways glance at Emily. 'You'll know Colin and I had different mothers? Colin was my half-brother – I guess that means Emily is my half-niece.'

Clarice sensed barely disguised animosity behind the words and the slanted half-smile.

Ruffian yowled, pushing against Clarice's ankles. She bent down and picked him up. 'Siamese make such a wonderful noise.' She drew her fingers back and forth along the cat's head to elicit a purr. 'They can sound like babies crying.'

Dawn and Emily watched as the cat first head-butted Clarice, then rubbed its whiskery face against her cheek.

'I understand this house has a huge connection to the breed.'

'Emily has told you about Bellatrix?'

'Yes, and about her great-great-grandparents having two kittens from the line of the first breeding pair of Siamese that came into the country.'

'There have always been Siamese cats in this house.' Dawn looked from Clarice to Emily, the red lips momentarily curving before she nodded. 'I'll see you both at lunch.'

Ruffian wriggled in Clarice's arms to signal that he wanted to be put down as Dawn walked away. Once on the floor, he eagerly hurried to follow his mistress.

'He is very much Dawn's cat,' Clarice observed.

'Yes, and he's the love of her life.' Emily smiled tightly. 'For the present.'

Clarice watched as Dawn, in her tight denim jeans and long black boots, left the hall to go outside. Handsome rather than pretty, she radiated self-confidence. She obviously looked after herself, with unblemished skin and a good figure, and it was clear she would have no problem attracting suitors.

'You said Colin didn't like Dawn – but what about you? How well do you get on?' Clarice asked. Emily had linked her arm to guide her across the hall.

'Not at all, probably because Tessa and Dad never did,' Emily said. 'In fairness, it was six of one and half a dozen of the other. I told you Dad would never have referred to Tessa as his sister or half-sister?'

'Yes,' Clarice nodded, 'and because the parents were at war, their children, you and Dawn, were drawn into it.'

'Tessa often tried to stir things up between Dad and Grandpa; the animosity divided the family into two camps. Naturally, I was on Dad's side.'

'Of course. Colin was your dad – and Dawn would be in her mum's camp, so she would hardly want to be your best friend.'

'Yup, and when arguments flared up, Grandpa and Aunt Ernestine fluctuated between the two sides, depending upon their mood at the time.'

'How awful.' Clarice had stopped by a door. 'Maybe they'll be nicer to you now that your dad has died.'

'I won't hold my breath. Tessa's beef was that Grandpa would favour Colin financially over Dawn. Dad always had an advantage, being both older and male.'

'I think Dawn could have challenged a will that didn't give her something,' Clarice said.

'That's true, but Tessa and Grandpa never married.' Emily raised her eyebrows meaningfully. 'It's a big deal to Tessa; she thinks it weakens Dawn's prospects of inheritance. Colin would have inherited the house, and it bugged Tessa that she couldn't change that. She said it was unfair.'

'But now that your dad is dead, won't you inherit?'

'No.' Emily was emphatic. 'The house can't be split; it goes to one person. Dawn is the oldest now. It's Grandpa's decision. I won't dispute it.'

'I see,' Clarice said.

As Emily pushed open the door, Clarice's attention was taken by the corridor, an exact match to the one on the opposite side of the great hall.

'You can see that this is the two-storey part of the building again, attached to the tower. Grandpa's office is on the opposite side.' Emily pointed to the other door across the width of the hall.

'So what's on this side?' Clarice asked.

'The kitchen, dining room, another toilet and a sitting room. Come and see the kitchen.'

Herbs, cooking oils and flowers combined to permeate the kitchen's air. Hanging upside down along one wall, tied at the stems in bunches to dry, were rows of lavender. It was a long room, made bright by fluorescent lighting and the light coming through the long windows. Clarice's eyes were immediately drawn downwards to the black, green and mauve floor tiles.

Emily introduced her to Mrs Fuller. Sturdy, with a pudgy red face, she wore carpet slippers, and a net that clamped sparse white hair to her skull. After looking Clarice up and down suspiciously, she returned to the preparation of lunch.

Taking the room in, Clarice thought it must have altered little over the years. At its centre was a large, solid pine table with plenty of space around it, allowing people to work and move quickly about the room. There were no modern built-in fitted units; instead, around the perimeter was imposing cabinetry: cupboards with open shelves, hooks for pots and pans, a large, deep sink, and a Victorian range cooker, obviously no longer used for its original purpose but as an extra surface for stacking plates and bowls. Next to it, incongruously, was a modern white conventional electric cooker.

'Mrs Fuller isn't used to visitors,' Emily said when they had left the kitchen. 'She's been the cleaning lady here since Dad was a boy. She comes on her bicycle every morning, with a net bag dangling over the handlebars containing her house slippers. There's also her sister, Mrs Banner, to call on if needed – they're like peas in a pod. I gather they both spent yesterday washing the floor of the great hall. Johnson usually does the family lunch, but when he's busy, he'll instruct Mrs Fuller.'

'Who cooks in the evening?'

'Usually Johnson,' Emily said. 'Although Tessa likes to think she's a good cook. Occasionally she'll decide to make dinner.'

Clarice wondered momentarily if Tessa's culinary skills were as debatable as Emily seemed to be suggesting. As much as she liked Emily, she was becoming aware that long-held hostility and the toxic nature of relationships between family members might have affected her judgement.

'It's a big house to keep clean.' She moved the discussion on.

'Yes, it is. Oh, and Mr Archer comes on weekday mornings for the garden and woods.'

'Was it him we saw when we arrived?'

'I assume so; he was too far away for me to make out.'

'Out of interest, what does Dawn do, work-wise?' Clarice asked.

'How long have you got?' Emily jested.

'That bad?'

'Dawn's forty-three. She gets obsessed with an idea, then suddenly goes off the boil!' Emily sounded cross. 'She got into university to study art history. Dad said it was all she talked about – then after the second year she dropped out.'

'How silly,' Clarice said.

'She then decided she wanted to do graphic design, and found a college that accepted her. That time she dropped out after less than a year. Among other things, she's also been a barmaid, done teacher training and was a budding thespian for a short while.' Emily looked reflective. 'I feel sorry for Grandpa, paying for all the career changes.'

'So she's resting now?' Clarice smiled. 'Between career changes?'

'You could say that,' Emily agreed, 'although supposedly she's writing a novel, I don't know what about. She's been at it for around four years.'

Clarice nodded.

'And then there's her love life.' Emily glanced around, as if ensuring nobody could overhear. 'I'm such a gossip.'

'That's OK.' Clarice matched her grin. 'Gossip on.'

'It's a bit like her working life, how she becomes obsessive about something. With relationships, in the beginning, it's always *lurve*.' Emily raised her hand dramatically to her forehead. 'Best thing ever. She seems to enjoy the chase, but she loses interest when she gets the bloke.'

Clarice waited.

'The most recent embarrassment was with a man called Ian Belling.' Emily folded her arms, implying it was a long tale. 'Ian's wife, Penny, was supposedly a good friend of Dawn's. Dad told me that Dawn and Ian started an affair that went on for well over a year, until Penny found out.'

'It finished?' Clarice asked.

'Not exactly. Ian and Penny have three children, and the oldest was then fourteen. There was a lot of going back and forth between Dawn and Penny before Ian finally settled with Dawn. He was a successful businessman when divorce proceedings began. According to Dad, Penny took him for everything she could get. She got the house, half his financial assets, and then—'

'Maybe she worked with him in the business, and in fairness, if they had three children, she would need a house and money,' Clarice interrupted.

'I'm sure it was probably fair. They'd been married a long time,' Emily said. 'But just a week after the divorce, Dawn dumped him. She said their relationship wasn't working – it was a mistake.'

'How long ago was that?'

'Around six months ago. Since then, things have turned sour. At first he phoned Dawn endlessly – she had to change her mobile number twice. To begin with, it was all about how much he loved her.'

'Before it turned to hate?' Clarice asked.

Emily nodded. 'He kept hanging around near the house, in the woods. Dawn said he'd become violent. He hit her once, slapped her across the face, but she couldn't prove it. She took out a restraining order.'

Clarice nodded as she followed Emily into what must have once been a grand dining room but was now in a state of decline. The red of the fabric wallpaper was muted and dark in the upper corners, the maroon carpet had worn in places, and the dado and frieze, once probably a dark gold, were dull brown, with light patches. When had the room last been decorated? Certainly not, Clarice imagined, within the previous couple of decades. Looking around at the furniture, it seemed a tale of two parts: while the decoration of the room was poor, the furniture was of good quality, with some value. The long table was oak, the eight chairs and two carvers elm and oak. The sideboard was on a grand scale, with high shelves containing blue and white porcelain. At the end of the room was a screen to one side, the bottom half and sides in oak, the top sections in a floral embroidery design.

The room compounded Clarice's sense that the house's problems – the damp, lack of heating, and issues with the damaged windows – would worsen if not fixed.

As they turned to leave the room, she saw that a small elderly woman had entered silently to stand and observe them.

'Hello, Aunt Ernestine.' Emily went immediately to embrace her and kiss her cheek.

Ernestine was small and neat, with short pure white hair. Her blue eyes were bright and inquisitive, and her porcelain skin remarkably unlined. She wore a pink floral dress with a red cardigan, below which slim legs and ankles could be seen. The black leather court shoes on her dainty feet were highly polished. She resembled an immaculate china doll.

'I'm her great-aunt,' Ernestine addressed Clarice, her voice sing-song and light, 'but it's a bit long-winded to call me that!'

'Yes.' Clarice smiled.

'I'm seventy-nine and a half,' Ernestine spoke with pride, 'and I have all my own teeth.' She gave a wide mock grin to demonstrate.

'This is Clarice Beech,' Emily said. 'She was a good friend of Dad's.'

Ernestine walked over to stand near Clarice. 'My goodness, you are tall. You make me feel such a little shrimp. I knew you were coming. My brother, Ralph, told me.'

As she talked, Ernestine frequently touched her necklace – diamonds interspersed with pearls. The stones were large; could they be genuine diamonds, worn so casually during the day?

'Yes, I've met Ralph, and Dawn with Ruffian,' Clarice said.

'We always have Siamese cats. You've seen Bellatrix?'

'Yes. Emily explained the family history.'

'They make an unusual sound; it would be strange not to hear them, especially during the night.'

'Are they a lot noisier then?' Clarice asked, puzzled.

'Dawn is quite good at getting Ruffian in at night,' Emily interjected.

'He loves to hunt.' Ernestine ignored Emily's words. 'We find quite a few decapitated bodies: mice, rats, voles, and their bits – the entrails.' Her face was alight; she clearly enjoyed talking about the subject. 'You're not squeamish, are you?' Her eyes fixed on Clarice's face; it seemed she relished the belief that Ruffian was a violent predator.

'No, not especially.' Clarice looked at Emily, who, standing behind Ernestine, silently pointed to indicate the door, hinting at their departure.

As Clarice moved to go around the old lady, Ernestine stepped in front to block her path.

'Colin was a delicate little boy, ever so squeamish.' She chuckled. 'I once made a finger puppet from the head of a dead mouse. I have tiny fingers – look.' She spread out her hands, palms downward, and held them in front of her. 'I snuck up on Colin to surprise him, wiggling the mouse's head on my finger.' She moved the index finger of her left hand in the air to demonstrate. 'He screamed and screamed, then wet his pants.' Ernestine's chuckle turned into a throaty laugh.

'Poor Colin, how old was he?' Clarice asked.

'Avril never usually lost her temper, but she turned quite nasty.' Ernestine suddenly looked sneaky. 'I can't remember how old he was, it was such a long time ago.'

Her gaze wandered away from Clarice, and she looked vaguely about the room as if suddenly lost in thought. After a few moments' hesitation, Clarice took the opportunity to follow Emily out. It felt as though the elderly lady had shifted in a moment from animation to losing the mental thread, her mind drifting.

Chapter 16

'She has a macabre sense of humour,' Emily muttered as they made their way to the sitting room.

'Poor Colin.' Clarice grimaced. 'He was only five when Avril left, so he must have been very young when Ernestine played that nasty trick.'

'You'll get used to Ernestine. I have.' Emily sighed with resignation. 'And you still have the pleasure of meeting Tessa.'

In the sitting room, Clarice's gaze went immediately to the ornate fireplace with its geometric side panels. The fire had been laid but was unlit. She guessed that the highly polished grey mantel was, again, limestone. In a line on the top were boxes of varying sizes and shapes, and moving closer, she realised they were snuff boxes, in either wood or metal.

'Grandpa collects them,' Emily said as she noticed Clarice's interest. 'There are more in his private sitting room.'

Clarice nodded, glancing around the room. Next to the fireplace, an old, worn wicker basket held logs. The furniture and the decor fitted with the style of the rest of the house. The carpet, which once might have been deep blue, was faded and worn, as were the wall-hung tapestries. An upholstered sofa with a carved frame stood facing a chaise with a dark oak end frame. Both sagged in the centre with age and use. A deep leather armchair with two squashed cushions and a red checked throw over one arm was nearest the fire. It was, Clarice assumed, Ralph's regular seat.

'I need to go up and get another layer of clothes.' She felt a shiver. 'This house is so cold.'

'I did warn you. I am sorry; maybe I shouldn't have pushed you into coming with me.' Emily sounded fraught.

'No,' Clarice said. 'First, you did not push me into anything; secondly, I'm glad to be here with you.' She did not voice her thoughts. In this house, without her father, Emily needed an ally.

'Great.' Emily sounded relieved.

After going to the bedroom to add an extra layer of clothing, they returned to the dining room. There were six places set at the table, and two heated trolleys were in position nearby. Johnson was in the process of spooning food onto a plate from a dish.

'Perfect timing,' Ralph said, having taken his place in one of the carvers at the head of the table. Cleaning his spectacles with a white handkerchief, he stared at them through clouded eyes, looking much like Floss, his elderly Labrador.

'We have poached cod with vegetables. Johnson is sorting mine out. When he's finished, go and help yourselves. Remember, Emily, guests first; help to serve Clarice, and then get your own.' Having given his instructions, Ralph turned away to talk to Johnson.

A woman suddenly stood directly in front of Clarice, her hand extended.

'I'm Tessa. We haven't been introduced.'

It was easy to see that this was Dawn's mother. At seventy-seven, she was slim, fit and attractive, with a strong bone structure, and her grey hair still had the wavy bounce of her daughter's.

'Good to meet you,' Clarice said.

'See if you're still of that opinion by the time you leave tomorrow.' Tessa spoke without losing eye contact and held on to Clarice's hand for slightly longer than was necessary. The slanted half-smile was the same as her daughter's. 'You should get your lunch before it goes cold.' She turned to walk away. 'Make sure you eat sufficiently; it's just sandwiches this evening.'

Emily served up lunch for Clarice and herself before they took their places at the table. With Ralph at the head, Clarice, Emily and Ernestine were opposite Tessa and Dawn.

'You'll have introduced everyone here to Clarice?' Ralph looked beadily at his granddaughter.

Clarice saw the now-familiar rise of pink in Emily's cheeks. 'Yes, thank you,' she cut in. 'I've met everyone.'

'Has Emily shown you around the house?' Ralph asked.

'Yes, it's splendid. I believe the peak of Gothic revival was in the 1860s and 70s – but this was built in 1890?'

'Yes, that's right. Queen Victoria's reign finished in 1901. The manor is Victorian Gothic.' Ralph spoke as if he had switched on autopilot, possibly from telling the story so often. 'George Compton, my grandfather, was good at making money, and when he married Emily Smythe, an affluent merchant's daughter, he acquired an even greater fortune. Emily was an only child, and as there was no male heir to carry her family name forward, she and George joined their surnames on marriage. With his wealth, George commissioned an architect and had Stone Fen Manor built. He moved his family from London.' He waved his fork in the air. 'My father, James, was the oldest of the three sons, so he was the one to inherit the house.'

Clarice nodded.

'We were born here, the three of us. I'm the eldest, then Ernestine, and we had a baby sister, Elizabeth – always known as Beth. Sadly, she died just after her seventh birthday.'

'I'm sorry,' Clarice said.

'High death rates among children were common then.' Ralph sounded unmoved. 'More of a shock with all the present-day medical resource was Colin's death at fifty-five, poor boy.'

A silence fell.

'I'm looking forward to Emily showing me the outside of the house and the garden later.' Clarice broke the silence.

'It's not at its best at this time of year,' Tessa said. 'There's not a lot to see – just trees, trees and more trees.' She gave a hollow laugh.

'A lot for the gardener to do, clearing up the debris.' Clarice smiled amiably. 'We saw him in the woods on our way in.'

'Can't have,' Ralph said. 'He's not here today.'

'What did he look like?' Dawn's voice was sharp.

Clarice and Emily glanced at one another as the room went quiet.

'I didn't notice,' Emily said.

'He was in his late forties, denim jeans, brown jacket and light-coloured trainers.' Clarice looked at their concerned faces.

'I think it's—'Tessa started.

'We'll talk about it later.' Ralph gave her a hard stare.

'Of course.' Tessa looked down at her food.

Ralph, Clarice realised, had silenced Tessa for a reason, one that he did not wish to discuss in the presence of a stranger.

'I'm looking forward to seeing the windows and the carved stonework.' She filled the awkward silence. 'A lot of mid-nineteenth-century Gothic buildings were red brick.'

'Yes,' Dawn looked at her intently, 'and other materials, iron and glazed tiles, became fashionable too.'

'If you're interested in architecture and the house,' Ralph spoke directly to Clarice, 'you should talk to Dawn. She did art history at university.'

Tessa's face assumed a smug expression.

'No, she's writing a book, Ralph – you're confused.' Ernestine sounded belligerent.

Ralph put down his fork and leaned forward to glower at his sister.

'I think I might remember what my daughter has and has not done. She is currently writing a book, but she spent two years studying art history. It's you who's lost your marbles, Ernestine, not me!'

Ernestine stared back, her twisting face conveying irritation. 'She chops and changes, never sticking at anything – not like our Colin. She's been writing a book for years. Why would anyone remember if she did some course at university?'

'For heaven's sake, Ernestine.' Tessa's voice was a low, controlled growl, and Clarice had a fleeting mental picture of a sleek but combative Dobermann. 'You cannot possibly compare Dawn and Colin. Dawn is sensitive and artistic. Colin was simply dreary. He started wearing those ridiculous blue-framed specs because he thought it might make him look slightly more interesting. Being an accountant suited his personality. He was such a dull little man – dull, dull, bloody dull.'

Clarice, glancing at Emily, saw her frame stiffen.

'Don't talk about my son like that!' Ralph boomed, waving his arms and knocking over his glass in his agitation. 'Now look what you've made me do.' He stared at the water spreading away from him along the table, his bushy eyebrows meeting in an angry line. 'Apart from it not being true, Colin's daughter – my only grandchild – is sitting opposite you. How insensitive of you to be so rude about her father.'

Tessa glowered. 'Your grand*daughter*, yes. I know Dawn didn't give you a grandson, but Colin didn't either.'

'I've never expected anything from Dawn.' Ralph's voice was clipped.

'And what, pray, is that supposed to mean?' Tessa snapped.

'Colin was a good boy.' Ernestine sounded confused. 'He gave us Emily.'

'Just shut up.' Tessa glared at her. 'You pathetic old woman.'

Like a shadow, another uneasy hush fell over the small gathering.

'My dad,' Clarice did not recognise the controlled pitch of Emily's voice as it pierced the silence, 'was never dull.'

Quiet came again, as if those present were taken aback by the rejoinder from someone usually so docile. Clarice saw that as she spoke, Emily cast her eyes downwards, as if not looking directly to confront anyone.

'Dad loved his mother,' she continued, 'and Avril's disappearance was never properly explained. It meant he never came to terms with her loss. That affected him.' She paused as she struggled to find the words to finish. 'But he was a lovely person, funny, clever, artistic – the best dad ever.'

Ralph and Tessa stared at one another before looking away. Tessa scratched her fork against her plate to scoop food into her mouth in an exaggerated gesture. Clarice sensed the tension seeping from Emily, and out of the corner of her eye she saw Johnson standing watching and listening near the door.

'Avril going away upset the boy.' Ernestine spoke with passion. 'But it was Bellatrix who made her leave. She would have taken Colin. Bellatrix made her leave without him.'

'Shut up, Ernestine!' Ralph stood up to shout at his sister. 'Avril made her choice when she buggered off in the company of Major Freddie Baxter, my so-called friend.'

His words made Clarice wonder if losing the friendship of the Major had been a more significant blow than losing his wife.

'Bellatrix always protects us,' Ernestine said. 'Out of love.'

Ralph's face twisted into an angry mask, but instead of responding, he raised his eyes in an expression of exasperation.

'Emily.' He turned to his granddaughter. 'What Tessa said was unforgivable. I know how upset Colin was about his mother, but it was her choice to leave. Try to remember your father was only five when she went. He found it hard to accept that I could not keep her here against her will, that it was her choice to go.'

'Dad never gave up wanting to know where she went and why she hadn't taken him with her.' Emily raised her eyes to look at him.

'If somebody does not wish to be found, they'll make damn sure they aren't,' Ralph said bluntly. 'Colin could have scoured the country or engaged a dozen detective agencies, but after my wife buggered off with the Major, they went to ground. Colin should have accepted it and moved on. I lost not only my wife that day, but also the man I'd considered my dearest friend.'

'Jam roly-poly?' Johnson was beside one of the heated trolleys, looking at Ralph.

'Have yours first, Emily,' Ralph said.

'I've lost my appetite.' She stood up.

'Why don't you take Clarice outside?' He sounded conciliatory. 'She wants to see the outside of the house. Come back to help set up when you're ready – though it's not obligatory.'

Emily nodded, and Clarice got up to follow her out of the room. She felt the intense gaze of five pairs of eyes watching their departure. Emily had been right in thinking her grandfather could not keep up the charm offensive for long.

Chapter 17

'We'll need to grab our coats from the cloakroom; it's cold out there.' They'd reached the great hall without speaking.

'Will you get mine?' Clarice asked. 'I have to make a quick call.' She held up her cell phone.

Emily nodded understandingly. When she returned with the coats, she asked, 'Did you get Rick?'

'It wasn't Rick. He'll be at work – I won't catch him until this evening. I wanted to speak to Micky.'

'Dad's mate from the ceramics class – with the snake tattoo?'

'Yes, I was checking that he and some of the others are still coming tomorrow for the funeral. You said they would be welcome.'

'Yes.' Emily was suddenly eager. 'Any or all of them. I'd love to see their friendly faces.'

As they approached the doorway, Emily indicated hooks to one side of the door.

'Those four blue jackets are waterproof, extra large, and have hoods,' she said. 'They can go over the top of a coat or jacket and are for anyone to use if you get to the door and it's raining – handy for diving out to the car.'

'That sounds sensible.' Clarice glanced at the row of jackets.

'Although like most practical plans, it does have a flaw. People often wander upstairs, or Grandpa to his study, forgetting to return the jacket on their way back in.'

'The best of plans has flaws.' Clarice grinned.

'Tessa never forgets to hang hers back up. Dad used to call her the jacket monitor; she'd get so grumpy if she noticed there were only three.'

'Trust your dad to put a humorous spin on it.' Clarice laughed.

They walked outside, and the garden felt still and silent after the earlier confrontations. The dark, overcast sky intensified a feeling of gloom.

'She is magnificent.' Clarice looked up at Bellatrix, her first opportunity to examine her properly. Earlier, Johnson had ushered them quickly forward, removing the chance to hover for a closer look. The cat dwarfed her. Close to, its stonework was pitted, but the almond-shaped eyes and profile of the head remained unmistakably Siamese. There was a quality of quietness and stillness as she gazed at the statue, perhaps because of the contrast with the earlier heated anger in the dining room.

'Yes, she is amazing.' Emily stood next to her.

'You have so much history.' Clarice rested her hand on the massive cold paw. 'Not just with her – but also with this house.'

'Yes,' Emily was hesitant, 'but with the history, I also get the not altogether pleasant relatives!'

'All families have at least one of those.' Clarice tried to sound cheerful as she turned towards the garage. 'There are some expensive cars here.' She observed the vehicles in a line inside.

Emily nodded, letting her gaze roam over them. 'Tessa loves her Jag; the Saab is Dawn's. Johnson uses the other two. The Range Rover is officially his, and he drives my grandfather in the Porsche. With his poor eyesight, Grandpa can't drive himself.'

'Has Ernestine given up because of dementia?'

'Aunt Ernestine never learned to drive; she always had to be driven – Johnson again.'

'Are you OK?' Clarice looked closer at Emily's pinched expression.

'I should be used to them by now. They're all pretty selfish and awful; everything is about them.' Emily cast her eyes back to the house. 'But that's the first time Tessa's been quite so rude about Dad.'

'Try not to allow her to get to you, otherwise she's won. But I know that's easier said than done.'

'Tessa is nasty. But Grandpa is annoying because he's insensitive about how difficult it was for Dad when Avril left.'

'Poor Colin, he was only five. It must have taken him a while to stop believing she might come back.'

'I think he was forced to confront it fairly quickly.' Emily stopped to look at Clarice as she spoke. 'Every day after she'd gone, he went upstairs to sit on her bed – he said the room still smelt of Mummy.'

Clarice nodded.

'One day, about a week after her departure, he went up to find them moving her bed. Aunt Ernestine said Avril's bed was much nicer than hers, so she was going to have it.'

Clarice nodded. 'I didn't think the two pine single beds matched the rest of the room.'

'Dad said he was in tears. He asked, if they took the bed, where would Mummy sleep when she came home?'

Clarice watched Emily's face contort with emotion.

'Grandpa told him to get that thought out of his head, Avril was never coming back.' Emily looked away, as if unable to meet Clarice's eyes. 'They bagged up all her things that day, cleared out the wardrobe, cupboards and drawers.'

They stood quietly for a few moments.

'Let me show you one of the routes through the woods.' She strode away as if needing to distance herself from the house.

Before they reached the trees, she pointed at a semi-derelict building. The walls were brick, with a tiled roof, part of which was missing, revealing rotting exposed beams. 'That was the stables,' she said.

'Is it used for anything now?' Clarice asked.

'Not for horses. It's more of a dumping ground for gardening tools.' Emily walked towards the building and pushed hard against the door. Clarice followed her inside to see four empty box stalls and rusting metal drinking troughs. The high windows were intact, dark and unwashed. On the sills, straw and twigs poked out, evidence of nesting birds. Light entered between the rotting beams. In contrast, the other end of the stables was open to the sky, part light and part shadow.

Evidence of the horses that had once been there was all around. Clarice stroked her hand gently against a halter hanging from a hook on the wall, feeling the thick leather hardened and cracked; on a window ledge was a lone stirrup and a broken curry comb. And over one of the horse boxes hung a leading rein. Tools the gardener might use, spades, forks and a hoe, were at the building's dark dry end. An aluminium wheelbarrow stood propped against the door of an empty stall. Lying next to it was a metal stake with a rounded end, possibly used in the past to be tapped into the ground and a rein from a horse attached, so that the animal might graze without wandering. Apart from the rattle of a loose window, shaken by the wind, the stable was utterly silent.

'You have barn owls?' Clarice bent, examining the ground.

'Have they left droppings?' Emily came near to look.

'Pellets. They're black, which means they're fresh.' Clarice let her gaze wander around the stables. 'This is a good hunting place, with the mice and rats; owls have more difficulty sourcing food in winter.'

Emily walked away to wander in and out of the stalls.

Clarice tried to imagine the place in its prime, the whinnying of the horses and the clank of horseshoes on the concrete floor, the movement and chatter of the stable boys, the smells of hay, manure and meal. With the people and horses long dead, the dilapidated building had become a monument to a different age.

They left to walk into the woods, the bare branches of the trees spreading high above, the heart-lifting beauty of colours that brought joy in the spring and summer months replaced by browns and a sunless grey sky. Now in the dying season, they walked on a carpet of soggy golden-brown leaves, taking a narrow path through the trees: alder, ash, oak, birch, chestnut and elm.

In a small clearing, the attractive, slightly twisty limbs brought Clarice's attention to a group of quince trees. Her mind went back to when the fruit from her own quinces had turned from light to golden yellow, with a delicate vanilla fragrance. As well as jelly, she had used some of them to make quince gin.

The chopped fruit was currently marinating with gin, herbs and sugar in a large plastic tub, to be bottled in December and given as Christmas gifts.

As they moved on, the wood became dense again, shadows enclosing them. Emily stopped where there was a choice between two paths.

'There's a well that way.' She indicated the left-hand route.

'Not in use?'

'Not now. It was used to fill the troughs for the horses that grazed in the field nearby. Over the years, a willow tree has grown close to the well, and Dad said its roots would take any water. The field is now part of the woods, and near the well, there's a cemetery.'

'A cemetery?' Clarice repeated with surprise.

'Not people.' Emily smiled. 'It's the pets, mainly Siamese cats and Labradors from three generations of Compton-Smythes. Beyond the cemetery, it's very wet and boggy, and then there's the Wash.'

'The family are more sentimental than I'd imagined they might be.' Clarice tried not to sound too cynical.

'I think,' Emily gave a wry smile, 'Grandpa has a greater affection for his Labradors than for any member of his family.'

'Talking of Labradors …' Clarice looked in the direction from which they had come. With a triumphant bark, as if it had been his quest to find them, Ben, Ralph's younger dog, charged towards them, scattering leaves in his wake.

Emily bent to pat him. 'You shouldn't be out here on your own,' she told him. 'He doesn't separate from Floss,' she said to Clarice. 'They're very much a pair.'

'Did Ben replace an older dog?' Clarice asked.

'Yes, Grandpa always has a pair, a bitch and a dog; when one dies, he gets another. The last dog, Max, died four or five months ago, and he got Ben at twelve weeks old.'

'I don't think he's on top of the training routine with Ben.' Clarice watched the dog dance gleefully in a circle around them. 'Let's see if we can teach him to sit and stay.'

Half an hour later, Ben understood the rudiments. Tempted by the reward of dog treats, he sat when requested, but was too excited to stay sitting for long.

'You've made some progress,' Emily said.

'Not a lot.' Clarice patted him. 'He needs consistency in his training, ideally at least several times a day for the message to take root in his brain.'

'Can I have a go?' Emily's face was momentarily devoid of angst.

Clarice gave her some treats to put in her pocket. Ben was happy to comply by sitting to command.

'He's a bright dog,' Clarice said. 'Training him should be a doddle.'

They walked back through the trees to the house. Ben fell into step beside Clarice.

'I still haven't shown you the outside of the house and the windows.'

'I'll see them before I leave.' Clarice looked towards the entrance. 'Are you sure you're ready to go back?'

'I would like to help. I don't want Tessa whinging that I wouldn't give a hand.'

'What needs doing?'

'I told you that Mrs Fuller and her sister cleaned the great hall yesterday?'

Clarice nodded.

'It has to be set up for a buffet and drinks. There are folding tables and chairs stored in a utility room off the kitchen. Mrs Fuller is on ironing duty for the tablecloths – some are well past their sell-by date. Then the crockery, cutlery and water jugs need to be washed. Don't under any circumstances mention bottled water in front of my grandfather – it's another one of his pet hates. He'll go ballistic, on and on about tap water and the money that people waste on bottled.'

'A bit like heating the house,' Clarice said.

'You've got it,' Emily said. 'It's a trigger. Once he gets started, it's not easy to shut him up.'

'Who will be doing the food?'

'They're having a caterer come in while the funeral is taking place. Johnson will stay behind to organise everything.'

'Not exactly cheap. That does surprise me.'

'No,' Emily agreed. 'What makes it more difficult is that Grandpa treats it like pick and mix. The caterers obviously charge for everything, so he tells them not to bring or do certain things so he doesn't need to pay extra. It all gets very complicated.'

'He's trying to keep an eye on costs?'

'Yes. Dad said that deaths and weddings were the only times Grandpa used caterers, and apparently he would moan for at least a week afterwards about the expense and …' She paused, then continued. 'Dad used to pull my leg about my wedding. He'd say, "When you get married, Emily, we're going to have such a cracking day, it will give your grandpa the opportunity to moan for a month."'

'His lovely sense of humour again,' Clarice said, and

noticing that Emily was teary-eyed, she linked arms with her to finish the journey back to the house.

In the great hall, they found Tessa and Dawn setting up a trestle table between them. Ralph and Johnson were carrying chairs in.

'You've decided to join us then,' Tessa hissed at Emily as she passed, quietly enough for Ralph not to hear.

Emily ignored her. 'Grandpa, let me help you,' she said.

Clarice walked through the hall, deciding to go upstairs to fetch a camera from her bag. She knew Rick would appreciate seeing photographs of the house. As she walked into the bedroom, she found Ernestine standing at the window.

'I've got all my own teeth, you know,' the older woman said.

Chapter 18

'I've got all my own teeth.' Ernestine repeated the words, then pulled her lips back, as she'd done previously, showing her teeth and gums. It was clearly a fixed part of her repertoire, part of the loop of the illness that was dementia, or perhaps just a misguided attempt at wit. Clarice remembered what she had said earlier about the mouse's head and her small fingers.

Ernestine was standing next to one of the long windows; it was as if she had been watching Clarice and Emily coming back from their walk, awaiting their return.

'I was born in this house,' Ernestine said. 'Ralph is the oldest; I'm five years younger than him, and Beth is four years younger than me.'

'She *was* four years younger,' Clarice gently corrected her. 'Your little sister who died. It must have been tough for you.'

'She loved me very much,' Ernestine said. 'I was always her favourite person.'

'How lovely.'

'She liked my dolls. I had to hide them from her.'

'You didn't like her playing with your things?'

'No, she had her own dolls, and anyway, nobody was allowed to touch Ralph's toys, he would go mad. It wasn't fair, her taking my stuff.'

'I think it's always a problem if you have younger siblings,' Clarice said.

'Mummy gave her my pretty dresses. She said because I'd grown big, they didn't fit me any more, I had to let Beth have them. I liked to see them in my wardrobe. She never looked after them properly.'

Clarice nodded understandingly.

'Her name should have been Jill. I was the baby before she came.'

'Do you like the name Jill better than Beth?' Clarice found the conversation odd.

'No, why do you say that? Beth is a much prettier name, or Liz, Lizzie even.'

'You said she should have been called Jill?' Clarice said.

'It's the nursery rhyme. Jack and Jill went up the hill.' Ernestine looked expectantly at her. 'Jack fell down and broke his crown.'

'Yes, I see,' Clarice replied, although she didn't understand Ernestine's point. 'Did Beth fall down and break *her* crown?'

'Don't be silly. She was stamped to death by a horse.' Ernestine looked past Clarice as though checking to ensure they were alone. 'I speak to her all the time, but we can't play any more.' Her eyes took on a momentary faraway look. 'We used to play games; the best was hide-and-seek. I always won – I liked winning.'

Clarice hid her surprise on learning how Beth had died. Ralph had talked vaguely of childhood mortality – but perhaps Ernestine was confused.

'Do you miss her – Beth?'

They stood in silence for what felt like an eternity.

'Yes.' Ernestine paused, examining Clarice's face, before going on. 'Nobody's ever asked me that before. I didn't think I would. Ralph got treats because he was the eldest, and Beth got hers because she was Mummy and Daddy's special baby girl.'

'What about you?' Clarice asked.

'I got treats sometimes. Mummy used to laugh and say I was her funny girl, and Daddy said I was clever when I danced or sang.' Ernestine's expression was one of bewilderment. 'Beth was my special little sister. I miss her.'

'It must have been an awful time. You were so young when it happened.' Clarice watched Ernestine, who had become distracted, looking across the room at her image in the wardrobe mirror.

'Do you like my necklace?' She smiled at herself.

'Yes, it's lovely. Are the diamonds real?'

'Of course they are – you don't think I'd wear crap. And the pearls, too.'

'Wow, they are special.' Clarice smiled while thinking how her initial perception of Ernestine as a delicate china doll did not fit with her language.

Ernestine walked closer to the mirror, smiling lovingly at her reflection.

'They belonged to Mummy.' She spoke with a sneaky, half-flirtatious look from under her eyelashes.

Clarice marvelled at the prettiness of Ernestine's unlined face, her pert nose and rosebud lips. Her eyeshadow matched the blue of her eyes; she wore a touch of rouge on her cheeks and pale pink lipstick.

'Do you wear them all the time?' Clarice asked.

'Always.' Ernestine's fingers crept up to stroke the necklace. 'It's not as if I go out anywhere to show them off. Although I don't wear the bracelet.'

'No – I see.' Clarice felt a moment's sadness.

'Nobody does the things they used to when they were young. Ralph doesn't play tennis any more. Johnson used to go to the bridge club in town on his evenings off.'

'I'd heard Ralph enjoyed tennis.'

'He doesn't go out much now he's half blind. He can't go anywhere unless Johnson or Tessa drives him,' Ernestine said. 'Years ago, he practically lived at Riverside, the tennis club in Spalding. I used to go there too, but not as often as my brother.'

'Were you good at tennis?' Clarice asked.

'No, I never won, and nobody really wanted me to be their partner in the doubles, so I stopped going,' Ernestine said. 'It's where Ralph met Tessa.'

'Avril,' Clarice corrected.

'Tessa first, then Avril. I'm not the one who's going gaga.' Ernestine appeared to have grown two inches, clearly enjoying the idea that she knew more than Clarice. 'Ralph met Tessa at the tennis club. He brought her here once.' She paused. Her fingers crept to her lips as she appeared to concentrate. 'There was an awful woman called Pamela, but he never brought *her* home.'

Clarice had stopped breathing; she willed Ernestine not to wander onto another subject.

'Then he met Pamela's younger sister, that was Avril, and he did bring her home.' Ernestine smiled suddenly. 'She was a quiet little thing. I liked her very much, the best of all Ralph's girlfriends. He wasn't a fool. He married her pretty damn quick.'

A quiet little thing until you played nasty tricks on her small son, Clarice thought, but she didn't say the words out loud. Instead, she said, 'You got on with Avril?'

'She was special, she liked me, and she took me with her whenever she went shopping. Sometimes we'd have lunch at one of the hotels in Spalding or Boston. It was only ever Avril who asked me to do that.' Ernestine clasped and unclasped her fingers; she was suddenly far away in memory. 'She let me wear her pretty shoes; she was small, like me.'

'You were the same shoe size?' Clarice asked.

'Yes, and she painted her toenails pink, like her fingernails. I'd never watched anyone do that, except in a movie.'

'Did you copy her?' Clarice asked.

Ernestine nodded. 'Little feet with pink toenails.' She put her hands out in front, palms down, as if to show Clarice her perfect, unchipped, pink-varnished nails.

'In open sandals, sticking out from beneath her skirt or trousers?' Clarice smiled.

'It's the special ones who always go away and leave me, although Ralph hasn't gone, he's still here.' Ernestine sounded distracted.

Clarice thought again about the trick Ernestine had played on Colin. There were doubtless other times she had done similar nasty things – it would go with her macabre sense of humour – but Avril had obviously forgiven her. She had included her difficult sister-in-law in normal domestic activities and treats. It seemed that Avril had been both kind and tolerant.

'Did you see Avril on the day she left?' Clarice again held her breath, wondering if the elderly lady would remember. 'Did she say goodbye?'

'She didn't say it.' Ernestine held her hands forward again, side by side. 'She was wearing pink, like me. When she was leaving, she waved goodbye.' She moved her hands up and down from the wrists. 'Ralph told me she was leaving and I mustn't get upset, that I should go back into the house – so I did.'

Ernestine had not mentioned the presence of the Major. Could it be that Ralph, aware of the relationship between his wife and his best friend, was taking Avril to meet him? Having known Ralph for only a short amount of time, Clarice thought it out of character. In his world, she imagined, what was sauce for the goose was not sauce for the gander.

'It was the last time I saw her.' Ernestine sounded regretful.

'I hope you're not making a nuisance of yourself, Ernestine?' Tessa was suddenly standing in the doorway, her face like thunder. Clarice wondered how long she'd been there. It seemed people were always hanging around doors in this house, eavesdropping.

'I'm not a nuisance, am I?' The words were directed to Clarice.

'No, of course not,' Clarice said. 'Do you need our help downstairs?'

'A bit late now.' Tessa sniffed.

'I didn't tell her anything.' Ernestine flung the words at Tessa before suddenly rushing past her. The pitter-patter sound of her small feet as she went down the stairs filled the silence.

Tessa observed Clarice, her gaze moving from head to toe.

'You shouldn't listen to what she says.' Her tone was hard. 'She's completely batty; even before dementia, she'd lost her marbles years ago.'

Clarice walked to the bed to open her bag and remove a small camera, which she slipped into her pocket. 'She seemed quite lucid to me.' She forced a congeniality into her voice that she did not feel.

'You wouldn't think that if you were traipsing about in the dark at midnight searching for her. She sometimes goes walkabout.' Tessa leaned against the door frame as she talked. 'Ralph worries that she might end up in some watery hole, or lost out on the mudflats.'

'I expect it must worry you as well. It would be awful if she became confused and couldn't find her way back.'

'She's not my sister – not my problem,' Tessa said, po-faced. 'Ralph often talks about quality of life with his Labradors but never thinks about applying it to his sister.'

'Are you suggesting he should have her put to sleep?'

'Don't be ridiculous! That's not what I meant at all,' Tessa said sharply. 'What I meant was that if something did happen to Ernestine, it wouldn't be the end of the world. It would be a release for her.'

'Ralph obviously doesn't think that.'

'No.' Tessa wiggled her fingers up and down. 'He has airy-fairy ideas about her joyful, charming personality, but I think she's getting worse by the day.'

'I didn't realise you knew Avril.' Clarice tried to make her words sound natural, with no hidden agenda.

'Not that it's any of your business.' Tessa straightened up. 'The Riverside tennis club was where everyone met when I was a girl; there were no nightclubs or online dating then. Everyone knew each other.' She gave Clarice one of her intimidating stares. 'You need to butt out of things that don't concern you.'

It was clear that Clarice was correct in thinking Tessa had been listening to her conversation with Ernestine.

Clarice said nothing; she moved towards the door to return downstairs. Tessa placed her arm across the frame, blocking her exit.

'I don't know what rubbish Colin told you about his mother.'

'Nothing.' Clarice smiled. 'Absolutely nothing.'

'I don't believe you.'

'You must believe what you choose.' As she spoke, the notion drifted through her mind that she could use Tessa's belief that Colin had confided in her to her advantage. 'Not that it's any of my business,' she said calmly, using Tessa's own words, 'but it seemed you disliked Avril. Perhaps your logic is the same as Pamela's – Avril's sister.'

'Have you met Pamela?' Tessa appeared astonished.

Clarice ignored the question, putting forward one of her own. 'Did you get an invite to the wedding? Pamela was offended, being the sister of the bride, when she didn't.'

'I was a friend of both Avril and Ralph. They did invite me to their wedding. Pamela had her eye set on Ralph. She was quite unforgiving when he chose Avril – such a silly woman.'

But you were shrewder than Pamela. Clarice thought, aware that Tessa would probably work out what she was thinking. When Ralph chose Avril over her, Tessa stayed close to both of them, waiting for her chance. Had they continued an affair after Ralph and Avril were married? Four months seemed a remarkably short amount of time from Avril's departure with the Major to Tessa's moving permanently in as Ralph's partner. And it was possible that if there was an affair, that was what had prompted Avril to leave. The thing that must rankle with Tessa was that Ralph had given Avril something he'd never given her: he'd made her his wife. Still, he couldn't suggest marriage because he'd never divorced Avril. Tessa's nasty attitude was doubtless due to festering discontent. Emily was the offspring of his legitimate first-born child.

Clarice stepped towards Tessa, who dropped her arm to allow her to pass. Going down the stairs to the great hall, her mind was full of possibilities. It was the first time she'd heard mention of Ralph knowing Tessa before Avril. Perhaps a relationship had started between the two before Avril arrived on the scene. If Tessa had been dumped for Avril, it could explain her animosity towards Colin and Emily, the son and granddaughter of her rival.

Chapter 19

Back in the hall, Clarice saw Emily deep in conversation with Johnson.

The lights were already on as the afternoon light started to slip away. The trestle tables were arranged in two rows, one on either side of the hall. Around the room were clusters of chairs to allow people to sit together in small, intimate groups. The tables were covered with the cloths so recently ironed by Mrs Fuller, in shades of beige and white. There were stacks of plates of varying size and colours, with an assortment of cutlery and piles of paper napkins. Vases had been placed on windowsills, filled with a mixed range of flowers: yellow and white chrysanthemums, blue thistle-like sea holly, yellow-centred asters with white petals, larkspur and tall green fronds. Having seen no evidence of a flower garden, Clarice assumed they'd come from the village florist.

Tessa had followed her down from the bedroom, and now went immediately to take Ralph by the arm. She put her face close to his to talk as they moved along.

Clarice decided not to intrude on Emily's conversation. Instead, she wandered outdoors to begin a walk around the house's exterior while it was still light enough to view it properly.

She stepped back, trying to decide where to take photographs from to show Bellatrix at her best. Realising that the fading afternoon light was not good enough, she determined to try again the following morning. As she strolled around the side of the building, deep in thought, pushing the camera and her hands into her jacket pockets, she found her mind bouncing from one idea to another. For the second time today, the house and the people appeared to reveal a tale of two financial opposites. There was little evidence that money was being spent on the upkeep of the building, either inside or out. The internal decor was tired and shabby; walls and ceilings required repainting and carpets replacing. Externally, the guttering looked in a poor state, and the windows needed to be assessed by experts to manage improvements after years of deterioration. Yet there were many signs of affluence. If genuine, the diamond and pearl necklace worn by Ernestine must be worth a small fortune. The cars in the garage were expensive models; keeping them in top condition, and the employment of Johnson and the staff for the house and garden, must be costly.

Emily said her great-great-grandfather George had bought farms and land. These had been sold over the years by his son, James, or his grandson, Ralph. Perhaps the only real assets Ralph now had were the house and woods and whatever came in from his business ventures.

'Can I help you?'

Clarice was so deep in thought that she had not observed Dawn coming up behind her.

'Despite what my Aunt Ernestine says, I was fortunate to have two years studying art history. I find the Victorian period especially fascinating.' Dawn's words and smile of encouragement appeared to be genuine.

'I imagine that being born in such a lovely house must give you a special awareness of the subject,' Clarice said.

'Absolutely. Have you worked in architecture? You seem to know a fair bit about Victorian Gothic Revival?'

'No, it's only an interest,' Clarice replied. 'I have London friends who live in a lovely early-nineteenth-century house. I always enjoy visiting them. And there are so many examples of Victorian Gothic in Lincolnshire, especially some of the small churches. But I'm no authority on it.'

'Strawberry Hill House in Twickenham was the first house built in Gothic style, in the mid eighteenth century,' Dawn said. 'It belonged to Horace Walpole; he wrote the first Gothic novel.'

'Ah yes.' Clarice smiled. '*The Castle of Otranto*.'

'You've read it?' Dawn said, pleased.

'Years ago.'

'I haven't read it for years either. I remember it felt so dated – the language.'

Clarice nodded.

'In the eighteenth century, the aristocracy saw the Gothic style as reaching back into the past – the medieval world, charming and romantic.' Dawn spoke with enthusiasm. 'The peak of Gothic Revivalism was in the nineteenth century; there was a moral and Christian element that would have appealed to Great-Grandfather George when he was newly wealthy, although …'

Clarice noticed a mischievous look in her eyes.

'Perhaps I shouldn't use the word "moral". Both George and his son James, although married with children, had reputations for chasing the ladies.'

'Red-blooded men,' Clarice remarked, remembering what Emily had told her.

'Yes, great churchgoers, upholders of the peace – they imagined, no doubt, that their naughty-boy reputation was a badge of honour.'

'The stained-glass windows are decorative, but I know many have a religious significance to deliver a Christian moral message,' Clarice said.

'Yes, very much so, but I don't think the monied few or those with power thought the same rules applied to them.'

Clarice could not help but feel that she was receiving an art history lesson. But Dawn's confidence and warmth when discussing her love of the building was revealing a different side to her.

'I love visiting Gothic cathedrals.' She looked at the windows. 'The light coming through the stained-glass, filling the length of the nave, always gives, even for the non-religious, a sense of the spiritual.'

'My goodness, you are my sort of girl!' Dawn's cool persona had gone. 'We're lucky to have an interpretation of early English Gothic so near – in Lincoln Cathedral.'

'Yes, it is beautiful.' Clarice smiled, warming to Dawn's enthusiasm. 'I love York Minster and Chichester too.'

'You mentioned Lincolnshire churches. My favourites are St Martin's in Ancaster and St John's at Corby Glen,' Dawn said.

'Who did your great-grandfather commission as the architect at the manor?'

'You won't have heard of him. He was once a student of William Burges, but the building was the creation of a master mason rather than an architect.' Dawn put her hand out to touch the stone wall. 'This is Lincolnshire limestone.'

'It was popular before the Victorian period,' Clarice responded, realising that Dawn had moved on, ducking away from answering her question. If the architect was someone she considered insignificant, his association with the great William Burges, if it even ever existed, was probably tenuous.

A silence fell between them.

'Have you ever wanted to leave here and live somewhere else?' Clarice asked.

'I have done.' Dawn gave her half-smile. 'I lived in Sheffield for two years, when I did art history, and later for a year in London.'

'Not a city girl.'

'I guess not. What about you?'

'I lived in London too – I studied ceramics for two years.'

'Two years? You didn't get your degree either, but you still carried on as a ceramicist?'

'I dropped out when my mother became terminally ill. I'm an only child,' Clarice said. 'I became her carer until she died.'

'Ah, that's sad,' Dawn said.

'In a way, I'm not so different from you. I live in a cottage with my husband. I was born and grew up there. It's not grand, but I love it.' Clarice's spirits rose, talking about her home.

'There you go. And,' Dawn squinted mockingly, 'I guess we're around the same age. I'm forty-three.'

'Good guess.' Clarice laughed. 'So am I.'

Dawn leaned back, smiling. 'You know where you're going,' she said, sounding regretful. 'You've established your career and have a husband.'

'No possible suitors lurking?' Clarice put her head to one side, observing Dawn's reaction to the question.

'I never had a problem finding suitors when I was younger. The older you get, the harder it becomes. I've made a few mistakes. All the decent men are in relationships or married.'

'Yes, a lot of things seem easier when you're younger.' Clarice remembered the six months she and Rick had been separated; the idea of starting life again without him had felt lonely and frightening.

'I think you might already know about my most recent disastrous relationship?' Dawn raised her eyebrows theatrically.

Clarice did not answer.

'His name is Ian Belling. There was an awkward moment at lunch when you mentioned that you'd seen him.'

'When?' Clarice asked.

'The description of the man in the woods was spot-on Ian – he stalks me.' Dawn's face twisted with emotion. 'There is a restraining order.'

'You must tell the police.'

'My father would have done that immediately after we finished lunch. I'm not letting Ian get to me, with all that's going on with the funeral.'

'Your dad obviously takes the threats seriously.'

'I can't live my life worrying. If I did as Dad wanted, I'd never leave the house even to walk around the woods or the gardens. Ian would love that, thinking he's got me cowering in my bedroom.'

'Being stalked must be terrifying.'

'If you allow yourself to be scared – yes.' Dawn nodded. 'He says that when he gets an opportunity, he's going to make me regret having made a fool of him. I won't let him get that close.'

'*Did* you make a fool of him?'

'Not intentionally. I'm embarrassed to admit his wife was a friend. I became the mistress for a while; the wheels fell off when he left his wife and we lived together.' She looked reflectively out towards the woods. 'When we became an official couple, Ian changed. He imagined I'd take the place of his wife – do the things she did: iron his shirts, pick up his dirty socks, sit at home watching telly while he went out to the pub with his mates.'

'He took the end of the relationship badly then?' Clarice said. 'Do you think he might turn up at the funeral?'

'He wouldn't do anything so public; he's far too clever. He wants to catch me on my own.' Dawn gave her half-smile. 'What amuses me is that the locals talk behind my back. They say the daughter's just like her mother, getting involved with a married man. They have never believed that Dad took up with Mum *after* Avril had gone.'

'Is that how it happened?'

'They'd known each other for years. Mum had wanted him, but he chose Avril – let's say she was there to pick up the pieces when Avril went away.'

Dawn looked back at the manor house.

'I'll have all this when my father dies. Now that Colin is out of the picture, I'll inherit this place.' Dawn waved her hand towards the building. 'I won't be a hypocrite. Colin and I never got on. If you hadn't already guessed, the elephant in the room was called Avril.' Her lips twisted. 'She was at the root of all the family arguments. But Colin's death was unexpected. It's a blow for Emily.'

'Do you think Emily might get part of the inheritance?'

Dawn stared, her eyes cold, then she flicked her hair from her face and banished the expression. 'That's not how it works, Clarice. It's the oldest child. The house can't be split. And we're not some illustrious aristocratic family, where, if there were no male heir in the immediate family, the house would go to a male cousin.' She looked down at the ground for a moment. 'Being brutally frank, Colin's misfortune is my good luck.'

'I think you and Emily could get on,' Clarice said. 'Perhaps never best buddies, but you could certainly have a reasonable relationship.'

'You think so?'

'Yes.' Clarice nodded. 'I might be wrong, but I think the ones who drew the battle lines were Tessa and Colin. It would always have been difficult, with Avril disappearing as she did when Colin was young and vulnerable. I don't know what happened between him and your mum, but I'm guessing it was probably a case of fault on both sides. I'm someone who always prefers having a friend to an enemy, and Emily is lovely, such an easy person to get on with.'

Dawn looked at her thoughtfully for a moment, then turned away. 'Let's look around the perimeter of the house before it gets too dark.' She led the way. 'Have a look at the windows that you've seen from the inside. I'm afraid they don't deliver the emotional response you described in cathedrals, that sense of the spiritual. The hall doesn't have either the length or width of a great church.'

'It does have height and an arched ceiling.' Clarice had stopped when they reached the windows to look up admiringly. 'It might be a scaled-down version, but it is beautiful and unique.'

They carried on to the back of the building.

'And that,' Dawn pointed, 'is what used to be the tennis court.'

Tall, rusty fences surrounded the long-neglected oblong court. The metal posts used for the net were still in place. The large square of concrete had long cracks sprouting grass and weeds.

'Your dad didn't want to keep it up?' Clarice asked.

'No, he preferred to go to the club, but my grandfather used to have social gatherings here, tennis and gin fizz – although I'm not sure those two things would necessarily have worked well together.'

They wandered on chatting until Clarice felt a touch to her bottom. Surprised, she turned to find a playful Ben.

'Hello, sweetheart.' She bent to make a fuss of the Labrador as he whipped his tail in glee.

'Looks like you're making lots of new friends today.' Dawn smiled as she spoke.

They walked back to the house with Dawn chattering away like a long-lost buddy and Ben trotting at Clarice's heels. Dawn's friendly overtures had seemed entirely genuine; it was only when the talk turned to her inheritance that there had been a flicker of hostility. Their shared interest in the appreciation of Stone Fen Manor's beauty had bridged a divide.

Back inside, Clarice caught sight of Emily descending the stairs from the tower. She took her leave of Dawn and walked along the newly created aisle, tables on either side, to reach her, Ben following a few steps behind.

'I've just been upstairs looking for you,' Emily said.

'Is everything OK?' Clarice asked.

'No problems. I've volunteered us to wash the glasses. They came on loan from the supermarket in town, with the alcohol Grandpa ordered. Johnson will take them back after the funeral.'

'Are they not from the caterers?' Clarice questioned.

'Grandpa would have needed to pay extra.' Emily smiled. 'Pick and mix, remember.'

'But I daresay they would have arrived clean from the caterers,' Clarice said.

'They were meant to be clean when they arrived from the supermarket.'

'Come on then,' Clarice said. 'We'd better get on with it.'

'You've still got your pal.' Emily looked at Ben.

'Yes, he found me in the garden. Sit, Ben,' Clarice commanded, and the dog obeyed. She slipped him a treat. 'Good boy.'

'There he is.' Ralph emerged from the corridor leading to his study. 'He hasn't been a nuisance?' he asked Clarice.

'No, not at all.' She was relieved to find that Ralph's demeanour after her recent encounter with Tessa was still friendly.

'We're on our way to the kitchen to wash the glasses for tomorrow,' Emily said.

'I thought you were on sandwich-making duty for our supper later?'

'Shh, Grandpa!' Emily whispered. 'I haven't told Clarice

that yet. I was going to drop it on her once I'd chained her to the kitchen table.'

Ralph chuckled as he bent to hold onto Ben's collar. 'Off you girls go, then. I'll keep hold of this one; he might try to follow. I'll see you for sandwiches in the sitting room.'

'Not the dining room?' Clarice asked once they were out of earshot.

'No, Grandpa used to like having dinner at eight in the evening, but the last four or five years he's changed to wanting a meal at lunchtime and sandwiches early evening. It's more informal in the sitting room; everyone helps themselves and sits around chatting – or that's the theory.' Emily smirked.

'Everyone bitching?' Clarice said.

'Mm.'

'Let's hope we got that out of the way at lunchtime.' Clarice looked around as they went into the kitchen. 'No Mrs Fuller?'

'She'll have cycled home before it got dark. Washing or drying?' Emily rolled back the sleeves of her sweater.

'You choose,' Clarice said.

'I'll wash, then. What did Dawn say to you?'

Clarice walked back to the door and closed it. 'Let's start with Ernestine and Tessa in the bedroom first.' She began methodically to repeat each of the conversations from her recent encounters.

'Why didn't I know that Tessa had met Grandpa first, before Avril? Dad never told me.'

'Probably because he didn't know.' Clarice was sombre. 'It's not something Ralph would have wanted to share with his son. Especially if he'd continued having a relationship with Tessa, which Avril found out about.'

'Which,' Emily picked up the thread, 'caused her to leave him.'

'But,' Clarice stood still, holding the tea towel, 'that still doesn't explain the connection between Avril and the Major. She apparently found out about an affair, days before she supposedly disappeared with him. What we haven't considered is that she might have had a long-term relationship with him. Finding out that Ralph had been in one with Tessa for the duration of their marriage might have been a crucial factor.'

'Making her decide to go with the Major.' Emily nodded.

They continued working, both thoughtful.

'I'm surprised Dawn didn't baulk when you suggested she and I might get on,' she said. 'I thought the idea might have been distasteful.'

Clarice shrugged. 'Things change. She's been going through a rough time with her ex, and so have you with Colin dying so unexpectedly; maybe she's as sick as you of all the bitching.'

'Yes, perhaps.' Emily nodded again. 'And I'm sorry I didn't tell you how Beth died. It must have been a shock, Aunt Ernestine telling you like that.'

'I can understand why Ralph wouldn't want to talk about it; she was his baby sister. He just mentioned that childhood death was more common years ago, which was why I assumed she'd died from an illness.'

'Not being trampled by a horse.' Emily grimaced. 'It was a horrible end.'

They had completed their task, the glasses having been washed and dried while they talked.

'What happened with Johnson?' Clarice asked. 'You seemed engrossed in conversation.'

'It was about Dad's funeral arrangements,' Emily said. 'There will be a car taking all of us to the church.'

'I didn't expect to be included as part of the family group,' Clarice said, surprised.

'It's already been arranged. Johnson will stay here to receive the caterers and make sure everything is in place when we get back with whoever else wants to come – the whole village, I expect.'

The door opened suddenly, and Tessa wandered in.

'Are you doing the sandwiches?' She looked from Clarice to Emily.

'Yes. I was just explaining the funeral arrangements for tomorrow.' Emily spoke without hesitation. 'Johnson told me the plan earlier.'

'Good.' Tessa looked suspiciously at Clarice. 'We can *all* talk about that over supper. And don't forget to do a few fingers of Patum Peperium on buttered white bread for your grandfather.' She turned without waiting for a response, leaving the door ajar.

'So,' Clarice looked to the empty doorway as she spoke, 'do you want to butter or fill?'

'Let's share and do both together.' Emily grinned before leaning closer to whisper, 'I asked Grandpa about the photo album. He's bringing it out to look at while we have our sarnies. There are some excellent ones of Dad as a boy with Avril.' She followed Clarice's gaze to the doorway. 'Although that might rattle Tessa's cage.'

Chapter 20

Later, in the sitting room, next to Emily on the chaise, wearing a thermal vest, woollen jumper and a bulky sweater, Clarice still felt the cold in her feet, fingers and nose. Neither she nor Emily had mentioned the coldness of the house again, perhaps both recognising that there was nothing more to be done. The fire now burned in the grate, and the woodsmoke smell from the logs made her feel homesick, thinking of Rick and her animal family.

Ralph arrived first, handing Emily a thick battered brown book.

'Stick it on the sideboard, and we can all have a look later. There are some good ones of my parents.'

'Thank you, Grandpa.' Emily took the photograph album.

Ralph looked at the plates stacked with sandwiches. Clarice noticed that his line of gaze did not focus in one place but hovered just above the food. She wondered if he could see well enough without the aid of Johnson to help himself.

Each sandwich was cut into four small triangles, arranged on large plates to form towers. There had been no discussion about the crusts, and Clarice realised that with the Compton-Smythes, the practicality of waste would trump drawing-room delicacy. There were various fillings – egg and cress, ham and chutney, cheese and pickle, tuna with mayonnaise – and a separate plate with the fingers of Patum Peperium. Two pots stood beside the plates, one containing tea, the other coffee.

The room had taken on the most potent smells, egg and tuna, along with the woodsmoke.

'I'm sure they're all yummy,' Ralph said. 'Did you leave a selection for Johnson in the kitchen? He prefers to take his back to his flat.'

'Yes, I remembered. Would you like me to pour you a coffee?' Emily reached for one of the pots.

'I'd prefer a cup of tea.'

'Let me get you some sandwiches.' Clarice went through the list of what was available.

'I am thoroughly spoiled,' Ralph said. 'You shouldn't help; you've done enough today. You are a guest.'

'I don't mind.' Clarice laughed. 'I like to keep busy.'

'In that case, I'll have my special, and one triangle of each type of sandwich.' Ralph went to sit in his leather armchair, equal in shabbiness to the one in his study. Emily, having poured his tea, put it on a side table next to him.

When Tessa, Dawn and Ernestine all arrived together, they found the three chatting amiably.

'Lovely.' Dawn's voice was friendly as she looked at the spread of food. 'Thank you, Clarice and Emily.'

Tessa glowered at her daughter.

'I'm starving.' Ernestine went immediately to take a plate and began to pile sandwiches onto it greedily.

'When are you not hungry?' Tessa spoke sharply.

'We're not having any fallings-out. I think there was enough unpleasantness at lunchtime. Clarice will go away with an odd impression of Colin's family,' Ralph said.

Tessa's mouth became a set horizontal line and she helped herself to sandwiches and coffee without commenting.

'Now, so everyone knows the plan for tomorrow, the funeral directors are sending the car at eleven. It holds six people, which is perfect; we will all, including Clarice, fit in comfortably.'

'Oh goody, we're all going to be together!' Ernestine said, pleased.

'The cars do hold six people, Ralph.' Tessa's tone was sharp. 'But if Clarice drove herself, the rest of us would have so much more room. After all, she isn't family.'

Ralph's sunny mood evaporated in an instant. He stared at Tessa for several seconds from under his thick knitted eyebrows, his expression cold.

'They are extremely large cars,' he said.

'We don't want to be squashed together like sardines.' Tessa spoke slowly, as though reasoning with a child. 'With only five of us, there would be extra space, so we wouldn't be squashed together. It should be family only travelling in the car.'

'Tomorrow is the day I lay my only son to rest, and you deliberately set out to humiliate me by questioning my decision to allow our guest to travel to the funeral with us.'

'Clarice is an intelligent woman; she won't think that. And anyway, it's nothing to do with what others want or think.' Tessa was not backing down.

'Exactly.' Ralph continued to glower. 'It has nothing to do with what others think. It's my son, and my money paying for the funeral. The decision has bugger-all to do with you.'

'Ralph, you're being silly. This funeral has rattled you – you're not thinking straight.' Tessa, as though suddenly drained of blood, was white with anger.

'It's not the funeral that's rattled me, it's burying my son, and your interference is not helping.' Ralph had risen to his feet. He'd moved the plate of sandwiches onto his lap, and they tumbled to the floor as he stood up. 'I never expected to outlive him.'

'I was just making a very obvious and sensible point!' Tessa snapped.

'I have invited Clarice to travel with us, and that's an end to it.'

'If you say so, although—' Tessa was cut off.

'You never cared about Colin; you never gave him a chance. It was because he was Avril's – mine and hers. He was so young when you first came here. If you'd been a mother to him, he could have loved you.' Ralph stumbled forward, crushing sandwiches into the carpet.

'I did try, Ralph, you know I did, but he only ever wanted Avril. *Mummy, Mummy, Mummy* – that's all that ever came out of him; *when will Mummy be coming home?* I couldn't compete with the perfect, saintly Avril.' Tessa reached imploringly towards Ralph. 'He was five when I came here, and he wouldn't so much as hold my hand.'

Ralph did not take the offered outstretched hand, and the silence between them expanded to create an unbearable tension. The only noise was the crackling of burning logs. Then he stepped towards the door. Before he reached it, Johnson entered the room. As Ralph staggered forward to grasp the back of a chair, Johnson was beside him, offering an arm to lean on. They left the room together.

For the second time that day, Clarice was aware that Johnson had been hovering near the door, listening to conversations.

Tessa dropped her hand and looked at the sandwiches squashed into the carpet; her face still pasty white, her sense of humiliation as radiant as the reddened logs in the fire grate.

'It's you stirring up trouble.' She turned on Emily. 'If you hadn't forced your grandpa to give your friend a place in the car to church, the subject need not have come up.'

'It was Grandpa's idea.' Emily's eyes were shiny with unshed tears, a crimson tide creeping up from her neck to her face.

'I can see both sides of the argument.' Dawn's calm voice was a surprising balm after the ranting.

'It's about what Ralph wants,' Ernestine said.

Earlier, Clarice had observed Ernestine's head moving, as it might while watching the ball in a tennis match, as the argument went back and forth between Ralph and Tessa, listening while munching her sandwiches.

'Colin was Ralph's son. Avril would have stolen him if Bellatrix hadn't stopped her.' Ernestine small, china-doll face was calm, unmoved by emotion.

'Shut up, you silly old woman!' Tessa could not disguise her anger. 'I don't know how I put up with you, day in, day out, your endless wittering, greediness and ridiculous remarks. Bellatrix is an inanimate object – it's made of bloody *stone*.'

'She protects the family. She sent Avril away and kept Colin here for Ralph. That woman knows what happened, Tessa.'

'Who, what woman?' Dawn cut in.

'Clarice, she knows, I can feel it – she knows the truth.'

'Clarice is here, Aunt Ernestine.' Dawn pointed. 'She's sitting just there.'

'No, not Beth.' Ernestine dismissed Clarice with a flick of her eyes. 'The woman in Avril's bedroom. I'm not making it up. Avril wouldn't like her being in her bedroom; she's sneaky and interfering. She knows what Ralph made Johnson do – I didn't tell her, but she knows.'

'That's Clarice. She was in the bedroom.' It was Tessa's turn to point. 'I saw her up there. And Ralph did nothing to Avril – she ran away with that scheming charlatan, the Major.'

'She wants my necklace.' Ernestine raised her hand to cover her throat.' She can't have it. That's why she came here, to my house.'

'Aunt Ernestine.' Dawn's voice was conciliatory. 'What did my dad make Johnson do – was it something connected to Avril?'

Ernestine quietly stood up, smoothing her skirt as her eyes darted around to rest for a few seconds on each individual. 'I don't know why you're all suddenly having a go at me. When I tell Bellatrix, she won't like it – she'll be angry.'

She walked from the room, leaving those left behind watching her exit before turning their attention to each other.

'Whatever did she mean?' Dawn looked at her mother. 'What did Dad make Johnson do?'

'She talks rubbish. You should know that after all these years.' Tessa took her plate to the table.

'You and I need to talk, Mother.' Dawn walked to the door, then waited for Tessa to follow. The sound of their heels clicking on the hall tiles faded as they left.

'Shall we clear these away?' Clarice asked.

'Yes, let's get the washing-up done.' Emily took some paper napkins and cleared the debris of the sandwiches from the carpet, while Clarice gathered up the plates.

Once in the kitchen, Emily looked back towards the closed door before she spoke. 'I'll wash again, if that's all right?'

'I don't think they'll come and bother us here,' Clarice said, picking up a tea towel.

'I shouldn't have involved you in this. I'm so sorry, Clarice.' Emily kept her head down over the sink while she washed cups, saucers and plates.

'Nonsense, I'm glad to be here with you. You mustn't let Tessa get to you. Remember what I told you earlier: Dawn was interesting and reasonable in the garden. If you get her away from her mother, she's a completely different person.'

'Yes?' There was doubt in Emily's voice.

'Go back to what you said about Tessa and your dad not getting on, the two camps – you and Dawn both had to take your parent's side.'

'I can't see myself rushing back here after the funeral,' Emily said, sounding defeated. 'Tessa and Dawn won't figure in my life after tomorrow.'

'No. I guess not.' Clarice paused. 'Can we still have a look through the photo album, though, before we go to bed?'

'Good plan. I wanted you to see the ones of Dad.'

'I want to see them too.' Clarice hung up the tea towel. 'I'm just going outside to clear my head, and I promised I'd call Rick.'

'I'll throw a couple of logs on the fire while nobody is watching!' Emily was suddenly brighter. 'Don't get lost.'

'I won't go far from the house, and I have a torch.' Clarice patted her arm. 'Don't worry – I'll see you back in the sitting room.'

Chapter 21

After collecting a torch from her bag in the bedroom and wrapping up against the cold, Clarice descended the stairs, relieved not to encounter any household members.

Outside, she flicked the torch beam high up against the manor's yellow stone, checking its range. Gargoyles leered down, the light creating eerie shadow lines, like black liquid seeping beneath grotesque melting faces. As she moved the torch over Bellatrix, the light and dark areas generated a sense of movement, giving an illusion that the seated stone cat, suddenly more immense and imposing, had sprung to life. She went to rest a gloved hand momentarily on the enormous cold stone paw before moving away from the house, taking the route that Emily had shown her earlier that day.

She felt an overwhelming urge to distance herself from the manor, to free her brain, stressed by the toxicity between the house occupants. The reason Colin had never talked about his family was now apparent. Clarice did not doubt that after the funeral, Emily would follow her father's example in having little to do with her relatives.

It had not rained, but it was bitingly cold, with the ground hard and dry. The quietness made each footstep resonate as it crunched down on dry leaves and twigs, exaggerating the sound. After passing the old stables, she stopped for a moment, turning in a circle to spread the light from the torch around her. There was nothing there but trees and undergrowth. In spring or summer, the sky above would be blocked by foliage, and on the ground level, away from the paths, there would be soft banks of green growth. Looking up now, there was only blackness, the moon doubtless hidden by the trees, and all around her, mist was beginning to form.

At the point where the track divided, she paused, and her thoughts went to Rick. Robert Frost's poem, 'The Road Not Taken', an analogy for life choices, was one of her husband's favourites.

As she set off along the left-hand fork, she listened for sounds – barn owls, foxes, badgers and other creatures moving about in the woods – but heard nothing. The curves of the pathway, first one way and then another, seemed to go on forever, and remembering Emily's words about not getting lost, she was about to turn back when she came to an open clearing.

The disused well was before her, a miniature circular red-brick tower, about waist high. Nearby, overshadowing it, was a large willow tree, its branches forming an umbrella a few feet above the opening. And further away, picked out by the light of her torch, were rows of small headstones: the animal cemetery. Clarice stopped; she would come back tomorrow and have a look when it was light. She imagined that what had been the field for the horses would be to her left, but the misty haze had blocked the view, and she suddenly became aware of how quickly it was building.

Leaning with her back against a tree, she took out her cell phone.

'Hello, sweetie.' Rick's voice lifted, giving away his delight at hearing from her. 'I was starting to get worried. How's it going?'

Clarice quickly filled him in on what had happened since her arrival that morning.

'Sounds pretty shit!'

'That's one way of putting it,' she concurred. 'I'm worried about Ernestine. I think I might have dropped her in it – put her in danger.'

'How, why? She hasn't told you anything of importance, has she?'

'She told me three things I didn't know. Tessa knew Ralph before he met Avril. The last time she saw Avril was when she left with Ralph. Also, that Ralph made Johnson do something. And I'm beginning to think Tessa was just as involved with Avril's disappearance as the two men were.'

'From what you've said, Ernestine's dementia makes her an unreliable source of information,' Rick said. 'When she watched Avril leave the manor for the last time, Ralph could have been taking her to meet the Major, don't you think?'

'That had crossed my mind, but it would have been out of character for Ralph to deliver his wife to her lover. And why did he lie to Colin, telling him his mother left that day with the Major?' Clarice tried to muster her thoughts into some sort of order. 'Ernestine's mind wanders, but she couldn't have lived so closely with her brother and Avril all that time without knowing what led up to the point when Avril and the Major left. The Compton-Smythes are a family who hide their secrets well, but dementia might cause her to unravel and say something she's kept quiet about for the last fifty years.'

'What are you suggesting?' Rick was sharp. 'That Avril and the Major didn't leave; they were murdered? And if so, who do you think killed them?'

'I've got nothing that makes it conclusive. I believed what Ernestine told me. I didn't think she was lying, but when I put it together, it somehow doesn't tally. It makes no sense.'

'Is there something else, something someone said or did?'

'I don't know; I need to think. I'll go over my list, the notes I made from Colin's notebook. Ralph would be my number one suspect. Something Avril's friend Pattie said made me believe Johnson would do as Ralph told him.' Clarice's voice trailed off. 'I need more time. With so much going on, I haven't had time to think. They are one highly dysfunctional family.'

'Be careful,' Rick warned. 'Don't go winding anyone up, especially if you have concerns about the possibility of at least one of them having murdered two people.'

'I will tread carefully, I promise.' Clarice tried to sound conciliatory.

After finishing the call, she stood still for several minutes, listening. She heard a scream from some way off: a barn owl out hunting for his supper. The mist was getting thicker, becoming a barrier that encircled her, and as she turned to retrace her steps the light from the torch hit a wall of white it could not penetrate.

Dragging her feet against the ground to ensure she kept to what felt like the rough pathway, rather than the banks on either side, she made slow progress. The fog wrapped around her like a velvet cape, making her torch redundant. How, she wondered, had it come in so quickly? It could not have been much over twenty-five minutes since she had left the house. Why had she wandered so far? She remembered what Tessa had said about Ralph's fears for Ernestine. She thought about the wet grounds beyond the trees, then the barren, uncompromising space that was the Wash.

There was a noise, short and insignificant: a small animal moving nearby, perhaps?

She shuffled forward again, and the noise, a footstep to her left, repeated like an echo. As she advanced, there was another footstep, then another, sounding nearer.

She stood perfectly still, her head at an angle, listening.

She heard the screech of the barn owl again. Could she use that noise to guide her back? But how would she know the owl was hunting nearby, or in the stables? Might she follow his cry and be going in the wrong direction? She switched off the torch before taking three strides forward, putting her feet down as quietly as she could. Time stretched endlessly; she mentally counted to thirty and had just decided to move on when the sound came again. Someone was stalking her. She remembered the man in the woods on her arrival, Ian Belling; then her mind went to Johnson and his dour expression.

She took three more long, silent strides, and waited again. She shuddered, feeling the coldness of the night seeping through her clothes into her flesh and bones. Was it likely that whoever was following her had come from the manor? They would know these woods blindfolded. But Ian Belling had also spent a lot of time here; he'd know his way around too, and might believe he was now stalking Dawn. A surge of heat seemed to flush through her body, making her forget the chill, her mind tingling fleetingly into panic mode while her chest tightened with fear. She mentally cursed her actions. Why ever had she come to this dismal house, with its peculiar family? She recalled Ernestine's words about Bellatrix protecting the family, and her amusement earlier when the torchlight had made the giant stone Siamese cat seem alive. Then Dawn telling her what Ian had claimed he would do to her once he caught her alone.

Having stayed where she was for what felt like an eternity, she began moving gradually forward again. There was a sudden scurrying behind her. She instinctively crouched, and at the same time swung quickly in a circle, turning the torch on and directing the beam towards the noise. The white wall revealed only a darting shape with an elongated head, accompanied by the cracking of leaves and twigs beneath running feet. Without uttering a sound, the form dashed one way and then another. Clarice rose to move forward again on what she believed was the pathway, and again there came a rush of feet from behind. The hot flush of fear ripped through her body, reaching down into her gut, and unable to quell it, she ran, hard and blindly, every instinct pushing her to get away from the stalker. Branches reached out like arms to catch her clothes and hair, and then something slammed hard into her stomach. Her upper body and knees continued travelling forward, and she found herself on the ground. The torch, gone from her grasp, was a small dot of light, now buried in the woodland debris.

She rolled to one side, away from where she thought her assailant might be waiting, ready to strike again, then lay still, winded by the blow. Her stomach hurt, and her face and back felt both cold and sweaty with fear. Her heart was beating so fast she found it hard to catch her breath. She could see the light of her torch and willed herself to get up and find it. Then another light and the slow rhythm of a heavy footfall moved towards her and stopped.

'Mrs Beech.'

The voice with the unmistakable Glasgow accent was without any doubt that of Johnson.

Still winded, Clarice rolled into a sitting position, then stood up, dazzled by the yellow light.

'Are you all right, Mrs Beech?' The words were mock sympathetic, Johnson's tone clipped.

'What do you think?' she responded, fighting to suppress a mixture of anger and fear.

'Let me get your torch.' His steps crunched away as he went to retrieve the fallen light.

'Someone attacked me.' Clarice drew long, even breaths, her stomach still feeling the effects of the blow.

'The only thing that attacked you was the branch of that tree.' Johnson directed the strong beam towards a tree with a thick limb protruding at waist height. 'You ran into it.'

'Were you following me?'

'Why ever would I do that, Mrs Beech?' His voice drifted to her. 'This is the route for my regular evening walk.'

'*Someone* was stalking me,' she persisted. It felt as if she was having a conversation with an invisible man. Johnson lowered his torch. She could hear his voice but still couldn't see him.

'I don't know why anyone would want to stalk you.' His voice was not hostile; still, it seemed to hold a threat. 'Perhaps you're suffering from a guilty conscience, asking questions about things that don't concern you, prying into other people's business.'

'I wasn't aware I'd upset anyone,' Clarice lied, knowing her presence had invoked hostility, at least in Tessa.

It was quiet all around. Clarice imagined she could hear Johnson's breathing, low and even.

'Follow me back. Keep going in that direction, and you'll end up on the mudflats.'

She saw the movement of light as Johnson pushed her torch into her hand. She watched the hazy beam of his torch through the whiteness as it moved away. Her mind raced, questioning: if she followed, would he lead her out and abandon her on the mudflats? She allowed a gap to open between them, neither of them speaking. Again it felt that she had been walking for a long time. The sudden unexpected screech of the barn owl made her body judder. It was close, and she became aware of the shape of the old stables. Past that, a few moments later, the light from Stone Fen Manor was the most welcome thing she had seen all day. Without pausing, Johnson went past Bellatrix and under the point of the arch to return inside the manor.

Following him, she stopped to watch as he continued through the aisle of tables in the great hall, which, but for a light halfway along, was in darkness. As he passed through the light, she saw that he was wearing the dark green quilted waterproof jacket he'd worn when she first arrived. He turned left before reaching the staircase, going through the door that led to Ralph's study.

Clarice remembered the row of four blue hooded waterproof jackets used by the family. Glancing to the side, she raised her torch to illuminate them. Two jackets remained on the hooks. Emily had told her that people often forgot to put them back; this might be what had happened to the two that were missing.

Having turned her torch off, she silently headed in the same direction as Johnson, but turned right to go to the corresponding corridor on the opposite side of the hall. Emily would be waiting in the sitting room. As she pushed the door open, light spilled out from the corridor, but she changed her mind, letting it clunk shut.

How much of what had happened should she tell Emily? She stood in the shadows, leaning against the closed door, thoughts racing through her jangling brain. They had to spend the night here. And there was Colin's funeral tomorrow to get through, which would be an emotional rollercoaster. What had happened in the woods would undoubtedly upset Emily; she might even feel that she must say something about it to her grandfather.

A noise from the main door alerted her to the entry of someone else. She stood still in the darkness, hardly daring to breathe. There was a noise as the shape of the person moved in the doorway, removing their outer garment; they were, Clarice realised, returning one of the blue jackets to hang it back with the others. She had a mental picture of the strange, elongated head, seen momentarily through the mist. It must have been the long hood of the jacket. In the next second, the figure emerged to walk past the light, and she saw it was Tessa. As she moved, she pushed gloves into her pockets and unzipped her padded jacket.

Clarice watched as she turned left. The door was open for as long as it took for her to walk through. From her vantage point directly opposite, she saw light and movement.

'Tessa?' It was Ralph's questioning voice.

'Has Johnson beaten me back?' Tessa asked.

Clarice did not hear the response. The door had closed.

Chapter 22

As Clarice entered the sitting room, Emily, who had been reclining in her grandfather's armchair next to the fire, stood up looking relieved.

'Clarice, I thought you'd got lost – are you OK?'

Sensing fear in the question, Clarice made her decision. She wouldn't tell Emily what had happened in the woods.

Her mind was alight with questions: why had Tessa and Johnson been stalking her, if indeed it had been them? She hadn't completely ruled out the possibility that it might have been Ian Belling. She was sure the elongated shape she'd seen through the mist had been the hood of the jacket worn by the stalker, but there were other types of jackets than the four in the hall, and two of those had been gone when she'd left for her walk. It was unfortunate that she could not gauge the height of the hooded stalker in her defensive crouching position.

Her instincts made her think it more likely to have been Tessa. If it had been Ian Belling, he would surely have noticed the height difference; Clarice was a good deal taller than Dawn. And it was Tessa, not Johnson, who'd been wearing one of the blue jackets. What had been the intention – to frighten her, to make her stop asking questions?

'No problem, I'm fine.' She rubbed her hands together. 'Bloody frozen, though. It's icy out there.'

'I'm not surprised. You're shivering. Come to the fire.' Emily went to the sideboard. 'I know where Grandpa keeps the brandy.'

'Won't he mind?' Clarice would not admit just how welcome the idea of a stiff drink was at this moment.

'Too bloody bad.' Emily went to collect two glasses from a side table. 'I brought these in earlier. They aren't the right glasses for brandy, but it'll taste the same.' After pouring the drinks, she passed a glass to Clarice. 'Don't worry, Grandpa won't run out; there are two unopened bottles in there. Cheers.'

'Cheers.' Clarice held up the glass before drinking, and enjoyed the burning sensation of the neat alcohol sliding down her throat.

'Clarice,' Emily was peering closely, 'you've scratched your face.'

Running her fingers down her cheek, Clarice saw a smear of blood on her fingertips. She pulled a tissue from the back pocket of her jeans and dabbed at the scratch. 'It's nothing. I must have brushed into something in the dark.' She kept her voice light and unconcerned.

'Are you sure you're OK?

'Absolutely.' She held up her glass again.

The room had lost the smell of food. But there was always an underlying odour of damp, even with the fire. The firelight brightened the room, but also highlighted the darker patches on the walls.

'Any thoughts while you were in the woods?' Emily asked after a few minutes.

Judging by her grey, drawn expression, it was clear Emily was seeking a distraction. The funeral was now only a few hours away.

'There was one thing: the numbers in your dad's notebook that we puzzled about.'

Emily leaned forward. 'You didn't think they were telephone numbers, or amounts of money.'

'I wondered if they could be measurements of distance,' Clarice said.

'Where to and from?'

'If your dad was considering the possibility that Avril and the Major never left – and we can't ignore that it has to be an option – he might have measured distances from the house to the various places bodies could be hidden.'

'What an awful thought.' Emily shuddered.

'It is, but realistically the numbers might mean something totally different – it's all guesswork,' Clarice said.

'Clutching at straws?'

'Exactly, and a practical consideration is that if the numbers *were* distances, your dad didn't know what we now know – that Ernestine saw Avril leaving, and she didn't mention seeing the Major. If there were only one small, light body – Avril's – it could easily have been carried.'

'Neither did he appear to be aware of what Ernestine mentioned about Tessa knowing Grandpa before he'd met Avril.'

'Yes.' Clarice remembered Tessa's words of a few minutes ago: *Has Johnson beaten me back?* Her voice had been so casual.

Looking at Emily's face, she felt an overpowering sense of gloom, like a sudden black shadow when clouds moved to cut the sunlight. She felt a responsibility for the young woman. 'I think we need to put it all out of our heads for the time being.'

'OK.' Emily's voice signalled she had lost interest in the subject. 'Do you want to look at the photographs or go up to bed?'

'Photographs, please.' Looking through the album might bring the evening to an end on a positive note, Clarice thought.

They sat close to each other, near the fire, to work their way through it.

'There are a lot of Ralph and Avril, on holiday, I think?'

'Yes, they enjoyed going abroad, Italy, France and Spain,' Emily agreed.

'They look so smiley and happy,' Clarice said. 'I love the ones with Colin and Avril.'

Emily nodded, her face sorrowful.

'And lots of your great-grandparents.'

'It seems that James and Elizabeth liked having their picture taken.' Emily put her finger on a group photograph. 'I especially like this one. Grandpa told me it was the last photograph taken with Beth – she must have been five or six.'

Looking closely, Clarice saw a small, pretty child with drooping socks; she had an abundance of golden curls and sported a lopsided ribbon.

'Grandpa said she was a real tomboy, climbing trees and so on. She wanted to be able to ride her father's stallion, Thunder, rather than Tuppence, her dapple-grey pony, but she was told he was too big.' Emily smiled sadly. 'She always has her socks falling halfway down, and her hair ribbons on the wonk.'

'A girl after my own heart.' Clarice nodded. 'I hated ribbons, or anything pink.' She moved her gaze to Ernestine, her feet in line, the bow in her hair sitting flawlessly, her hands joined primly in front. 'Ernestine is the opposite. The sisters look almost identical, both incredibly pretty, but Ernestine is so demure, absolutely perfect. She must be nine or ten here.'

'She was ten when Beth died. Grandpa said that she was devastated by what happened.'

'Understandably, but with childhood mortality being higher back then, it would have been more common for children to have to get over the loss of a sibling, even if it was in such horrible circumstances.'

'Yes, I suppose.' Emily looked again at the photograph. 'Beth wasn't killed immediately; she died the next day from her injuries after Thunder trampled her. She was completely fearless. She would go into the stall with an apple or a carrot.'

'Poor kid,' Clarice said. 'But surely, if she went in and out of his stall with apples and carrots, he would have grown used to her. I wonder why he reacted as badly as he did on that occasion.'

'Grandpa told Dad that the horse had been ill – out of sorts. He had warned both of the girls not to go near. It was a huge upset for all the family. Grandpa said that despite him occasionally getting cross with Beth, he'd always admired her spirit. He said she was the one who took after him.'

'Daddy's favourite?' Clarice asked.

'Apparently.'

'There are some benefits to being an only child. There's never any doubt about who's the favourite.'

'Absolutely,' Emily agreed. She turned the pages of the album. 'Now we come to the photos of Ralph and Avril with their mothers.'

'They do make a handsome couple.' Clarice looked from Avril to a young Ralph. The pair were flanked by two older women. 'That's Elizabeth, Ralph's mother, so this side must be Avril's mother?'

'Yes, that's Helen. They had just become engaged when this one was taken. Sadly, both their fathers died before they married.'

'I love the jewellery. They knew how to impress back then – if you had the money. Ralph's mother, it seems, was a big fan of pearls – she wears them in all the photographs – and Helen is wearing what looks like jet.'

'Yes,' Emily agreed, 'but Helen loved diamonds, too. She isn't wearing them here, but she does in the wedding photographs.'

'Did you inherit her jewellery?' Clarice felt awkward asking the question.

'I have a diamond brooch that belonged to Avril, but Dad said she must have taken the diamond necklace she wore on her wedding day with her when she left.'

'Understandably,' Clarice said.

Emily was frowning. 'They've gone.' She had turned the page to find two blank spaces where photographs had been removed. 'How odd that there should be two from the wedding day missing. Avril looked radiant in her wedding dress.'

'Your grandfather must have taken them.'

'I can't imagine why.' She went slowly through the book again before closing it with a puzzled sigh. 'They aren't here.'

They talked for another half an hour, and the fire had reduced to embers before Clarice suggested they go to bed.

'We've still got to use the bathroom without waking anyone up, and you'll have a stressful day tomorrow.'

'It's nearly ten thirty.' Emily looked at her watch. 'Let's wash these glasses. I'll put Grandpa's brandy back.'

Clarice watched as Emily slid the photograph album into the sideboard alongside the brandy.

Later, when they were in the bedroom, they looked in amusement at each other's fleecy pyjamas.

'I didn't realise you'd have such an enormous pair of jimjams.' Emily bent over in a fit of the giggles before clambering into bed.

'You can talk. Yours look really cosy – flannelette?' Clarice felt fleetingly warmed by Emily's spontaneous burst of laughter.

'Don't forget, I've slept here before. There may be a lot of heavy bedding' – Emily lifted the thick duvet and layers of blankets to demonstrate – 'but I still find my face and nose get cold.'

'The reason these are so big,' Clarice held out her arms, 'is because they're Rick's. The only time he's ever worn them was an overnight stay in hospital. We always call them the hospital jimjams. I've never owned a pair.'

'What are you doing?' Emily watched, puzzled, as Clarice, having walked around her bed, moved the chair from across the room to place it tightly against the door.

'It's just in case anyone wanted to pay us a visit,' she said. 'It'll make a lot of noise if they try to push the door open with the chair there.'

'You don't think anyone would come in while we're asleep?' Emily pulled the bedding close to her chest defensively.

'No, I don't, but it doesn't hurt to be careful.'

A few minutes later, lying in the darkness, Clarice was relieved that Emily had accepted that using a chair to block an unlocked door was a standard precaution. The problem with telling lies – or withholding the truth about what had happened earlier – was that it had a knock-on effect, but she could hardly tell the young woman that her step-grandmother had stalked her in the woods, and might attempt to murder them both in their beds.

Chapter 23

After thinking that the anxiety permeating her mind, like the buzzing of an angry wasp, would never allow her to unwind and sleep, Clarice succumbed, waking with a jolt. It took her a few moments to remember where she was; the room was in blackness, the only noise Emily's gentle snoring. She lay motionless, listening, wondering what could have woken her. After the encounter in the woods, her imagination, she concluded, was getting the better of her. Turning on her side, she slithered down into the bed's belly of warmth and tried to relax.

The sound of the door handle turning was so quiet that had she not been fully awake, she might have missed it. There followed a soft *click, click, click* as the door made contact with the back of the chair she'd positioned as a barrier. Had it been that noise that had roused her from sleep? It brought recognition that her mind was not playing tricks; somebody outside the door was trying to get in.

She slid out of bed. Grabbing the heavy sweater she'd worn earlier, she pulled it over her pyjama top and picked up the long torch next to the bed. It wasn't much of a weapon, but a swift blow from it might deter an attacker.

Going to the door, she stood quietly behind it. The silence of the house was heavy and oppressive, making her edgy. Emily's regular snores continued; the young woman was deep in slumber, oblivious to Clarice straining in agitation to catch any further sounds. After waiting for what felt to be infinity, she gently lifted the chair to move it away from the door.

Outside the bedroom, she turned on the torch, allowing the beam to bounce around, taking in every surface and nook. There was nobody out there. On impulse, she pulled the door shut behind her and moved silently down the staircase, pausing on each landing. She felt tension with every downward step, believing that someone, possibly concealed from view, might be creeping along after her. She stopped every few seconds to shine the light behind her, and stayed for longer on the landing leading to Tessa, Dawn and Ernestine's bedrooms. All was silent and undisturbed.

Reaching the bottom, her bare feet felt icy cold as she stepped onto the stone floor of the great hall. Houses were rarely utterly silent at night; there might be the gentle hum made by the central heating or fridge, the snuffling or snoring of sleeping pets, or the wind rattling against the roof. None of those applied here. She'd remembered that Johnson took the dogs to his flat above the garage and felt relief that Ben's barking would not reveal her night-time wandering. The light halfway along that had been on early in the evening had been switched off, and the hall was now in complete blackness. Looking at the dense black wall before her, she imagined who might be watching her from the blackness: Johnson, Tessa, or some deviant intruder.

Her steps were hurried as she crossed the hall. As if she'd

imbibed the darkness into her being, she fancied numerous eyes watching, burning into her back. Within a few moments, she was in the corridor that led to Ralph's study, holding the torch low as she moved so that she could see her way along.

A feeling of guilt swept over her as she entered his private domain. Whatever she might find of interest in here, if she was caught, she would be humiliated by her actions. Still she progressed across the room, shining the torch onto the rows of books. They covered what she imagined were Ralph's interests and hobbies, including hill-walking in Scotland, grouse shooting, dogs, and collecting porcelain, furniture and snuff boxes. Nearing the desk, she stopped, remorse overwhelming her. She would not sneak a peek into the drawers. As she hovered for a moment, she became aware that Johnson might see the beam of her torch across the driveway in his flat. Dipping the light down, her attention was caught by what appeared to be two pieces of blank paper on the desk. Curious, she picked them up and turned them over, revealing the two wedding photographs missing from the family album.

She studied them to find something that would make them controversial, necessitating their removal. In both, Avril stood next to a young Ralph, their expressions radiating joy. In the first, the couple's mothers, Elizabeth and Helen, stood on either side of the newly married pair. Avril wore a beautiful white silk wedding dress with a brocade bodice, and Ralph, taller by a head, the handsome groom, was holding her hand. Elizabeth, as in images Clarice had seen previously, wore a pearl necklace. This one, in three strands, had large, regular-shaped gems. Helen wore a single-strand choker made up of individual rose-cut diamonds.

Her mind went to Colin's before-and-after lists. Pearls and diamonds were in both. It appeared to be something common in the Compton-Smythe household in past and present generations. Ernestine's necklace combined diamonds and pearls, Tessa had earlier worn a neckpiece containing large cultured pearls, and Emily had inherited a diamond brooch from her grandmother. Clarice shone the torch close to the photograph: neither Emily's grandmother nor either of her great-grandmothers was wearing the brooch on the wedding day.

In the second photograph, the couple were again at the centre, with friends and family grouped around them. Ernestine was easily identified, a younger version of the china doll; she had altered little, still perfectly turned out. There were four young men and three women. Something was familiar about one of the women, partially hidden at the rear: slim, with her hair swept up, wearing a sleeveless blue dress. It might have been Dawn. Clarice examined it more closely. It was a young Tessa.

She turned the photographs face down again on the desk before leaving. Back in the great hall, she paused with her foot on the bottom step, her eyes darting unseeing against the blackness. Then, abruptly changing her mind, she scurried across the hall to enter the other corridor. She found the kitchen lit naturally by moonlight. Turning off the torch, she went to the window to stand quietly looking out.

Her mind drifted. It was odd that Ralph had removed the photographs; he must have realised his granddaughter wanted to show them to her. It seemed that Emily had not recognised Tessa in the second photograph – she had certainly made no mention of her. What was it Ralph had not wanted Clarice to see? After the confrontation in the bedroom, Tessa would have already informed him that Clarice was aware he'd met her long before he'd known Avril.

Wiggling her toes, she realised her feet were now unbearably cold, and she decided to return upstairs to the bedroom. As she turned, a movement in the garden caught her attention. Backing rapidly away from the window to become invisible in the shadows, she watched as a figure moved unhurriedly between the trees. From this distance, it was impossible to work out if it was a man or a woman, and she waited motionless to see them emerge. She waited in vain. The figure appeared to have melted into the dark camouflage of trees.

Remembering that the woods would make it possible for someone to work their way around the edge of the house, she considered that the intruder might come out and cross to the manor further on. But why would anyone be outside during the night? The kitchen clock showed that it was ten past two; even Johnson would not be about at this hour. Should she raise the alarm, get Ralph from his bed? And if she did, how would she explain her presence downstairs at gone two in the morning?

Taking a step back, she sensed the presence of someone close; then froze as the fingers of a warm hand touched, then grasped her shoulder. Her chest felt the tightening grip of terror, and with panic overwhelming her, she swung sharply around, raising the torch as a weapon.

'Shh.' Dawn stood there, holding her finger to her lips, urging her not to scream. 'It's only me. Did you see him?' Her voice was anxious.

'I saw movement between the trees.' Clarice glanced back out of the window.

'It's Ian Belling. He's been there for at least twenty minutes. I spotted him from my bedroom window. Is that what brought you down?'

'I wondered who it was,' Clarice hedged, not wanting to give the real reason for her presence. 'Can he get inside the house?'

'He hasn't managed it yet.' Dawn followed Clarice's gaze. 'But he knows the place well. He stayed here with me when we were a couple. After we broke up and he started stalking me, Johnson fitted new locks to make it harder for him to break in.'

They were both whispering. Clarice looked at Dawn's thick brown towelling dressing gown and matching fluffy slippers, and reflected with envy that the other woman's feet would be pleasantly warm.

Dawn, still watching the window, unexpectedly grabbed Clarice by the arm, causing her to wince as her nails dug through the thick sweater into her flesh. Dawn's expression had altered, distorting with panic as she stared forward over Clarice's shoulder. Clarice turned around to see a face against the glass pane; dark eyes staring hard and unblinking. An unremarkable-looking man in his forties, turning his head this way and that against the glass, was trying to see inside. Clarice put her arm around Dawn to quietly shuffle them further back into the shadows. She felt the tremor of terror running through the woman's frame and realised that despite all her earlier protestations about not allowing Belling to upset her, she was genuinely frightened of him.

'He won't be able to see us this far back,' she whispered encouragingly. 'Don't move about.'

Dawn nodded.

They stood silently watching as Belling progressed slowly along from window to window. When he disappeared from view, they stayed fixed to the spot for several minutes before Clarice stepped away.

'Do you want to go up to your room?' she asked. 'I'll walk back upstairs with you.'

'Not yet. I won't be able to sleep now. Come to the sitting room with me. The curtains will be closed, and they're thick; he wouldn't be able to see inside.'

Dawn switched on a small table light in the sitting room, then knelt and prodded the dead fire with a large poker until it revealed red in the ashes. Shuddering with cold as she broke twigs from the wood basket, Clarice considered that the act of rekindling the fire was a distraction from what had just happened.

Passing her father's armchair, Dawn picked up the rug resting on its arm and handed it to Clarice. 'Wrap that around your legs and feet,' she said. 'I'm used to this cold house.'

'We should contact Johnson or tell your father,' Clarice said as Dawn added logs to the blazing twigs. 'They'll contact the police.'

'Wake up two old men? I don't think that's a good idea.' Dawn shrugged dismissively. 'We all have such a long day tomorrow with the funeral and the wake.'

Clarice nodded.

'I think Dad is under enough stress after Colin's death without me adding to it.' Dawn finished with the fire and went to the sideboard. 'I know where he hides his stash of brandy,' she added as she took out the bottle before reaching to bring out two glasses.

Clarice smiled inwardly. Where Ralph stored his brandy was not a very well-guarded secret.

After pouring two generous measures, Dawn passed one to Clarice.

'What are you two doing down here?' Emily stood in the doorway, her torch beam bouncing around the ceiling. Her voice expressed both annoyance and surprise. Like Clarice, she had put a thick sweater over her pyjamas. 'I woke and found you'd gone. I was worried.'

Was she worried, Clarice wondered, because she imagined her to be fraternising with the enemy? 'You don't mind if I tell her?' She looked at Dawn.

'We both saw Ian Belling,' Dawn said in response.

'I couldn't sleep,' Clarice lied. 'I looked out the window and saw someone moving in the woods. I came downstairs to watch from the kitchen window.'

'Dawn, you *must* wake Grandpa and get him to call the police,' Emily said urgently. As she spoke, Dawn handed her a glass of brandy before returning to the sideboard to fill another for herself. Clarice and Emily watched in silence.

They settled in a circle, with Emily next to Clarice on the chaise and Dawn in her father's armchair. Dawn finally spoke.

'I'm embarrassed to admit that this is my regular nightly ritual.' Her voice was flat, unemotional, her eyes cast downward. 'After the break-up with Ian, when I first spotted him wandering outside, I told Dad and Johnson, and they phoned the police, but …'

'By the time the police arrived, he'd gone.' Clarice had guessed how the story would end.

'That's right.' Dawn sipped her brandy. 'It's difficult for a police car, with headlights blazing, to creep through the woods and catch someone unaware. Ian was on his toes as soon as he saw it coming. The police organised two officers to be here, hiding at the house. That happened several times. I don't know how he knew, but when they were here, he never came.'

'You took out a restraining order?' Clarice asked.

'Yes, and it seemed to work for a while. He doesn't come and lurk every night. There is no set pattern.'

'But he does it often enough to keep you up at night, checking the garden,' Clarice said.

Dawn nodded, her eyes still cast down.

'That's awful.' Emily was outraged. 'Evil bastard … he shouldn't get away with it.'

'It was my own fault. I had an affair with the husband of my best friend. Such a despicable thing to do; I must have been demented.' Dawn's lips curved into a sad half-smile. 'I broke up their marriage, and then, after a few months, I dumped him.'

'That's like saying that when a woman is raped, it's her fault – because she wore a short skirt or a low-cut blouse.' Emily was suddenly strident. 'Yes, it was a shit thing to do to a friend, but there were two of you involved in the affair, and he was the one who cheated on his wife. The relationship between you and Ian didn't work out; he needs to man up and move on.'

'My thoughts exactly.' Dawn raised her glass, and Emily joined her, lifting her own.

'Why don't you leave the dogs in the house?' Emily asked. 'Ben would make a great guard dog; he'd let you know if you had an intruder.'

'We did give that a go, but we can't separate them, and Floss is completely deaf, while Ben starts barking at nothing and everything as soon as it gets light.' Dawn smiled kindly. 'They're used to going to their basket in Johnson's flat overnight. He takes them out in the morning for their first walk and feeds them.'

'Floss is an old lady,' Clarice agreed. 'It would be confusing to change her routine after fifteen years.'

'There must be something you can do.' Emily's exasperation was evident in her tone.

Dawn leaned over to pat her knee. 'It's OK, I can wait him out. He has to run out of steam sometime, and …'

They waited.

'Dad, as you know,' Dawn looked at Emily, 'is notoriously tight. Mum has nagged him incessantly about installing security cameras, but with this being such a big house, the cost made his eyes water.'

'He's agreed?' Emily asked.

'After months of research, Johnson has found a company that can do it, and at a price Dad finds acceptable. They're coming in next week to install the cameras.'

'That's brilliant,' Emily said.

'What does he do for a living?' Clarice asked. 'Ian Belling.'

'He had a property business, but it went under.'

'I'm not surprised, if he wastes his energy wandering around here half the night,' Clarice said. 'And I expect he blamed you. I doubt he'd admit that it was his actions that caused it to collapse.'

'You've got it,' Dawn said. She stared down at her glass for some time in contemplation. 'We should all go back to bed;

I don't know what the time is, but we need to get to Colin's funeral in a few hours.'

'There is one thing,' Clarice pondered. 'I know you're having the cameras installed next week, but has your dad or Johnson never seen Belling?'

'Ian is clever. Don't forget he lived here with me for a few months. He knows my mother has regular habits, walks at set times, and that Dad's half blind.' Dawn paused, thinking. 'Johnson said he'd seen him from a distance a couple of times. He told the police, but as it wasn't close to, they wouldn't use him as a witness. It's always my word against Ian's.'

'But I've seen him close to. I would recognise him again, no doubt about it,' Clarice said.

Dawn became alert. 'Would you make a statement to the police on my behalf?'

'Yes, of course I will.'

'Thank you so much.' Dawn's hands flew to her face, which was suddenly alight with hope. 'I can't tell you how much that would mean to me. The police will take it seriously that he's breached the conditions of the restraining order.'

'Yes!' Emily punched the air triumphantly.

'I'm so glad you brought Clarice with you, Emily,' Dawn said.

'Me too.' Emily winked at Clarice.

Dawn smiled encouragingly, her voice warm. 'Tell me about your dad when you were growing-up, the big brother I never knew.'

Crouching down in front of the fire, bed forgotten for a while, Emily told them stories of her childhood, places she'd visited and fun things she'd done with her dad. Despite his growth in confidence over the years, there had always remained a reserve to his persona. Clarice learned about a Colin previously unknown to her, teaching Emily to swim and ride her bicycle. When, aged fifteen, she went to a party at the home of one of her school friends, but was too shy to take to the dance floor alone, Colin had demonstrated his 'dad dancing' skills.

'It was excruciatingly embarrassing, but also hilarious.' Emily laughed.

'Something to tease him about.' Dawn's eyes were mischievous.

'You bet – I never let him forget.' Emily looked wistful as she spoke, as if a part of her was back watching her father dance.

Clarice's mind went on an irrational curve to consider how she introduced a new cat into a multi-cat household to encourage them to bond. She would put the incomer into a room on its own for a few days, stroking the whiskers and cheeks of all the cats to mix up the scent from their glands, and swapping blankets around daily, between the newcomer and the clowder, to mingle smells. Watching the two women, now leaning into one another, talking animatedly, Clarice marvelled that their bonding was progressing at a rapid pace. The cracks from years of animosity appeared to be showing signs of healing. Ralph would be delighted, but not, she suspected, Tessa.

'Can we leave telling Dad about Ian until after the funeral?' Dawn asked. 'It'll only delay it by a few hours. Everyone is stressed out, especially Mum. I won't mention anything about this until after the wake, when all the guests have gone.'

'No problem,' Clarice agreed.

'Shall I wash these?' Emily looked at the glasses.

'No, better not put the light in the kitchen on,' Dawn cautioned. 'If Ian's still out there, it will attract his attention. Leave them on the sideboard. First one down in the morning can wash them.'

Guided by the light from their torches, they moved as a group back up the staircase. As they reached her floor, Dawn peeled away with a wave of her hand, disappearing into the corridor that led to her bedroom.

Back in their own room, Clarice put the chair against the door before she climbed into bed.

'I don't think you need to worry about that chair now.' Emily yawned. 'We didn't need it earlier; nobody bothered us.'

Half an hour later, curled into a foetal position, Clarice once again listened to Emily's regular snores. The image of the face at the kitchen window lingered in her mind. Such an ordinary countenance for a man with such evil intent, and there was every likelihood it had been him stalking her in the woods earlier.

Her last memory before she slipped into sleep was of Tessa's contemptuous expression when she'd spoken of Colin over the lunch table, her eyes hooked into Emily. *He was such a dull little man – dull, dull, bloody dull.* The words went around in a loop, accompanied by the memory of the *click, click, click* sound of the chair hitting the bedroom door.

Chapter 24

Awakening with light creeping around the curtains, Clarice's first thought was what had happened last night in the woods. Closing her eyes, she mentally considered every action, which included her foolish behaviour in going so far from the house in darkness. The image of the hooded head of the stalker attached to a blurry shape mingled with the face at the kitchen window. Had Belling been the stalker in the woods? The discussion with Dawn in the early hours had convinced her that he was a strong candidate.

Creeping silently out of bed, she walked across the creaky floorboards, feeling their coldness under her bare feet. For a moment she envisaged Avril doing something similar over fifty years ago, the thought inevitably taking her back to Colin and his funeral. She peeked around the curtains to look at the light blue sky; it was impossible to judge the likelihood of rain. Weak sunlight filtered through above, and an elongated furl of grey clouds lay low on the horizon. The ground was frost white.

Johnson was walking towards the house. He was well wrapped up, a dark scarf showing above his jacket collar, his hands covered by black gloves. His bearing, as always, was upright, his craggy pockmarked face set; she could not imagine him slouching, even when he was alone. Fleetingly she wondered if he ever smiled.

Emily was snuggled down under her duvet in the next bed; only her ruffled hair was visible, making Clarice imagine a small brown rabbit half out of its burrow.

It was just after seven when she took her toilet bag to head for the bathroom. Returning twenty minutes later, she discovered that Emily was up.

'You beat me.' The young woman's face was glum as she dived past Clarice to take her turn.

Dressed, and waiting for Emily's return to go for breakfast, Clarice decided to send a text to Rick. But her phone, which should have been in the pocket of her trousers, was missing. Panic set in for a moment. She remembered that the last time she'd used it was the call to Rick in the woods. It was probable that when she fell and dropped the torch, she'd also dropped her phone.

'Are you OK?' she asked when Emily returned.

'Not really. I've been dreading today.'

On their way downstairs, they agreed that they would go out for a walk after breakfast and search for the lost phone. 'I'll ring your number using my phone, and we can follow the sound,' Emily said.

At the bottom of the stairs, they encountered Johnson.

'Good morning, Emily and Mrs Beech,' he said, his voice formal and polite. 'I hope you both slept well.'

'Yes thank you.' Clarice was an echo to Emily.

'Mrs Fuller is sorting out breakfast.' He nodded towards the kitchen. 'She and her sister will spend the day here helping out.'

As she followed Emily, Clarice considered Johnson's self-control; she imagined very little would rattle him.

'Shall we go for that walk?' Emily asked after they'd breakfasted on eggs and toast.

'Definitely,' Clarice said. 'It'll be good to get out for a bit.'

'Where do you want to look for the phone?'

'I phoned Rick when I was near the well, so it's on the way back from there. I might have wandered off the path – it was a bit foggy.'

'You went a long way. I'd imagined you going about as far as the barn.'

'It was a mistake,' Clarice said sheepishly. 'Let's walk to the well and then retrace our steps. It's a while before we need to leave for the funeral.'

Clarice noticed as Emily set off that she'd turned away at the mention of the funeral.

'It's going to be a difficult day for you,' she said as they walked.

'Too right. You only bury your dad once.' Emily sounded bitter. 'I didn't think he would leave me like this – so suddenly.'

Taking the same route as the previous day, Clarice felt the difference with the morning light after her fear in the misty darkness.

It was not until they'd passed the old stables that Emily spoke again.

'Sorry for being grumpy, Clarice.'

'Don't worry.' Clarice slowed her pace. 'Today there'll be so many mixed emotions.'

'I shouldn't be grouchy with you. You've come to this poisonous place and been such a good friend to Dad.' Emily used the back of her hand to wipe her face.

'I'm here for you too, not just Colin. You've become a friend.' Clarice rested her hand gently on Emily's arm.

'Yes. That's what I think too.' Emily did not speak again until they entered the clearing to reach the well.

In daylight, Clarice could see that there were fractures through the brickwork and ivy growing up one side, its state of disrepair making it obvious it had not been in use for many years. The willow tree was more prominent than she remembered from the previous evening. With its height and proximity to the well, its roots would absorb any water.

'Come over here.' Emily walked to the furthest point of the burial patch to point out two of the small headstones.

'Dana, 1890 to 1903, and Preeda, 1890 to 1905.' Clarice read out the names on the worn memorials.

'I told you that the first pair of Siamese cats were brought to England in 1884. They were given as a gift to his sister by the British consul general in Bangkok; Dana and Preeda were direct descendants.'

'And they were given suitable Thai names.' Clarice nodded. 'They're a popular breed now.'

'They became fashionable very quickly, enough for the owners club to be set up in 1906.'

'All that time ago,' Clarice said. She glanced towards the solid wooden shed at the end of the line of graves. 'What's the shed used for? I didn't notice it last night with the mist.'

'It's where the gardener keeps spades and stuff he doesn't want to carry from the old stables,' Emily replied.

Clarice nodded, then wandered along the lines of headstones. The Compton-Smythes had repeated some names; there were two Sams and four Bens.

'They're the Labradors. Both my grandfather and great-grandfather had them in pairs – you've met the present Ben, of course.' Emily grinned, her face brightening.

'Did they all have small coffins – like people?' Clarice asked.

'Goodness, no. I've no idea how the great-grandparents did it, but Grandpa wraps the body in an old blanket, always the dog or cat's favourite, taken from their basket. The idea is that they go back to nature – to become, over time, part of the earth.'

'What about the possibility of foxes or other animals digging them up?'

'The gardener always digs a deep hole. After the soil has been put over the body, Grandpa puts a layer of broken bricks in, then more soil – it would have to be the Houdini of foxes to get down to where the body is.'

'I think Houdini used his skills to get out, not break in, but I take your point.' Clarice laughed. 'Your grandpa paid a great deal of attention to every aspect of the burials.' They'd finished their walk around the gravestones. 'I suppose we should wander back; it might take us a while to find the phone.'

'It's only half eight.' Emily looked at her watch, as if hoping that she could put off their return.

Looking at her, Clarice thought again of a delicate, spindly whippet. One that wanted to bolt and hide, fuelled by fear.

Emily lifted her shoulders. 'You're right, though.' She took out her phone. 'I'll trail behind – tell me when to ring.'

In daylight, Clarice found it difficult to work out the route she'd taken the previous evening. Looking from side to side, she was not sure at which point she'd roamed away from the path. The way through the trees, away from the track, was dotted with bushes and large clumps of vegetation, making it less easy to negotiate. It made her more certain that only someone who knew these woods well could have pursued her. Above, the branches, naked of leaves, moved with the wind. Taking long strides, she moved right and then left. It was no good; she could not work out the way she'd gone, and guesswork would not take her to the place where she'd fallen.

'Try calling my number now, Emily.'

Emily obliged, without success. After much wandering, on the eighth attempt Clarice picked up the sound of the ringtone and spotted the phone in the undergrowth. As she reached to pick it up, her eyes were drawn to the stout waist-high branch jutting out, the one she had run into. Her mind went again to the figure she'd glimpsed, the person stalking her and the reason for her alarm.

'You could have wandered to the Wash.' Emily pointed. 'It's that way.'

Clarice glanced at the phone. Rick had sent a text to wish her good morning before he'd left for work, and there was also one from Micky, who had asked her to put a suggestion to Ralph on his behalf. She slipped the phone into her pocket and tried not to think of what might have been if she'd wandered onto the mudflats.

They had reached the stables when a delighted Ben ran towards them as if he hadn't encountered them in weeks.

Clarice welcomed him. 'Are we going to do some sitting?' She gave him the command, and he followed the order immediately. 'What a good boy.' She slipped him a treat.

'Hello there.' Ralph came into view, wandering towards them from the old stables. 'You need to go in and get yourself ready, Emily,' he said gently. 'I understand today will not be easy for you, so stiff upper lip, eh?' He patted her shoulder.

Emily and Clarice moved towards the house.

'Mrs Beech – Clarice, I would like to talk to you,' Ralph said, walking after them. 'Let's go to my study.'

Emily turned, frowning. 'I'll come too.'

'No, Emily, just Clarice. She'll see you soon.'

Emily's glance was ominous as she left them to walk on alone.

After giving her a head start, Ralph followed in the direction of the house. Clarice fell into step behind him on the narrow path.

Entering the great hall, she caught sight of Tessa near the entrance. Looking casually to the side of her, she counted four blue jackets in a row; the jacket monitor had been active. For a fraction of a moment, she met Tessa's gaze; the older woman's eyes were blank, conveying neither warmth nor animosity.

Following Ralph in silence, Clarice mentally braced herself for what was to come. She'd not felt this sensation since she was twelve years of age, when she'd been sent to the headmistress's office for scrumping strawberries from the council allotments behind the school. The feeling was a mixture of bravado, a pretence that she did not care, laced with humiliation for having been caught in the act of doing something she knew to be wrong. Had Tessa told Ralph that she was causing trouble by asking awkward questions, giving Ralph no option but to ask her to leave, with immediate effect? Knowing Emily would be upset, Clarice felt determined to fight her corner.

Trotting unbidden behind her, Ben trailed them to his master's study, where they found Floss sleeping on a blanket in the pool of sunshine that spilt through the window. He immediately went to the older dog, jumping around in the hope that she might want to play. It felt peaceful there, with the sun's brightness warming the office and picking out the layer of dust across Ralph's desk. He went to sit in his battered old armchair.

'Sit down, sit down.' He spoke to Ben. The dog ignored him. 'Do take a seat, Clarice.' He indicated the chair opposite.

There followed a few minutes of silence during which Ralph appeared to be ruminating. The silence became uncomfortable, and Clarice had almost decided to ask why he wanted to talk to her when he spoke.

'A couple of things,' he said. 'You've put the cat amongst the pigeons. You probably know that.'

'In what way?' Clarice decided to pretend innocence.

'Clarice, you are far too intelligent to play that game.' Ralph leaned back in his armchair, his bushy eyebrows knitted as he observed her over his glasses.

'I am sorry if I've upset anyone,' Clarice said.

'I've got my family telling me to ask you to leave immediately. Apparently you're a disruptive influence …' Ralph raised his hand as Clarice opened her mouth. 'But I have no intention of doing that.'

They sat studying each other for a few moments.

'I believe you're helping Emily.' He put his head to one side. 'It's two votes for you to go and three for you to stay, mine included. She needs support to get through the funeral; she's had enough to deal with already.'

'Thank you,' Clarice said. Ralph, as head of the household, was surprisingly democratic. Obviously it was Tessa and

Johnson who wanted her to leave. It was interesting that Ralph included Johnson in the family count, rather than as an employee.

'This time tomorrow, the funeral will be over and done with, and you and Emily will have gone, after which the household can return to its normal routines.' Ralph looked at her as if in contemplation. 'She's always been such a shy little thing.' He scratched his head absent-mindedly, looking as if his mind was far away.

'You said a couple of things?'

'Yes, I want to ask you something … rather awkward,' he said, uncharacteristically hesitant.

'OK.' Clarice gave her most encouraging smile.

'I would prefer that you didn't repeat this.' Ralph's tongue-tied discomfort made her think of him as a rather elderly schoolboy. What could make him feel so embarrassed?

'It's the dog,' Ralph said at last.

'The dog – Ben?' Clarice pointed.

On hearing his name, Ben came to stand beside her.

'Sit,' she commanded. The dog sat.

'That's it exactly, don't you see?'

Clarice looked from Ben to Ralph.

'He's my blithering dog, and he won't do that for me. Always had dogs, all my life.' Once he'd got started, it seemed that Ralph was not going to stop. 'I always train them up, never had a problem, but this one won't do a damn thing I tell him. You turn up, and within a few hours you've got him eating out of your hand – literally. Does exactly what you tell him.'

Clarice held her hand up to stop Ralph talking. He had turned a deep shade of puce.

'How long ago was it that you trained your last puppy?' she asked kindly.

'It was Floss.' He nodded towards the elderly dog. 'Lovely old girl.'

'That was quite a long time ago. Maybe you're a tiny bit rusty.' She smiled. 'No offence intended.'

'None taken.' Ralph listened intently.

'You're not training him to one command at a time. You say "sit down" – that's two separate instructions. He's highly intelligent. How often do you give him treats when he obeys instructions: sit – stay – down, that sort of thing?'

'Used to do it.' Ralph scratched his chin. 'Did it with Floss when she was a pup. I do give him a biscuit after dinner.'

Clarice stood up. 'I'll show you my secret stash.' Ben, who had wandered to the other side of the office, immediately came to her.

'Sit!' she commanded. Ben sat, and she slipped her hand from her pocket to the dog's mouth. Not taking his eyes from her, Ben swallowed the treat.

'Stay.' She put her hand up palm forward as she gave the command, then walked to the door, where she turned and waited for a moment. 'Come.' Ben leapt forward, and Clarice rewarded him. 'Good boy.' She scratched him behind his ears.

Ralph stood up. 'What are you giving him?'

Clarice brought out a handful of small treats from her pocket, and Ben's tail started to swish. She handed them to Ralph.

'Bacon-flavoured. One treat every time he obeys. He's picked up "sit" and "stay" very quickly, but I haven't been here long enough to teach him more.'

'Sit.' Ralph gave the command. The dog sat, and his master gave him a treat. 'Well, it's pretty damned obvious really,' he blustered. 'Should have worked it out, remembered the treats.' He was quiet again for a few moments. 'You must think I'm a real old ditherer.'

'No, not at all.' Clarice smiled again. 'If you haven't done something for fourteen years, it's easily forgotten.'

'Why did you hold your palm up when you said "stay"?'

'Because it got his attention. If he'd been a good distance away when I told him to stay, he might not have heard, but he would understand the visual command.'

'I get it.' Ralph smiled briefly before the smile slipped into a sad expression. 'So – now there's just the funeral to get through.'

'Yes.'

'Please don't tell anyone about our little talk.' He tapped the side of his nose. 'I don't want them to think I'm an old fool.'

'I wouldn't dream of it.'

'If there is ever anything I can do for you ...'

Clarice sat down again. 'Actually, there is. Not for me, for Emily, but I don't know if you'll be happy to agree to it.'

'Go on,' Ralph said.

'I know you're giving the eulogy in church.' She gave her hopeful smile. 'Might it be possible for one of Colin's friends to say just a few words?'

'Impossible,' Ralph said. 'The order of service has already been printed. It's too late, and I can't change it.'

'But,' Clarice spoke decisively, 'you did say you wanted to support Emily to get through her father's funeral. If a friend of her dad, someone she knows well, were to speak a few kind words about her father, how could that not help?'

'You mean not like Tessa, calling him dull.' Ralph glowered. 'Dreadful.'

'Yes, I do mean that, but also, who really knew Colin locally?' Clarice paused to let him take in what she was saying. 'He went away to school at twelve, then on to university, and then never came back home.'

'Yes, there is that.'

'Emily knows all of Colin's friends. They watched her growing up, they love her.'

Ralph contemplated. Then he said, 'Tessa shouldn't have said that – it was spiteful.'

Clarice realised he was going to say no. At least she could tell Micky she had tried, and Ralph wasn't throwing her out.

'I'm sorry, but I have to say no,' he said at last.

She nodded, accepting his decision.

'It's highly irregular, and I would be worried about someone I've never met – wouldn't know what to expect. They might say something terrible.' He looked at her over his glasses. 'But you can say a few words if you wish.'

'Me!'

'I've seen you with Emily. I'm confident you would only have her best interests at heart. Still highly irregular, but it's you who speaks or nobody.'

'If that's what you want, then yes, I'd be pleased to do it,' Clarice said, and was surprised to be rewarded by a rare smile.

Chapter 25

Leaving Ralph's office, Clarice walked into the great hall. She saw Mrs Banner making her way out. There were minor physical differences between her and Mrs Fuller, but both were square and solidly built, very much alike. Clarice looked about. All was calm and tranquil. Ralph had gone upstairs to his bedroom; everyone was getting changed, preparing themselves for the arrival of the car.

Walking behind a row of tables, she lifted the lid of one of the wooden boxes with upright backs, useful both for storage and seating. Finding what she had expected, she could not suppress a grimace. The chests, like the wall tapestries hanging above, had been in place since the property was built. The long gouges and deep scratch marks were evidence of well over a hundred years of cat activity, sharpening their claws on the wood. It was one of the hazards for cat lovers; their much-adored domesticated animals had bad habits.

At the bottom of the staircase, the door leading to the kitchen and dining room opened and Mrs Fuller peered into the hall.

'Are you all right, Mrs Fuller?' Clarice asked.

'I'm looking for Johnson or my sister. I need someone to give me a hand moving a table.' She spoke with urgency, looking past Clarice. 'Johnson said he had stuff to do outside.'

'Can I help you?' Clarice asked. 'I just saw your sister going out, and I don't know where Johnson is. Everyone else is upstairs getting changed for the funeral.'

Mrs Fuller backed away into the corridor. 'Come on then.' Evidently she was not interested in the finer points of politeness, such as please or thank you.

Clarice followed her to find a long, narrow pine table, too much for one person but easily managed by two.

'OK,' she said, 'I've got this end.'

Mrs Fuller put her large, work-worn hands under the lip of the table edge. 'He wants it near the door to put out a photograph of Colin.'

'That's a nice idea.' Clarice thought from the expression on Mrs Fuller's face that *she* probably judged it a silly notion. 'Did you know Colin?' she asked.

'Course I did.' Mrs Fuller put her end down, Clarice doing the same. 'I've worked here since I was a girl.' She looked at Clarice, weighing her up. 'I liked him, quiet boy, liked his mother too.'

Clarice smiled encouragingly.

'I liked the Major.' Mrs Fuller's eyes sparkled.

'Major Freddie Baxter?'

She nodded eagerly, then looked around to check nobody was listening. 'Such a handsome man, reckon he could have been in the movies. I'd have liked to have seen him in uniform.'

'Well!' Clarice couldn't hide her surprise. Mrs Fuller had clearly been smitten. 'He does sound a bit special.'

'If it's gossip you want, you should talk to Albert Wilson. He'll be here today – short man, always wears a checked jacket, gingery orange hair.' She cackled, her reticence gone. 'He's seventy-eight, can't bear the thought of white hair. Every few months his sister helps him dye it.'

'I'll look out for him. Thank you,' Clarice said.

'Too mean to pay a hairdresser.' Mrs Fuller suddenly folded her top lip back in what might have been a smile, displaying perfect dentures. 'Albert's sister was a friend of Colin's mum.' She nodded knowingly. 'They went to school together.'

'Thank you.' Clarice spoke with sincerity as she picked up her end of the table again, manoeuvring herself through the doorway and into the space below the curved staircase. It felt that Mrs Fuller was pushing much harder than she was pulling.

'Bugger, it's stuck,' Mrs Fuller said, before giving the table an almighty shove. The unexpected movement propelled Clarice backwards, leaving the table in the centre of the stairwell and throwing her onto her backside.

At the moment she was flung back, Clarice had felt the sensation of a rushing noise and movement in front of her. She watched, stunned, as the bronze cat from the fourth floor landed on the table, smashing it in half. Chips of wood flew upwards. The noise of splintering wood and the deafening bang of impact as the sculpture hit the floor was followed by a moment of utter silence. Then Mrs Fuller screeched.

In a daze on the floor, Clarice looked upward; she could see no movement above. Mrs Fuller, her hands over her eyes, was now gasping and crying. For a moment Clarice felt confused, then nauseous. She pulled herself up from the floor. The cat sculpture seemed to be undamaged. Table legs were lying at odd angles some distance from each other, and fragments of tiles were scattered in a wide circle.

'Christine – Christine!' Mrs Banner was suddenly there, taking hold of her sister. 'Stop, stop – you're all right.' She gave her a firm shake.

'I could be dead!' Mrs Fuller pointed at the debris.

'Not you, Christine, you hadn't come out.' Mrs Banner pointed at Clarice. 'Her. It would have hit her – she'd be dead.'

The sisters stood side by side in shock, staring at Clarice, and then there were voices and movement as the family, alerted by the noise, came rushing down the stairs, Emily first, with Dawn a few steps behind.

'What happened?' Emily asked. As she spoke, she saw the bronze cat amid the mess of broken wood and tiles, and her hand flew over her mouth, her eyes round with shock.

'They were moving that table, her and Christine.' Mrs Banner pointed at Clarice. 'The table was stuck. As they jerked it, she fell over onto her arse and skidded backwards, then that came flying down – smashed right through the middle of the table.' Mrs Banner now pointed at the sculpture.

'My God!' Ralph, the last downstairs, pushed past Tessa, Dawn, Ernestine and Johnson, who had arrived seconds before him. 'The last time that happened was over seventy years ago.'

'It was Duncan.' Ernestine looked at her brother. 'That boy you were at school with.'

Clarice marvelled that the elderly lady could remember quite clearly events of almost seventy years ago, but probably not what she'd eaten for breakfast that day. She looked smart, attired in a navy-blue suit with court shoes; around her neck she wore her diamond and pearl necklace. The others, apart from Johnson, had also changed their clothes in preparation for the funeral.

'How the hell did it happen?' Ralph looked around. 'It couldn't have just toppled and fallen by itself.'

'Are you OK, Clarice?' Emily asked.

Still feeling the shock of what had happened, Clarice did not answer.

'I only let her help me with the table because I thought you were outside,' Mrs Fuller snapped accusingly to Johnson.

'I was in the storage rooms upstairs looking for some extra glasses.' Johnson glowered back at her.

'The floor's badly damaged,' Tessa said.

'It's awful – it could have killed Clarice.' Dawn, who was carrying Ruffian, turned to her father, who had gone to examine the debris more closely. 'I was with Emily in the guest bedroom. I didn't hear anyone outside.'

'The door was closed. We wouldn't have heard if there was someone there,' Emily added.

Tessa frowned, looking from Dawn to Emily.

'I need to get changed.' Clarice spoke, her mind still in a daze.

'Do you still want to go to the funeral?' Tessa sounded kind. 'Everyone will understand if you decide to stay behind.'

'I'll be fine.' Clarice headed for the stairs. Behind her, she could hear Ralph's angry voice asking again and again who had toppled the sculpture.

On the top landing, Emily stopped Clarice with a hand on her shoulder to ask the question again. 'Are you OK?'

'Bit shocked, if I'm honest.' Clarice went to the stone plinth where the bronze cat had sat and looked over the balustrade. Below, the group had not dispersed, but they were talking more calmly now, no longer arguing. 'I'm not going to let whoever did this stop me going to the funeral,' she said.

'As Grandpa said, it couldn't have fallen unless someone gave it a deliberate almighty push.'

'It was top-heavy. If a ten-year-old schoolboy could do it, anyone could.' Clarice was thoughtful as she went into the bedroom and began changing her clothes. 'I do think your grandpa was shouting the loudest – could it have been for a reason?'

'You mean that if he was the one who pushed it over, he wanted to put on a good show at being outraged, to be sure no one would imagine it was him?' Emily said.

'Yes, something like that.' Clarice glanced at her image in the wardrobe mirror, then pushed her hand through her hair distractedly. 'What Ernestine told me keeps going around my mind. The last time she saw Avril, she was leaving with Ralph – nothing to do with going with the Major, or going to meet him. Where did your grandfather take her?'

'Like you said yesterday, Ernestine might just have been confused.'

'Yes, I know.' Clarice paused and looked at Emily over her shoulder. 'But I'm worried about her.'

'About seeing Avril leaving for the last time with Grandpa – or because she said Grandpa made Johnson do something?' Emily said.

'Both. I'm worried that by bringing all this out into the open, we're putting Ernestine in danger.'

'Are you accusing my father of something?' Dawn was suddenly next to Clarice, still carrying Ruffian. 'I came to make sure that you're all right.'

'I'm fine.'

'But you wouldn't have been if Mrs Fuller hadn't shoved that table ...'

Clarice looked at her, not responding.

'You can't really think my dad pushed the bronze sculpture over?'

'Not necessarily,' Clarice said. 'I don't know who did it. I'm just going through the people it might have been – trying to work it out.'

'Everything goes back to Avril.' Dawn looked towards Emily. 'It's somehow connected to her.'

'Yes, it puzzled Dad,' Emily rushed the words out, 'Avril suddenly deciding to run away with the Major. But perhaps she didn't. Maybe neither of them actually left.'

Dawn's stony expression was unreadable; she stepped close to look into Emily's eyes. 'I really can't imagine that my dad – your grandpa – would have done anything to harm Avril, can you?'

After a moment of hesitation, Emily averted her gaze. 'I find it difficult to believe, but I feel I only know the story Grandpa wants me to know. I don't know the whole truth.'

Dawn frowned. 'I need to lock Ruffian in my sitting room,' she said. 'He's not used to a lot of people, and the house will be full after the funeral.' She turned as she was leaving. 'They're waiting for you downstairs; the hearse and the car are here.'

Clarice nodded. 'Let's go down. We don't want to keep them waiting.'

Emily watched Dawn disappear down the stairs. 'I can't do this.' She held onto the door frame. 'Someone tried to kill you, Dawn's having a wobbly – and I'm burying my dad ... it's my dad.'

'You can do it.' Clarice gently guided her out of the room. 'Forget about everything else; just concentrate on laying him to rest. Today should only be about him.'

They crossed the landing. Clarice avoided looking at the plinth where the bronze cat should have been. As they walked down the staircase, Emily glanced along the corridor to where Dawn had her bedroom.

'Dawn came into the guest room while I was changing. She said very much what you had – why are we fighting a battle we didn't start? It was between her mother and my father.'

'And?' Clarice waited.

'I was honest and told her what I said to you. I agreed with her and said I don't want the bloody house – she's welcome to it.'

Clarice stopped to look at her.

'She said we'd work that out between us when the time came, and that we should leave the past behind us, see my dad's funeral as a line in the sand, and try to get on and be more supportive of each other in the future.'

'That's great.'

'But after what she's just overheard, she might change her mind. I've upset her.' Emily stopped to look through the open doorway to the hearse.

'Forget all that for now,' Clarice said. 'If Dawn is genuine, and I hope she is, it's better for you to have her as a friend than an enemy. Concentrate on saying goodbye to your dad.'

'I will,' Emily said. 'What did Grandpa want to talk to you about? I was scared he might be asking you to leave.'

Clarice thought about the promise she had made Ralph about not mentioning Ben's training. 'It was mainly about the eulogy. I asked if one of Colin's friends, Micky perhaps, might be allowed to say a few words about your dad.'

'And?'

'He found the suggestion "highly irregular". He didn't like the idea of someone he'd never even met standing up to talk publicly about Colin.'

'Yes, I see,' Emily said, disappointed.

'But he said it was OK if I would like to speak.' Clarice looked closely at Emily to gauge her reaction.

'You will do it?' Emily eagerly caught her hand. 'For Dad?'

'I did say yes,' Clarice said.

'I'm so pleased it will be you.' Emily hugged her, and they continued outside.

Chapter 26

The hearse was by the entrance to the manor; behind it, the long black limousine. In the back of the hearse, the dark wood of the coffin with brass handles was visible through the glass sides, partially hidden by the many floral wreaths. Four employees of the funeral company, dressed appropriately in black, hovered with sombre expressions as they awaited the family.

Dawn had joined the small gathering, dutifully following her parents and aunt, their feet crunching over the frosty ground. She watched them getting into the car before ushering Emily inside, then following her to take her own seat. Clarice came last.

'You should sit over there next to your grandfather.' Aunt Ernestine, sitting between Emily and Clarice, pointed.

'Don't worry about that.' Emily patted her aunt's knee. 'I'm happy to be here with you.'

Just as Clarice was thinking how compos mentis Ernestine seemed today, she ruined the thought.

'I've got all my own teeth.' In the now-familiar gesture, she gave a wide fake smile.

'You have,' Emily said. She patted Ernestine's knee for the second time, looking out of the window as the car moved forward.

'For God's sake,' Tessa hissed.

Ralph glowered first at Ernestine, then at Tessa, but remained silent.

The funeral director, wearing a top hat and carrying a cane, walked with the requisite amount of pomp in front of the hearse. As they were about to enter the wooded area, the vehicle stopped, allowing him to climb into the passenger seat, rejoining his colleague, and lead the funeral procession to Sealsby village church.

Emily looked out of the window distractedly, her mind undoubtedly reflecting upon her father.

Ernestine appeared like a child in receipt of a treat on an outing, smiling as she turned her head first one way and then the other, looking out to the fields.

'This is my best suit.' She spoke aloud, but did not seem unduly concerned whether anyone was listening, appearing not to require a response. 'I never get fat, so it still fits me. I've got a good figure – always have.' She took a piece of fudge from her bag and popped it into her mouth. 'Look, sheep.' She pointed. 'I never wear clothes out, not like Ralph and Beth; they're so rough with their clothes.'

Clarice noticed Tessa rolling her eyes, her lips pinched in a tight line, before she tried mentally to switch off in an effort to blank out the incessant drone of Ernestine's chatter. The now grey and sunless sky loomed large over flat fields, seemingly stretching away forever. Her mind went automatically over the events of the previous evening and earlier that day. She tried to concentrate and remember conversations with each individual since her arrival. To find pointers to what had made her the target for someone with murder on their mind. In contrast to Ernestine wittering with joy, Emily, her fingers pressed to her lips, seemed steeped in despair.

'Colin didn't like church. And he didn't know any hymns. I know lots.' Ernestine rattled on. 'Colin should be buried at home. Bellatrix would have wanted that, and he wouldn't have needed that ugly brown box, just an old blanket. He won't like the box. He was frightened of the dark; wet his trousers when I locked him in the wardrobe.'

Looking at the thunderous expression on Ralph's face, Clarice felt it must be taking every ounce of his self-control for him not to let rip at his sister.

Ernestine giggled as she chewed. 'He wouldn't play hide-and-seek again. Suki was my favourite girl cat. She's in the graveyard in the woods; she was fourteen when she died.' She popped another piece of fudge into her mouth. 'Ralph wrapped her in her blanket, it was blue. He folded it over, so Suki was all covered up. The hole was ever so deep – so foxes couldn't dig her up again. I haven't had a cat since she died.' She sounded sad.

'Ernestine.' Ralph had leaned forward to look directly into her face. '*Shut up.* I don't want to hear another peep out of you for the rest of this journey.'

Ernestine became rigid; the angry menace in her brother's voice was unmistakable. The rest of the five-mile journey passed in silence.

As the car entered the village, Clarice looked out for the church, remembering its position from having passed through previously. There were numerous cars and a coach parked on land next to it, and a small group of people were gathering around the wrought-iron gates. The hearse slowed to turn onto the entrance pathway; the limousine did the same.

'What a lot of cars,' Ernestine said, pressing against the window, forgetting Ralph's command. Her jaw, as she spoke, moved ceaselessly. 'There's a coach. Why is that here? Is something else happening today? Are people going on their holiday?'

Clarice watched Emily's face as she took in the coach and then looked the other way to see a crowd gathered next to the church doorway.

'Look, Clarice, there's Micky. Simon, Denise and Gill ... they've all come.' Emily half rose in excitement. 'And that's Len and Milly, Dad's neighbours.'

'That bald man has a big snake on his head.' Ernestine's mouth hung open. Her voice was filled with awe.

'Where the hell did this bloody rabble come from?' Tessa glowered.

'They're my dad's friends,' Emily said.

'And they are all very welcome.' Ralph's look of shock had been replaced with one of mild surprise as he attempted to smile at Emily.

Clarice took Emily's hand for a moment. 'The ceramics crowd and your dad's neighbours know one another through the summer parties he held in his garden over the years.'

'Did they come on the coach?' Emily asked.

'Yes, but Henry could only get a thirty-seater. Micky sent me a text. He said more people wanted to come, but Henry couldn't get a bigger coach at such short notice.'

'Micky's husband?'

'Henry took on the organising, phoning around,' Clarice said.

Tessa's intake of breath sounded much like the hiss of a snake.

There was a second, larger crowd on the opposite side of the doorway. Clarice presumed them to be people from the village.

As the car stopped, the driver climbed out to walk around and open the door. Before he could reach it, Emily had flung it open to leap out with the agility of a greyhound leaving the traps. She sprinted across the drive towards the group, decorum forgotten. Clarice heard a sound like the ripple of wind over grasses, as voices joined in repeating *Emily, Emily, Emily*. And when she reached them, Micky and Gill, both with their arms wide open, caught her, the rest of the group closing around, swallowing her into their midst.

Once out of the car, Clarice followed her over.

'I think she's pleased to see us.' Micky sounded tearful, as he peeled away to greet her.

'She is.' Clarice smiled. 'I spoke to Ralph about your idea.'

'What did he say?'

'He said it was highly irregular, and he'd be delivering the eulogy himself.'

'So no go?'

'I pushed it, but he was unhappy about someone he'd never met speaking. He told me that I could do it – it was that or nothing.'

'Please tell me you said yes, Clarice?'

'He phoned the vicar before I left. The vicar agreed to say that Colin's friend Clarice would like to say a few words.' She looked around to find Emily coming her way. 'I have told Emily.'

'That's great.' Micky grinned. 'I sent you a text this morning to suggest some things Colin's mates might have liked me to say; they wanted his family to know how much we all loved him. Maybe you can say them instead of me.'

'I saw it. I can't promise to cover it all, but I'll do my best to fit in as much as I can.' Clarice turned to Emily. 'You should join the family.'

'Yes. Everyone's coming to the house after the service. I'm so pleased,' Emily said as Clarice guided her back towards her grandfather.

They watched in silence as the coffin was carried into the church.

Ralph took Emily's arm. 'We'll walk in together,' he said kindly.

'Thank you, Grandpa,' Emily said.

'I blame you for this,' Tessa hissed at Clarice when Emily and Ralph were out of earshot. Not waiting for a reply, she turned and followed them, shepherding Ernestine much as a sheepdog might a wandering member of its flock.

Clarice looked back at the ceramists. She belonged to their group; she wasn't a member of the family. She'd half turned to walk over to join them when she felt a touch to her elbow.

'Come on, Clarice.' Dawn was next to her. 'I don't think my niece will forgive me if I let you wander away. You're one of us today – the family.'

Looking at her, Clarice did not doubt that she was genuine in her intentions, while Tessa's feelings were transparent from her glare as she glanced back to see that Dawn had linked arms with Clarice to walk into the church.

Inside, the bearers had put the coffin in place. The family went to the front pew, moving along in a line to sit. Dawn followed them, with Clarice seated at the end, next to the aisle.

The music was a recording of an organ recital, which Clarice suspected might be by Bach. Before sitting down, she picked up a pamphlet left on the pew giving the order of service. On the front was a photograph of Colin smiling, wearing his glasses with the signature kingfisher-blue frames. She eyed the hymns, 'Jerusalem', 'Dear Lord and Father of Mankind', and 'Guide Me, O Thou Great Redeemer', all completely inappropriate for Colin, an entrenched atheist. She shuddered involuntarily, aware that Ralph had organised the service to uphold not what Colin had believed in but what he himself thought acceptable. He lived his life by a rule book that was all about how he would be perceived by society.

The shuffling of feet, coughing and whispering continued as people trooped in to find a seat. Glancing along her row, Clarice could see Ralph sitting rigid, staring straight in front. Tessa was doing the same. Emily was dabbing her eyes, Dawn reading the order of service, while Ernestine was fiddling in her small cardboard box to extract another piece of fudge.

Ralph's agreement that she could say a few words during the service had surprised her. She knew that he thought her intelligent, articulate and presentable, someone who could offer a respectable image. Micky, with his bald tattooed head, wouldn't have done at all.

She pulled her thoughts back to the church, looking to the altar, above it an image in glass of Jesus on the cross; below, the trestle bearing the coffin containing Colin's remains. The church was cold, and smelled of damp and artificial lemon floor cleaner.

The vicar, a slim, neat man with a short goatee beard, known to his flock as Terry, had moved forward to have a few quiet words with Ralph. His body language was obsequious; the Compton-Smythes obviously still held some sway in the community. Having finished talking to Ralph, Terry moved along to stop in front of Clarice.

'You're Clarice Beech?'

'Yes.' Clarice nodded.

'I understand you will be saying a few words about Colin. You were a friend?'

Clarice nodded again.

'I'm going to drop you in here after the third hymn, "Guide Me, O Thou Great Redeemer".' He pointed to the place in the pamphlet. Clarice could not help but notice that his nails were bitten to the quick.

'That will be fine,' she replied, thinking his choice of words odd.

There was the sound of the church door slamming shut. Glancing behind her, Clarice saw that every seat was full, and people were standing in a row at the back.

What might Colin say if he could see the crowd gathered here because of him? 'I always knew how to make an exit.' Clarice smiled as she remembered the tone of his voice, then watched as Terry mounted the three steps to take his place at the lectern.

Chapter 27

Terry spoke of Colin James Compton-Smythe, a much-loved son, stepson, father and nephew. In his mid thirties, the vicar had an unexpectedly high voice and a tendency to touch the side of the lectern with his fingertips while talking, possibly a nervous habit along with his nail-biting. Clarice glanced at Ralph; eyebrows knitted in concentration, he listened intently. Emily had said her father had never attended church when he visited his old family home. Clarice realised that Terry would not have met Colin; he would have put together biographical information given to him by Ralph. Had Ralph, she wondered, included Avril in those details?

During the singing of the first hymn, 'Jerusalem', Ernestine, who clearly knew the words by heart, put her head back and joined in with shrill but joyful abandonment. Dawn's expression was sombre and severe, Tessa's fraught. Emily kept her head down, her lips unmoving.

After the hymn had finished, Ralph walked unaided to take his place at the lectern, and faced the congregation. He took his time, and Clarice could see his eyeline was somewhere above the audience's heads. She imagined what he saw might be a blur. She wondered if he'd practised climbing the three steps. Johnson was not here to offer support; had Tessa suggested she assist him? Perhaps Ralph had rejected any such help, not wanting to be seen so publicly as a doddery old man.

He talked about the family's history, his father James and grandfather George, their place in the community for over a century and his joy at having his son born at Stone Fen Manor, continuing the line. He moved on to Colin's school and university days, after which he had become an accountant. He concluded by saying that he had been a wonderful son and a devoted father to Emily.

After the third hymn, Terry introduced Clarice Beech as Colin's friend, and she stepped out of the pew. Although she was used to talking to student groups, this was different. The idea of standing in front of Colin's family and friends to speak so personally about the man she'd known made her hands feel clammy. As she climbed the stairs, she felt a rush of panic, imagining the eyes of the congregation boring into her back. She was suddenly fearful that her voice might wobble with emotion.

She took a deep breath and willed herself on.

'I teach ceramics, or pottery as it used to be known, which is how I met Colin. He joined a new evening class, telling me that he'd give it a try for a term. Ceramics suited him. He was hooked, and after that first term, he continued coming to the classes for the next eleven years, during which time he created a fantastic range of pieces, including plates, cups and vases.

'Colin told me that he found his job as an accountant to be rewarding and satisfying, but working with ceramics he unexpectedly discovered his artistic side. He enjoyed the creative process of designing and following a piece through, from the drawing stage to manipulation of the clay and glazing and firing. He had a particular love of nature, and many of his designs featured flowers.

'During the eleven years I knew Colin, he became a dear friend, and I have been privileged to watch his daughter grow up. I first met Emily as a shy young schoolgirl; she is now a lovely young woman in her first year at university.

'Colin made friends very easily. His fellow students, most of whom started with him in the first class, became part of his circle outside of class. A couple of years ago, during a discussion, one of the students commented that they were a diverse bunch of people from completely different backgrounds. Colin, he said, was the group's centre point, bringing them together; he was their heartbeat. His sense of humour and fun could lift even the lowest of spirits.'

She paused for a moment to look at the back of the church, where the ceramics group were sitting.

'Colin's friends have asked that I say a few things about what he meant to them, the difference that he made to their lives.

'Micky confided in Colin that he'd always wanted to do a university course. Colin was absolutely convinced that he could do it and succeed. It gave Micky the self-confidence to enrol with the Open University. It took him eight years to attain his degree. During that time, he met Henry at one of the university summer schools. Micky and Henry married last year. Colin was their best man.

'Gabriel was a mechanic in a garage in town. When the garage was due to close, Gabriel believed he would become unemployed. Colin got together with Simon, a fellow student, a solicitor, to help Gabriel make a business plan, working out the overheads and costings to obtain a mortgage and buy the garage. That was five years ago. The business is so successful that Gabriel has now taken on two employees.

'There are so many other stories: how he helped his neighbours, his baking skills – his lemon drizzle cake was terrific – his legendary garden parties during the summer. The list is endless.

'A small number of Colin's friends have taken on the task of summing up the man they knew in under five words.'

Clarice paused again for a moment, looking around.

'Here they are. Diane said "kind and compassionate". Gabriel described Colin as "the very best of friends". Mandy called him "a delightful man". Simon said Colin was "always great company". Gill spoke of his "wonderful sense of humour". And finally, Micky said that Colin was a "diamond geezer, an irreplaceable one-off".

'Speaking on my own behalf, I found Colin to be a man who was extremely decent and kind. With his dry humour and awareness, and a wonderful sense of the absurd, he could bring classes to a standstill. He treated all those he came into contact with with equal dignity and respect. And he was unstinting in supporting others when they needed help. I'm proud to be able to say that Colin was my friend. I loved him. He was one of those rare people who enriched the lives of all he came into contact with, my own included. I shall miss him.'

There was a gentle ripple of applause at the back of the church, like rain hitting the windows. Clarice nodded towards Terry, and as she returned to her seat, she saw that Tessa had turned around to glower at where the noise had come from. Emily, with tears running down her cheeks, put out her hand to take Clarice's and squeezed it. Tessa turned back, her eyes down as if suddenly finding something interesting to read in the hymn book. Ralph sat rigid. What she'd said, Clarice mused, might perhaps have been hard for Ralph, a man who struggled to show emotion.

Later, outside, the congregation gathered around as the coffin was lowered into the grave and Terry concluded the funeral service. Afterwards, Ralph, Emily and Tessa stood near the church door, talking to mourners. The sky was ominously dark, but the rain had held off.

Dawn stopped Clarice on her way to talk to Micky and Colin's other friends.

'I liked what you said about Colin; he was a lucky man to have a friend like you – loyal and kind.' Despite her warm words, Dawn looked upset. 'We need to talk – not now, later, at the house. I can't get the idea out of my head that my father might have been involved in Avril's death.'

'Dawn, it might not be him,' Clarice whispered urgently. 'We were only working through the possibilities. But somebody is rattled, and that bronze sculpture didn't fall by itself.'

'Speak later.' Dawn squeezed her arm, slipping away as the ceramics class converged.

'Thank you, Clarice, you did Colin proud. I couldn't have done better myself.' Micky hugged her.

'We're coming back to the house – Emily invited us,' Diane said. 'We won't be able to stay long, maybe an hour or so. She won't mind, will she?'

'I know how delighted she was that you came, and I'm sure

she'll understand that you still have the journey home,' Clarice reassured her. 'And your grandchildren come to your house after school, don't they?'

'I give them their tea,' Diane nodded, 'and they stay until my daughter collects them after work.'

'I'm just glad we could come.' Simon, slim and dapper in his best suit, looked around at the others, who nodded in agreement. 'Thank you, Henry, for doing the organising.'

'It was a pleasure,' Henry said.

'Hello, ducky, it's Clarice, isn't it?' A man in his seventies, with badly dyed orange hair and wearing a checked jacket, sidled up to Clarice. The greeting gave away his Lincolnshire roots, and she smiled, remembering Mrs Fuller's accurate description of his hair. 'I'm Albert Wilson.' He lifted his hand as if to touch an imaginary cap. 'I knew Colin as a little boy – shy lad, but nice. What you said about him today was lovely.'

'Thank you,' Clarice said. 'Did you know all the family – his mother?'

'Yes, I knew her as a child; Avril was the same age as my older sister, Jane. They were in primary and middle school together. Avril went on to the grammar – Jane didn't.'

'She passed her eleven plus?'

'Her parents could've afforded private education; they were well-heeled, but the father was a tight bugger. He wouldn't pay out for girls. They'd get married so didn't need a good education, he said. He didn't have a son, just the two daughters, Avril and Pamela.'

'Was Avril quite shy, like Colin?' Clarice asked.

'She was quiet,' Albert glanced around as he spoke, 'but she was nobody's fool. Because she was quiet, there was the odd kid that thought they might manipulate her. Jane told me that Avril wouldn't be pushed around.'

'That's interesting. Did you also know the Major?' Clarice asked.

'I could tell you a thing or two—'

'Did you say Avril?' Ernestine was suddenly next to Albert, interrupting the conversation.

'Yes,' Albert said.

'She was my best friend,' Ernestine said; and then, suddenly remembering, 'She was my sister-in-law. She used to take me shopping, and we'd sometimes go out for lunch.'

'Did you go on holiday with her?' Albert asked, smiling kindly. 'She liked flying – going to sunny places, Italy, Greece, for holidays.'

'What?' Ernestine's face had taken on a bemused expression. 'That's silly!'

Albert looked at her, puzzled.

'Avril couldn't fly.' Ernestine lifted her arms up and down in imitation of a bird flapping its wings.

'Ah.' Albert looked to Clarice. 'Yes, very good.'

Clarice wondered how she might go about shutting Ernestine up.

'Did you know that I have all my own teeth?' Ernestine showed him her mock smile. 'I'm nearly eighty.'

'Everyone to the car!' Dawn came to herd Ernestine away.

'I'll see you at the house.' Albert raised his hand to tip his imaginary cap again and disappeared into the crowd.

Heading towards the limo, Clarice stopped to watch Dawn following her parents into the vehicle. It was clear that catching the end of the conversation between her and Emily had unsettled her. She moved her eyes from the car to take in the newsagent's opposite the church, and next to it the war memorial she had noticed yesterday. The monument was probably similar to those in many Lincolnshire towns, bearing the names of soldiers who had died in the two world wars.

'Come on, Clarice,' Emily called.

Clarice moved forward, then stopped to look back. The man she'd seen in the wood on her arrival, and a few hours ago staring in through the window at Stone Fen Manor, was standing in the half-shadow of the memorial. She now knew his name was Ian Belling. His gaze was fixed on the car with Dawn, unaware of his presence, sitting inside.

The journey back to Stone Fen Manor was quiet, apart from Ernestine's intermittent chatter, with Clarice's mind returning to what she'd seen.

Tessa appeared to have decided to detach herself from the others. Her gaze was directed through the window throughout the journey.

'Ralph, you didn't ask me to speak,' Ernestine said. 'I could have said something nice about Colin.'

'No, we had enough people speaking,' Ralph was blunt before turning his head to copy Tessa and stare out of the window.

Dawn caught Clarice's eye and raised her eyebrows.

'Don't worry about it, Aunt Ernestine.' Emily gave her aunt's knee a reassuring pat.

'It's just the lunch to get through now,' Clarice said quietly. Emily nodded.

'Ralph you should have asked me.' Ernestine pouted. 'I wanted to tell everyone what a lovely boy Colin was. I'm his aunt, and I didn't get the chance to speak.'

'Ernestine, enough!' Ralph snapped.

'Please don't worry about it.' Emily tried to distract her. 'There will be lots of food when we get home.'

'Thank goodness.' Ernestine's face lit up. 'I'm starving, and I've run out of fudge.'

Chapter 28

The caterers had done their work. Within half an hour of the family's return home, the rest of the congregation were pouring into the great hall, chattering and filling their plates.

Clarice had gone immediately to find Ralph, following him to his office, where he discarded his coat.

'I need a quick word,' she said.

'I think we've heard enough of what you've got to say.' Tessa came in behind her, clearly annoyed.

'That man, Ian Belling.' Clarice looked from Tessa to Ralph.

'What about him?' Tessa's demeanour changed to one of concern.

Clarice told them what she'd seen, and for a moment they looked at each other without speaking.

'I'll give the police a call,' Ralph said. Tessa nodded. 'Thank you, Clarice,' he said as she turned to leave. 'I don't think he would come here, but that's not a certainty – and don't tell Dawn, I don't want her being upset.'

Clarice nodded and left them. She had not broken her word to Dawn; she had not told Ralph about the night-time sighting of Belling. It was ironic that Ralph had also asked for her silence. Later, after the wake, there would be time for father and daughter to talk properly. She went upstairs, where Emily was in the bedroom, freshening her make-up. After telling her what had happened, they returned downstairs to find Ralph with Tessa at his side, talking to guests, and Ernestine eating sandwiches.

They went to join Colin's friends, Emily filling plates and glasses to be sure they had something to eat and drink before their journey home. Watching her, Clarice realised she'd relaxed, mixing with friends, going from one familiar person to another to receive a hug. The weight of the family arguments over the last two days seemed to have lifted from her.

Clarice observed Ernestine approach Micky; as she watched, Micky bent down so the elderly lady could stroke the snake tattoo on the top of his head. She then pulled her lips into the fake smile, and Clarice knew what she would be telling him. Ralph was working the room, trailed by Tessa, carrying a wine glass. The perfect host, he talked to each individual, shaking their hand and thanking them for coming.

After just over an hour, the group departed on the coach. Clarice and Emily, having gone outside to say goodbye, stood next to Bellatrix.

'Will you get something to eat now?' Emily asked.

'In a bit,' Clarice said. 'What about you?'

'My stomach feels wobbly. I'm not hungry.' Emily let her eyes wander over Bellatrix. 'I'm just going to have ten minutes on my own to get my head together; I'll have a wander to the old stables and back. I have to talk to the others, the ones I don't know – people from the village. Grandpa will expect it.'

'You don't need to do anything unless you want to.' Clarice was firm.

She watched Emily leave before going back inside. Ernestine was at the buffet table, piling her plate with sandwiches and sausage rolls before moving on to receive a glass of sherry from one of the catering staff.

Walking to the staircase, Clarice found the bronze sculpture of the cat standing upright on a square piece of board that covered the damaged floor. She wondered who had helped Johnson put it in place.

'Now then, ducky.'

She turned to find Albert Wilson, carrying a glass.

'Hello, Albert, have you eaten yet?'

'I've had something. Waiting for the queue to go down before I go back for seconds.' He indicated the crush around the food tables. 'It's a good spread; they won't run out. I've got wine – there isn't any beer.'

'Ernestine is busy,' said Clarice, watching as the elderly lady, who was now seated, concentrated on working her way through the pile of food.

'That's good. We can talk properly.' Albert leaned nearer to her. 'You mentioned the Major.'

'Yes.' Clarice's expression gave away her interest.

'The ladies loved him,' Albert said. 'I didn't get it; he only had to snap his fingers and they'd be twittering around him like a load of daft birds.'

'Really?' Clarice said.

'He'd been in the army, smooth talker. He'd done this, that and the other.' Albert snorted. 'He was from away, a foreigner,

247

so he thought he could say anything and get away with it. I knew Janice, his wife, before he'd even met her.'

Clarice nodded, noticing another Lincolnshire habit – calling people from other parts of the UK 'from away', or foreigners. 'Did Janice tell you a different story?'

'Let's say she was a snob. Lively girl, thought local boys were all clods, and when Freddie came with his money, posh talk and fancy ways, she thought she'd caught herself a big fish.' Albert took a sip of wine and wrinkled his nose. 'I don't know why folk shout about this.'

'I understand she was a beauty,' Clarice slipped in, waiting for Albert's reaction.

'She was all right,' he sounded sour, 'but she knew it; wouldn't go out with the likes of someone like me.'

'The Major had money?' Clarice raised her eyebrows.

'Plenty, but he didn't spread it around. He became a partner in the Compton-Smythe business; he and Ralph were old friends.' Albert took another sip, swilling the wine around his mouth before swallowing. He spoke conspiratorially. 'Course, Janice thought she'd gone up in the world, started putting on airs and graces. She joined the tennis and golf clubs; they got a house in the village, nice garden. Didn't last, though.'

'Didn't she leave him?' Clarice asked.

'Leave him? Don't talk daft. She thought the sun shone out of his backside. She went up north to look after her mum, who had cancer. Freddie was to join her later. He was waiting to get his money back from the business. Word was, he wasn't getting enough profit from his investment in Ralph's company.'

Clarice could not help but wonder how reliable Albert's information might be. If the Major was independently wealthy, why would he be so desperate to get his money back from Ralph? It didn't make sense.

The room was getting noisy, with voices raised in conversation.

'I believe her brother moved in with her at some point in Yorkshire,' Clarice said.

'You don't know much, ducky.' Albert was dismissive. 'Peter moved to Australia. He married and had five kids. Maybe he came back for a while, after their mother died. Nobody heard from Janice after she went up north to look after her.'

'I see – I've got it wrong,' Clarice said. 'I thought the Major left here with Avril, and I heard Janice might have got herself a boyfriend.'

'No, Avril just did a runner when Ralph took up with Tessa again. And Janice would have crawled through broken glass if the Major had told her to; she was never interested in anyone else. The story did the rounds that Avril and Freddie had left together, and he was such a charmer with the ladies, the rumour was believed.' Albert waved his glass around. 'A lot of women around here would have thrown themselves at him if they'd had the chance. I always thought Avril was much too level-headed.' He glanced to one side as an elderly woman who matched him in height and hair colour came to join them. 'This is my sister, Jane.'

Clarice wondered if brother and sister had shared one bottle of the hair colour, splitting it between them. Whatever shade of dye they'd used, it turned orange when applied to their fine white hair.

'This the lady who knew Colin?' Jane spoke while putting a half-eaten sandwich back onto the plate she was carrying, the better to scrutinise Clarice.

'This is her, ducky.' Albert's eyes wandered back to the food. 'I'll catch you again in a bit; there's a space at that table,' and he was gone.

'I liked what you said at the funeral.' Jane cocked her head to one side, reminding Clarice of a wise old owl. 'It was nice that Colin made a good life for himself and had so many friends.'

'You knew Colin?'

'No, not really. I saw Avril with him in town a few times. She always stopped for a chat if she saw me.' Jane assumed a smug expression. 'She was no snob, never forgot her roots and her friends.'

'Albert said you were at school with her.' Clarice smiled.

'Primary and middle school,' Jane agreed. 'Avril passed her eleven plus, so she went on to the grammar. I went to the secondary modern.'

'I understand they were a wealthy family.'

'Rolling in it. Avril's mother had a mink coat, and her dad was on the council. He was the mayor at one time.' Jane picked up her sandwich again to bite into it. 'They could easily have sent her and Pamela to a private school …' she talked and chewed simultaneously, 'but they were girls, so they wouldn't waste the money.'

'Because they wouldn't have a career?' Clarice nodded. 'Albert told me.'

'That's it. Back then, it was thought girls just got married, and their husband would be the breadwinner. But,' Jane rubbed her finger and thumb together meaningfully, 'those girls would have inherited a lot of money. The father bought properties and did them up to rent or sell on.'

'I didn't know that,' Clarice said, storing this information away.

'The mother, Helen, was a widow when Avril married Ralph. She died not long after their wedding. Avril would have brought a tidy sum to the marriage.' Jane pursed her lips to push her point. 'Pamela blew her share of the inheritance on rotten husbands – she had a few of those.'

Clarice smiled without comment. If Ralph had had access to Avril's family money, it might have been absorbed into his business. Could he, after all, have married not for love but in the knowledge that his bride would bring a sizeable sum to the marriage?

After Jane had moved on, the room began to get crowded and noisy, which made Clarice, who suffered from claustrophobia, feel uncomfortable. She looked around, unsuccessfully, for Dawn. Ralph, without Tessa, was now seated with two other elderly men, engrossed in conversation.

The wake was in full flow. Entering the corridor that led to the toilet, Clarice saw that several people had had the same idea as her; there was a queue outside the door. She returned to cross the hall, going towards the passageway on the opposite side, only to find that door locked. Ralph, understandably, must have decided he didn't want people going into the corridor leading to his study and private sitting room. She made her way upstairs to the next floor, to the bathroom nearest the unused bedrooms. A few minutes later, as she emerged, she stopped, and with curiosity getting the better of her, and a guilty backward glance, headed towards the first of the four bedrooms.

Sharing with Emily had not bothered her, but when she had arrived, it had seemed odd, given that the property had four spare bedrooms, that it could only offer one guest room. Now she realised that having even one overnight visitor staying appeared to be a rarity.

Entering the first room, she found the darkness of the corridor carried on inside. The curtains were partially closed, and two large wardrobes near the windows blocked outdoor light from getting in. Flicking the light switch exposed a sad state of neglect. The condition of this room was worse than the others she had entered in the rest of the house. The wallpaper had possibly been in place since the first or second generation of Compton-Smythes. Its faded design revealed various shades of pink flowers on a background of pale green. High up, near the ceiling, it had peeled to droop limply down, and in the corners, areas of grey mixed with beige and brown mould. Cobwebs clung above the wardrobes, travelling up to anchor against the ceiling. The outside-facing walls felt damp.

After the noise and activity in the great hall, the room felt unnaturally silent. Clarice shuddered; it was bitterly cold, and as she looked out of the window, she breathed in the fusty, mildewed air of the neglected room. Running her finger along the windowsill made a clear line in the dust and dirt. If all four rooms were in a similar state of neglect, it was clear why none were viable for use by overnight guests. Thinking about the layout of the building, she had noticed some decay in the rooms directly below, but not to this extent. At least the downstairs rooms benefited from some form of heating. Here, what looked like an old pillow was stuffed into the fireplace to block the chimney, possibly to stop birds foolish enough to nest above from entering the room. Her mind moved to the opposite side of the central tower. Ralph had his office on the ground floor, and above were the bedrooms used by the family. She hadn't noticed the level of decay on that side; perhaps this wing of the house had problems with subsidence or a structural crack?

She moved around a stack of chairs, all damaged; why had Ralph not got rid of them? She remembered Emily repeating Colin's words to describe the rooms: *the cemetery for dead furniture.* Judging by the styles, they could be over a century old. Many appeared to have been part of a set; several had broken armrests or legs, and deep scratches probably made by cats. So a large number of chairs suggested that George or James, the first and second of the Compton-Smythes, must have held grand gatherings. Clarice imagined music, dancing and laughter in the great hall, or a long dining table laid with sparkling silverware and fine china, with the chairs seating the numerous guests.

There were double beds, abandoned sofas and armchairs in the next two rooms, the beds half buried under a jumble of unwanted cast-offs. The state of decay was in keeping with the first room, and furniture once cherished had been abandoned and stacked haphazardly, like junk. There were tennis racquets, a rolled-up tennis net, a doll's pram filled with damaged dolls, a train set and various other toys.

Clarice picked up a small blue box at random and recoiled as the bottom fell open, allowing glass marbles to escape. With horror, she watched as they crashed noisily to the floor. The noise continued as they rattled across the bare floorboards to roll in different directions. She froze to the spot, her stomach suddenly queasy with shock. After waiting for what felt like an eternity and hearing no approaching footsteps, she crawled around the floor to collect the marbles before dropping them into the pram.

The fourth room evoked a sense of poignancy. Although Clarice had never known Ralph and Ernestine's younger sister, she had felt moved by the story of her unnatural demise. Amongst the collection of junk was a small desk. Carved into the wood, in a wobbly style recognisable as a child's hand, was the name *Beth*. Clarice smiled; it would have to be Beth the naughty tomboy who would deface the desk; she could not imagine Ernestine doing such a thing.

As she ran her hand over the surface, she heard the door of the bedroom opposite quietly closing. Her breathing quickening, panic flushed through her body as she turned to leave. Too late; the door was thrown open.

'Found you, found you!' Ernestine, her face alight with glee, was before her. 'I'm the best at hide-and-seek.' She bounced up and down on the spot, clapping her hands like an over-excited toddler who'd eaten too many sugary sweets. 'Nobody can beat me.'

'Yes,' Clarice smiled, 'I can see that.'

'You haven't done it properly.' Ernestine was suddenly serious. 'You should have told me before you hid, and I would count to one hundred then come to look for you.'

'It's a long time since I played hide-and-seek,' Clarice said apologetically. 'How did you know I'd gone to hide?'

'I saw you going upstairs – you weren't in any of the other rooms I looked in.'

'That was clever.' She smiled. 'A process of elimination.'

'I've got nobody to play with now.' Ernestine looked sneaky. 'You can be my new friend; we can play together.'

'I came up to use the toilet; the one downstairs had a queue. We'll have to go back down now.'

'That was my little sister's desk.' Ernestine, suddenly distracted, walked to open the lid. 'She was very naughty and scratched her name on it, and she got into such trouble.'

'With your parents?'

Ernestine nodded. 'She was always Daddy's favourite. The desk was new; he told her in the morning to take care of it, and later, in the afternoon, he found she'd done that!'

'I suppose if it were brand new, he would be annoyed,' Clarice murmured.

'I was glad it was her turn, not mine again.' Ernestine looked self-satisfied.

'Why, were you always in trouble?' Clarice asked.

'It was usually about food.' Ernestine had wandered to the window. 'If Cook made cakes or biscuits and I took them without asking, Mummy said, "Ernestine, leave some for everyone else – you are a very greedy little girl."'

'All children like those,' Clarice said.

'Look, there's Tessa.' Ernestine pointed to where Tessa was walking away towards the stables. Clarice wondered if she had become bored playing the role of hostess.

'Does she often go for walks?'

'All the time.' Ernestine nodded. 'Ralph has to go with Johnson, because he can't see properly. Dawn walks in the woods sometimes.'

'At night?' Clarice ventured.

'The others walk at night. I don't do it very often.' Ernestine was suddenly serious. 'Ralph gets cross if I go out too late in the dark. He thinks I'll end up in some boggy hole.'

Clarice smiled, waiting.

'Ralph, Dawn, Johnson and Tessa – they've all gone out to find me, to bring me back, when I'm not really lost. It's very annoying.'

'It's good they care about you,' Clarice said.

'Yes, I suppose.' Ernestine became reflective. 'Dawn doesn't go out so much now since that man keeps turning up.'

'Ian Belling?'

'I can't remember his name. Dawn used to be his girlfriend, but she's not now. Dawn said he hates her.'

'That's not good.' Clarice was non-committal.

'Ralph said we must tell him if anyone spots him, so that he can phone the police.' Ernestine shrugged. 'By the time they get here, he's gone.'

'It must be difficult for Dawn.'

'Tessa thinks Dawn will inherit the house now that Colin is dead.'

'I expect she will. She's the second eldest,' Clarice said.

'But she's a girl. It always goes to the eldest boy; that's how Ralph got it!'

'I would think it could only go to Dawn or Emily. Dawn is the oldest, and anyhow, Emily is also a girl.'

'Tessa told Ralph that it's Dawn's birthright, but Ralph doesn't see it that way.'

'How do you think he sees it?' Clarice asked.

'He said, "It's not a done deal."' Ernestine's lips curved into a crafty smile as she imparted her knowledge, gained no doubt from eavesdropping.

'You think the house might go to Emily rather than Dawn?'

'How should I know?' She shrugged again. 'Are we going to play hide-and-seek, just one game? You've had your turn to hide; it's my turn now.' Her voice wheedled, and the sneaky look had returned.

'No, we must go back downstairs,' Clarice said kindly. 'If you remind me later, when the guests have left, I promise I will play then.'

'You'll forget.'

'No,' she led the way out, 'I won't, and there is still a lot of food downstairs.'

'I'd forgotten that.' Ernestine's steps quickened. 'I'm starving.'

On the way down the staircase, Clarice pondered. Dawn had talked about her inheritance as being assured. After Colin's death, she believed she'd be next in line to inherit. Emily had agreed. The decision was down to Ralph, but from what Clarice had just heard, he had not yet made a final choice. Since her arrival, working on the premise that Dawn would inherit, she had considered Tessa's belligerent attitude towards Emily odd. The response Ralph had apparently given to Tessa changed everything. Tessa's attitude was more understandable if she saw Emily as a threat to Dawn's expectations.

Clarice's thoughts moved back to the appalling state of the four bedrooms. As with other parts of the building, they would require a considerable amount of money to get them into good order. Would ownership of the property be a poisoned chalice?

Reaching the bottom of the stairs, she looked down at her clothes and quickly brushed away the dust picked up from crawling around the bedroom floor collecting the marbles.

At the buffet tables, Ernestine was pushing her way to the front of the queue. Clarice hoped that later, when the guests had departed, the old lady would have forgotten about her promise to partner her in a game of hide-and-seek.

Chapter 29

Finding her way to the kitchen, Clarice discovered a scene of turmoil, every surface piled high with plates, cups and glasses. The room was warm, and the windows were misted over. Mrs Fuller and Mrs Banner stood side by side, each like an identical reflection of the other, washing and drying plates.

'Are you all right, duck?' Mrs Fuller gawped at her as she might an odd museum exhibit.

'I'm fine,' Clarice said. 'I thought the caterers were cleaning up?'

'We decided to make a start,' Mrs Fuller said. 'My daughter, Kirsty, brought us here today. She went to the church and is out there having something to eat.'

'You won't have to cycle home in the dark?' Clarice asked.

'No, Kirsty will drive us.'

'Bet you're glad,' Mrs Banner moved her head, swinging all her chins, 'that our Christine pushed that table when she did. She saved your bacon.'

'I was extremely lucky,' Clarice said.

She stayed for a further ten minutes. It was clear that the sisters wanted to talk more about the incident, but with little new information, there was not a lot to add. She did not doubt it would be exaggerated dramatically over the weeks as it became village gossip. When she eventually escaped outside, she took out her phone. There was a text from Rick: *Call to let me know all is well.*

Walking away from the house, she decided to follow Emily's example and get some air. She headed towards the woods, remembering the last time she had gone there on her own; but this time, in the light, she told herself, it would be fine. Not having passed Emily, she assumed she might be back in the house.

The wind had got up and was whipping the grey clouds along; she could hear the movement of the branches above as she passed the old stables to enter the trees. She looked up at them as she walked. In the daylight, they revealed their secrets; naked of leaves, abandoned bird's nests, misshapen trunks and twisted limbs were exposed.

As she reflected, raised voices made her look about. Someone was shouting. She turned full circle, trying to catch from which direction the sound came. She heard it again, a high voice from near the stables.

'Don't you walk away from me when I'm talking to you!'

It was Tessa. As Clarice hurried back the way she'd come, she saw the door closing and could no longer hear Tessa's voice. When she reached the building, she pushed open the heavy door. Light spilled in through the gap in the roof, and the smell of damp and decay assaulted her.

'You can fill Dawn's head with all that shit – not giving a toss about inheriting the house – but I'm on to you, lady!' Tessa was growling. In the corner of the stables, Emily, looking terrified, had backed into what had been one of the horse boxes.

Tessa picked up the metal stake that Clarice had noticed earlier and waved it dramatically in the air.

'And you can drop the simpering act you put on for Ralph – *yes, Grandpa, no, Grandpa, three bags full, Grandpa*. It doesn't wash with me.'

Emily shook her head as if in denial, her lips moving but no words coming forth.

'You're in a special place there. That was Thunder's box – the horse that trampled your great-aunt Beth. How does it feel to stand on the spot where a little girl died?' Tessa cackled suddenly, at either the grotesque image she had created or the distress on Emily's face.

Quickly and silently, Clarice moved across the stable, slipping past Tessa to step between her and Emily.

'If it isn't Miss Nosy Bitch,' Tessa sneered when she spotted her. 'All that twaddle you came out with in church about Colin – what a load of shit.' She looked at Emily. 'And you – Daddy's pathetic little princess. Even your mummy left you behind when she moved on.' She watched to see her words hitting home.

'That is not true,' Clarice cut in. 'It's a sad fact of life that marriages break down. Emily chose to stay with her dad.'

'And you can stop cosying up to Ralph. He took you into his office before the funeral to tell you to sod off, and you wormed your way out of it.'

'He didn't ask me to leave, so I had nothing to worm my way out of.' Clarice shot the words back defiantly.

'Crap – and I bet you made up that story about seeing Ian Belling after the funeral just to try to get into Ralph's good books.' Tessa appeared to be determined to let rip with all her anger.

'We're going back to the house now.' Clarice moved sideways, holding Emily's arm.

'You can leave when I say so.'

'What do you want from Emily?' Clarice tried to moderate her voice to sound reasonable. 'You and Colin didn't see eye to eye, which was a shame, but Colin's dead – why don't you try to move on?'

'If Ralph didn't get you in his study to tell you to leave, I'd like to know what you *were* talking about. You were with him long enough. You're worse than *her*.' Tessa used the metal rod to point at Emily. 'You've been stirring up trouble, planting the seeds of mistrust in this family from the moment you arrived.'

'That was never my intention,' Clarice said. As she spoke, she pulled Emily closer to the door. Tessa moved sideways. Back and forth they went, as if engaged in a surreal dance. Then Tessa turned her head momentarily to look towards the door as it opened and closed. Clarice seized her chance to pull Emily past. Two steps further forward, a shadow loomed. Whoever had come in was directly in front of them, blocking their path.

There was a long moment of silence. Clarice sensed Tessa behind her, watching and listening.

'You do have a habit of being in the wrong place at the wrong time, Mrs Beech.' Johnson's Glaswegian voice was, as usual, dour. He stepped towards them into the light.

Clarice looked back at Tessa, then at Johnson. Her chest tightened. It felt like a replay of last night in the woods, but today she was trying to protect Emily.

Johnson moved slowly forward, then, stepping aside, he walked around them to put himself between them and Tessa.

'Your grandfather will be wondering where you are, Emily.' He spoke without turning.

'Stay where you are!' Tessa shouted.

'We'll have no more of this nonsense.' In one stride, Johnson was beside her, snatching the metal rod from her hand. 'Off you go, Emily.' He threw the stake into the corner, where it hit the wall before clattering to the ground.

As they walked away from the stables, they could hear Tessa cursing and berating him.

'She's so angry. She said it's my fault that she and Dawn have had a massive falling-out,' Emily whispered.

'That's nothing to do with you.' Clarice was firm.

'Dad saw her angry once as a child; it frightened him.' Emily glanced back as they moved quickly forward. 'Grandpa told Dad that Tessa keeps everything bottled up then can't control her emotions – she just ends up exploding.'

Walking in silence, Clarice thought about what had just happened. If Johnson had been working with Tessa last night to stalk her, why had he let her go now? He appeared to be protecting Emily. She needed to reassess his involvement with Tessa; if it wasn't the pair of them working together last night, who else could it be? Her thoughts went again to the man she'd seen in the woods when they first arrived, and earlier today, after the funeral: Ian Belling.

Emily led the way to the back of the house, going in through the kitchen door. They walked along the passage to come out at the bottom of the stairwell, where they both looked at the bronze sculpture. The noise in the great hall was like a wall of sound, making it impossible to talk.

Suddenly the clashing of metal rose above the clamour, over and over again, bringing an abrupt silence.

Clarice and Emily moved past the sculpture and around the edge of the staircase to find Ernestine standing on the fifth step. She'd raised herself high enough to be seen. In her hands were the metal lids from two saucepans, which she'd banged together like a pair of cymbals.

'Hello, everyone, I'm Ernestine Compton-Smythe, Colin's auntie.' Her voice was high and excited. 'Colin is dead, so I want to say a few words about my darling nephew.'

Clarice and Emily looked at each other.

'Oh my God!' In despair, Emily brought her hands up to cover her face.

'Hellfire,' Clarice muttered.

'Herrumm.' Ernestine cleared her throat and placed the saucepan lids down on the step beside her.

Looking at her, Clarice revisited her first impression of her as a flawless bone-china doll. The room was silent.

'I didn't say anything in church, so it's my turn now. Colin, my nephew, is dead. I was his favourite auntie. He was a lovely boy, he was special – just like his mother, Beth. Daddy's horse killed her. It was horrible, because there was a lot of blood, it was all over my dress, the one Mummy gave to Beth because it was too small for me … Colin didn't get kicked by a horse, but he is in a brown box in the ground next to Beth. They are back together. He won't like the dark. When he was little, he would wet his pants and sometimes—'

'Ernestine! What the hell is going on?' Ralph's voice reverberated around the hall as he came out of the door from the passageway leading to his office, followed by Dawn.

'I'm telling everyone about Colin.' Ernestine smiled with the innocence of a child.

'Stop making a bloody fool of yourself. Where the hell is Tessa?' Ralph strode towards her.

'I haven't finished, Ralph.' Ernestine's bottom lip drooped.

'Come on, Aunt Ernestine.' Dawn walked past her father to reach her first. 'Let's go upstairs for a lie-down.'

'I don't want to lie down. I want to talk about Colin. He didn't like the dark.'

'That was when he was a little boy, Aunt Ernestine, a very long time ago.' Dawn put her arm around her aunt's shoulders.

'But I haven't finished.'

'I have some sherbet bonbons in my room,' she said in a stage whisper.

'Have you?' Ernestine's face lit up. 'My favourites. Are they for me?'

'Yes, let's go and find them.'

Having watched the two figures disappear upstairs, Ralph turned to address the guests.

'I'm so sorry about that.' Standing where Ernestine had stood, he cast his eye over the depleted gathering. 'My sister has dementia. One of the many joys of old age.'

There was a weak ripple of laughter. As Ralph walked back down the stairs, people started to chatter again.

'Emily,' he stopped next to his granddaughter, 'it's just gone four o'clock. Tell the caterers to start clearing the tables. It'll give the hangers-on a nudge. Three hours for lunch is more than sufficient.' He turned to follow his daughter and sister upstairs.

Emily walked to each of the catering staff and spoke to them quietly; they nodded and began removing plates. A small gathering around the table holding the alcoholic drinks looked at one another with disappointment.

Clarice noticed that Albert Wilson seemed to have left. Taking out her phone, she texted Rick. *Everything OK here. Will fill you in on the details in an hour or two.* Having sent the message, she joined Emily in helping to clear the tables. As they worked, she told the young woman about her earlier encounter with Ernestine.

'No, that can't be true.' Emily could not hide her surprise on hearing what had been said about the inheritance of the house. 'It automatically goes to the oldest male, and if there isn't one, the oldest female.'

Still, as they continued stacking plates and glasses, Emily seemed deep in thought. Might she be thinking that her grandfather was considering changing the rule because he favoured her over Dawn, or was she worried that if Dawn were to find out there was a question mark over her inheritance, their blossoming relationship would falter? More fundamentally, did Emily really want to be stuck with the responsibility of owning Stone Fen Manor?

Chapter 30

As the caterers continued clearing up, Clarice saw Mrs Fuller and her sister emerge from the kitchen. A few minutes after they left, Tessa entered the great hall, walking through with a fixed scowl, and climbed the stairs, head down, hands clasped in front. She carried misery in every step. Johnson had taken up position by the front door, standing ramrod straight, arms folded, to watch the caterers load their van with trays and utensils.

It was an hour before Clarice and Emily went upstairs to their bedroom, each carrying a mug of tea and a plate of sandwiches. Having removed their shoes, eaten the sandwiches and drunk the tea, they lay wrapped in duvets on their beds.

'It's been a long day.' Emily yawned.

'Do you want to stay here and have a sleep?' Clarice asked.

'Just half an hour.' Emily turned on her side to look at her. 'Do you think Johnson will tell Grandpa about Tessa in the barn?'

'I don't honestly know,' Clarice said. 'I can't help but feel that Johnson is very dutiful; he does his best for his employer.'

'Grandpa – not Tessa?'

'Your grandfather is his employer. I doubt he'd stay if Ralph died before Tessa.' Clarice met Emily's gaze. 'Dawn said she wanted to talk when the funeral was over; we haven't had a chance yet. I wonder what she's told Ralph about our conversation – what she overheard.'

'Or what she might have asked Aunt Ernestine. She heard us talking about Ernestine seeing Avril leaving with Grandpa. It was the last time she was seen alive,' Emily said.

'Judging by the speech your aunt gave earlier, she'd mixed up Avril and her sister Beth. It must have been a bewildering day for her, with all the people, when she rarely sees anyone.'

'I just think she's lost the plot.' Emily sounded distracted. 'It must be difficult living with her when she has a bad day.'

'Tessa said much the same. In fairness, you'd have to be a saint not to get wound up by someone talking nonsense and constantly repeating themselves.'

Emily didn't reply. Clarice looked at her.

'It feels strange that it's all over – the funeral.' Emily was reflective. 'Since Dad died, I've felt as if I've been in a dream, but now it feels real.'

'Yes,' Clarice agreed. 'Colin's death was so sudden and unexpected, it's not surprising it took a while.'

'I still can't believe I'll never see him again,' Emily said. 'That sounds silly.'

'No, it's normal to feel that.'

'All the other family stuff hasn't helped,' she mused. 'I thought finding out what happened to Avril would be a distraction, and …'

Clarice waited.

'It gave me an objective – I thought I would solve the riddle for Dad …'

They lapsed into silence. Clarice lay on her back, looking up at the ceiling and contemplating. Emily had so many mixed emotions, and Tessa's aggression would not have helped her to deal with them. Her thoughts turned to Ernestine. She wondered if Avril leaving and waving with her pink-varnished nails had been something she'd witnessed – but not on the day Avril left Stone Fen Manor for the last time. Avril and Ralph must have gone out on many occasions when Ernestine saw them leaving. Had she drawn the wrong conclusion?

It was 6.30 when Emily decided to go back downstairs.

'I'm going to give Rick a quick call.' Clarice took out her phone. 'I'll see you down there.'

'I need to use the bathroom anyway. I'll wait for you at the bottom.'

It occurred to Clarice while pressing the button to dial Rick that Emily did not want to face the family alone.

'Clarice, are you OK?' Rick's voice was apprehensive.

'Yes, I'm fine. I got caught up earlier, and I then thought you might be working, so I've left it until after six.'

'I'm just leaving home with my overnight bag. I'm going up to Newcastle.'

'Why?'

'It's part of the nightclub murder case. The main suspect legged it; they've caught up with him in Newcastle. There's also a second man who might have been a witness to the stabbing. I'm going to interview both of them. It'll be late by the time it's all wrapped up, which means an overnight stopover.'

'Great that the case has moved on,' Clarice said.

'Never mind that; tell me how things have gone with you. I've been worrying about it all day.'

'Well ...' Clarice hesitated. She had been undecided about whether to tell him everything, even knowing it would upset him, or to hang onto some of the information until she got home. Knowing that he hated to be kept in the dark – he always preferred honesty – she'd decided to give him all the facts. But the news that he had a long car journey ahead and would be worrying about her while driving altered her decision.

'Funerals are always depressing,' she began. She told him about the service and Ernestine's wittering on the journey to the church, before repeating the information given to her by Albert Wilson and his sister Jane. Rick stayed silent until she'd finished.

'So apart from Ernestine driving you mad, everything is running smoothly?'

'You could say that.'

'Good.' He paused thoughtfully. 'I phoned an old friend earlier today, Graham Digby.'

'He was a sergeant in Lincoln the same time as you, and you played rugby together, for the police team,' Clarice recalled.

'That's him,' Rick agreed. 'He moved down to Spalding when his promotion to DI came through. I filled him in about what you're up to – just in case.'

'In case things here get messy.' Clarice felt guilty for withholding the truth; things were already messy.

'Phone and leave a message if you need to.' Rick spoke quickly. 'I'll have my mobile turned off during the interviews.'

'I will. Have a good journey.' She realised from his voice that he wanted to get on.

Going downstairs, she found Emily sitting on the bottom step.

The smell of food and alcohol still lingered, but the great hall was empty of people, the folding chairs arranged in lines along the walls on either side of the grand fireplace. As on the previous evening, the place was in semi-darkness, with just one light halfway along. Clarice followed Emily into the family sitting room, where there was a fire blazing. Walking in, they were immediately pounced on by Ben. Floss followed behind at a slower pace.

'Hello, we've not seen you since this morning.' Clarice scratched both dogs on the scruff of their necks.

'Been in Johnson's flat,' Ralph said from his chair by the fire. 'Too many people would confuse them. He's had them out for their walks.' He was nursing what looked like a whisky.

'Is everyone else still having a rest, Grandpa?' Emily asked.

'Johnson's around somewhere.' Ralph raised his glass. 'He just brought me this. Dawn was here a while ago. She's looking for Ruffian. Haven't seen Tessa or Ernestine.'

'Did you want something to eat? I could make you something.'

'No thank you. There are piles of sandwiches and picky things left over. They're in the kitchen if you're hungry.' He took a sip of his drink. 'Suggest you get in first, before Ernestine discovers them and starts working her way through.'

'Shall we go and help ourselves?' Emily turned to Clarice.

'I'm not desperately hungry, after what we had upstairs earlier,' Clarice said.

'No, me neither,' Emily agreed. 'Maybe later.'

'Why don't you sit down?' Ralph peered at them. 'I need to speak to both of you.'

They went to sit on the sofa opposite.

'Was Auntie Ernestine OK?' Emily asked. 'I was worried how confused she'd become, talking about your sister Beth.'

Ralph's forehead furrowed. 'She usually remembers things from the past quite clearly, while an event that happened the same day might get her in a muddle; it's the same thing I said about the dogs – too many people here. It confused her.'

'I thought that was it.' Emily nodded.

'I'm sorry about what happened with Tessa earlier.' Ralph cast his eyes downwards. 'When you were in the barn – you must have been frightened.'

'Johnson told you?' Emily asked.

'No, Tessa did.'

Clarice suspected that Johnson would have allowed Tessa an opportunity to tell Ralph herself, and that if she hadn't done so, he would have said something. The relationship between the three was complex.

'Did she say why she was so angry?'

'She didn't need to say why; it doesn't take a genius to work it out. She didn't get on with Colin. She was jealous of him, and you.' Ralph took another sip of his drink. 'It's been a trying few days for her; she and Dawn had a set-to earlier.'

'What about?' Emily asked.

'I think she feels that you and Dawn are getting on rather too well.'

'That can only be good,' Clarice interjected.

'Not to Tessa's way of thinking. She said she'd shouted at Dawn, another meltdown. She'll apologise and make up with her later.' Ralph stared down at his glass, looking every bit his age. 'She keeps everything bottled up, then her emotions just explode.'

'That's awful. Poor Dawn, being on the receiving end.' Emily's voice was trembling.

'Now don't you get upset.' Ralph peered at his granddaughter.

'Where is Tessa? Is she still upstairs?'

'She went for a lie-down. After the caterers left, Johnson took her up a pot of tea and some food. She went outside a while back to get some fresh air.'

'Oh. OK.' Emily sounded a little calmer.

'I don't think you've helped the situation, Clarice.' Ralph gave her a beady look. 'You asked Ernestine about Avril, encouraged her to talk about her. No good can come of it, raking over ancient family history.'

'It's me, Grandpa, not Clarice,' Emily said. 'I found information after Dad died about his continued search for Avril. I showed it to Clarice.'

'Well, I'll repeat what I said, no good comes of digging up something so painful to us all – Avril leaving.'

'With the Major?'

'My dear child, what have I just told you?' Ralph's eyebrows were locked in perplexity. 'I don't want to dredge up the past, and I certainly don't walk to talk about Major Freddie Baxter.' Agitated, he passed his glass from one hand to another. 'When Dawn and I took Ernestine upstairs earlier, after she'd made a complete ass of herself, Dawn practically accused me of murdering Avril – she asked me outright!'

Emily stared at her grandfather, her face flushing pink.

'Coffee and tea.' Johnson appeared, wheeling a small trolley into the room bearing the two ceramic pots, milk, sugar, cups and a plate of biscuits. He seemed to have a knack of arriving at tense moments.

'Everything OK?' Ralph asked.

Before he could answer, Tessa entered the room, having changed from the dark funeral suit she'd been wearing earlier into blue slacks and a thick cream-coloured sweater; she had also repaired her make-up. She paused for a moment, looking around. Ralph glanced at her meaningfully and nodded.

'I want to apologise.' Tessa's voice was soft; her eyes, like Ralph's earlier, were cast downwards. 'I behaved in a completely unforgivable way.' She turned to look at Ralph, and he nodded again. He had, Clarice realised, instructed her to apologise. 'It's been such a stressful couple of days, but it's all over and done now.' She pushed her fingers through her hair, sounding hesitant and awkward. 'I shouldn't drink alcohol. I had a couple of glasses of wine.' She turned to face Emily. 'I am so sorry, to all of you.' She waved an arm to include Clarice and Johnson.

'All over and done now,' Ralph repeated, looking relieved. 'Let's just move on and put everything behind us?' His voice held a question mark; his eyes, hopeful, were directed towards Emily.

'Yes, Grandpa, I want to forget about it too.'

'Good, thank you, Emily.' Tessa spoke quickly, as if trying to move hastily away from the topic. 'Have any of you seen Dawn, by the way? I can't find her.'

'I just told the girls that she came in earlier looking for Ruffian,' Ralph said.

'Yes, she locked him in her bedroom before the funeral. When she went up later, he'd gone. Someone let him out. Dawn was annoyed and worried. Why would someone go into our private part of the house to take her cat?'

'I know someone who might – bloody Ian Belling!' Ralph snorted with annoyance.

'He wouldn't have come into the house with all those people here,' Tessa said. 'Everyone knows there's a restraining order against him – and he would have needed to walk through the great hall to get upstairs. It would be only a possibility if he got someone to do it for him.'

'Sit down for five minutes.' Ralph made fussy hand movements towards a chair. 'Have a coffee first, then Johnson can go with you to look. It's not like Ruffian to stray far from Dawn's side. He must have got out accidentally. Having all those people here today has been disruptive.'

'We'll go with you,' Emily volunteered, looking at Clarice. 'I'm sure we'll soon find them.'

'Yes, of course,' Clarice responded, but her spirits sank. The thought of going out into the woodland in the dark, after the events of the previous evening, filled her with trepidation.

Chapter 31

A short while later, with Dawn not having returned, the group donned their coats, scarves and gloves. Johnson, wrapped in his padded jacket and scarf, was waiting for them in the great hall. He passed heavy-duty torches, similar to the one he'd used the previous evening, to Emily and Clarice, the beams of which would radiate a strong, broad light.

'Where's Ernestine?' Tessa asked.

'I saw her earlier,' Johnson said. 'She was going from room to room looking for Ruffian. She might have gone outside.'

'Oh God help us!' Tessa was immediately tetchy. 'It's bad enough searching for Dawn without having to worry about bloody Ernestine as well.'

'I did ask her to go and keep Ralph company.' Johnson nodded towards the sitting room. 'I'd hoped she heed the advice.'

'I'll head towards the main gate and take the circling route to the back,' Tessa informed them, regaining some of her haughty manner.

'We'll go into the woods to where the path divides,' Johnson said to Clarice and Emily, 'then split up. You two stick together; you don't know the woods as we do.' It was not a request, but an order.

Before leaving, Tessa stopped to take one of the blue waterproof jackets. Glancing at the pegs, Clarice saw there was only one left. Perhaps Dawn and Ernestine had the others.

Johnson turned to leave the house, taking long, measured strides. Outside, as they crossed the lawn, Tessa walked away from the group, heading towards the drive that circled round to the main road. Clarice thought about Johnson's instruction that she and Emily should stay together. Was he suggesting she was less of a target with Emily, or that Emily on her own might be given a hard time by Tessa?

As on the previous evening, it was bitingly cold, and the darkness closed around them. But yesterday she had gone out later in the evening; tonight the mist had not yet begun to build.

As they walked the now-familiar route past the stables, Clarice became lost in thought. The Compton-Smythes were such a strangely dysfunctional family. But while they often appeared to dislike one another intensely, they could show generous support. Tessa had been utterly vile to Johnson in the barn, yet after her outburst, he had taken tea and sandwiches to her private sitting room. The relationship between Ralph and Johnson was interesting. Two elderly men, one employing the other for over fifty years. Time had given them a bond in which words seemed redundant; they appeared almost able to read each other's thoughts. Remarkably, the relationship between employer and employee held no hint of servility. Although she didn't much like Johnson, it was obvious that he knew his worth and would not kowtow to anyone.

It was challenging to work Tessa out. Ralph calmly telling them that she had verbally attacked Dawn said something about his relationship with her. Dawn was his daughter. He appeared to accept that his partner might occasionally blow a fuse. Clarice could not help but ponder on how often Tessa had in the past shown verbal aggression towards Ralph; she had already seen some evidence of it. It was clear when Tessa had apologised that she had done it under duress; the apology did not feel honest, making it meaningless.

They continued in silence to where the path divided.

'I'll see you back here when you've worked your way around,' Johnson said, and then was gone, disappearing into the blackness, going towards the well and the pet cemetery. The light of his torch in the darkness appeared detached, bouncing like an errant fairy.

Clarice and Emily took the other route, swinging their lights from side to side. Stopping occasionally to listen, they made their way steadily around the pathway until it came out near the manor.

'Should we go back?' Emily asked.

'We said we'd meet Johnson at the fork.' Clarice looked to the path leading back through the trees. 'I hope he's had more luck than us.'

'Dawn may already be in the house.'

'We'll go back inside once we've seen Johnson,' Clarice said.

They walked back towards the manor to rejoin the path taken earlier. As they passed the stables, the screech of the barn owl startled them.

Emily let out a nervous giggle. 'It's really creepy at night.'

'Let's check in there.' Clarice led the way to the stables

and pushed open the door. The smell of damp and decay seemed more potent in the bleakness of the evening, and the appearance of abandonment and decline, as the torchlight picked out spider's webs and dust, made Emily's description feel apt. She noticed that the young woman held back, waiting outside, perhaps thinking about what had happened there earlier. Shining the torch into the box where Tessa had cornered Emily, Clarice saw that the metal stake had gone from where Johnson had thrown it. Had he perhaps hidden it in a place Tessa might not find?

Entering the woods, they moved quickly, and had covered half the distance to the junction where the path divided when, out of the darkness, a light danced towards them. The sound of feet crunching on the cold, dry ground came closer, and waving their torches over the figure, they recognised her.

'Aunt Ernestine,' Emily said as she drew close. 'We imagined you'd be back in the house.'

Ernestine stopped, looking from one to the other. She was wearing one of the blue waterproof jackets, but she had not zipped it up, and it hung off her shoulders. She was still dressed in the dark suit she'd had on for the funeral. They'd lowered the torches so as not to dazzle her, and Clarice was reminded of the gargoyles she'd seen the previous evening. The torchlight underlit Ernestine's face, her slightly slack mouth and empty-looking eyes adding to her appearance of menace.

'Are you all right, Ernestine?' she asked.

'Let me fasten this for you.' Emily stepped forward to pull the jacket closer around her aunt and zipped it up. 'It's freezing out here.' She pulled up the hood. 'You should have a scarf or hat.'

Ernestine stood still, watching her. Clarice, noticing that she'd dropped her gloves, bent to retrieve them.

'And you should be wearing those, not carrying them,' Emily said gently.

Ernestine looked from one face to the other. 'Ding dong bell,' she sang in a hoarse whisper, as if divulging a secret.

Emily glanced at Clarice, puzzled.

'Ding-dong-bell,' repeated Ernestine, before rushing past them, heading back towards the manor.

'What was that supposed to mean?' Emily asked, baffled.

'Ding dong bell.' Clarice repeated the words. 'Pussy's in the well.'

They both turned to look along the path along which Ernestine had come.

'Ruffian must have fallen into the well,' Clarice said.

They carried on at the divide, hastening along the path that Johnson had taken earlier. The mist had now started to build, and Clarice hoped they would be able to get back inside the house soon – and that Dawn might already be there.

Just before they reached the clearing, Johnson's outline bore down on them. He was carrying something in his arms while still managing to hold his torch, dazzling them.

'We need to get back to the house.' He moved forward in an attempt to herd them back, his voice hard and abrupt.

'Why, what's happened?' Clarice said. The sound of the high-pitched Siamese yowl alerted her to Ruffian, clasped in Johnson's arms.

'She's deed.' Johnson's voice, at its most Glaswegian, contorted the word.

'Dead?' Clarice repeated. 'Who? Dawn? Are you sure?'

'I said so, didn't I?' He looked from Clarice to Emily. 'Most of her brains are on the outside. Now go back, I don't want Emily to see, and I need to find Tessa before she comes out here.'

'Wait here, Emily,' Clarice instructed before skirting around Johnson.

'Can you not take my word for it?' he shouted angrily.

'No.' Clarice moved on, throwing the words as she ran. 'If there's even a slim chance she's alive and I didn't check, I'd never forgive myself.'

Advancing into the clearing, she felt her heart racing. Ian Belling's face came into her mind, pressed to the kitchen window, peering in. The torchlight picked up Dawn's booted feet first, then, moving up, illuminated one of the blue jackets kept in the hall. There was no possibility that she was still alive. Her prone body was spread-eagled, face down, her head touching the base of the well. The back of her skull was a mush of blood and bone, the blood having encircled her head, halo-like, spilling against the well's brickwork. The metal stake from the barn was next to the body. Clarice knelt to feel for a pulse; there was nothing. Dawn's wrist still felt warm, but she was dead.

'Come on.' Rejoining Johnson, Clarice took Emily's arm.

'Satisfied?' he snapped.

'Yes, you're right: we must get to Tessa before she comes out here.'

Clarice, pointing her torch, followed Johnson. Emily, remaining silent, allowed herself to be guided forward. In front of them, Ruffian continued his cry. Was he howling, Clarice wondered, in grief for his dead mistress?

Johnson muttered, cursing as he strode on. Clarice, digging into her pocket, found her phone.

'I'll call the police.' She addressed her words to Johnson's back.

'Do it.' He spoke over his shoulder without stopping. 'I've left my phone in the house.'

'Police, I want to report a murder.' Clarice continued to give information as they passed the old stables.

Johnson appeared to stagger as the house came in sight, then corrected himself to lead them back inside. He went through the darkened great hall, turning into the passageway and heading straight to the sitting room, Clarice and Emily trailing behind.

Ralph was still in his armchair. Tessa, alerted by Ruffian's yowling, rose from a nearby seat.

The dogs bounded over. 'Come here!' Ralph shouted, the fierceness of his voice making them obey the command. They went to stand near him.

'You found him. Ruffian, you are a very naughty boy. You've sent us all on a wild goose chase.' Tessa walked forward with her arms outstretched; Johnson placed the cat into them.

'I need to talk to you.' Johnson's voice cracked with emotion as he looked at Ralph, whose body immediately stiffened. 'It's Dawn,' he said.

'Why is this cat so wet?' Tessa, who had been returning to her seat, stopped, then moved her hand away from Ruffian, holding it out to show it red with blood. She looked closely at the cat. 'He's been in an accident. He's bleeding.'

'No,' Johnson said. 'It's not the cat. He wouldn't leave her; he was sitting on her body, crying.'

'Dawn?' Ralph stared from Tessa's bloody hand to Johnson.

'Dawn? No – don't be silly, Ralph,' Tessa chided him, incredulous.

'Is she badly hurt?' Ralph put his glass on the side table and stood up.

Johnson looked from Ralph to Tessa, unable to say the words.

'No – no!' Ralph shouted, while beside him Tessa appeared to fold, and was suddenly a crumpled heap on the floor, still clutching Ruffian.

'Clarice phoned the police on the way back,' Johnson said to Ralph as he walked past him to the door. 'I need to put the lights on and wait for them.'

Ralph nodded, as if in a daze, before going to kneel next to Tessa on the floor. In a rare show of intimacy, he put his arm around her. Her body shuddered as she turned to press her face against his shoulder, sobbing loudly.

Emily stood a few feet from Clarice, tears spilling silently down her cheeks. Her arms were wrapped defensively across her body, as if trying to protect herself from an invisible assailant. It felt to Clarice that time had momentarily stopped.

Tessa suddenly pulled herself up, her eyes filled with torment. Her face was streaked with tears and make-up, her hands still red with Dawn's blood. Ralph kept hold of her.

'There are rats, foxes, badgers out there.' She made an attempt to tear herself from her husband. 'I can't leave Dawn there by herself.'

'The police will be here in a short while,' Clarice said.

'The police are on their way,' Ralph repeated. 'You can't go outside; if he's still out there, he might attack you too.'

'That man – Belling,' Tessa mumbled.

Ralph nodded. He struggled to his feet before silently guiding Tessa to the chaise. They sat side by side, with her tightly clutching his hands.

For something to do, Clarice walked to the fireplace to rake the ashes with the poker and place more logs on the fire. Emily, brushing her face with her sleeve, went to sit opposite her grandfather and Tessa.

Looking around, Clarice recalled the small gathering here less than twenty-four hours earlier. She thought of the optimism in Dawn's voice when she'd agreed to act as a police witness. Then, her mind filled with images of the body on the ground near the well, she was engulfed by a feeling of utter desolation.

Chapter 32

At last, the door opened. Johnson came in, followed by two uniformed constables. Behind them, in a suit and tie, walked a heavily built man with short brown hair and a flattened nose: DI Graham Digby, Rick's colleague and erstwhile rugby buddy. He introduced himself and his officers, PC Danny Morris and PC Leanne Rickman.

Ralph introduced himself and everyone in the room.

Graham's eyes met Clarice's, and he moved his head slightly in recognition before addressing Ralph.

'Dawn was your daughter?'

Tessa looked at him, her eyes conveying the wretchedness of her grief.

'Yes,' Ralph said. 'Dawn was our daughter.'

'I am so sorry for your loss.' Graham paused for a moment before continuing. 'When they get to her, they'll erect a tent over her.' His voice was gentle as he looked at Tessa. 'And a police officer will be with her until she's moved – she won't be left alone.'

'I'll take you to the well.' Johnson had been stationary since they came in, standing behind Ralph's armchair, gripping onto its back, his fingers white.

'It's Mr Johnson?'

'Everyone just calls me Johnson. I work for Mr Compton-Smythe.'

'I see.' Graham studied him. 'We'll go outside and talk to the team.'

Johnson moved towards the door.

Ralph said nothing, but his eyes glinted, suddenly filled with unshed tears. Both his children were now dead. Clarice looked from him to Tessa, wondering how long their relationship would survive – but perhaps they were tighter as a couple than she'd assumed.

As Johnson left the room, he stopped to speak to someone in the hall outside. 'You should go in.'

Ernestine entered slowly, looking around like a sly, curious cat. Having changed into a skirt and matching pink sweater top, she fiddled with the necklace that, as usual, adorned her neck.

Graham, who had been following Johnson, stopped.

'I'm Ernestine.' She spoke to him as she walked towards him. 'I've got all my own teeth.' She gave the stretched smile.

'No, not now, Ernestine, please,' Ralph begged.

'You're such a big man.' Ernestine ignored her brother and eyed Graham, moving her gaze from his feet to the top of his head. 'You're as tall as Beth.' She pointed towards Clarice.

'Clarice,' Emily corrected her.

'She calls herself that now, but her real name is Beth.' Ernestine stepped closer to Graham, still staring. 'I met a man today with a snake on his head. I patted the snake, and it was warm.'

'Please, Ernestine, we don't need all this now.' Ralph rubbed his hand across his face, his voice feeble.

'I'm nearly eighty, and I'm slim. Mummy says I have a lovely figure.' She patted her stomach.

Tessa started to moan, quietly at first, the noise building. She turned on the chaise to press her face down, as if trying not to let the sound escape.

Ralph stood up. 'I'm going to phone our doctor.' He went to Emily, glancing back indecisively at Tessa. 'I don't want to leave her. Will you keep an eye on her?' he asked.

Emily appeared uncertain. Clarice thought she was probably questioning whether Tessa would allow herself to be looked after by her.

'Leanne, our PC, can stay here with your partner, Mr Compton-Smythe.' Graham nodded towards the female officer.

'I'd rather it was someone she knows.' Ralph was querulous. 'I'm quite blind. Johnson makes phone calls when necessary, but you need him outside.'

'Where is the number for the GP?' Clarice asked. 'I'll phone for you. You can stay here with Tessa.'

'It's a private number. My address book is in the top left-hand drawer of my desk in the office – under Arnold Maid.' Ralph spoke quickly. 'Please explain the situation – I know he'll come.' He went to kneel next to Tessa. His old body looked like a crumpled, discarded sack as he draped himself over her, whispering while gently stroking her hair.

Clarice left the room and made her way to Ralph's study. After being brought to the phone by his wife, Dr Maid listened as she explained the situation and Ralph's concern about Tessa.

'And how's Ernestine dealing with all that's going on?' he asked.

'Not well,' Clarice said.

'I'm not a bit surprised. Tell Ralph I'm on my way. I should be there within twenty-five minutes.'

Returning to the hall, Clarice found Graham talking to Johnson.

'I'll need you to guide me and the officers to the well. Can you find your way there through this mist?' he asked him.

'Yes.' Johnson nodded. 'No problem.' His expression was dour, as if he didn't relish the prospect of returning to the bloody scene. 'Tell me when you're ready to go.'

'Can we drive there, take a van with equipment?'

'You can't get a vehicle through the woods; the path is too narrow. You could take the one around the edge, approaching from behind the pet cemetery, but not at night. There's a lot of wet, marshy ground.'

'OK, wait at the door. I'll join you in a minute.'

As Johnson walked away, followed by PC Morris, Graham moved towards Clarice.

'Rick phoned me yesterday.'

'He told me,' Clarice said. 'I spoke to him earlier. He was just leaving for Newcastle.'

'The nightclub case he's working on?'

Clarice nodded.

'He doesn't know about this?'

'No. I phoned the main 999 police emergency line immediately after we found Dawn's body.' Clarice watched Johnson as he reached the door at the end of the hall. 'There's a lot Rick doesn't know, and I couldn't fill him in earlier because he had enough on his plate with his own work. I didn't want him driving for hours upset, worrying about me.'

'You can tell me everything that's happened when I get back.'

He had been professionally courteous rather than friendly. Wearing his police inspector's face. Clarice watched him walking away, knowing he would be talking to Johnson about getting a tent and lighting to the murder scene. He needed the team to preserve the area and safeguard the site for forensics.

'Did you reach the doctor?' Ralph asked as soon as she entered the sitting room.

'He'll be here within twenty-five minutes,' Clarice told him.

'Thank you,' he muttered.

Tessa had not moved, but she was now silent. Ralph had sat down next to her on the chaise again. Leanne, the PC, stood near Ralph's usual armchair, saying nothing.

'Emily has taken her aunt into the kitchen to make some tea,' Ralph told Clarice.

'I'll go and make sure she's OK.' She started to move back towards the door.

'Clarice,' Ralph spoke urgently, 'can you find something to occupy Ernestine until Dr Maid arrives? Please don't bring her back in here.'

In the kitchen, Emily was putting cups and saucers onto a tray. She turned as Clarice entered. The room was well lit, and the two rows of fluorescent lights seemed suddenly cold and dazzling after the muted light in the sitting room.

'Is the doctor here?' Emily's voice was hushed.

'Not yet,' Clarice muttered.

'Who?' Ernestine became animated. 'Is it visitors, someone to see me?'

'No, I'm afraid not.' Clarice spoke casually. 'Can you help Emily make some more tea? I'll take these, but we need a few more.'

'I don't know,' Ernestine said. 'If we have visitors, I'll have to entertain them. Daddy loves me to do that – he says, "Ernestine, you always *enchant*."'

'How do you entertain them?' Clarice asked, latching on to this as a distraction.

'Ralph plays the piano while I dance.' Ernestine's face lit up with the memory. She stepped away from the table and bent to lift the edges of her pink skirt. 'Da, da, da, de-dum, de-dum, de-dum.' She started to twirl around the kitchen, her tiny feet encased in their shiny patent-leather shoes tapping on the black, green and mauve tiles. Her head was back, looking up at the ceiling as around she went, again and again.

While she danced, Clarice relayed Ralph's instructions to keep Ernestine's attention and not allow her to return to Tessa. The doctor was on his way.

Finally Ernestine came to a halt.

'Bravo!' Emily clapped her hands, but Clarice noticed a flicker of contortion on her face. A woman lay dead in the woods with her head caved in, and they were pretending to be happy to occupy an elderly lady with dementia. It felt surreal.

'I'm a beautiful dancer.' Ernestine beamed happily, glad to be the centre of attention.

'Yes, you are.' Clarice smiled. 'I didn't realise that Ralph could play the piano or that you could dance.'

'Ralph wasn't very good; Mummy said he wouldn't practise enough. And Beth was sometimes a nuisance. When I danced, she used to follow me around, trying to copy me.'

'Little sisters do that,' Emily said. 'I expect she looked up to you – her big sister.'

'Yes, she did. Is there anything to eat?'

'Lots of sandwiches.' Clarice went to the old range to find two plates. 'Here we are.' She placed them on the table, taking off the paper napkins that had been covering them.

'Yummy.' The food immediately took Ernestine's attention. 'I'm starving – I didn't realise they were there.' She opened up the ends of several sandwiches before coming to the ones she liked. Taking them from the plates, she laid them in a row in front of her on the wooden table. 'Ham and cheese, my favourites.'

'Shall I take these teas?' Clarice whispered to Emily, who nodded. 'I'll be back in a tick.' She picked up the tray.

As she reached the sitting room, Tessa was following a white-haired man from the room. Ralph trailed behind, looking haggard and unwell. He hung back when he saw Clarice.

'That's Dr Maid. We're taking Tessa to her room. He'll give her sedation, help her get through tonight.' He glanced towards the kitchen. 'How is my sister? Driving you mad, no doubt?'

'Eating sandwiches,' Clarice said.

'I'll ask him to see her next. She'll be spinning into orbit all night if he doesn't give her something to calm her down.'

Clarice watched him shuffling away. He seemed to have become even more stooped, and she remembered Tessa coming in earlier from the old stables, carrying misery in every step. She could not help but feel sadness at the desolation at the heart of this strange, complicated family. Turning into the sitting room, she placed the tray on the side table. There was nobody there.

Chapter 33

Back in the kitchen, Emily had pulled up a chair to sit next to Ernestine.

'I've finished my sandwiches,' Ernestine announced when Clarice walked in, much as a child might tell her mother she'd eaten all her dinner. 'I want to go back to the sitting room, to the fire.'

'OK.' Clarice held the door open.

'Where is everyone?' Ernestine's lips drooped.

'Tessa's gone to bed,' Clarice said.

'What about that big man? I liked talking to him.'

'He'll be back in a minute or two,' Clarice told her.

A log had fallen forward, and the room had taken on the smell of the drifting smoke. Clarice used a poker to prod it back in place, and added another. Emily sat and patted the chaise next to her. 'Let's wait here for him,' she said to Ernestine.

Ernestine stared hard at her, considering the suggestion.

'Shall I sing you a song while we wait?' she asked.

'Why not?' Clarice said.

The songs were hymns, and Ernestine was word perfect with each. She stood up as though entertaining a large audience, her hands laced together across her chest, gazing at some distant point over their heads. After clearing her throat, she began with 'Amazing Grace', moving on to 'All Things Bright and Beautiful', and was just finishing 'Morning Has Broken' when Ralph returned with the doctor.

The two men applauded. 'Well done, Ernestine,' Ralph said.

'I've been entertaining everyone.' Ernestine spoke with solemnity.

'Sit down, my dear.' Ralph's voice was gentle. 'I have to tell you something – it's serious.'

'Oh dear, I don't like this.' Ernestine sat back on the chaise, looking worried. 'You said that when you told me Colin had died.' She peered at her brother.

'Yes – yes, I did.'

'Was it because I upset Tessa earlier? I'm in trouble – I'll say sorry.'

'No.' Ralph looked lost. 'When you were here earlier, I don't think you understood what had happened, why Tessa and I are upset.'

'Is Arnold here because Tessa is sick, like when Daddy died? He was ill, and the doctor came.'

'No, it's Dawn.' Ralph spoke as though trying to deliver the news before his sister wandered to another subject. 'Dawn is dead. She died earlier today.'

'Dawn!' Ernestine stared at him, her mouth slightly agape.

Ralph could not say anything more.

'It's a sad time,' Arnold said. 'Not just for Ralph and Tessa, but also for you.'

'It's Colin that died, Ralph.' Ernestine put her head to one side, speaking clearly. 'I know you think I get muddled, but I went to the church today. I had a ride in a lovely big car and I saw his coffin.'

'After that, my dear …' As Ralph moved closer, Emily stood and stepped away to allow him to sit next to Ernestine. 'After that, Dawn was killed while she was out looking for Ruffian.'

'Did Bellatrix take her because she tried to run away – or was it that man?' Ernestine looked around nervously.

'Which man?' Ralph asked.

'The one she used to go out with,' Ernestine said. 'I didn't much like him. I saw him in the woods.'

'Today?' Clarice asked.

'When I was looking for Ruffian.'

Ralph exchanged a look with Emily and Clarice. 'Are you sure it was today that you saw Ian Belling – in the woods?'

'Ian … who's that?'

'The man Dawn used to go out with,' replied Ralph, trying to be patient. 'You just said you saw him in the woods when you were looking for Ruffian.'

'I think it was today. Stop being cross with me, Ralph.' Ernestine's bottom lip quivered, as though tears were not far away.

'I'm sorry, my dear. I'm upset about Dawn.' Ralph patted his sister on the knee. 'We're going up to your room now, and Arnold is going to give you something to help you sleep.'

'I don't want to go to sleep.' Ernestine twisted her face like a naughty child. 'Dawn's dead. She'll be sleeping forever, and Colin's asleep in his brown box with the shiny handles. He won't be waking up.' She looked around. 'Shall I sing?' Her face suddenly lit up. 'I know a song called "Little Boxes".'

'No, Ernestine, no more singing.' Ralph was firm.

'What about Ruffian?'

'We found Ruffian, my dear. You don't need to worry about him.'

'I know that.' Ernestine was forthright. 'Dawn is dead, so that means I can have Ruffian. He'll be my cat. It's a long time since I've had one of my own – apart from Bellatrix.'

'We don't want to talk about that now.' Ralph, his face tense, looked at Arnold for help.

'Look, it's the big man. He's come back to see me.' Ernestine gawped excitedly past Clarice.

Graham was followed into the room by PC Rickman.

'Hello again,' he said to Ernestine.

'I've got all my own teeth.' Ernestine grinned at him to demonstrate.

'That's good.' Graham smiled back at her.

'I'm just going to give Ernestine something to help her sleep,' Arnold said. 'She has a heart condition. We don't want to overtax her.'

'I don't want to sleep. I told you that.' Ernestine balled her fists. 'I want to stay here with Ralph.'

'No, I'm afraid not,' Graham said. 'We need to speak to your brother alone.'

'It's not fair.' Ernestine started to cry.

'Let's walk upstairs together.' Ralph nodded at Arnold, who took Ernestine's arm to guide her out of the room. 'I'll be back in a few minutes,' he said to Graham.

As they walked her along the corridor to the stairs, Clarice could hear Ernestine's voice complaining noisily.

'Are you OK?' she asked Emily once it had gone quiet.

'Aunt Ernestine's been hard work,' Emily said. 'Too much has happened today. It's confused her.'

'Johnson told me she has dementia,' Graham said.

'She said she saw Ian Belling in the woods today when she was looking for Ruffian.' Emily looked at Clarice for confirmation. 'She might be mixing it up with another day.'

'Even if she is, she's not the only person to confirm Ian Belling has been hanging around in the woods,' Graham said. 'Do they often give her something to help her sleep?'

'No, not that often; only when she gets very confused. They've had to search for her after she's wandered away in the dark,' Emily said. 'Grandpa always goes with the doctor when she has to take pills, otherwise she'll pretend to take them, then get up and wander around again.'

Graham sat down to await Ralph's return.

'Is Johnson still out there?' Clarice asked.

'Yes, he's helping guide the crew to take everything to the well. We've left it all just outside the area. We don't want to trample the crime scene. We did see Dawn, though,' he added gravely. 'I need to talk to Ralph. Leanne, my constable, will sit in. I want to hear what he has to say while the memory is fresh, and the same applies to both of you.'

'Can I stay with Grandpa while you talk to him?' Emily asked. 'He's putting on a brave front, but he's in a bad way.'

'Yes,' Graham agreed. 'Just as long as he's happy for you to be in the room. Can I ask you a few questions while we're waiting for him?'

'Yes, of course.'

'Shall I leave you to it?' asked Clarice. 'I can have a cuppa in the kitchen.' Her eyes went to the tray she'd brought in earlier. 'That will be cold and stewed.'

'Yes, if you don't mind. I'll come to see you after I've spoken to Emily and Mr Compton-Smythe.'

Clarice picked up the tray to take it to the kitchen. Once there, she found her phone and called Rick. It went straight to voicemail. He would, she realised, probably be in bed, and had left the phone to charge. After leaving a message about Dawn's murder, she busied herself making tea.

Half an hour later, the kitchen door opened.

'Ralph's only just come back.' Graham raised his eyes. 'Apparently his sister was playing up. The doctor's left. They had to bribe her to take the pills.'

'With fudge?' Clarice asked.

'It'll be on the bedside table when she wakes.'

Graham looked at the empty mug.

'When we've finished with Ralph and Emily, I might have a cuppa,' he said cheekily. 'I suspect I'll find out a lot more from you, Clarice, than anyone else.'

'I'll make you one when you get back,' Clarice agreed. 'Have you heard anything about Ian Belling?'

'They've picked him up.' Graham gave her a long look. 'It's common knowledge; he was at a busy village pub in Sealsby, five miles from here.

'So he's having his clothes checked for possible blood and DNA,' Clarice pushed.

'It's early days.' Graham was non-committal as he left.

Clarice felt that mix of confusion that came when she knew someone well as a friend, but police business kept her on one side of a line she couldn't cross. Graham and Jenny, his wife, had been friends when they lived in Lincoln, going out for the occasional meal together. Due to Rick and Graham's long working hours in different parts of the county, however, they had seen less of one another over the years. If Rick were here, he would have told her, in confidence, what progress was being made, but she couldn't expect Graham to do that. She would have to rein in her nosy nature.

She settled back in her chair. It might be a long wait before Rick returned her call, or Graham came back to interview her.

Chapter 34

'I'm ready for that tea,' Graham said to Clarice when he finally strode into the kitchen.

'How did it go?' she asked.

He gave her a guarded smile. 'You know I can't share information with you, Clarice. Although I know you well enough to believe you had no involvement in Dawn's death, you are still potentially a suspect.'

'Can you move her body yet?' Clarice looked over her shoulder as she filled the kettle. 'That can't be giving me too much information.'

'The pathologist and SOCOs are on site.' Graham was blunt. 'They won't be able to move it until it's light enough to get a vehicle in to drive around the back way. It'll only be a few hours now.'

Clarice nodded as she popped a tea bag into a mug.

'Emily wants a quick word with you. Go and see what it's about, then come straight back,' Graham said. 'I think I can manage to make myself a cup of tea.'

As Clarice arrived in the sitting room, Ralph and Emily were preparing to leave.

'We're going to Grandpa's private sitting room – it's opposite his study.'

'Yes, I remember you pointing it out.'

'I expect you're up next for an interview?' Ralph said.

'Yes,' Clarice said. 'He's waiting for me.'

'I just wanted to tell you I'll be with Grandpa,' Emily said. 'Don't worry about me.'

'Tell the police officer he can use this room for your interview if he prefers it to the kitchen – it's warmer.'

The log basket next to the fire had been filled, probably by Johnson. Clarice noted that for the time being, Ralph appeared to have ditched his parsimonious ways.

Returning to the kitchen, she told Graham what Ralph had suggested, and he grabbed his mug of tea and moved with alacrity back into the sitting room.

'This house is bloody freezing,' he said, throwing a couple more logs onto the fire before settling himself in Ralph's armchair.

Clarice sat opposite on the chaise.

'I'm assuming you've left a message for Rick?' Graham spoke once he was settled.

'It went straight to his voicemail service.'

He nodded. 'Leanne will come and join us in a minute. Before we get to Dawn, Rick told me yesterday that Emily wanted to find out more about Avril, her grandmother – she'd gone missing, I gather.'

Clarice nodded. 'Yes, fifty years ago.'

'Can you go through it from the beginning, and then tell me everything that has happened since you arrived here?'

'No problem.' Clarice started with getting to know Colin

at the ceramics classes, and Emily giving her his box to go through.

As she spoke, there was a low tap on the door and Leanne looked in.

'Come in and join us,' Graham said.

Once she was seated, Clarice continued. Graham didn't speak again until she'd brought him up to the present moment.

'That is a sad and complicated tale.' He sat stroking his chin. The silence stretched for several minutes. 'My concern is with the murder of Dawn Compton-Smythe; I can't be distracted by a murder that *might* have happened fifty years ago – unless it had some connection to Dawn's killing.' He looked at Clarice for a few moments, his face inscrutable. 'From what you've told me about the metal cat sculpture falling, and being stalked in the woods, you might be in danger.'

'Yes.' Clarice got up, suddenly agitated, remembering Dawn's bloodied, battered head. She paced back and forth.

'Where are you going to be until it's light?' Graham looked at his watch. 'It's gone two now. If you want to go to your bedroom, Leanne could sit with you.'

Clarice had been turning over the options before he asked the question. With Emily downstairs with her grandfather, she would be alone. The bedroom, at the top of the tower, away from the rest of the house, might isolate her and give the murderer a fresh opportunity. But she didn't want an officer with her; she needed space to mull over the events of the last forty-eight hours.

'It's been manic since I arrived here.' She spoke at last. 'I've had zero time to think and put my thoughts in order. I've a couple of things to collect from the bedroom, then I'll settle in here. It'll be good to have some time alone.'

'You sure you'll be OK on your own?'

'Yes, absolutely.'

After Graham and Leanne had gone, Clarice went upstairs, retrieving from her bag the notes she'd made from reading Colin's notebook. Downstairs again, she moved to the sideboard. The photograph album was still where Emily had left it. She put it on the table next to Ralph's armchair, and after going to the kitchen for a glass and helping herself to some brandy, she threw a log on the fire.

Settling into the armchair and wrapping the red-checked rug across her legs, she opened the album.

Avril stared out at her from the photographs, with Colin standing nearby looking up at her adoringly. She went again to the family groups, some with Ralph and others that included Ernestine. There were several photos of Ralph and Avril, their arms linked, in foreign locations; one looked like St Peter's Square in Rome, another had the Eiffel Tower in the background. Clarice remembered Albert Wilson, after the funeral, talking about Avril's love of foreign holidays. Working through the pictures taken at home, she saw that Johnson was not in any of them, and she imagined that it might have been him behind the camera, watching and recording the visual images. Not so different from when he lurked in doorways, listening, storing away information.

From the moment she'd arrived, she'd sensed Johnson didn't trust her. She was the enemy; but why? She put the album aside and leaned back in the chair, bringing her knees up to wrap the woollen throw tighter and close her eyes.

Had he been told that she and Emily had been digging into Avril's past? If so, by whom? The only people aware of their quest were Dennis Simpson, Avril's sister Pamela, and Pattie Freeman. Although having got to know Johnson's attitude over the last forty-eight-hours, what she had taken as hostility might just have been his sceptical nature. He had been following her in the woods, but he had also led her back to the safety of the house.

Her notes reminded her about Colin's observations on each individual. One Christmas, as a small child, he'd watched his father and mother dance cheek to cheek, a fond recollection. His view that his father had a nasty temper was echoed by what Emily and Pamela had said. But Clarice had not found Ralph to be as extreme as she'd been led to believe. His hackles appeared to go up with the mention of Avril, but he'd been reasonable in allowing her to talk in church about Colin, and had sought her advice about his dog.

She made a mental list of what people had said about Avril, where their recollections agreed and where they differed. Pattie had pointed out that Avril loved shoes and dancing, and there had been a common thread regarding jewellery. When Colin had itemised shoes and clothes in his lists, did it mean he was making some kind of comparison? What had been his purpose?

Colin had disliked Tessa, which was hardly surprising. Tessa was defensive, bitter and angry. She had been quick to take another woman's place – possibly imagining Ralph would seek a divorce and marry her. The breakdown of Ralph's marriage to Avril was feasibly due to her discovery of an affair. Emily still believed that it might have been with Tessa. Dawn had been clear that this was not the case; it was anyway irrelevant. The critical issue was not who he'd had an affair with, but what had happened to Avril. The thought that her remains were in the well and that Ralph had been the one to put them there had become lodged in Clarice's mind. But why? What had happened or been said to make her suddenly now feel so sure?

Ernestine was hard to slot into a set type; her dementia made it difficult to know what to think of her. She craved attention and gained it by saying or doing outrageous things. But she had given more away with her macabre sense of humour than she had through the confusion of her dementia. The knowledge that Ralph had known Tessa before meeting Avril might be significant, and Clarice also remembered Ernestine's innocent ramblings in the car on the way to the funeral about the death of her favourite cat. The image came to her again of a perfect china doll. Ernestine dancing in the kitchen, holding the hem of her skirt, twirling in circles while her small feet moved around the floor.

She worked through, examining every conversation, sifting sand to find a hidden gem. There were also confrontations she been told about but had not witnessed, between Tessa and Dawn, and Ralph, Dawn and Tessa. She could only surmise the content.

There had been conflicting accounts about the Major. Clarice did not believe everything Albert had told her. His dislike of the man was probably motivated by jealousy. He had been keen on Janice, but his feelings hadn't been reciprocated.

She got up to pace back and forth, as in her mind she shifted the pieces of the jigsaw around. Then, stopping in front of the fireplace and looking down into the dying embers, she knew that understanding had finally come.

Hearing movement in the hall outside the door, she went to investigate. Two young male officers, a constable and a sergeant, were walking past.

'All right?' the sergeant asked. 'The boss said to keep an eye on things out here.' He allowed his gaze to travel along the corridor, past the kitchen.

'I'm fine, thank you.' Clarice returned to the sitting room. She felt edgy; her head and back ached. At the window, she moved the heavy curtain to look outside, staying there for a while to watch the movement of bobbing torchlight. Then, coming to a decision, she put more logs on the fire, before lying down on the chaise, placing a cushion behind her head and covering herself with the blanket. It was nearly 4 a.m. Her last thought was that she only needed to stay awake for a couple more hours.

She awoke with a start with light coming into the room. Her phone, nearby on the floor, was ringing.

'Clarice.' Rick's voice was tense. 'I've just picked up your message. Are you OK?'

'I'm fine.' She spoke quickly, filling him in on everything that had happened.

'Hellfire, why didn't you tell me about the stalking and the bronze statue yesterday?'

'You were just setting off for Newcastle. I didn't want you worrying about me.'

'And do you really believe I would have gone if I'd known what was happening at your end?'

'You had to – it's your job.'

'I would have asked someone else to go in my place.'

'Did it all work out yesterday?'

'Yes, one man is being charged with manslaughter, the other with aiding an offender. Anyway,' Rick changed track, 'never mind that. Have you told Graham your theory – what you've just told me?'

'No. I worked it out after he'd left, and I know he won't want me poking my nose into police business.'

'I don't blame him; he's a professional and has a job to do.' Rick was curt. 'You must tell him what you've told me, at the first opportunity, but then step back, don't interfere.'

'Yes,' Clarice said. 'I understand.'

'I'm just about to leave. The earliest I'll be with you will be about nine thirty.'

After he'd rung off, Clarice gathered her paperwork and made her way upstairs to the bedroom.

The house felt even colder this morning, if that were possible. Perhaps, with the police coming and going, the main door was being left open. On the way up, she glanced at the door that led to Tessa's room, and at the corridor where Ernestine had her bedroom, imagining them both still to be asleep.

In the guest room, she found Emily wrapped in a duvet and propped up by pillows, absent-mindedly plucking at the corner of the duvet as she looked at her phone.

Chapter 35

'What time did you go to bed?' Clarice asked.

'I came in here to see if I could sleep maybe two hours ago.' Emily sat up, swinging her legs from the bed to the floor. 'Grandpa wanted to talk; then we just sat together quietly. I didn't like to leave him alone.' She looked devoid of energy. As if she had nothing left to give.

Clarice sat on the bed to listen.

'The police were back and forth all the time. I could see lights through the window and hear their voices.'

'What about Johnson?'

'He came in a couple of times, asked Grandpa if he was OK, then went back outside to help the police.'

'Has your grandfather gone to bed now?'

'Yes.' Emily nodded. 'We came upstairs together. He says he'll have a lie-down for a few hours. Tessa and Ernestine will be up and about soon.'

'Yesterday was a very sad day for your grandfather.' Clarice grimaced.

Emily looked pale and listless, her eyes going back and forth from Clarice to the blank screen of her phone distractedly.

'Ernestine was hard work, but Grandpa did say that when she's had the medication, she's generally calmer the following day.' She stared hard at Clarice. 'Grandpa was upset by Dawn accusing him of killing Avril.'

'That's pretty much what he told us before we went out searching for her.'

'Clarice,' Emily looked at her with pleading eyes, 'I never knew Dawn that well, and I'm sorry she's dead, but I don't think I'll be able to bear it if it were Grandpa who killed Avril.'

'I know,' Clarice said.

'I didn't realise that I loved him until last night.' Emily's eyes were filled with tears of desperation. 'The relationships with Dad's family have always been so horrid, I never connected the word love to any of them.'

'What did your grandpa talk about?'

'He mentioned Avril's name for the first time without being asked.' Emily gave a weak smile. 'He told me she was a gentle soul who was incredibly thoughtful and kind.'

'It sounds like Pattie got it right. Do you think he cared about her?'

'He said that he loved her but let her down.'

'The relationship she found out about?'

'He didn't say that; just that he had failed her. It has to have been with Tessa.'

'Does that matter after all this time?' Clarice asked. 'Everything points to it being Tessa, with her moving in so quickly after Avril's departure. But whoever the affair was with was only relevant as the catalyst – the reason that prompted Avril to go, that set other things in motion.'

'I wanted to ask, but I couldn't, not outright: "Grandpa, did you kill her?"'

Clarice didn't answer, and they sat in silence for a while.

'I'm going to use the bathroom, then go down for something to eat,' Clarice said eventually. She retrieved her toilet bag and went to leave.

'What were you thinking about?' Emily stared at her.

'I think we should talk later today to bring everything into the open,' Clarice said. 'No more secrets.'

Walking down the stairs, she stopped at the window on the next floor down to look outside. The sun had risen and the frost-covered ground sparkled. She thought about Dawn and the manner of her death. She had hardly known her, but had found her to be a far better person than Colin had believed; their lives had been locked in an endless cycle of acrimony. It felt sad that Colin, so empathetic with his friends, neighbours and classmates, could not have bridged the divide between himself and his half-sister. Although with Tessa in the mix, it might have proved impossible.

A sense of guilt prickled. She had not been able to protect Dawn. If she had only been able to put the jigsaw together sooner …

Johnson passed her on the stairs. 'Breakfast is in the kitchen from the heated trolley – tell Emily.' In an instant he was gone, not waiting for a reply.

Emily took her turn in the bathroom before they went down for breakfast together.

On the pine table in the kitchen, knives and forks had been placed in cups, sticking upwards. Nearby, on top of the heated trolley, was a pile of plates. The room held the smells of coffee and bacon. A Calor gas heater had been lit and stood at one end of the room, making a hissing noise and taking the edge off the cold.

'Johnson's been hard at work.' Graham pointed to a cafetière.

Clarice poured coffee into two mugs, handing one to Emily. 'That's decent of him.' She looked around. 'No sign of the family yet?'

He looked at his watch. 'Give them time.' He downed the remains of his own coffee. 'I'm giving everyone the same information. Nobody will be able to leave the house after nine this morning. If you want to go outside for a breath of air, do it straight after breakfast. And don't go in the direction of the old well. Each household member must come for their interview when asked. Come sooner if you prefer, and wait in the sitting room; it's the warmest place. Or stay in your bedroom until you're called. The interviews will take place in Mr Compton-Smythe's study from 9 a.m., and will be recorded.' His phone rang as he spoke.

'Can I talk to you before then?' Clarice asked.

'It'll have to wait, Clarice; you'll have your chance to talk later.' He left holding the phone against his ear.

'Having Ernestine and Tessa cooped up together is going to be hell,' Emily said.

'Tessa will probably stay upstairs. I imagine Graham is trying to be sensitive. Ralph and Tessa have just lost their daughter in the most horrible way; they can hide in Tessa's private sitting room until they're asked to come down.'

'Losing her daughter won't make Tessa hide away.'

'Really?'

Emily deliberated. 'We'll see – you don't know Tessa like I

do. She's the most combative person I've ever met – hates to miss anything.'

Ten minutes later, they were sitting at the large kitchen table, having chosen eggs, tomatoes and beans from the trolley. Emily wore an overlarge blue sweater, the sleeves long enough to cover most of her hands. Only her fingers were visible, holding the fork to push baked beans around her plate. She stared broodingly at the gas heater. Although she had brushed her hair, she'd not applied her usual make-up, making her complexion appear pallid, and the limpness of her movements reflected her mood.

'No appetite?' Clarice asked.

'No.' She placed her fork onto the plate. 'Everything is such a mess. I came here to bury Dad – now Grandpa has lost both his children.'

'It's not your fault,' Clarice told her. 'There was nothing you could have done to prevent Dawn's death.'

'Do you know if they've arrested that man – Ian Belling?'

'He was taken to the police station yesterday evening; they found him at the pub in the village.'

'How could someone possibly feel that much hatred?' Emily's voice wobbled with passion.

'When relationships turn sour, there's so much bitterness and anger. It happens more often than you'd imagine,' Clarice said.

'But to kill someone so cold-bloodedly ...' Emily sounded deeply shocked.

'Let's wait to hear from Graham,' Clarice said quietly.

After they'd finished eating and had washed the plates and cups, Clarice suggested that they go out to stretch their legs.

'We obviously can't go down the path towards the well. Let's do a couple of laps around the house, passing the old tennis court at the back.'

In the great hall, they met Johnson returning to the house. He was looking down as he walked, and didn't see them until the last moment. He was wrapped in his usual outdoor attire, his dark woollen scarf showing from the top of his jacket. Like Ralph, he appeared to have aged in the last twenty-four hours. His face and voice gave nothing away, but his demeanour had lost its self-assurance.

'You won't be able to go down to the area where the police are working.' He was abrupt.

'We're just going to walk around the boundary of the house,' Emily said.

'It's cold out there.' He looked towards the door.

'Is Grandpa up yet?'

'I've taken him his breakfast in bed.'

'He's not himself. He's even more of a grouch,' Emily said, watching Johnson walk through the hall towards the kitchen.

'It would be very odd if he weren't upset,' Clarice replied. 'And from what you said, he didn't go to bed at all. He's not a young man; he'll need some rest.'

'I hadn't thought about that,' Emily said quietly.

Once outside and away from the house, Emily came straight to the point.

'Were Dawn and Auntie Ernestine wearing identical jackets? I didn't see Dawn after …' Emily's voice trailed away.

'Yes,' Clarice confirmed. 'They were both wearing a blue jacket from the hall.'

'Do you think Ernestine was the real target, then, rather than Dawn?'

'That had occurred to me.'

'And?'

'I don't think it's relevant, if you look at the height difference.'

'In the mist, the murderer might have been confused.'

'I don't think that's what happened.' Clarice moved forward, pushing her hands deep into her pockets.

Emily gave her a curious sideways look and followed.

When they reached what used to be the tennis court at the back of the house, they stopped. Clarice's thoughts went to yesterday afternoon, when she had stood here with Dawn talking about Victorian Gothic architecture. There had been passion and enthusiasm in Dawn's voice as she spoke. Now Clarice and Emily stood looking around, both listless, the cold air pressing against their exposed faces and creeping through their clothing.

'Do you want to go back inside?' Emily asked a few minutes later as they drew near to the entrance.

'Let's do one more lap; I want to clear my head.' Clarice checked her mobile phone. 'There isn't much time before the interviews start.'

As they spoke, a large white van came through the trees and stopped. Graham appeared from the house and climbed in, and the vehicle moved slowly back into the woods and disappeared from sight.

The two women exchanged a look, neither speaking. They were both aware that Dawn's body was due to have been removed at first light, three hours earlier. Perhaps Emily too was wondering where Graham was now going.

They walked unhurriedly around the building again in silence. So much had happened in the last two days, leaving Clarice feeling drained, her body aching with tiredness and tension. It was clear that Graham would be too busy to speak to her before the formal taped interview, and when he did, would he be prepared to take her theory seriously?

Chapter 36

Coming back into the hall with Emily, Clarice recognised the white-haired doctor from the previous evening sitting waiting.

'I've come to check on my patients.' Arnold Maid spoke to the constable introduced yesterday as Danny Morris. 'Ralph asked me to come back this morning.'

'Thank you, Doctor,' PC Morris said. 'You were expected. One of the officers will give you a shout when we've finished the interviews. They'll be running a bit late.'

Clarice thought of Graham getting in the van a few moments earlier. She doubted they would start the interviews until he arrived back.

It was exactly nine when they entered the sitting room. Outside in the corridor, Leanne and another PC were huddled together talking quietly. The fire had been banked up with logs, and chairs had been arranged around it. For the first time since she'd arrived, Clarice saw that Johnson, rather than waiting in attendance, was sitting with the family. Another armchair had been moved near to Ralph's to accommodate Tessa. Sipping from a teacup, she looked pasty and lifeless.

Clarice wondered why they were all here when Graham had suggested they might go elsewhere and come when called.

The room felt warm. As well as the open fire, the Calor gas heater, previously in the kitchen, gave a low hiss from the corner. Two ceramic pots and discarded cups stood on trays on the sideboard.

Ernestine, in a bright ochre-coloured sweater and black skirt, sat on the chaise. She was chattering as they arrived. Open on her lap was a nearly empty box of fudge that she dipped into while talking.

'Emily and Beth.' Ernestine pointed in delight.

'This is Clarice.' Emily corrected her again.

'You can't have my fudge.' Ernestine put her hand over the open box. 'I haven't got much left. I can't share it.'

'Ernestine, nobody wants your blasted fudge.' Ralph spoke sharply to his sister.

Emily indicated two straight-backed chairs near the sideboard. They each moved a chair to include themselves in the family circle around the fire.

'We understood you'd be in your sitting room, waiting to be called.' She looked from her grandfather to Tessa. While her eyes were knowing, her voice managed to convey a hint of surprise.

'We decided to come and wait in here and get our interviews over with first. *She* was already here.' Tessa indicated Ernestine as she placed her cup on the small side table next to her. 'And you, Emily, kept poor Ralph up half the night with your wittering.'

'Tessa, I told you, we could have spoken to the inspector first even if we'd waited upstairs.' Ralph kept his voice low and even. 'And you know that Emily did not keep me up; she kept me company.'

Tessa snorted and looked towards the logs burning in the grate.

'We talked about Avril last night.' Emily's voice was high, and a pink flush rose up her neck, creeping into her cheeks. 'Grandpa told me she was a gentle soul, thoughtful and kind.'

'We don't want to hear about that damn woman at a time like this!' Tessa snapped.

'Perhaps, Emily, this is not the most appropriate time.' Ralph's eyes swivelled from Tessa to his granddaughter.

'When *is* an appropriate time?' Emily was defiant. 'Dad waited fifty years, and the time was never right.'

'I've just lost my daughter.' Tessa dabbed her eyes with a tissue.

'And I am genuinely sorry about that.' Emily was not going to be silenced. 'I got to know and like her over the last couple of days. I think we might have become good friends.'

'Rubbish.' Tessa looked at Clarice. 'It's *her* bloody fault that I argued with Dawn. She had no right to go poking around in family business, stirring up trouble.'

'I asked Clarice to look at the information Dad had saved about his investigation into Avril's disappearance.'

'What information?' Ralph turned his attention to Clarice. 'Emily mentioned that yesterday – what bloody information!'

Clarice looked at each of the faces in turn. Ralph's was grey and unwell, while Johnson stared blankly at the floor, avoiding eye contact; his head seemed to have shrunk uncharacteristically into his collar, like a creature becoming smaller to be unobtrusive. Tessa appeared to be boiling over with anger, perhaps as an outlet for her grief. Ernestine's eyes darted from one person to another, her jaw moving as she chomped on the fudge.

'Dawn described Avril's disappearance as "the elephant in the room". Everyone was aware of how passionately Colin wanted to discover what had happened to his mother. Everything begins with and leads back to Avril.'

Tessa's head lifted at the mention of her daughter's name, but said nothing.

'I asked you what information,' Ralph snapped.

'After Colin's death, Emily asked me to go through a box of his things. Having done that, she invited me to come here for his funeral.'

Emily looked straight ahead as Clarice spoke, her face still resolute, although her neck and cheeks now revealed a full scarlet flush.

'The box contained a report from a detective agency, a postcard, a locket, two photographs and a notebook.'

Ralph leaned forward.

'The first thing that struck me as odd was why Avril would leave the locket, which contains a photograph of Colin as a baby. She's wearing it in every picture that I've seen after he was born. If she had gone away with the Major, she would have taken it with her.' Clarice paused briefly to allow this to sink in. 'It was so incomprehensible that it drew me into the mystery of her disappearance.'

Apart from the hiss of the heater, the room was soundless.

'Emily and I went to visit Dennis Simpson at the detective agency in Lincoln. He could offer us no further information other than what was contained in the report. But you knew about the agency, Ralph.' Clarice turned her gaze to him.

'Colin didn't tell me!' Ralph said, his tone sharp.

'You mentioned it to us at lunch on the day I arrived here. What was it you said to Emily?' She waited for a moment. 'Something about how Colin could have engaged a dozen agencies, but if his mother didn't want to be found, she wouldn't be.'

Ralph glowered.

'That was far too good to be a shot in the dark. You knew that Colin had contacted the agency, because someone told you.' Clarice left another pause, but Ralph remained silent.

'Then there was the postcard. Colin was disappointed with the report's findings. He went to an address in Roundhay, Leeds, where Janice, Major Freddie Baxter's wife, lived. According to his notes, he stayed overnight in Leeds and sat in his car for hours over two days to watch Janice's comings and goings.'

'Silly boy, wasting his time,' Ralph spluttered.

'He spoke to Janice when she left the house. She told him to go away.' Clarice straightened in her chair. 'He couldn't leave it, and kept going back until she agreed to a meeting, which she later cancelled by sending the postcard.'

'I'm not surprised she told him to go. She might have complained to the police if he'd kept it up.'

'Yes, that's what Janice said she would do. My theory is that she agreed to meet him to give her and the Major a bit of space, so he could go away for a while until Colin had given up.'

Ralph regarded her, his expression sour.

'Once her husband was well out of the way, she cancelled the arrangement. I expect the Major told you all about it?'

'Why would that man contact me? I'm the last person in the world he would have wanted to speak to.'

'Because,' Clarice replied, 'the suggestion that he ran away with Avril is pure fiction. When Avril found out about your affair, she did intend to leave you – but not with the Major, and she would have taken Colin with her.'

'How dare you!' Ralph shouted. 'I don't have to answer to you about my relationships.'

'It's none of your bloody business,' Tessa chipped in.

'I don't give a fig about your infidelities, Ralph; it's Avril's murder I wanted to talk about.'

'Murder, ridiculous!' Ralph snapped, his bushy eyebrows knitting together, his face twisting.

'Janice had moved north to care for her sick mother. She anticipated her husband joining her there. You try to give the impression that you hated the Major because of what you say he'd done. But he was your best friend; there was never a falling-out between you. After Avril died, he had your back, played along with the story that he and she had left together.' Clarice stared stonily at Ralph. 'He was hanging around here at your invitation. And the truth is, he was here when Avril died. If he wasn't, he knew she'd been murdered because you confided in him – your best friend.'

'What an offensive suggestion! You put that idea into Dawn's head, that I was involved in Avril's death. She would never have come up with that that on her own. And who I do business with is my own concern,' Ralph growled.

'I know Avril didn't leave. I got that from Ernestine.'

'No – I didn't say anything,' Ernestine protested, flustered.

Clarice ignored her. 'Ernestine told me that Avril painted her toenails as well as her fingernails. She said that the last time she saw Avril was when she left the house with Ralph. Avril didn't say goodbye, but she waved.'

'I didn't.' Ernestine looked petulant. 'No, no, Ralph, I didn't say anything.'

'She waved like this.' Clarice held her hands in front of her, side by side, as Ernestine had done, showing her varnished nails. She then lifted her fingers up and down. 'I didn't get it at first, but then I realised that Ernestine was talking about feet. She meant Avril's feet, with the painted toenails, were waving up and down as Ralph carried her body wrapped in a blanket. Ernestine's sense of humour is priceless.' Clarice's voice was without mirth. 'And you told her not to be upset.' Clarice stared at Ralph.

'It wasn't me. I didn't do it!'

'Do shut up, Ernestine!' Ralph glared at his sister.

'In the car on the way to the funeral, Ernestine talked about Colin. Rather than the church funeral, he could be wrapped in a blanket and buried in the garden, she said. It sounded like what Emily told me happened with the family's dogs and cats, buried wrapped in a blanket in the cemetery. I realised that the last time Ernestine had seen Avril was when she was dead; her body wrapped in a blanket with her feet sticking out.'

'You're making this up.' Tessa looked smug. 'Pathetic, just enjoying the sound of your own voice.'

'When the police go down into the well, Avril's body will be all the proof that's needed.'

'I won't permit that,' Ralph blustered.

'They won't need your permission if it's part of a murder inquiry.'

'You killed her, Grandpa.' Emily was crying quietly.

'Putting her into the well was probably done in a panic – I guess if you'd thought it through, you might have buried her in the woods or out on the mudflats,' Clarice said. 'But Colin was due back from his friend's, and then there was the gardener, who might have questioned what, or who, you'd wanted to bury.'

'No, no!' Ernestine waved her hands, her voice shrill. 'Stop her, Ralph.'

'Do you want to give her a heart attack?' Johnson glowered at Clarice. 'She has a heart condition. And you shouldn't put him through this.' He looked towards Ralph. 'He's just lost both his son and his daughter.'

'Grandpa.' There was hurt in Emily's voice. 'Why did you kill her?'

'It was your grandfather who put Avril's body into the well, Emily,' Clarice said. 'But he didn't kill her. I only worked it out last night, when Dawn was found dead there.'

'I don't understand ... but ... then who?'

'Your Aunt Ernestine killed Avril.'

Emily's eyes jerked in shock to stare at her aunt.

'Don't look at me.' Ernestine moved her hands, fanlike, across her face. 'I don't like it – don't look at me.'

'A detail listed in Colin's notebook was that the day his mother died was the hottest of that year.' Clarice looked at Ralph. 'Another detail I learned was that when it was hot, she always opened wide the tall double windows in her bedroom.'

'We don't need to hear more.' Ralph spoke loudly. 'Enough is enough.' He pushed himself up from the chair.

'Shut up!' Tessa shouted, her eyes ablaze, 'I want her to finish ... to hear what else she has to say.'

'I believe that Avril was packing to leave when Ernestine came into her bedroom. They probably argued, and while Avril stood next to the open windows, Ernestine ran at her and pushed her out.'

'I didn't do it – it was Bellatrix!' Ernestine shouted. 'She was protecting Ralph because Avril was going to take Colin away from him.'

'No, Ernestine,' Clarice said. 'You shoved her out, and she fell onto the stonework of Bellatrix, which killed her.'

The room had become silent. Ralph had put a hand over his eyes, as if trying to block out what was going on.

'There is generally a grain of truth in whatever Ernestine says, and it is her macabre sense of humour that gives her away.'

Ernestine looked blank, as if unable to comprehend Clarice's words.

'What was it you said to Albert Wilson after the funeral, Ernestine?'

'I don't remember.' The old lady looked at Ralph, still with his hand over his face shielding his eyes.

'When Albert said that Avril enjoyed flying off on foreign holidays, you said, "Avril couldn't fly". You laughed because you thought it was funny. It was one of your little jokes; because, having been pushed from the window, Avril *couldn't* fly – she fell and *broke her crown*.' You got your wires crossed there; you said it was Beth who should have been called Jill, from the nursery rhyme. My guess is that when the police recover Avril's body, she will have a broken skull – from hitting it against Bellatrix.'

'It was Bellatrix who stopped her leaving and taking Colin.' Ernestine looked again at her brother for help. 'Tell them, Ralph.'

Ralph finally lowered his hand to look coldly at his sister, then sat down again, slowly.

'You're very good at pushing people *and* things.' Clarice stared at Ernestine as she spoke.

Tessa turned, her eyes hard. 'It was you,' she said. 'You pushed over the bronze cat – you saw Clarice downstairs and tried to kill her.'

'She's nosy.' Ernestine's voice was sneaky. 'We told you, Ralph. Tessa and I both said you should make her leave before the funeral.'

Her words surprised Clarice. She had believed it was Tessa and Johnson who had voted for her banishment from the house. But it made more sense that Ernestine wanted her gone.

'It was your second attempt – or third if you count trying to get into the bedroom when you thought I'd be asleep.' Clarice spoke directly to Ernestine. 'It took a while to work out who was stalking me in the woods on the first night. Last night, you dropped your gloves while Emily was helping you with your jacket. When I picked them up, I was bent down looking up at you – just like I did on the first night in the mist. I wasn't completely sure then, but I am now.'

Ernestine put her hand to her throat. 'She wants my necklace … You can't have it.'

Johnson, Tessa, Ralph and Emily all stared at her.

'It's no good, Ernestine,' Ralph said. 'If Clarice has worked out what happened to Avril, I'm quite sure she'll know that the necklace was never yours in the first place.'

'You had a jeweller redesign it using a combination of the diamonds in the necklace inherited by Avril when her mother died and her own pearl choker,' Clarice continued. 'Avril's mother is wearing the diamonds and Avril the pearls in the photograph taken on her wedding day.'

Ralph nodded. 'I realised you might notice – I took the photos of the wedding day out of the album.'

'The diamonds have a Victorian gipsy setting,' Clarice said. 'The setting type can seem a little crude in today's market. I imagine because Ernestine was so greedy, she wanted both necklaces. You had a jeweller make one using pieces from both. Although the possibility was low, there was a risk that if someone saw her wearing Avril's diamond necklace, they'd have asked why Avril hadn't taken it with her.'

'I'm not greedy.' Ernestine looked at Clarice, her hand still covering the necklace.

'I'm afraid you are,' Ralph said sadly. 'Envious, greedy and avaricious.'

'You are covetous, Ernestine,' Clarice said. 'It's been that way since you were a child. You couldn't even accept your little sister wearing your hand-me-downs.'

'They were my things,' Ernestine said, suddenly sounding spiteful. 'Mine.'

'Was Colin one of your things?' Clarice asked. 'You didn't want his mother to take him with her?'

'He was special, and he belonged here with us. Bellatrix wouldn't allow him to go.'

'Stop saying that!' Tessa broke in angrily. 'I've had that crap year in, year out. It's rubbish, and you could have caused Ralph to get into trouble for a murder he didn't commit.' She turned to Ralph. 'Why the hell did you protect her? You should have called the police.'

'I couldn't have done that to my own sister.'

'She killed your wife.' Tessa's voice was sharp. 'We could have got married, had a normal life. Things could have been so different. She,' she pointed at Ernestine, 'could have landed you in prison for murder.'

'No, it was me who saved him, Tessa. *I saved him.*' Ernestine sounded childishly happy.

'How?' Tessa asked.

'I wouldn't let Ralph go to prison. He's my brother. I had to stop it.'

'Ernestine.' Tessa had reached her limit with the confused ramblings. 'You're talking your usual tripe.'

'No.' Ernestine patted the side of her nose. 'It's a secret – but I saved Ralph.'

Tessa looked around, mystified. Ralph and Johnson exchanged a sudden look of comprehension.

'I know,' Clarice said.

Tessa turned her gaze towards her.

'You heard Dawn accuse Ralph of killing Avril,' Clarice said to Ernestine.

Ernestine shook her head in denial. 'No, don't say it out loud – it's a secret.'

'You took Ruffian from Dawn's room and hid him in the graveyard shed. Then you helped her search for him. You told her that he'd fallen into the well – *Pussy's in the well.* Then, when she leaned over, shining her torch down into the darkness, you hit her over the head with a metal stake.'

Tessa visibly jerked, her eyes widening.

Ernestine had dropped the empty fudge box onto the floor. Her lips were moving, but no words came out.

'Is that what you meant?' Emily's eyes too were wide with shock. 'You said you only worked it out last night – after Dawn's body was found next to the well?'

'Yes, last night I became convinced that Avril's body was in the well – but why, what triggered that feeling?' Clarice said. 'Once I'd worked out it was Ernestine who'd killed Dawn, everything fell into place. I realised that with Ernestine's confused logic, having knocked Dawn out, she believed she would tip her into the well.'

'Like Avril.' Ernestine spoke quietly. Her eyes, moving around the room, were devoid of emotion.

'Yes, like Avril. You thought she would simply disappear. It didn't work, though, because after you hit her, Dawn fell to the ground and was far too heavy to be lifted into the well. You probably hit her again then, to be sure she was dead.'

'No!' Tessa moved her head frantically, as if in pain. 'Don't let it be her – please say it was that man Belling.'

'Get out of here.' Ralph stood up again, his reddened face filled with murderous intent, his voice a bellow. 'Get out of my sight – now!' He pointed at Ernestine.

Tessa stood too, steadying herself on the nearby side table. 'You disgusting, evil old woman!' she screamed.

There was a moment of silence before a voice boomed from the doorway.

'What the hell is going on in here?'

Clarice turned to see DI Graham Digby stride into the room, followed a few feet behind by two police constables – and finally, Rick.

Chapter 37

Everyone in the room turned to look at Graham. The gathered group fleetingly appeared to have frozen. Then Emily spoke. 'Aunt Ernestine killed my grandmother fifty years ago. Last night, she killed Dawn, my aunt.'

As if a painting had come suddenly to life, everyone moved at the same time.

'I hope you rot in hell!' Tessa shouted the words.

'Stop that now!' Graham bellowed.

Tessa remained immobile. PC Rickman darted across the room to stand between her and Ernestine.

Ernestine shook her head. Her lips still moved, but no words came forth as she crumpled to the floor.

'Dr Maid's in the hall,' Graham said to one of the constables. 'Fetch him in here now.'

Clarice went to kneel at Ernestine's side. She picked up her hand.

The room became quiet again for a few moments.

Then Ernestine opened her eyes to clutch at Clarice's sweater, trying to pull herself upright. Clarice helped her into a sitting position, with Emily pushing cushions, grabbed from the chaise, behind her back.

'Ralph!' Ernestine called, her voice beseeching. She looked around in confusion, her mouth agape.

Ignoring his sister, Ralph turned towards Tessa. 'Leave her alone.'

The PC stepped away, and Ralph took Tessa's hand. She immediately snatched it back.

'Don't touch me,' she hissed. 'You've allowed that woman to live here with our daughter all these years when you knew what she was capable of.'

'I'm sorry …' Ralph mumbled.

'Don't touch me again … ever.' Tessa cast a glance around the room as she left.

Ralph hurried after her. 'I have to speak with her,' he muttered frantically.

As Ralph left, Dr Maid entered the sitting room.

'After what I've just heard,' Graham said, 'if she needs to go to hospital, a couple of officers will be going with her.'

The doctor, his expression confused, went directly to Ernestine.

'Leanne and Stacey.' Graham directed his words to the two PCs. 'Stay here and report back to me. I'll be next door. Clarice and Emily, please go to the kitchen now.' He stepped back to allow them to pass before following them out.

'Ralph, I want Ralph,' Ernestine started calling; her voice was silenced when Graham closed the kitchen door.

'Now tell me,' he looked from Clarice to Emily, his face surly, 'what the hell just happened in there?'

* * *

Once they had told Graham everything that had been said in the sitting room before his arrival, Leanne joined them briefly to tell them that at Dr Maid's request, she had put in a call for an ambulance. She and Stacey would follow it to hospital, and remain with Ernestine until told to do otherwise.

After waiting in the kitchen for a seemingly endless amount of time, Clarice and Emily were taken separately by one of the police constables to Ralph's study, where they made formal recorded statements.

Later, Graham left to talk to Ralph and Johnson, and then the men on site. Emily went back into the sitting room to wait for her grandfather.

'Hellfire, Clarice,' Rick stormed when they were alone, 'what happened to you having a quiet word with Graham?'

'I did try,' Clarice protested, 'but he said it would have to be later, and I didn't expect the family to be together in the sitting room. It all just kicked off.'

'At least it's out in the open now.'

Clarice had made them both a mug of tea. Rick nursed his thoughtfully as they sat at the kitchen table.

'What's happening with Ralph and Johnson?' Clarice asked.

'They've been cautioned and taken to the station to be formally interviewed. Ralph will be facing charges. He might not have murdered Avril, but he did cover it up and hide her body'

'And Johnson?'

'I don't know. He didn't admit to anything.'

Graham walked back into the kitchen, interrupting their conversation.

'You're free to leave, Clarice, now that we've got your statement.'

'Thanks.' Clarice looked from Graham to Rick. 'I'll wait until Emily is ready.'

'Is Ernestine still at the hospital?' Rick asked.

Graham's expression hardened. 'She's had a minor heart attack. She'll need to remain there for a few days.'

A hush fell momentarily. 'She is clearly mentally ill.' Rick broke the silence.

'That's not for me to say,' Graham said. 'A case worker will be assigned to organise a psychiatric report.'

Clarice looked down, remembering Ernestine's tiny feet dancing on the tiles the previous evening.

'Avarice appears to be one of her main characteristics,' he continued. 'It would seem she becomes jealous of people's possessions, wanting them for herself.'

'Yes,' Clarice agreed.

'I don't know how she could not have sociopathic tendencies, from what I've heard about her macabre sense of humour and her lack of remorse,' Graham said.

'Does Ralph know how Ernestine is?' Clarice asked.

'He's been updated at the police station.' Graham looked tired as he leaned heavily against the kitchen table. 'He's been charged with perverting the course of justice and assisting an offender. He's not considered a flight risk, so he'll be allowed to come home.'

Rick held his mug up invitingly. Graham attempted a grin. 'A cuppa would be most welcome.'

'I was surprised by what Clarice told me about yesterday evening – how Ernestine wanted Dawn's cat.' Rick grimaced as he went to switch on the kettle. 'The cat still covered in the blood of its mistress, the woman she'd just murdered!'

'Yes.' Clarice nodded. 'Pattie Freeman's summing-up of Ernestine was "mad as a box of frogs but harmless enough".'

'She certainly got that wrong,' Graham snorted.

'Indeed she did.' Her voice was forlorn. 'Are you OK if I go and have a word with Emily?'

'I'm due a break,' Graham said. 'I'll have a cuppa with Rick.'

Leaving them talking, Clarice could not help but think how chatty and forthcoming Graham had become once Rick had joined them. Still, the case was now resolved. The image of Ernestine from the previous evening, dancing around the kitchen, remained fixed in her mind.

Chapter 38

Back in the sitting room, Clarice found Emily alone, her legs and feet tucked under her on the chair.

'Are you OK?' she asked.

'Apart from being completely gobsmacked?'

'Yes, apart from that.'

'Relieved.' Emily rocked her body as she spoke. 'Rick thinks Ralph will be charged with conspiring to cover the murder up by hiding Avril's body.'

'Yes,' Clarice said.

'I know what he did was wrong, but I'm still relieved that he wasn't the one who killed Avril.'

'I understand,' Clarice said.

They sat for a few minutes, both with their thoughts.

'I've been up to the bedroom and packed my bag.' Emily sounded glum.

'I'll go and do mine in a minute,' Clarice said.

The fire had died to embers, and to keep busy, she again set about breaking pieces of sticks from the log basket to get it to catch before putting fresh logs on.

'That's the second time,' Emily said. 'You'll be in trouble for doing Johnson out of a job.'

Clarice forced a smile.

'Why did you not tell me what had happened in the woods, when Ernestine stalked you?'

'Because you still had to get through the funeral. You were upset enough, and I didn't think at that point that it was Ernestine.' Clarice sat back on her heels, watching the fire take. 'I was torn between Johnson, Tessa and Ian Belling.'

'Ah, hence the chair at the bedroom door?'

'You've got it.'

'You've been so kind and thoughtful.' Emily's voice shook a little.

'The trauma's behind you now,' Clarice said. 'The worst is past.'

Ralph's return was heralded by the two dogs. Ben bounded into the room in front of him; Floss plodded at the back. Although his step was slow and sluggish, his voice was strong.

'Settle down, settle down,' he shouted at the dogs.

Ben came to Clarice to press his body against her legs; Floss chose to settle in front of the fire.

'You know I've been charged,' he said to Emily.

'Yes,' she said. 'What about Tessa, is she still here?'

'Upstairs in her private sitting room.'

Emily bit her bottom lip. Clarice wondered if she was trying to hold back tears.

'What my sister did is beyond belief.' Ralph was wretched as he lowered himself into his armchair. 'Dawn was always good to her. Never for a moment unkind.' He stared into the flames of the burning logs.

The three of them sat in silence, listening to the sound of the fire crackling. The sunlight coming through the long windows brightened the room, showing up the shabby furnishings.

'Why did you cover up for Aunt Ernestine when she killed Avril?' Emily asked. 'You could have just contacted the police.'

'It happened so quickly.' Ralph turned to stare at Ben as he spoke, perhaps unable to meet Emily's gaze. 'I'd been outside to get something from my car. Walking back along the drive, I heard someone scream. Ernestine was standing at the open windows in Avril's bedroom, looking down. Avril was below – on the ground. She was dead, her head cracked open.' He turned to look at Clarice. 'As you surmised, when she was pushed, she fell backwards, smashing her skull on Bellatrix.'

'But why didn't you call the police?' Emily insisted.

Ralph appeared to struggle to find the words. 'She was my sister; she would have gone to prison. I had to protect her.'

'It was a habit that was hard to break,' Clarice said.

'Yes. I'd copied my parents. Ernestine was not the easiest of children, but however difficult she was, they never gave up on her. I somehow believed I had to do the same.'

'Not even after Beth?'

'That was grim. Mother cried for days.' Ralph sighed, his face hung with sorrow. 'Father had told us we mustn't go near his stallion. Thunder had been ill and was fractious. Mother said the girls must have forgotten and gone in there to play hide-and-seek. Beth went inside Thunder's stall.'

'You didn't believe that?' Clarice asked.

'Not completely,' Ralph said. 'I think Ernestine might have encouraged or dared her to go in. My mother said that being the middle child was a problem.'

'How?' Emily asked.

'I was top dog, getting a lot of attention as the eldest and much-wanted son and heir. Beth was the baby; she was so delightful, and I think my mother, knowing it would be her last child, wanted to enjoy her.'

'And Ernestine?' Clarice asked.

'I expect if Beth hadn't come along, Ernestine would have got all the extra attention lavished on her little sister – but that's life. Ernestine was jealous as hell. Mother just told her to get over it.'

'But she got on with Avril – in the beginning?' Clarice asked.

'Always. I could not have anticipated what would happen. Avril had been so amazingly kind to Ernestine; she bought her treats, took her shopping and on outings – she could not have been a more considerate sister-in-law.' Ralph grimaced. 'It all came about because she said she would leave and take Colin with her.'

'Ernestine took things into her own hands?'

'She adored Colin.'

'A strange word to use, if you consider the horrible tricks she played on him?'

'I know it might seem difficult to believe, but she did love him. Ernestine always had a strange sense of humour.' Ralph was reflective. 'Bottom line is: she just snapped. It might have been because she'd believed she was losing one of her *things*.'

'And then there was Tessa?'

'Yes.' Ralph nodded. 'Tessa was the complete opposite of Avril. Ernestine drove her mad with her inane wittering.'

'I thought that was due to dementia?'

'That has naturally made her more confused. She always wittered, prattling on about some nonsense or other. In fairness, it was irritating, but inoffensive.'

Clarice remembered again Pattie Freeman's description of Ernestine as 'mad as a box of frogs'.

'Life must have been frustrating for Tessa,' she mused. 'Not only because of Ernestine, but because she could never be your wife – you weren't divorced.'

'Impossible,' Ralph mumbled. 'Getting married was a priority for Tessa, but I couldn't prove Avril was dead without getting Ernestine and myself in trouble.' He fell silent for a moment, as if his mind were elsewhere. 'If I could turn the clock back, I'd do it in an instant.' He snapped his fingers. 'I would be on to the police the moment I'd found Avril. Tessa was right: our lives would have been different – and Dawn would still be alive.'

Clarice and Emily listened, not breaking into his contemplations.

'What was it?' Ralph asked Clarice. 'What made you realise Ernestine murdered Avril? I know it was a mistake to keep the locket, but I couldn't hide it – it was so personal to her that I wanted Colin to have it.'

Clarice gave a small smile. 'In the end, it all came down to Avril's dancing feet and Ernestine's greed.'

Ralph stared at her, puzzled.

'I knew there was something that didn't fit. It was annoying. I kept wondering if it was something I'd seen or heard. Finally, last night, I understood. In Colin's notebook, there was something he'd observed but couldn't make sense of.'

'What was that?' Emily asked.

'It was in his before-and-after lists,' Clarice said. '"Before" when Avril was still here, and "after" when she'd gone. He had jewellery on both lists. His grandmothers loved it, and so did his mother, Aunt Ernestine and Tessa. I think he'd half worked it out. The jewellery worn by Ernestine was familiar – but different. The ruse of having the pieces worked into one design threw him off the scent, as intended. But shoes and dancing feet were on both the lists as well, and that made sense last night when I watched Ernestine dance around the kitchen. She was the one who told me she took the same size shoe as Avril.'

'Avril's friend Pattie Freeman said she loved shoes, especially unusual ones,' Emily recalled.

'Ernestine's greedy nature meant that once Avril was dead, she took her shoes. It might have only been one pair, but they were ones with unusual gold-coloured buckles, and as a child, it stuck in Colin's mind. If his mother really had left, why was his aunt dancing around wearing her shoes?'

'Poor Colin.' Ralph snorted. 'I didn't know that. So much for my sister believing she was a good aunt. She really was a terrible woman.'

'Tessa seemed obsessed by who would inherit this house. Is she aware that you're practically bankrupt?' Clarice asked.

For several minutes Ralph said nothing. Eventually he looked up. 'Strangely, she didn't want to know. I tried many times to broach the subject, and I think it's pretty bloody obvious, really. A house like this needs money. Anyone can see it requires repairs and upkeep, so much needing to be done. I think Tessa didn't want to face those facts, the reality. But that's irrelevant; she won't stay now Dawn has gone. The relationship's been difficult for years. Dawn was the glue that kept us together.'

'She might change her mind,' Emily said.

'No, she won't.' Ralph spoke with certainty. 'She says I'm to blame for not protecting Dawn against Ernestine. She has a point.'

'What about the Major? You said he was a friend. Did he know about Avril's murder?'

The expression on Ralph's face softened. 'Freddie was a good man, the best friend I ever had. He died just over two years ago, a year after Janice. Colin adored him. He was like a favourite uncle. Did magic tricks with cards, and finding a coin from behind Colin's ear – that sort of caper.' He smiled sadly. 'Freddie had been staying here while his wife was in Yorkshire, taking care of her mother. Janice was a practical woman. With her mother nearing the end, she wanted Freddie out from under her feet. He left for London the day Avril died; he'd gone to visit a friend.'

'Did you tell him what had happened?' Emily asked.

'Yes, I told him, and he begged me to go to the police. But it was too late.'

'You'd already hidden Avril's body in the well,' Clarice said.

'Yes. How would I explain that?'

'You could have told them the truth.' Clarice shrugged. 'That you'd panicked.'

'No, out of the question; it would have been in all the newspapers,' Ralph blustered. 'I would have been made to look like an idiot!'

Clarice remembered what Emily had told her about Ralph before they arrived at the manor: that he considered the reputation of the Compton-Smythe family, and his own standing in the community, to be paramount.

'Did he mind you using his name as the man Avril had been having an affair with?'

'It was Colin who started it. I told him his mother had gone away and wouldn't be coming home. He couldn't accept it – just went on and on. I was pretty rattled after what had happened – didn't handle it at all well.' Ralph rubbed his bent, arthritic fingers together thoughtfully. 'Before he went to bed, he asked where Uncle Freddie was. I just said he'd gone away, and Colin immediately came back with "With my mummy?"'

'It went from there?' Clarice asked.

'The next day, I found he'd told the cook, the cleaner and the gardener that his mummy had gone away with Uncle Freddie. He was a little boy who talked too much.'

'Innocence,' Clarice interjected.

'When I told Freddie what had happened, it was his idea to continue the lie. And he passed the whole tawdry tale on to Janice. She was bright – smart as a whip. Freddie said she'd know when he was lying; that unless she had the whole story, it wouldn't work.' Ralph patted Floss's head. 'She took a lot of persuading. I know she was furious about it, but in the end, she went along with it.'

'She sounds like a strong lady.'

'Yes.' Ralph nodded. 'Freddie met his match with Janice. He never looked twice at another woman once he'd met her – despite what people thought.'

'What about the business?' Clarice asked.

'It was obvious Freddie could no longer be a partner.' Ralph's forehead furrowed, remembering. 'We simply backdated the paperwork to the day before he had supposedly left with Avril. It terminated his interest in the company. I paid him his share.'

'Avril didn't have anyone to go looking for her?'

'Both parents were dead, and she didn't get on with Pamela, her sister,' Ralph said. 'Freddie never came here again, and Janice cut links with the few friends she'd had in the village. Then …'

'Forty years later, Colin went looking for her,' Clarice finished.

'That's it. First the man from the investigative agency, then Colin turning up in Roundhay. Janice panicked, arranged to meet him, then cancelled the meeting. She and Freddie went to stay in London. They had a flat there.'

'Grandpa …' Emily's voice trembled; clearly she was unable to say more. Tears began to fall as she came to sit on the floor by his chair and rested her head against his knee. Ben watched them, wagging his tail, confused.

For a moment, Ralph's arthritic hand hovered near her head, and Clarice imagined he might pat it, but instead he gently began to stroke her hair.

'I told you that Avril was a lovely person. Colin inherited so many of her qualities, and I loved him very much. The parallels between Avril going when Colin was five and your mother leaving when you were thirteen would not have escaped him. He was a sensitive boy. Meeting his friends yesterday made me realise I didn't actually know him – my own son. There was so much I'd missed.' Ralph seemed far away again. 'His friends seemed so … unrestricted, natural and free. I envied them. And the worst thing is that I never told Colin how very much I loved him.' He bent to kiss the top of Emily's head. 'And I love you, Emily – very much indeed.'

After Ralph had given up another secret, there was a

quietness. It felt as if they were trapped in time, in a silent, sealed room where dust might be allowed to settle.

Clarice thought of Rick waiting in the kitchen.

'I'll go and bring down our bags,' she said.

Ralph did not look up.

It took only ten minutes to pack her bag. Before leaving, she stood for a moment looking through the long bedroom windows out to the Wash, thinking about Avril. Halfway down the stairs, she met Johnson on his way up.

'Let me take those, Mrs Beech.' He leaned in and took the baggage.

She stopped for a moment to look at him.

'Can I say something?'

Johnson stopped. 'If you insist.'

'Thank you for helping me in the woods.' Clarice spoke gently, a tone she had not previously used with Johnson. 'I believed, wrongly, that you were stalking me – that you meant me harm.' She looked at him for a few moments. 'It was the complete opposite: you were trying to protect me from Ernestine. And the next day in the barn, you were looking out for Emily.'

'I couldn't possibly comment,' Johnson said.

'Loyal to the end.' Clarice gave a sad smile. 'Protecting the family.'

'In …' Johnson paused. 'In the end, it's impossible to protect someone when the person you're protecting them from is themselves.' His expression was, as usual, dour.

'Yes, I understand.'

Following Johnson downstairs, she found Rick was waiting.

Chapter 39

Half an hour later, sitting in the car waiting for Emily, Clarice took one last look at Bellatrix. Her eyes moved up to the house, the central tower and the long windows from which Avril had fallen, pushed by Ernestine. In the short time she'd been a guest, she had fallen in love with the building's unique beauty, and felt a sadness remembering Dawn and her pride in it.

'It feels strange to leave a house I've stayed in without thanking my hosts for their hospitality,' she said to Emily when she joined her.

'It can't be often that your host has been charged with colluding in a murder and concealing the body.' Emily sounded remorseful as she looked at the house. 'I feel terrible leaving Grandpa, but he told me I must go.'

'He needs time to grieve, and he's not alone; he has Johnson.'

Johnson stood next to the giant Siamese stone statue, ramrod straight, his usual sardonic scowl in place. He had loaded the bags into the car. There were two police cars in the driveway, and Rick had said there was still a police presence at the well.

Looking at the tower again, Clarice imagined Tessa lurking at one of the windows, watching their departure from behind a heavy curtain.

Rick leaned in through the car window. 'I'll set off with you, but drive at your own pace; the road will be busy and it's starting to get dark. I phoned Sandra and Bob to let them know we're on our way home. Sandra is making something for supper. She said she'd put clean sheets on one of the spare beds in case Emily wanted to stay over.'

'That's our Sandra.' Clarice smiled.

She pulled out, heading along the drive. In the rear-view mirror, she saw Rick's white BMW tuck in, following.

'I don't know whether I'm feeling hungry or sick, and part of me feels I could sleep for a week, but then I'm too edgy to sleep at all. Everything in my brain feels scrambled,' Emily said.

'It's not surprising.' Clarice glanced at her. 'You're upset by all that's happened.'

They passed a police van hidden amongst the trees. Then the place where, on their arrival, they had seen Ian Belling. Clarice suppressed a shudder; so much had happened since then. She thought about Colin again, and imagined him walking through these woods with his daughter. She fleetingly wondered if he would have been pleased that Emily finally knew what had happened to the grandma she'd never known, the mystery resolved. Perhaps not; with Dawn's death, it put matters in a different light. Then her mind moved on to her last conversation with Ralph and Emily in the sitting room. It was painfully clear that Ralph had regrets about his relationship with Colin; the fact that he had never shown his love.

'Are you OK?' Emily asked.

'I'm fine,' Clarice said. 'I was thinking about you. Do you want to go home tonight, or would you prefer to stay over with us and go back tomorrow?'

'You must be sick of the sight of me,' Emily said drily.

'Don't be silly.' Clarice glanced in the rear-view mirror, reassured as she pulled onto the main carriageway to see Rick's car following. 'Maybe have a hot bath, something to eat with us, and try to unwind. Head home tomorrow morning.'

'Thanks, Clarice, I'd like that.' Emily settled down into the seat, closing her eyes.

The journey home was slow, Friday afternoons always being the busiest of the week. Clarice caught occasional glimpses of Rick's car following, disappearing behind vehicles that overtook, dipping in and out of the heavy traffic. There was the smell of diesel, and her mind felt overloaded and stressed.

Emily, awake now, occasionally broke into her thoughts to go over aspects of what had happened during their stay at Stone Fen Manor.

As they neared the cottage, the undulating softness of the Wolds gave her comfort. She loved the Lincolnshire flatlands in the south of the county, with the miles of openness and big skies, but here was where she felt at home.

It was early evening when they arrived; the light had gone. Rick was a few minutes behind them. Bob came out to the car, offering to take their bags indoors. Going into the cottage, they were mobbed by the dogs, receiving a noisy welcome and much tail-lashing. Blue and Jazz danced gleefully around them.

'We've just come back from the cat barn. They've all been fed, watered and walked, so you can relax,' Bob told Clarice.

'There'll just be the usual cat check in the barn, and the dogs needing to go outside, later, before you go to bed.'

'You are wonderful, Bob, both of you.' Clarice felt a sense of peace at being in her own home, with all those she loved and trusted.

Emily went to the barn to see Napoleon and Josephine. On her return, she joined the others around the pine kitchen table, sitting with large mugs of tea. Rick and Clarice gave Bob and Sandra a brief version of what had happened. Clarice was aware that Emily might not want to relive the events of the last forty-eight hours in depth.

'Sounds like it's been a nightmare.' Sandra patted Emily's hand. 'Do you regret wanting to find out what happened to Avril?'

'No,' Emily said firmly. 'But I'm sorry that it wasn't my dad who found out ten years ago. It might have given him some closure. Although learning that his father had hushed it up and dropped Avril's body into the well would have finished their relationship. And I feel desperately sad for Dawn.'

'You weren't to know that would happen, darlin',' Sandra said. 'The only one to blame is Ernestine.'

'Yes, I know. I had a feeling I might get on with Dawn in the future. We were building bridges.' Emily looked at Clarice. 'It was Clarice who told us that we should try to move on from the animosity between Dawn's mother and my father to make sure it didn't continue into our relationship – and she was right.'

'Colin was the kindest of men,' Clarice said. 'Growing up in that toxic atmosphere would have affected anybody. It would have been impossible for him not to feel animosity.

And I also feel sad for Dawn. She trusted Ernestine, and was sweet to her.'

'I think everyone trusted her,' Rick said. 'Ralph had put Avril's death behind him. He'd moved on.'

'Not completely,' Clarice said. 'I thanked Johnson for trying to protect me from Ernestine. He said he couldn't possibly comment. I realised that if he'd found it necessary to keep me safe from Ernestine, Ralph must have known about it.'

'That's true. You said Tessa was shocked when she found out Ernestine had been the one to topple the sculpture, while Ralph didn't say anything.' Rick considered. 'But you don't believe Ralph ever imagined Ernestine would harm Dawn.'

'He said much the same about Avril.' Emily joined in. 'He believed Ernestine really cared for her.'

'Don't forget Beth, their sister.' Clarice said. 'She was trampled by Thunder, their father's horse. I imagine Ralph originally convinced himself it had just been a childhood prank that went wrong.' She became pensive, fiddling with her empty mug. 'Because I was asking too many questions, I think Ralph thought it a precaution for Johnson to keep an eye on me – but I don't believe he thought for one moment Ernestine would harm Dawn.'

'It's all come back to haunt him now,' Rick said.

'I think Johnson summed it up,' Clarice said quietly. 'He said, "It's impossible to protect someone when the person you're protecting them from is themselves." I believe he had Ralph in mind. If Johnson was there when Avril was murdered, he may have attempted, unsuccessfully, to persuade Ralph to contact the police. As Tessa said, if he had done that, their lives would have been entirely different.'

'The Major tried to persuade him to go to the police too,' Emily chipped in.

'That detective agency bloke didn't find out much,' Sandra said.

Clarice looked at Emily. 'We weren't overly impressed when we met him.'

'There was one thing we didn't get to the bottom of.' Emily looked from Clarice to Rick. 'The downward spiral of Ralph and Avril's marriage started when Avril discovered Ralph was in another relationship – he was having an affair. Tessa never admitted it was her, although I'm convinced it was.'

'I think you'll never second-guess Tessa.' Clarice smiled sardonically. 'She is a very complex lady.'

'And we don't know what it was that Grandpa made Johnson do,' Emily continued. 'Ernestine mentioned that.'

'I suspect it was something to do with the disposal of Avril's body,' Clarice said. 'He might have been there after the fall from the window and helped Ralph move her. We'll never know.'

Later, Clarice heated up the fish pie Sandra had prepared, and they gathered again to eat it with broccoli, followed by apple pie and custard. Emily had become quiet, and watching her, Clarice noticed she ate little, appearing tired and listless.

Bob and Sandra, perhaps aware that they had said enough about Emily's family, chatted instead about the dogs and cats.

'Thank you, Sandra.' Clarice helped her diminutive friend into her coat and hugged her. 'Not just for the meal tonight, but for looking after all the beasties and Rick.'

'I've loved it, darlin'. I had Rick all to myself – bliss.' Sandra gave a cheeky grin.

'You could stay.' Rick smiled. 'We do have two spare bedrooms.'

'Thanks.' Sandra returned his smile. 'We've enjoyed our stay, but we'd like to get back to our own beds tonight.'

'It's already dark out, and cold.' Rick grinned. 'Nice and warm in here.'

'Very tempting, darlin'.' Sandra laughed, going to Rick to pat him gently on the cheek. 'We'll see you tomorrow afternoon.'

'They are so lovely,' Emily said after the couple had departed.

'They are family,' Clarice said. 'Are you OK?'

'Do you mind if I have a hot bath and go to bed?' Emily yawned. 'I feel shattered.'

'Go for it. Help yourself to any smellies in the bathroom. There's some avocado foaming bath oil, smells lovely – towels are on your bed. Rick and I will be going across to check the cats, then walking the dogs. You'll be in bed by the time we've finished.'

'Thanks, Clarice,' Emily said. 'For everything. I couldn't have got through it without you.'

They watched her go up the stairs.

'Cat barn first?' Rick suggested.

'Good plan.' Clarice followed him out.

Chapter 40

Once in the barn, they split up. Clarice went to check on the food and water for cats in two sections of the building, leaving Rick to stay with Sassy. On her return, she found he'd made himself comfortable on an old garden lounger, while Sassy was equally relaxed sprawled across him, purring and dribbling in equal measure.

'He made a beeline for me.' Rick smiled at the cat, who was now paddling happily with his large paws against his chest. He gave Clarice a knowing gaze. 'So, how are you bearing up? You've had a rough time over the last couple of days.'

Clarice tilted her head enquiringly.

'Come on, Clarice, you look shattered.'

'I can't hide anything from you.' She looked around broodingly.

'Nope.' He took his attention from the cat to give her a lopsided grin.

'You're right.' Clarice pulled a chair from across the room to sit facing him. 'I feel completely exhausted. The same might be said about Emily. Although she actually seems more normal now.'

It was Rick's turn to look enquiringly.

'She's been quiet, subdued and weepy since we left the manor.'

'She's grieving.'

'Yes, it's how she should have been since Colin died, rather than trying to put up a brave front.'

'I get it,' Rick said. They sat peacefully for a while, listening to Sassy's rumbling purr. 'You said that when you arrived, Johnson appeared to be suspicious of you?'

'I realised that it's in his nature.' Clarice shrugged. 'He's especially distrustful and wary of strangers. When the caterers were leaving after the funeral, he was checking every item being loaded onto their vans. I think he was making sure they'd not stolen so much as a teaspoon.' She shrugged again. 'He was distrustful because he didn't know me.'

'From what Ralph said, it sounds like the end of the road for his relationship with Tessa.'

'Yes,' Clarice agreed, 'he's quite sure it's over.'

'What about you?'

'What about me?'

'Are you going to tell Emily what you told me this afternoon, in the kitchen at the manor. About Ralph's lover? It was the spark that ignited this whole damn thing, Avril discovering Ralph's secret lover. Emily still thinks it was Tessa.'

'No.' Clarice spoke with certainty. 'It's none of my business, and I suspect Ralph will tell her himself at some point. Anyway, I have no proof.'

'Do you think Tessa knows?'

'Yes. I can't imagine that after fifty years, she hasn't worked out that Johnson is and always was the true love of Ralph's life.'

'She turned a blind eye?'

Clarice nodded. 'Up until now. As Ralph said, it was because of Dawn that they remained together. Dawn's death has changed everything. I never met Avril, but the picture I formed of her is far different from that of Tessa. Avril was innocent, not worldly. Tessa had been around the block a time or two before getting together with Ralph. She knew what she wanted from the relationship – although she was ultimately disappointed. She always imagined she'd get a ring on her finger, and she became deeply embittered over the years. With Avril and Ralph, it was a love match. I remember Pattie talking about seeing them together in the garden.'

'And Johnson watching and scowling.'

'Yes. He was probably jealous. Pattie said Avril felt threatened by him. She surmised it was because Johnson knew Ralph's lady friend's identity, and Avril was upset because he'd shared the secret with him. In fact it was because Avril had discovered he was Ralph's lover but she was far too embarrassed to tell anyone. I suspect that Ralph and Johnson got together when they both lived in London. Ralph moved to Stone Fen Mansion after his father died; Johnson moved in – as an employee – a couple of weeks later.'

'How did you work it out?'

'It was the tenderness.' Clarice smiled sadly. 'The touch on his arm when Johnson, this seemingly sour elderly man, put his hand out to help Ralph. He hovered around doorways, always nearby to support him. I believe there were two love matches, a triangle, with Ralph at the centre. Of course I could have got it completely wrong – it is only my gut instinct.'

'If you're right, it's sad that they felt they needed to hide it all these years,' Rick said.

'I realise now that I'd got it the first time I looked properly at the photograph Emily showed me. It was the family gathered in front of Bellatrix. I questioned then whether Ralph, having inherited the house, wanted to put all the other things in place; be like his father and his grandfather.'

'A wife and an heir?'

'That's it: the grand house, a landowner, a wife, a son and a couple of Labradors. Not forgetting the odd Siamese cat. What he hadn't anticipated was falling in love with Avril. He tried to muddy the waters. Pattie said Ralph hinted to Avril that Johnson had a lady friend he visited, but she never met her. I think that was an outright lie. And when Avril found out the truth about Ralph and Johnson, it was, for her, the end of the marriage.'

Rick smiled ruefully. 'It must have been hard for Johnson when Ralph fell in love with Avril.'

'Homosexuality only became legal in 1967. Emily talked about the Compton-Smythes being red-blooded men. For Ralph, that description created a pretence he could hide behind, and it helped when he moved Tessa in. He'd want an heir too, of course, as you say. He's never dared to own his love for Johnson – but then he was part of a different generation. And as you say, life could not have been easy for Johnson either. At the funeral, I was reminded by Albert Wilson about people "from away", a term commonly used in derision until recent years for people who'd moved here from maybe Norfolk or London. Can you imagine how hard it must have been fifty years ago for a gay, mixed-race man to move to Lincolnshire!'

'I remember coming from London and being called a foreigner,' Rick said.

'There is some positive news.'

'Please, tell me – I badly need positive news,' Rick, grinning, sounded dramatic.

'Emily told me on the drive home. Ralph will give a home to Napoleon and Josephine, just until she can get a flat in her second year at uni. She'll have them herself then.'

'That is good news. It means Emily will be seeing a lot more of her grandfather.'

'Yes, plus Ralph and Johnson are used to a multi-animal household, and the cats will love the woods. He told Emily he would arrange to visit her at Colin's home, bail conditions allowing, and Johnson would drive him there. They'll take the cats back with them. Maybe, if I've got it right, Ralph wants to reveal his biggest secret – who knows.'

They sat quietly, with only the sound of Sassy's throbbing purr filling the air.

'Can you remember what I said when you first became involved in this?' Rick smiled. '"I don't think something that happened half a century ago will be dangerous; no mad murders lurking in the shadows."'

'Ha!' Clarice grinned.

'Do you think we should go back to walk the girls?' Rick asked.

'Yes, it's getting on.' She stood up, while Rick slowly put Sassy down.

'And when do you want to move this old boy across to the house?' He watched the elderly cat stomp away to his food bowl as he spoke.

'Is it on the cards?' Clarice smiled.

'We both know it always was.'

Outside, they stood for a moment feeling the chill of the night while looking up into the starless blackness.

'I'm glad to have you home.' Rick's voice was soft. 'I missed you.'

Clarice slipped her hand into his, feeling his fingers instinctively spread, allowing hers to slip between and interlock.

'Even with Sandra's extra-large steak pies and the special puff-pastry topping to compensate?' There was laughter in her voice.

'It's close-run thing – but you win every time.'

Acknowledgements

Thank you to my agent, the amazing Anne Williams. Also, to Krystyna Green of Constable, for her invaluable support. To all the Constable/Little, Brown team, especially Amanda Keats. And thanks to Kate Hordern of Kate Hordern Literary Agency.

It has been a challenging time with Covid lockdown, during which I had a fall and broke my arm. My gratitude goes to all the friends who helped me get through doing my shopping, dog walking, driving me to hospital appointments, and long telephone calls with shared laughter. I could not have got through it without you. Especially to brother Stephen, Brian and Sue, Stephan and Jenny, Sue and Chris, Nicola and Nick, Lyn, Steph and Les. Thanks also to my book club friends – it is always great to get together!

Thank you to Dr Hilary Johnson, a fellow dog-lover, for her support, good advice and encouragement over the years.

Also, thanks to my vets, Nigel Turner and Maxine Briggs, for looking after my rescue waifs and strays.

I said my last goodbye to MC and Dan this year. I have loving recollections. I shall never forget the joy you both brought.

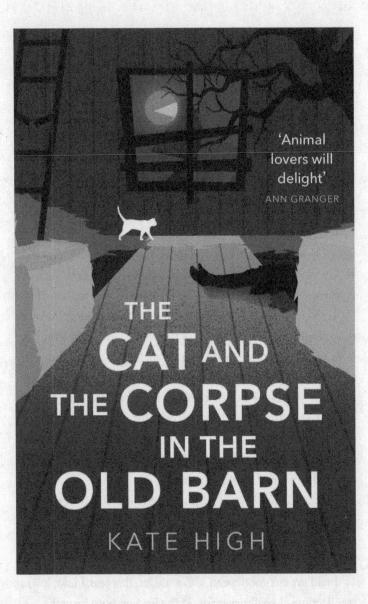

'Animal lovers will delight'
ANN GRANGER

THE CAT AND THE CORPSE IN THE OLD BARN

KATE HIGH

The Cat and the Corpse in the Old Barn

Book 1 in the Clarice Beech series,
set in the Lincolnshire Wolds

Clarice Beech has two passions in life: animal rescue and Detective Inspector Rick Beech. She is devoted to the first but she and Rick have been separated for the past six months – and life without him is hard.

Clarice shares her other love, for contemporary ceramics, with the charming Lady Vita Fayrepoynt. When Vita's adopted three-legged ginger cat Walter disappears from Weatherby Hall, Clarice is called in to find him. Walter, snug in an old barn, is quite well. But his discovery ends with Clarice in hospital, and Rose Miller, late of the Old Vicarage, in the morgue. There is nothing natural about Rose's death . . .

Putting their differences aside, Clarice and Rick are drawn together to try to understand the murder that has shaken the rural Lincolnshire community. As she explores Rose's past, Clarice is pulled into a shady world of blackmail, scams and violence. And, as the secrets of Weatherby Hall and the Fayrepoynt family threaten to spill out, Clarice finds friendships tested, and her own life at risk . . .

KATE HIGH

THE **MAN** WHO **VANISHED** AND THE **DOG** WHO **WAITED**

'Animal lovers
will delight in this'
ANN GRANGER

The Man Who Vanished and the Dog Who Waited

Book 2 in the Clarice Beech series,
set in the Lincolnshire Wolds

Available now

Summer in the Lincolnshire Wolds and Clarice is rung by her friend Louise, asking whether she can look after Susie, her son's lively Boxer, as 41-year-old Guy has gone missing from the family home.

His mother thinks he has been suffering from depression but more worryingly, in his professional life, he had been working on a high-profile case, defending a known criminal. His home life was beset with problems, too, which is why his mother has asked Clarice to look after the dog; Charlotte, Guy's wife, just can't cope with her as well as their three daughters.

Getting drawn into the puzzle of Guy's disappearance, Clarice wonders how Susie received a nasty cut to her back leg, and who is the mysterious Charles? Guy apparently did not trust him enough to let him into his home, and he had not been seen since he was driven away in Charles's car. Guy's friends all say that he was a good, honest man, but as Clarice looks further into the murky criminal world he inhabits, she questions if Guy has been pulled in out of his depth. And – why does Susie keep returning to the private woods, where she had spent so much time with her beloved master?